# The Almost Perfect Crime

# The Almost Perfect Crime:

## TRUE CRIME FEATURING PHILO VANCE, WITH OTHER STORIES

## S. S. VAN DINE

Introduced by
**Tony Medawar and Brooks Hefner**

P. O. Box 532057
Cincinnati, OH 45253
2025

For information contact:

Crippen & Landru, Publishers

P.O. Box 532057
Cincinnati, OH 45253 USA

Web: www.crippenlandru.com
E-mail: Info@crippenlandru.com

ISBN (softcover): 978-1-936363-95-7
ISBN (clothbound): 978-1-936363-94-0

First Edition: May 2025
10 9 8 7 6 5 4 3 2 1

# Contents

# The Wise Guy

By Tony Medawar

WILLARD Huntington Wright was born on the fifteenth of October 1888 in Charlottesville, Virginia. His parents were Archibald and Annie Wright, respectively of British and Dutch descent. In Virginia, Archibald managed several prestigious hotels and in 1901, he moved to California to take over the lease of the famous Arcadia Hotel in Santa Monica, which is where his family joined him in 1902.

As a teenager, Willard Wright attended Pomona College and later St Vincent's, California's oldest college, where he played baseball and was known as a prankster —once faking a student's death —and where he dreamed of becoming… a conductor; in 1904 – aged fifteen – Willard "composed, copyrighted and published" *Zululand*, a march described in the press as "abound[ing] in Ethiopian syncopation." After St. Vincent's, Willard went to Harvard for a year where he regularly missed classes and failed to graduate. In his spare time, he continued to write music as well as short stories —indeed, in an interview published in 1928, he claimed to have been writing "since the age of four, when a poem of mine was printed in my home paper. I wrote a full-length novel at nine and illustrated it myself. Luckily it was never published— it was worse than the poem."

Whatever the merits of these early works —now all, apparently, lost —and discounting that early poem, Willard first appeared in print in March 1906 when *The Pacific Monthly* published "No Story at All."

He was seventeen.

In August 1906 *The Bohemian* carried another story, "At the Edge of the Canon." Others appeared in *The Gray Goose* and the *All-Story Magazine*. But at this time fiction was of less interest to him than culture. On leaving Harvard, Willard spent a year studying art in Paris and Munich and, after returning to America, he married Katherine Belle Boynton on the thirteenth of July 1907. In October 1908, their daughter Beverley was born; in 1909, a second daughter —Maria —was born but she died the following year.

Willard became a journalist, and in December 1908 his first article was published in the *Los Angeles Times*, albeit with the by-line "Wilbur Huntington Wright." In 1909, he was appointed literary editor of the *Times* by the newspaper's president and general manager, Harrison Gray Otis. He would have his own column, "New Books and Book News," but he wrote other articles for the newspaper as well as for other publications, including *West Coast Magazine* and *The Pacific Monthly*. He was also becoming known as a speaker, for example taking part in a panel discussion about "The Book" at a meeting of the Women's Press Club in February 1910.

Life was good. But everything was about to change. At seven minutes past one in the morning of the first of October 1910, a bomb went off in an alley in the offices of the *Los Angeles Times*, just when the morning edition was going to print. Twenty-one people were killed. Willard had left the building only ten minutes earlier.

Happily, the newspaper continued to be published and Willard continued to write for them. He was becoming increasingly outspoken and in January 1911, he was accused by the *Times* of exploding "a loaded bomb" of a different kind when he praised the misogynistic attitudes of the nineteenth century German philosopher Friedrich Nietzsche at a meeting of the Arroyo Dinner Club, a Californian society for women. A few months later, he delivered an even more inflammatory speech at another meeting of the Women's Press Club where the pros and cons of giving women the vote were to be debated. He spoke first and against the motion. In the words of the *Alexandria Gazette* "there were hisses and cat calls, cries for him to quit and every one of the 125 women present had something to say" in response to his assertion that "suffragists are mainly women whose attractiveness is so run down at heel as no longer to command attention," *The Gazette* reported that as the chair of the meeting fainted, "whatever else he said was not heard even by those on the platform with him," and he was booed from the room as the debate was abandoned.

While continuing to write for the *Times*, Willard became associate editor of *The Smart Set* magazine where he worked from 1912 to 1914. In March 1913, *The Smart Set* published a lengthy article by Wright called "Los Angeles—the Chemically Pure" which sneered snobbishly at the "commonplace people [in the city] with rural beliefs [and] bourgeois prejudices" as well as the "faddists and mountebanks, mediums, astrologists, spiritualists, phrenologists, palmists and all other breeds of esoteric windjammers" that Willard felt had taken over Los Angeles. Predictably, his views were received badly and six months later Willard decided to move to New York where he became literary editor of the *New York Evening Mail*. His departure was reported gleefully in the Los Angeles newspapers, one of which welcomed it with two words —no, not those two words, they just said "Thank God!"

These were busy years for Willard Huntington Wright. As well as ad hoc journalism and editing *The Smart Set* and *International Studio*, he became the literary critic of *Town Topics* … and he also produced nine books, including a volume of poetry, *Songs of Youth*, and a travel memoir *Europe after Eight Fifteen*. The most important of these, as far as Willard was concerned, was *What Nietzche Taught,* published in 1915, the same year that his *Modern Painting* appeared. Towards the end of that year, Willard also wrote a series of articles for *Reedy's Mirror,* attacking *Encyclopaedia Britannica* while advocating "a declaration of intellectual independence for those who aspire to an American culture." The articles were collected in *Misinforming a Nation* but, by expressing what were essentially anti-British views. In 1916 Willard was seen as pro-German. This caused some of his friends to distance themselves and prompted the authorities to investigate his possible involvement in spying. Earlier in the same year he had edited the catalogue for *The Forum Exhibition of Modern American Painters,* and the year ended with the publication of *The Creative Will,* a volume intended to undermine his credibility as America's self-styled "First Aesthetician."

And 1916 was also the year that Willard published his first novel. *The Man of Promise* is about a young man who does not wish to live the life his father had lived, much as Willard had not gone into the hotel trade, and who complains about how women get in the way of a man's intellectual activities and achievements, much as Willard felt that his own wife held him back.

In *The Man of Promise,* the central character abandons his cultural ambitions and settles down to writing popular novels. In real life, Willard had already taken steps in this direction himself. He had a secret alter ego, a name which echoed that of the editor of the *Los Angeles Times,* Harrison Gray Otis. And, as "Albert Otis," Willard wrote a series of eight criminous short stories for *Pearson's Magazine.* These early stories are collected in this volume for the first time, and they are introduced by Brooks Hefner.

In 1918, Willard contracted influenza but by the following May he was well enough to lecture on art in San Francisco and in the following two years he would write for the *San Francisco Bulletin* and *Hearst's International Magazine* while working on *The Future of Painting,* which came out in 1923. In 1920, Katherine and Willard separated. This might have contributed to his breakdown in 1923 which he claimed was the result of "nervous exhaustion" However, in the masterly *Alias S. S. Van Dine,* his biographer John Loughery has suggested that it may have been because of an addiction to cocaine.

Whatever the truth, Willard was certainly confined to bed until the middle of 1925 by which time he had lost almost a third of his body-weight. The upside was that during his long illness, as Willard had been barred from reading cultural subjects (so he said), he discovered the pleasures of detective fiction. Deciding that he could do better than other writers "with far less experience or training." Willard worked out the plots for three books and made a 30,000-word synopsis of each, which he sent to Maxwell Perkins, a Harvard friend who was now a publishing editor at Scribner's. Perkins and his colleagues were impressed and offered an advance of $3,000 (equivalent today to $50,000 or £40,000).

Willard was delighted and set to work on the first book for which he decided to use a pseudonym. As he said to a journalist in 1927 – "a man who is working in other subjects would hardly be expected to write a mystery story!"

Thus, the art and literary critic Willard Huntington Wright became the detective story writer "S. S. Van Dine." Willard always claimed that Van Dine was a family name but there's no evidence of that and he may simply have chosen a more euphonious variation of his mother's maiden name, Van Vranken. As for "S. S.," Willard sometimes said it stood for "Steam Ship" and sometimes for nothing at all.

When it came out in 1926, *The Benson Murder Case* was promoted as the first of a series of "Philo Vance novels." Vance was described as "not only an expert in criminal psychology and in the various Continental and American methods of crime detection but a thoro[ugh] student of the literature of crime, both historical and fictional." The novel was a fictionalised version of a celebrated crime, the murder in 1920 of Joseph Browne Elwell, an expert in card games and the author of several books on bridge. Elwell's body was found behind the locked doors of his apartment. Without alluding specifically to the Elwell case, the novel's publishers stated that *The Benson Murder Case* had been written by a lawyer "in a position to know the 'inside story' of a number of New York's famous murder cases." As well as Philo Vance, the stories feature a district attorney, John F. X. Markham, and Ernest Heath of the Homicide Bureau. And to add to the fun, the novel's author "S. S. Van Dine" is also a character, a device currently being used by Anthony Horowitz.

While Vance and his mannerisms would come to grate, even on his most devoted admirers, *The Benson Murder Case* got "Van Dine" off to a flying start. The novels, at least the earlier ones, are characterised by everything we love about the Golden Age: an ingenious puzzle, a closed cast of suspects, double-edged clues and mysterious weapons, alibis that aren't and atmospheric settings.

In parallel with *The Benson Murder Case*, Willard Huntington Wright wrote a trenchant analysis of crime fiction for *Scribner's*

*Magazine* while at the same time and in a widely circulated interview "S. S. Van Dine" set out what would turn out to be a first draft of a set of "rules" for detective fiction, identifying clichés of the genre while drawing on Carolyn Wells' statement of the "Rules of the Game," first published in 1913. Willard later formalised his relatively light-hearted commentary into "Twenty Rules for Writing Detective Stories," which were published in *The American Magazine* in September 1928, more than six months before Ronald Knox's rather better known decalogue appeared in the introduction to *The Best Detective Stories of 1928*.

The second Van Dine mystery – *The Canary Murder Case* – was published in 1927. Like the Benson case, the Canary case was also based on a real crime, the unsolved murder of Dorothy King, the so-called "Broadway Butterfly" who had been killed in March 1923. While the first two Van Dine novels were the only books directly inspired by real life, Willard – as "S. S. Van Dine" —often wrote newspaper articles on real-life crimes and even a series for *Cosmopolitan*, using Philo Vance's voice to suggest lines of investigation and possible solutions. And by an amazing coincidence these articles were sometimes coincident with publication of a new Philo Vance mystery. They are included in this present volume together with Willard Huntington Wright's speculations about certain other notorious crimes.

*The Canary Murder Case* was a huge success, even more so than the first book. It was adapted for the stage and while it is unclear if the play of the book was ever staged, it was filmed, coming out in 1929 with the glamorous but rather wooden Louise Brooks as "The Canary," and William Powell as Philo Vance. Willard was more than willing to help with publicity for the film, posing for press photographs with the cast and even developing a *Canary Murder Case* cocktail, which is basically a variant on an Ampersand. However, and even by the standards of the time, the film of *The Canary Murder Case* is dull. It is also blighted by appallingly racist portrayals of minor characters, all childlike fear, rolling eyes and babbling incoherence.

While "S. S. Van Dine" was becoming the most prominent voice in American mystery fiction, Willard Huntington Wright was also taking an interest in crime fiction, editing *The Great Detective Stories – A Chronical Anthology* and using his own name he also wrote a fascinating introduction to *Some Famous Medical Trials* by Leonard Parry. Journalists started to smell a rat and one working for the *New York Evening Post* eventually broke the secret, claiming to have recognised Willard Wright from a portrait of "S. S. Van Dine" that had been used to illustrate an article about *The Canary Murder Case* in the *Chicago Tribune*.

1928 also saw the publication of Philo Vance's third and arguably greatest case. *The Greene Murder Case* involves multiple murders in a decaying house and features a family bound together by greed and mutual loathing. The book was also filmed, while at the university in Virginia students improvised a trial of the murderer. In interviews to mark the book's publication, "S. S. Van Dine" suggested that "The appeal of a mystery novel is almost wholly emotional while the appeal of a detective novel is almost wholly mental." Which he felt was why "scholars, statesmen, professional men, college professors —indeed the most cultured men of today read and enjoy detective stories."

Multiple murder was also a feature of the fourth "Van Dine," *The Bishop Murder Case*, published in 1929. It is a complex story involving archery, chess ... and nursery rhymes —indeed, the novel was originally announced as The Mother Goose Murders.

Later that year, after making a trip to Europe, Willard was sailing back to America on a French ship, the *S. S. De Grasse*. He found himself on deck, seated next to a woman who was reading *The Greene Murder Case* – by S. S. Van Dine —while her daughter was engrossed in *Modern Painting* by Willard Huntington Wright. The three fell into conversation, in the course of which Willard was disparaging about "trash" mysteries. When he revealed himself to be the author of both books, the younger woman felt he had been mocking her mother, and they parted on cool terms. So much for shipboard romances.

In 1930, *The Scarab Murder Case* was published. A philanthropist is found murdered in a private museum in Gramercy Park, New York. Everything points towards the head of the museum but Vance senses "a trap ..."

By the late 1920s, Willard must have felt on top of the world. While his first marriage had failed, he had undoubtedly achieved his goal of creating an American detective to rank alongside Gaboriau and Sherlock Holmes. As he said in an interview, "each one of the [books] made more money that all of [my] more serious books put together," and Philo Vance and his creator had become household names, with the first of numerous pastiches appearing in 1928 under the title "Who Killed Cock Cardinal?" His first four novels had been filmed: three with William Powell who in all would play Vance in five films, including 1930's Paramount on *Parade*, a musical revue showcasing the best of Paramount Studios; he had been played by Basil Rathbone. and Ramón Pereda had played him in a Spanish language adaptation of *The Benson Murder Case*. Nonetheless, what was expected to be the final Philo Vance novel was announced in June 1930 as… *The Autumn Murder Case*. However, no book with this title ever appeared and the next "Van Dine" would not be published until 1933. Clearly Willard was derailed by someone – or something —around the end of the 1920s….

It could have been Ogden Nash, a humorist who derided "S. S. Van Dine" in the *New Yorker* in 1929 and suggested —not inaccurately —that "Philo Vance needs a kick in the pance."

It could have been Corey Ford, a satirist who wrote *The John Riddell Murder Case*, a novel published by "John Riddell" in which Philo Vance investigates the murder of a writer called… John Riddell.

Or it could have been what happened in Bradley Beach, New Jersey, This is where Willard had a holiday home and where, in April 1929, he put up the prizes for the best games in the International Chess Congress which was to be held at a hotel in Bradley Beach. The guest of honour was the then world chess champion, Aleksandrovich Alekhine who happily posed with Willard while holding the black bishop in a convenient allusion to the fourth "Van Dine" novel, *The Bishop Murder Case*. The tournament came to an end with a gala dinner where – in his guise as "S. S. Van Dine" and "in recognition of his services in untangling murder mysteries," Willard was sworn in as police commissioner.

In accepting the honorary role, Willard said that "I fully realise that there are no murderers in Bradley Beach and that my powers of detection will not be needed in that direction, but I insist that my police duties include the inspection of bathing beauties and the measuring of the height and length of their [swimming costumes]. I hereby promise that my decisions will be neither short-sighted nor narrow-minded."

In saying that there were "no murderers in Bradley Beach," Willard spoke too soon… In August 1929, a handyman employed by a local pajama factory —was murdered en route to the factory from the Bradley Beach Bank where he had collected the payroll. As police commissioner —and as a regular commentator on crime in the press — Willard had no choice but to assist the investigation. Despite the fact that someone had actually died, the press had a field day, ridiculing the failure of the great "S. S. Van Dine" to solve what they– inevitably – called "The Pajama Murder Case." Willard resigned.

The case and his involvement had been widely reported and many friends sent him supportive letters, including the young woman he had met on the S. S. De Grasse, Eleanor Rulapaugh. However, she didn't include her address …

Humiliated by what had happened in New Jersey, Willard went to California where one of his neighbours showed him a portrait of a child painted by a local woman, Claire de Lisle. He was entranced but when he met the artist he was simply astonished to find that she was none other than the young woman he had met on the *De Grasse*, Eleanor Rulapaugh.

At least that is how Willard told the story.

In 1931, one of his closest friends, Florence Ryerson – who had written the screenplay for *The Canary Murder Case* – told a gossip magazine that Willard and Eleanor had certainly met on the *De Grasse* but it had been at a Valentine dinner rather than on deck, and they had continued to see each other after the voyage… Whatever the truth, it was time for Willard's marriage to come to an end. He and Katherine had been separated for around ten years and, somewhat belatedly, she charged him with desertion and they were divorced on the twenty-fourth of October 1930. Willard and Eleanor were married a month later, in New Jersey.

After the marriage, the couple went to Hollywood where, working with Florence Ryerson, Wright wrote scenarios for the Vitaphone Company for a dozen "two reelers" featuring Donald Meek as "Dr Crabtree" and John Hamilton as "Inspector Carr." Some were subsequently adapted for a series of possibly unauthorised cartoons featuring … Philo Vance, and these are included in this volume also.

While in Hollywood, Willard also worked on a scenario for Warner Brothers – *The Blue Moon Murder Mystery* – but this was not taken forward and, chastened, he returned with Eleanor to their New York home, a duplex penthouse apartment overlooking Central Park.

Willard needed to get back to what "S. S. Van Dine" did best. Writing books. A few years earlier, Philo Vance's next investigation had been announced as *The Autumn Murder Case*, but when the sixth book came out in 1933, it was titled *The Kennel Murder Case*. As well as collecting walking canes, art and books, Willard was a breeder of Scottish terriers and his dogs won many championships in America and Great Britain —*The Kennel Murder Case* features Willard's eighteen-month-old champion terrier "Heather Reveller of Sporran."

Years earlier, Willard had said that he would only write six books because he doubted "any writer [had] more than six good detective-novel ideas in his system." The late and much-loved author Christopher Fowler said much the same thing once about his "Bryant and May" stories and thankfully he didn't stick to it either.

So the casebook of Philo Vance should have ended with *The Kennel Murder Case*. But happily (on balance), it didn't.

The next novel to appear was *The Dragon Murder Case*, published on Friday the thirteenth of October 1933. As well as much piscatorial and draconine lore, the novel features an impossible disappearance. In the same way that *The Kennel Murder Case* had been inspired by Willard's hobby, *The Dragon Murder Case* was inspired by Eleanor's. He enjoyed breeding terriers and she enjoyed breeding fish. In their apartment, she had more than 60 tanks and upwards of 2,000 fish, and she had won two first prizes at the New York Aquarium Society's annual show in 1932, an achievement that the society marked by sending an invitation to become president to … her husband!

As "S. S. Van Dine," Willard contributed the foreword to a handbook on raising tropical fishes and home aquaria although it may have been written by Eleanor.

At around this time, Willard contracted for Vance to appear in various campaigns advertising a distiller, Hiram Walker & Sons. And he also licensed several board games. This frenzy of commercialisation reflected the simple fact that Willard needed money to maintain his lifestyle and because he had lost the larger part of his royalties from the first six books in the Wall Street crash of 1929. In an interview he quipped that this had made him realise that the only thing he could do with his so-called gilt-edged certificates was to write on the back of them.

And so to book number eight, published in 1934. This was *The Casino Murder Case*, and it was touted as S. S. Van Dine's best mystery, which is always a bad sign. The novel deals with poisonings —three of them —but there are too few suspects. Critics were disappointed. One even suggested that it had been ghost-written, leading the author to refute the allegation and protest that the novel had been inspired by his collection of shaved dice, weighted tables, and other devices used by fraudulent casinos.

The following year, Willard was one of six authors involved in *The President's Mystery Story*, a round robin novel based on an idea by Franklin Delano Roosevelt. 1935 was also the year in which the ninth Philo Vance novel, *The Garden Murder Case*, was published. It is set against a background of horse racing but the initial murder occurs in a garden above a New York penthouse, rather like Willard and Eleanor's apartment.

When it came to publicising the tenth book, Wright's press agent came up with "a cunning plan." Ahead of its publication, the publishers reported that a copy of The *Kidnap Murder Case* had been stolen from the *New York Times Book Fair*, and they even offered a reward! The book deals with the kidnapping of a New York playboy, Kaspar Kenting, who disappears from his ancestral home in New York's West 86th Street, the so-called Purple House. Indeed, the novel had originally been announced as T*he Purple Murder Case*.

In 1936, Warner Brothers – the company that Willard had worked with in the early 1930s —announced their intention to invite "S. S. Van Dine," Dashiell Hammett, "Sax Rohmer" and G. K. Chesterton to appear in a film based on *The Smiling Corpse* by Bernard Bergmann and Philip Wylie but originally published anonymously. In the novel, the four authors attempt to solve the murder of a critic but are beaten by a police officer. It is unclear if any of the writers was actually approached. Certainly the film was never made.

When *The Kidnap Murder Case* came out it was announced that the next book would be The Linden Murder Case but a year later the publishers revealed that the title would be The Powwow Murder Case, and it would be published in October 1937. Given that new title, it is possible that the plot would have been related in some way to the so-called "pow wow murder case" of 1928 in which a so-called witch doctor was killed by three teenagers.

But October 1937 came and went, and no book was published. A few years later The Powwow Murder Case was again announced as coming soon. The publishers even mocked up a unique copy of the book perhaps in an effort to inspire Willard to complete it. If it was, it didn't work.

By the mid to late 1930s, the well of inspiration seemed to have run dry. However, although no new Philo Vance novel came out in 1937, that year did see publication of surely the rarest "book" by "S. S. Van Dine"… a short pamphlet comprising half a dozen "original" Viennese recipes, made available for free to readers of *This Week* magazine. The recipes included "Eggs Philo Vance", "Perch Philo Vance", "Chocolate roll", "Christmas turkey" and "Breast-of-Chicken paprika", a dish that *This Week* thought was "as exciting as" one of Van Dine's plots.

Then, out of the blue, Willard received a surprising offer from Paramount Pictures —$25,000 to write a script in which the popular fictional detective Philo Vance would be partnered with the popular non-fictional comedienne "Crazy" Gracie Allen, "S. S. Van Dine" would provide the plot and Gracie's husband George Burns would write her lines. Far from being insulted by the suggestion that he would be unable to write comic dialogue, Willard accepted in the hope that the fee would take him a little faster to the retirement he craved. Although the film was not a success, Paramount decided to continue the series and requested another script from Willard, this time for a mystery to feature Sonja Henie, a Norwegian figure skater who had won gold at three Olympic Games and been world champion ten times since 1927.

Willard duly sketched out a story in which Henie's character is charged with murder and saved by Philo Vance. Although the film was not made, in part because of suspicions that Henie was a Nazi sympathiser, Willard's 30,000 word synopsis would eventually be published, albeit posthumously for Willard Huntington Wright died of a heart attack at home in New York on the eleventh of April 1939.

When *The Winter Murder Case* came out —on Friday the thirteenth of October 1939 —the publisher made the absurd claim that the book was actually better than the novel that Willard would have written if he'd lived because "the story is complete; it is only the usual decoration that is missing, and this last book proves that Mr. Wright's books would have been better if they had been left simpler."

It was an ignominious end. Philo Vance never appeared in print again. Except, arguably, in disguise as Ellery Queen. Vance did however appear on American radio in the late 1940s and many of the episodes are available online. He also appeared on screen. *Calling Philo Vance* had been announced before Willard's death; it starred the British actor James Stephenson and is a loose adaptation of *The Kennel Murder Case*.

In 1947, there was a trio of films with original plots: *Philo Vance Returns* featuring William Wright; and two with Alan Curtis: *Philo Vance's Gamble*; and *Philo Vance's Secret Mission*. None made much of an impression, and, while all but two of Willard's original novels have been filmed, there have not been any further English language appearances of Philo Vance. In 1974, a series adapted from the books was broadcast on Italian television, and in 2002 the first three novels were the basis of a six-part series on Czech television.

Today then, Philo Vance is largely forgotten but, as the stories are no longer in copyright, he may yet return. Vance played a part in taking the detective story past the First World War, particularly in America, and while he may well still deserve that "kick in the pance," his creator is surely deserving of a clap on the back.

Tintagel
August 2024

# The True Crime Cases

By Tony Medawar

In 1929, "S. S. Van Dine" was invited to write a series of articles about real-life crime for *Cosmopolitan* magazine. The series comprised pieces, which were published "as by Philo Vance."

These were historical mysteries, spanning a century and undoubtedly some were among the many cases he had read about while an invalid, bed-bound and contemplating the writing of a detective mystery of his own. These were in the main cases that offered little by way of mystery but had some quite extraordinary features. Van Dine's commentary provides a synopsis of the facts and there is comparatively little speculation. This is contrast with his earliest venture into the world of true crime cases when, in 1926, he set out his views on one of the most sensational crimes in American history, the so-called Hall-Mills Murder Case, which would provide the basis for several mystery novels[1] and almost immediately was recognised as "a classic of scientific criminology."[2]

The facts are these. A little after seven on the evening of Thursday, fourteen September 1922, a telephone call was made to a second floor flat of a house near the Protestant Episcopal Church of St. John the Divine in Middlesex County, New Jersey. The flat was home to Eleanor Mills, principal soloist in the church choir, and her husband James, the church sexton. Eleanor Mills told her husband that the call had come from Henry's, the neighbourhood grocery store, and she went upstairs to her room. Around half an hour later she came downstairs, wearing one of her newest dresses and her newest hat. Her husband, James, asked where she was going and, perhaps playfully, his young wife suggested that if really wanted to find out he should follow her. Mills did not do so and stayed at home with their two children, Charlotte aged fifteen and Dan aged twelve.

At two in the morning and unable to sleep, James Mills decided to go for a walk. "Thinking she might have gone there for choir practice,"[3] he headed in the direction of St. John's where he later claimed to have

---

1 For example, *The Bellamy Trial* (1927 by Frances Noyes Hart, *About the Murder of the Clergyman's Mistress* (1931) by Anthony Abbott and *The Crime* (1959) by Stephen Longstreet

2 *Buffalo Evening News*, 1 November 1922

3 *Washington Times,* 17 September 1922

waited until dawn. It would also emerge later that, in what her husband would later concede looked "like an elopement,"[4] Eleanor Mills had taken a trolley car, reaching the end of the line at 8.20pm. The terminus was a short distance from a deserted farm known as the Philips Place near the Delaware and Raritan canal in the western outskirts of Middlesex County.

When Mills returned home, he found that Eleanor had not returned and so, at nine the next morning, he went back to the church. On arriving he found Frances Hall, the wife of the rector of St. John's. Mrs. Hall asked Mills if he had seen her husband and, when Mills told her that his wife was also missing, they decided to go together to the police station.

Two days later, Pearl Bahmer and Raymond "Ray" Schneider, initially – and wrongly—described by the press as a "boy and girl, neither as yet in their teens,"[5,6] —discovered two bodies lying side by side face upward a foot apart in an orchard under a gnarled crab apple tree in a field about fifteen feet from a private road, De Russey's Lane, which led to an unoccupied farmhouse and was known as a local "trysting spot."[7]

The first body was that of a soberly dressed man, his coat was buttoned and his eyeglasses were in place while a Panama hat was over his face. The other was that of a young woman wearing a blue velvet hat and a blue dress with red polka dots, which had been smoothed down, and a brown scarf was covering her face.

The man had been shot once from behind, the bullet entering about three inches above his ear, while the woman had been shot three times, once in the centre of her forehead, once in the upper right cheek and once in her right temple; her throat had been cut with a sharp knife in what some medical examiners would later describe as a "necklace incision,"[8] and her tongue had been cut out. There was also bruising on her left arm, suggesting that someone had held her tightly.

It was evident from the condition of the bodies, the blood

---

4 *New York Daily News,* 26 September 1922

5 Pearl Bahmer was sixteen years old, and Schneider 21

6 Washington Times, 17 September 1922

7 *Central New Jersey Home News*, 25 September 1922

8 Some other medical examiners contended that Eleanor Mills' throat had not been cut at all

that had drained from the wounds and the flies that (sic)
bodies had lain where they were for about thirty-six hours[9]

While no weapon was found, there were two exploded .32 calibre cartridges near the woman's body was found and a third dropped
from Hall's clothes when the body was moved. Scattered near the
bodies – "in the greatest confusion"[10] —were several unaddressed and
unsigned letters, apparently written "in a woman's hand," and a number of visiting cards, one of which was lying on the rector's body and
would later be shown to bear a fingerprint.

Pearl Bahmer and Raymond Schneider went immediately to the
New Brunswick Police station where officers concluded that the case
was not theirs to investigate because the location at which the bodies
had been found was in Somerset County. The identity of the victims
was quickly confirmed and they were named as Eleanor Reinhardt
Mills, aged 32, and the Reverend Edward Wheeler Hall, aged forty-
one, who lived with his wife, her brother William Stevens, and several
domestic servants.

Lead responsibility for the investigation was transferred to Somerset
County and put in the hands of a detective called George Totten who,
perhaps surprisingly, immediately discounted James Mills as a suspect.

At the inquest, Totten "advanced the theory that robbery may
have been the motive for the double slaying ... Hall usually carried a
considerable sum of money and a watch. No watch was found on his
body and there was but 61 cents in cash in his pockets."[11]

The coroner agreed that suicide was not the explanation:

> There is no doubt that this was a double murder. The shots
> entered the body in such a way that any theory that one
> of the pair shot the other and then committed suicide is
> absurd. I am of the opinion that the murder was not com-
> mitted where the bodies were found, but that the bodies
> were transferred to the spot in an automobile.[12]

At the inquest, Totten revealed that some of the scattered letters

---


9  (New York) *Evening World*, 16 September 1922

10  *Billings Weekly Gazette*, 21 September 1922

11  *Washington Times*, 17 September 1922

12  *Salt Lake Telegram*, 17 September 1922

had been written by Mrs. Mills, including one that left no doubt as to her feelings for him:

> *There isn't a man who could make me smile as you can. I have the greatest of all blessings – a noble man's deep, true and noble love, and my heart is his. I am his forever.*

With the police openly admitting to being confounded as to the explanation of the murders, journalists were more than ready to offer theories:

> Although [the authorities] are convinced that jealousy was the motive and that a jealous woman played a leading role in the tragedy, they have failed to follow this theory to its conclusions and find the woman. They admit, also, that while most of the circumstances, such as the love letters written by Mrs. Mills, points to jealousy as the motive, there are other circumstances pointing to other motives. The disappearance of the rector's money and watch might mean robbery, if these articles were not taken merely to confuse the investigators. The gossip that had existed about the rector and Mrs. Mills might indicate the opportunity for blackmail. It is even considered possible by the investigators that the murders may have been committed by some volunteer moral censor or censors, either acting as an individual or concertedly in some such organisation as the Ku Klux Klan. That a religious fanatic might have committed the crime is another theory.[13]

Everyone known to the rector or the choir leader—other than James Mills —was considered a suspect: a couple who had heard screams in the woods on the night of the murders; a woman with whom Mrs. Mills had had an altercation in St. Johns, ostensibly about a prayer book but gossips muttered darkly that it was in reality about considerably more than that; Hall's widow Frances, whom Eleanor Mills' daughter Charlotte had "bitterly assailed"[14] ; and even Henry Stevens, Frances Hall's other brother, who was a well-known rifle marksman and had left New Brunswick immediately after the Reverend Hall's funeral.

---

13  *New York Times,* 25 September 1922

14  *Central New Jersey Home News,* 25 September 1922

Every incident was mined for clues, such as the occasion when Mrs. Mills and a number of women went camping with the rector and, after he had offered to drive one of the women home, Mrs. Mills "threw herself down on her cot and sobbed hysterically."[15]

And every stranger was a suspect, such as the drivers of two cars seen speeding near the crime scene on at 1am on Friday morning, or the two Italians who, it was alleged, had been seen boarding a small boat on the canal that ran close to the murder site but had not been seen since.

On the twenty-fourth of September, Pearl Bahmer and Raymond Schneider were called to the Somerset Prosecutor's Office. Schneider, described in press reports as a roustabout, had married two months earlier but he was already separated from his wife and he admitted to having visited the old Philips farmhouse with Pearl Bahmer on several occasions before sixteen September. However, he claimed that he had not in fact been with her when she discovered the bodies because at about nine o'clock he had left her girl near the trolley line terminus. After that, he had met up with a friend —Clifford Hayes —and another boy named Leon Kaufman, though he conceded that the three had then gone for a walk close to the old Phillips farmhouse before returning home by 9.45pm. Unsurprisingly, Schneider too became a suspect.

After questioning, in the first of what would be many extraordinary developments Pearl Bahmer was arrested on a charge of juvenile delinquency apparently unconnected with the murders. Her father, a pool room keeper called Nicholas Bahmer, had claimed that his daughter was incorrigible and had sent threatening letters to Annie Messler, a woman who lived in the same house as him; Pearl was charged but Bahmer withdrew his claim and, after one night in the care of the matron of the jail, she was released from the county jail into her father's custody. She would later bring a charge of incest against her father, who was convicted and jailed.

After the questioning of Pearl Bahmer and Raymond Schneider, three new theories emerged:

> 1. That the parson and singer were slain by blackmailers whom they had gone to the farm to meet. In this connection, it was conjectured that perhaps the torn letters, said to have been love epistles, had been stolen by the black-

---

15 *New York Times,* 25 September 1922

mailers and were to have been delivered to Rev. Hall for a sum of money he is known to have had on his person;

2. That the crime was committed by a jealous woman who resented the attention that the Reverend Hall had been paying to the pretty wife of the church sexton;

3. That the two had gone to the farm and been surprised by robbers who, after a struggle, killed the pair and robbed the clergyman.[16]

Then everything went crazy.

The King Kleagle of the New Jersey Ku Klux Klan issued a denial of any involvement in the murders.

Nicholas Bahmer admitted that he had gone "gunning" for Schneider on the night of the murder.

And the man who had discovered the body, Raymond Schneider, said his friend Clifford Hayes had shot Edward Hall and Eleanor Mills after mistaking them for his sweetheart and her lover.

And then everything went even crazier as one Jane Gibson, an eccentric known as the Pig Woman came forward, claiming to have been an eye witness to the murders. Her statement led Ray Schneider to retract his claim and, more importantly, led Frances Hall to employ the former assistant district attorney of New York County to investigate the case. He did and his investigations led the authorities to arrest Frances Hall, her brothers Henry and William together with a local man, a Wall Street broker called Henry Carpender, on a charge of murder.

Before the trial of the Stevens siblings began, the Newspaper Enterprise Association approached S. S. Van Dine who authored two pieces on the Halls-Mills case, which were published while the trial was proceeding. Carpender won the right to a separate trial and in fact was never placed in the dock.

During the trial, it was revealed that the fingerprint on the card found on Hall's body belonged to William Stevens who, it was disclosed, owned a .32 calibre pistol. And it was also confirmed that Henry Stevens had an apparently perfect alibi—he had, he said, been fishing in Lavallette with several friends. Frances Hall did not have an alibi but she was related to many of the wealthiest and most influential families in New Brunswick, which might or might not be entirely irrelevant.

Van Dine's first article, credited to "Philo Vance, The 'psychological

---

16 *Little Rock Daily News*, 25 September 1922

detective' hero' of 'S. S. Van Dine,'" deals particularly with the importance of individual psychology in crime detection and a generalisation on its application" to the specific case. The second article, also credited to 'Vance', examines the individual figures in the case. Both articles, which were syndicated and published across America, were prefaced with the blithe statement that "It is to be understood that any theory presented is purely conjectural".

For perhaps obvious reasons, Van Dine didn't complete the article by identifying the murderer or murderers and one can believe that he was far from surprised when, on 3 December 1926, the jury returned a Not Guilty verdict and the three defendants were acquitted. Carpender died in 1934. Henry Stevens in 1939 and his brother William in 1942. Frances Hall also died in 1942 and she was buried, like her husband, in Green-Wood Cemetery in Brooklyn, New York. No one has ever been convicted for the murders.

Van Dine also wrote about two other crimes. One very well-known, a classic of the true crime genre and the other now almost forgotten but in its time the focus of extensive speculation across the United States. ior completeness, these short pieces have been placed in an annex.

Tony Medawar<br>February 2025

# The Hall-Mills Case

*By Philo Vance, The "Psychological Detective" of
"S. S. Van Dine"*

Why were there three bullets in the body of the slain choir singer and but one in the corpse of Dr. Hall?

And why those after-touches of needless cruelty: the slitting of a slim, feminine throat and the slashing out or gouging out of a tongue that once spoke soft words from a mouth that once sang alluringly?

Was it not, then, at the "woman in the case" that all fury and hatred was directed?

Remember, too, it was a dark night, penetrated only now and then by a fickle moon! Throughout the long history of crime you will find that there are crimes of the dark and crimes of the light! And those who would tremble at their deeds, faced in the clear light of day, have been known to do amazing and terrible things behind the drape of darkness. I believe Shakespeare and others have had something to say on the subject. Certainly, in looking at the psychological phases of this remarkable case, the nature of the night cannot be overlooked.

In the little courthouse here the question still goes begging: Who killed Mrs. Mills and Dr. Hall? True, four defendants face a charge of murder; but that does not solve the mystery in many minds. One asks: Are they guilty, or the victims of circumstance? Does any or all seem to fit this particular crime?

A brief courtroom study and a glimpse into background can, perhaps, breed this conclusion: the Stevens clan have a great tenaciousness, as did their forebears. Through trial and travail, through accusation and tragedy, this instinct to hold fast prevails—prevails in matters of life, property, and reputation. Would it have been strong enough in love or pride to bring them to this crime?

And again: Is Mrs. Hall really unemotional or are her emotions merely pent up? But we shall come to this in greater detail later.

NOW LOOK briefly at the crime itself.

Every murder differs from every other murder—each has its own set of conditions and circumstances, as well as peculiarities, which indicate the character and temperament of the person who committed it.

The East Indian dacoit strangles, the Sicilian stabs, and so on. Just as it is possible to tell that Corot painted this or that picture, or that Ibsen wrote this or that play, from the internal evidence of the picture or play itself, so it is possible to look at the features of a crime and tell what manner of person committed it.

Clues count for very little against the psychology of a crime, for even without material clues, like fingerprints and foot-marks, or even with false clues (for remember, clues can be faked), the psychology of the crime and of the murderer remains the same, and cannot be changed or obliterated.

No one may have seen Corot paint a picture or have evidence that he actually wielded the brush but the feathery foliage of his trees, his idyllic atmosphere, and the delicate coloring tell us unmistakably that he did paint it.

In the Hall-Mills murder case, the clues are four years old. Many of them are contradictory. The evidence is conflicting. The stories of witnesses vary. A hundred warring circumstances and arguments are jumbled together in what appears almost chaos.

Leave all clues, material evidence, and stories of witnesses to one side, and look at the case psychologically. First, we have the small-town atmosphere—social climbing, gossip, scandal, a home about to be wrecked, jealousies and illicit love. Then two prominent people are murdered—not one or the other of these unhappy lovers, but both. They were shot, the man once and the woman three times! (Ordinarily would it not be the other way around?) Their bodies are not left as they fell but carefully, almost lovingly, rearranged side by side and with locked arms. Their love letters are scattered over them with a gesture of poetic melodrama. The minister's card is placed near the body, perhaps to identify him. It is like a grim tragic stage setting—a scene in a drama—a theatrical tableau. And if all these facts were not strange enough, the woman's throat is cut! And tongue too.

Here, then, is a double murder with a definite psychological aspect —and a definite personality. If you were able to read the indications they would inevitably point to the exact nature and character of the person who committed it. Just as the foliage, the coloring and the atmosphere would point inevitably to a Corot painting.

Therefore, try to ask yourself: Would this or that person, as I know his or her nature, have murdered Mrs. Mills or Dr. Hall in just the way they were murdered?

Another point: was it a man's crime or a woman's crime? Would a woman have used a gun in this direct and efficient, and murdered both of them? On the other hand, would a man have slashed the woman's throat and arranged the bodies and strewn them with love letters?

But suppose all these strange facts do not seem consistent with one person, suppose you could conclude some of the details of the crime are consistent with one person's psychology, and other details consistent with another person's psychology. What then? Do not forget that more than one person may have had a hand in the murders. One may have done the shooting, another may have arranged the "tableau" ad still another may have done the throat slashing.

Thus, from the psychology of the crime and its setting you may reconstruct a terrible partnership murder, with two or more people participating. But rest assured that every detail of the crime must inevitably reflect the personalities and natures—in short, the psychology—of the persons who did it.

But if you conclude from the psychology of it that more than one guilty person was present, then it might well have been an unexpected crime, brought about on the spur of the moment. If so, there is the indication that the actual murderer was an extreme person, one given to taking desperate measures, cool-headed in an emergency (as the accuracy of the shots show) and of considerable nerve.

Only a confession will clear the Hall-Mills murder mystery to the satisfaction of any considerable percentage of persons.

And, I will hazard the opinion that if this confession ever comes—which I doubt—it will completely upset the picture thus far drawn of the murder scene.

This does not mean that I make so bold as to acquit the defendants with a gesture or a theory, any more than I would similarly imply guilt.

I am seeking answers purely on the basis of individual psychology, and I find it difficult—almost impossible—psychologically to fit all of these persons to the hysteria of the scene that must have been enacted under the crabapple tree that fatal night. If, perchance, Prosecutor Simpson is on the right trial, then something somewhere is tangled. There has, of course, been so much "covering up" by dozens of people so much that has been hidden, so much that is still hidden, that such confusion is only natural. Anyone can note the undercurrent of furtiveness on the part of several witnesses.

I feel that here is a crime that one type of person could have committed by that type of person, but several, perhaps, added finishing touches.

Or it could have been committed by that type of person and others, surprised and startled by what had happened, could actually have gone to the means without participating.

Or thirdly, it could have been committed by more than one person, each using a different method of death and different degrees of violence, based on their different psychologies.

Again let us briefly reconstruct the scene: a small town milieu, full of social climbing, gossip, jealousies, sub rosa liaisons—a minister and his inamorata are shot… one bullet enters the man's body, three penetrate the woman's… her throat is slashed and her tongue torn or cut. Their bodies are lovingly placed side by side and their arms are interlocked.

Now the question is: Just what type of person would have committed the murder in this strange fashion? Does any one of the defendants now on trial fit the psychology of this particular crime?

First this is Mrs. Hall—aristocratic, polished, well mannered, immobile, poised, dominant woman—proud, rich and with social position, seemingly unemotional. But perhaps one who keeps her emotions in check; perhaps far more motherly than appears.

Secondly, there is Henry Stevens—a man of the same proud blood as Mrs. Hall, a fire-arms expert, a hunter and fisherman, a rugged outdoor sportsman, aggressive and forthright and cool-headed.

Thirdly, there is Willie Stevens, a weak-minded, pampered and protected, who has always been mothered by Mrs. Hall, and who, in turn, adores and worships her.

Which, if any, of these three would seem to possess a nature consistent with all the features of the crime? Visualize each of them, one at a time and try to fit them in the following conditions of the murder: (1) seeking or finding Dr. Hall and Mrs. Mills at their rendezvous, (2) drawing a gun and shooting, first Dr. Hall, (3) then shooting Mrs. Mills three times, (4) slashing Mrs. Mills' throat, presumably with a razor, (5) laying out the two bodies with linked arms as if for burial, (6) scattering the love letters of the murdered pair over them, and (7) placing the dead minister's card near his body.

And what are the implications of this amazing list of conditions?

That the murderer was a cool and accurate shot; all four bullets took vital effect. On the other hand, the revolver was a small one, and the shots were fired at close range.

That the murderer was not content with killing either Dr. Hall or Mrs. Mills, but killed both of them. Here is an interesting psychological fact when considered in connection with the present defendants.

That after both of them had been killed, the woman's throat was cut. Why shoot her three times and also cut her throat? Is this mutilation consistent with the efficient shooting?

That after the shooting the bodies were carefully rearranged. This would imply that the danger of being caught at the murder scene was not the foremost emotion of the person who arranged the bodies.

That some kind of sentiment or jealousy, or poetic idea, or hopelessness, or even viciousness may have entered into the heart of someone present. Otherwise, why were the love letters scattered over the bodies?

That several apparently conflicting, and even opposite, emotions actuated whatever person or persons were present at the scene—one emotion being murderous and vindictive, another emotion being hysterical and disorganized (as attested to by the useless mutilation of Mrs. Mills' body); and still another emotion being sentimental and dramatic (as attested to by the arrangement of the bodies and scattered letters.)

Now it is possible to harmonize these varying and diverse psychological facts into a definite and realistic portrait of a single possible murderer? And after you have completed this imaginary personality who fulfills all the psychological conditions of the crime, does it perfectly fit any of the defendants? Or does it coincide with any other person who might have committed the murder? Or again, does it imply a murder by more than one person?

And yet, even if you felt you had accomplished this difficult feat of psychological analysis, you well might be wrong, for the probing of the human mind is a tremendous and tricky task. As yet we know little of the hidden impulses of the heart and intellect working in conjunction.

# The Scarlet Nemesis

ON THE eighteenth of December, 1923, Germaine Berton—a slim beautiful girl of twenty-one, the tragic victim of strange passions and distorted ideals—was put on trial in Paris for cold-blooded and deliberate murder. The case created one of the greatest legal sensations of modern times, for not only did it involve many of the foremost figures in the post-war life of France, but it undermined the nation's most powerful political machine.

Germaine was born on June seven, 1902, in Puteaux, an old *faubourg* of Paris, where her father ran a little repair-shop. *Père* Berton was an unruly spirit. After the manner of the true French bourgeois he was forever grumbling at the existing governmental institutions, which he regarded as unwarranted restrictions on personal liberty. But, like the great majority of French bourgeois grumblers, he was industrious and thrifty; and though he preferred the independence of his own workshop to a better paying position in a factory, his ability as a mechanic and his frugal businesslike methods enabled him to open a little factory in Tours where he employed ten workmen.

Thus Germaine grew up amid dynamos and motors and the clangor of machinery, all of which had a deep effect on her sensitive nature. She was a charming, vivacious child, full of life and avid curiosity, gifted with a keen intelligence, and endowed with a poetic mysticism and a deep compassion for human suffering. Her mind was astonishingly versatile and precocious. She was an omnivorous reader, and at twelve was familiar with the works of Voltaire, Lamartine, Rousseau, Zola,. Kant, Victor Hugo, and Anatole France. She was an exceptionally talented pupil, and won two prizes at the local school of art and design.

At an early age the true quality of her character revealed itself. Like her father she was a *révoltée*, impatient of authority and opposed to all restrictions. From a letter of her mother we learn that she was obstinate and intractable, disobedient, and recalcitrant. Her relations with her mother were far from cordial, and during her trial she stated that she had received no kiss from her mother since her tenth year.

She had her own life, flouted the conventions and followed the ignis fatuus of her innermost promptings. The ties of home were but shackles which held her to a drab routine against which her adventuresome nature rebelled. Herein we see the ominous beginnings of an ardent and fanatical child who, a few years later, was to add another bloody page to the scarlet history of her country's crimes.

The first violent act that revealed her wild and abnormal nature came during the World War. At the age of fourteen she fell madly in love with a young man of Tours. When he was called to the front she suffered her first great weariness of life—what the Germans call *Weltschmerz*—and attempted to commit suicide by throwing herself into the Loire. But she was rescued; and in a short time her youthful energy overcame her despondency.

Just after the armistice her father died. Forced to work for her living, she separated from her mother and became a sign painter. Here her genuine talent in the graphic arts stood her in good stead. But her nature was unstable, and a short while later we find her acting as secretary of the Revolutionary Syndicalist Committee at Tours—a post that seemed to gratify some secret desire in her heart.

Also, her experiences in this connection sowed the seed of that stubborn plant which later bore the red bitter fruit of her splendid tragedy. Afterwards she confessed that the numerous victims of the war, whom she met returning from the hospitals and prison camps, aroused in her a passionate hatred of war and its instigators, and turned her into an apostle of the brotherhood of man.

In 1921 she heard the mysterious and haunting call of Paris, and to that city, with its welter of human emotions, she went, to pit her fragile beauty and blazing hopes against the sordid realities of entrenched power. At first she worked in the offices of a chemical company; but routine clerical work was not suited to her mercurial temperament.

She was not lazy, but intolerant of jurisdiction: her refractory spirit would brook no interference with her whims and wishes. And it was at this time, when she turned her back on ledgers and filing-cabinets, that she began to tread the path which was to lead her to the triumph of a startling murder and the apotheosis of a modern sainthood; for there can be little doubt that she will go down in history not as a criminal but as a martyr who sacrificed herself on the altar of a flaming ideal.

TOWARD THE end of 1921 Germaine came in contact with a group of young fanatics who were conducting a rabid anarchist propaganda at 123 *Rue Montmartre*, in the heart of the newspaper district. She soon became one of its leading spirits.

During the two years that followed no one seems to know exactly how she lived. But knowing the subterranean life of Paris and being familiar with the unconventional nature of the girl, one may surmise. She shares an apartment with Gohary or Charles d'Aoray today; tomorrow she becomes the *petite amie* of Lecoin or Rondel; later she is the "*confidante*" of other members of the radical group.

She was ever reaching forth for some illusory idea. But she was restless and dissatisfied; and even during this emotional search for permanency beneath the evanescence of sexual pleasures she never lost sight of the guiding star of her colorful destiny.

She wrote fiery pamphlets of a communistic character. She contributed articles to the revolutionary *Reveil d'Indre et Loire*. At night she met her comrades at the little café in the *Rue du Croissant*, where, on July thirty-first, 1914, Jean Jaurès, the leader and hero of the socialist party, was assassinated. She was at once arrested and sentenced to three months' imprisonment for assaulting the police; and later she served two months for carrying prohibited weapons.

Germaine Berton during this period was an uneasy and turbulent soul, marked with vivid contrasts and violent contradictions—beautiful and piquant, but with steel-cold eyes and an arctic mien of grave determination. Her mind was incisive and intelligent, calculating and logical; but her woman's heart was racked with fiery, devastating passions. She was prude and virgin, yet overflowing with sensual desires—at once a queen and a *grisette*. She belonged to that age-old hierarchy of women who wreck empires by day and subjugate the hearts of men by night.

In this strange and abnormal mind, swayed by the eloquence of fanatics and blinded by the visions of dreamers, there was slowly but inexorably developing an overpowering passion —a consuming and colossal hatred, without reason or restraint, for one man and all he stood for. To her he was the symbol of everything corrupt and vile and cruel in human nature. He represented the injustice and the tyranny against which her fervent spirit had always revolted. This man was Léon Daudet, the editor of *L'Action Française*, a member of the *Chambre des Députés*, the leader of the so-called *Bloc National,* and perhaps the most powerful political influence in all France.

Léon Daudet was born in 1867. Though there seems to be little doubt that he was the son of Alphonse Daudet, the creator of the immortal *Tartarin*, his enemies insist that he was only a stepson of Alphonse Daudet, the illegitimate offspring of a Levantine Jew. But this genealogy does not matter, for Léon Daudet at an early age carved for himself a deep niche in the hall of French literature and public affairs. As a dark-faced, vulture-beaked boy he showed marked literary ability; and in the days of the Dreyfus case he became one of a revolutionary group centered round the famous salon of Madame de Loynes—a salon which included such men as Lemaitre, Marchand (of Fashoda fame), Déroulède (afterwards foreign minister), Rochefort, Maurice Barrés, and Ernest Judet. Daudet soon became noted for his fanatical views on political and religious questions. He was a violent monarchist: nothing short of a return of the Bourbon dynasty would satisfy him.

He wrote many novels of unquestioned merit and was elected a member of the *Academic Goncourt*—one of the highest literary honors in France. A number of his books, however, were suppressed because of their obscenity and placed on the *Index* by Papal decree. His newspaper, *L'Action Française,* was a rampant Royalist sheet, the official organ of the Clerico-Royalist party, and the center of most of the intrigues and cabals against the government of the Republic. Lies, slander, blackmail, and even incitement to murder were its weapons; and there is little doubt that the murder of Jaurès was largely the work of Daudet's gang of "patriots."

But his activities did not stop at journalistic vilification. He organized a Royalist league of young people from good families, on the model of the German *Jugendwehren* and the Italian Fascisti, who were trained in arms, and who perpetrated numerous outrages and acts of violence.

At the outbreak of the war Daudet distinguished himself by leading bands of rioters to loot German and Swiss shops and to assault generally those persons whose political views differed from his. His ambition was to become a French Warwick at whose nod rulers were seated and unseated; and for a number of years he was the undoubted power behind the French government.

It was his attacks that drove Malvy into exile and Caillaux into prison. Clemenceau owed his dictatorial powers to Daudet; and after the war it was Daudet who drove first Clemenceau and then Briand into retirement, and who put Poincaré in power. His influence forced the latter into the occupation of the Ruhr, his aim being to break up the Anglo-French alliance.

Aided by the war hysteria, Daudet wreaked wholesale vengeance on his political enemies, and many a prominent man felt the weight of his mailed fist. Marcel Cachin, the famous socialist deputy, was imprisoned; and even conservative leaders like the Marquis de Lubersac were ruthlessly prosecuted as pro-Germans.

Schoolbooks on history were purged of everything reflecting on the Bourbon dynasty; and films like Griffith's *Orphans of the Storm* and Lubitsch's *Passion* —both well known to American audiences —were barred as German propaganda.

Daudet's political machinery was called the *Bloc National*. It was an irregular assemblage of all parties—an outgrowth of the famous *Union Sacrée* founded in 1914 for the energetic prosecution of the war.

Leon Daudet, vitriolic and vulgar, powerful and unscrupulous, constituted, in Germaine Berton's eyes, a menace to the Republic and a subverter of all the dreams of idealistic youth. And Germaine decided that he must die.

She had long since adopted the doctrines of Russian Nihilism, which advocated individual action as opposed to propaganda among the masses; and for months the idea of Daudet's murder had been germinating in her mind. At length, the conception having ripened, she gave herself up to it rapturously; and for weeks thereafter she lived in a trance of religious ecstasy, devising ways and means, and watching for her opportunity.

Now, Daudet was easily accessible in public, but Germaine wanted to be alone with her victim —she must have him entirely at her mercy. So on the morning of January twentieth, 1923, she presented herself at his home with a letter which offered valuable revelations concerning the anarchist movement. Thus, by baiting his prejudices, she thought to lure him into a private conference from which he never would come out alive.

But Daudet, canny by nature and cautious of necessity, was suspicious. Did he sense danger? Did some inner voice warn him against this girl who professed to have information of his enemies? Perhaps. In any event, he did not see her, but sent word to her that he was at his office and that she should call there.

Believing this message, she went to his bureau in the *Rue de Rome,* and was received by Daudet's assistants, Roger Allard. and Marius Plateau. But here again she met with temporary defeat. These two henchmen of the great dictator paid scant attention to her confused ramblings and dismissed her curtly.

Again in the street, her grim Messianic mission unfulfilled, she laid new plans. And now the romantic side of her nature dictated her course. At the old church of Saint-Germain-l'Auxerrois a mass is read each year on the twenty-first of January—the anniversary of the execution of Louis XVI; and it was the custom of Daudet and members of the Royalist party to attend the services in full regalia.

Churches always had held a fascination for Germaine, and she felt that no other place was as appropriate for her act of martyrdom as the church of Saint-Germain-l'Auxerrois. Here Marie Antoinette had come to pray when the mob was parading the streets to the strains of "La Carmagnole." And the bell of this old church had given the signal for the massacre of St. Bartholomew in 1572.

Here again, thought Germaine, a tragic and glorious page of French history would be written. Unwittingly she had chosen almost the exact day of this sacred annual mass to carry out her vengeance against

Daudet; and the next morning she went with eager haste to the famous sanctuary in the Place du Louvre.

But for some reason Daudet did not attend the mass that year; and Germaine for a time despaired of her mission. She felt no doubt that the forces of evil were triumphing against her righteous crusade. Desperate and dismayed, she returned the next day to the office of *L'Action Française* and demanded to see Daudet. But again it was Plateau, the head of the secret police of the League, who received her.

The girl hesitated but a moment. If the arch-enemy himself could not be reached, then his chief aide must fall as a warning—thus reasoned her inflamed mind. Drawing a revolver from beneath her cloak, she fired at Plateau. He fell instantly—dead. She had accomplished her great act of immolation.

Swiftly she decided that she too should now die, and she immediately turned the weapon on herself. But fate had other things in store for her; and she succeeded only in wounding herself slightly before she was seized.

Germaine took her arrest philosophically and offered no resistance. She was first taken to the Hôpital Beaujon; but, as her wound healed quickly, a few days later she was transferred to the famous Saint-Lazare prison and placed in the cell where Madame Caillaux had awaited trial in 1914—a distinction of which she was not a little proud. Her ceaseless energy and personal charm did not fail her in prison; and soon she was surrounded by an admiring circle of nurses, nuns and matrons. One of the nuns, a Sister Claudia, was delegated to bring her back to the religious fold which she had deserted years before; and the result of this attempted reclamation revealed the strange power of the girl who had sacrificed everything to a political ideal. It was the reformer who was eventually reformed. One morning Sister Claudia fled the prison, renounced her sacred sisterhood and joined the group of young fanatics whose priestess was in jail awaiting trial for murder!...

And now there occurred a somber and mysterious event that lifted the Berton-Daudet case into the realm of true Shakespearian tragedy. To this day it has not been satisfactorily solved; but its influence, both psychological and material, was destined to play an important and romantic part in the life of the girl who had enacted the role of the scourge of God.

On the afternoon of November 24 —ten months after Germaine's incarceration —Philippe Daudet, Léon Daudet's son, was found dead in a taxicab, shot through the head.

At first the identity of the body could not be established; and the following day there appeared merely the formal notice of the suicide of an unknown young man. But on Tuesday, the twenty-seventh, the press of Paris carried the following announcement:

We learn with regret of the death of young Philippe Daudet, son of our colleague, M. Léon Daudet, director of *L'Action Française*, deputy of Paris...

Five days later there appeared in *Le Libertaire*, the radical paper, an article signed by Georges Vidal, the well-known communist; and straightway the "death" of Philippe Daudet took on the aspect of a national scandal and became an intimate part of the Berton murder. Vidal stated that on Thursday, two days before young Daudet's death, a youth of eighteen or twenty had called on him, declaring himself to be an ardent anarchist. He had confessed that he loved Germaine Berton, and had stated that he wished to avenge her and sacrifice himself for the cause.

Vidal had spent the evening with him and attempted to calm him, but without success; and the next day the young man, who had given his name merely as Philippe, had called again.

This time he had left several manuscripts and letters in Vidal's keeping, as well as two hundred francs, although he had retained sixteen hundred francs in his own possession. This was the last Vidal had seen of him.

Immediately after the announcement of Philippe Daudet's death Vidal sent to Léon Daudet a letter addressed to Madame Daudet, which had been among the papers left with him by his unknown visitor. In the letter Philippe begged his mother's forgiveness for the pain he was about to cause her, and explained that his duty demanded that he take his life.

The police investigation into Philippe's death established the following facts:

Philippe left his home in Paris on the twentieth, four days before he was found dead, and went to Havre, where he registered under a false name. The object of the trip was never ascertained. He returned to Paris two days later and paid his first visit to Vidal. That night he sought shelter with a young anarchist, Jean Gruffy, to whom he confided that he had come from Havre for the purpose of killing Léon Daudet.

At four P.M. Saturday afternoon, November twenty-fourth, he took a taxi-cab on the *Boulevard Magenta* near the *Gare du Nord*. A few minutes later the driver, named Bajot, heard a shot and found the youth slumped in a corner of the seat.

A policeman was called, and the taxicab was driven to the Lariboisière Hospital; but the victim died without regaining consciousness. The bullet had traversed the front of the skull from the right to left; and, in the opinion of the hospital authorities, it was a case of suicide.

Several witnesses declared that they were near the taxicab when the shot was fired, but that no one had been seen to enter or leave the car.

No papers were found on the body; and the pockets of the clothes yielded only two cartridge-clips and eighty-three francs. The driver stated that the young man had been shabbily dressed and without an overcoat; but the hospital's inventory of the patient's possessions included an overcoat which was later identified as having belonged to Philippe Daudet.

Other facts, some of them curiously contradictory, were brought out. The police reported that Philippe had gone to a cabaret on the night preceding his death had borrowed ten francs from one of the porters; and had returned the next morning to ask where he could sell or pawn his overcoat.

The porter had lent him twenty-five francs more, and Philippe had written to Vidal asking him to repay the thirty-five francs from the two hundred deposited with him. (One wonders what became of the sixteen hundred francs during the few hours between his second visit to Vidal and the time he borrowed ten francs from a cabaret porter. And one also wonders whence came the eighty-three francs found on him after death.)

Another mystery centers about the bullet by which Philippe died. The taxicab driver found the exploded shell of the fatal bullet; but the bullet itself, which, after traversing the skull, should have lodged in the cab, was never discovered.

The police reports did not satisfy Léon Daudet. At first he had asserted that an autopsy was superfluous and that no suspicious circumstances surrounded his son's death.

But on December 4—ten days after the tragedy—he declared that the case was clearly one of murder, and made a formal demand that an immediate investigation be held by the attorney-general. Monsieur Barnaud was appointed examining magistrate, and a thorough inquiry was instituted. But though the young man's body was exhumed and a postmortem performed, no evidence of murder could be found.

A curious new fact, however, came to light. *L'Action Française* published a statement that, after a more careful inspection of Philippe's clothing, a small slip of paper had been discovered in one of the pockets, containing several names and addresses in an unidentified handwriting. One of the names was that of Henry Torrès, the attorney of Germaine Berton.

Thus the girl in prison was again connected with the mysterious death of Léon Daudet's son. Monsieur Torrès naturally issued a vehement protest, denouncing the implied accusations against his client and her political associates.

One other episode is worth recording here. The police during their second investigation unearthed a witness who swore he had seen the taxi-driver, Bajot, outside of the offices of *Le Libertaire* two days prior to Philippe's death; and *L'Action Française* at once hailed the fact as clear proof that Bajot had been in league with Daudet's enemies.

On cross-examination, however, the witness admitted that his testimony was wholly imaginary, and that he had been hired to give this false evidence by Léon Daudet himself. Whereupon *L'Action Française* characteristically accused the police of aiding and abetting the radicals.

The investigation by both the police and Monsieur Barnaud proved, practically beyond doubt, that Philippe had committed suicide after having planned to murder his father. This conclusion was strengthened by Vidal who, having talked with the boy without suspecting his identity, asserted there could be no question that Philippe, who had been in a state of fanatical exultation, had first decided to kill his father, but after a tragic inner conflict had chosen suicide.

Even, however, in the face of overwhelming official and unofficial proof Léon Daudet was not content to let the matter drop. He proclaimed in several articles that his anarchistic foes had lured his son to death and had taken advantage of the nervous spell under which he was laboring to force suicide upon him. He also declared that Philippe's letter to his mother had been dictated to him.

We may better understand this tragedy of young Philippe if we know something of his nature and his mental struggles. The descriptive record of him at the hospital gave him as between eighteen and twenty, with blue eyes and a regular nose and mouth. He had always been an abnormal, sickly child, and his poems and other writings, posthumously published by *Le Libertaire*, revealed an astonishing morbidity of temperament and a precociousness almost unique in one of his age. According to an article in *L'Action Française* he had, since his eleventh year, been suffering from a *tendence morbide à la fugue*—a morbid tendency toward flight—the attacks of which lasted from twelve to forty-eight hours. Under the influence of these spells he had several times run away from home. He was unable to resist these flight impulses, and often begged his father to keep him under strict observation.

It is said that his trip to Havre just before his death was due to one of these attacks. That he hated his father we know; and it is in keeping with his abnormal psychology that, when Germaine was imprisoned for what amounted to an aborted murder of Daudet, he should have committed suicide to save himself from an overpowering instinct toward patricide.

But whatever the explanation of the workings of his tortured, unbalanced mind, his net of self-renunciation was fated to redound to the advantage of the imprisoned girl for whom he had declared his love. Perhaps he had felt some such premonition during those last black hours.

In any event, his death gave glamor and extenuation to the murder she had committed through hatred for Daudet, Senior. And it enshrined Philippe forever in her heart.

He became for Germaine a saint and martyr. She believed herself to be his bride. His picture was her constant companion during the last days of her imprisonment.

Then came the final scene when this embittered girl was brought before the tribunal of justice to face her accusers. Among the many *causes célèbres* of modem times the trial of Germaine Berton takes a unique place. For melodrama, for spectacularism, for emotional appeal, it has few equals in the whole history of jurisprudence. The presiding judge was Councilor Georges Pressard, a jurist of wide repute. The prosecutor was Attorney-General Joseph Sens-Olive; and César Campinchi acted as attorney for the mother of Plateau, the murdered man. Henry Torrés, one of the greatest criminal lawyers of France, represented Germaine.

At the very outset of the trial it was evident that far more was at stake than the conviction or acquittal of the defendant. French politics was to have its day in court, and Germaine was to be made a symbol of vengeance. Monsieur Torrés not only defended his client; he launched an impassioned attack upon the party against which Germaine had fought in the battle of the political factions. His fervor spread beyond the court and its spectators: it was taken up by all Paris. It was felt in the distant cities of the Republic.

In vain the attorney-general objected. There was no stemming the avalanche of Torrés' venom and denunciation. It swept on and on, converting the murder trial of a mechanic's daughter into a political tribunal of national and even international importance.

The girl in the prisoners' dock was soon forgotten; but withal she was a picture worth studying.

She sat very erect, her shoulders noticeably narrow, her oval face, of the true *gamine* type, lifted defiantly toward the array of counsel. In her little gray dress with its white Eton collar and tie, her red cheeks almost hidden beneath a bell-shaped hat, she looked more like a schoolgirl than a militant Nihilist.

When she was called on to testify her expression was calm and untroubled. Her voice had a metallic ring, and her statements were terse and to the point. She exhibited no sentiment. She made no appeal to the sympathies of the court; nor did she seek to arouse the pity of the jurors. She said frankly that she had nothing to regret, and even gloried in her act. Bravely and resolutely she stood by her ideals.

She admitted her previous sentence of three months for striking a police officer and her arrest for carrying weapons. She told—not without pride—that she had once received a saber-cut in a street riot. She boasted of her revolutionary activities and acknowledged her various incendiary articles in radical publications. But, above all, she voiced her hatred of war and all those who preached war...

Then came her peroration, magnificent and tragic, futile and sublime—the courageous *morituri-te-salutant* of a lost cause. Yes! She had killed a Royalist, a defender of militarism, a hater of the common people. She had avenged the many victims of *L'Action Francaise* who had suffered imprisonment for their anti-war activities. She had dipped her banner in the blood of the enemy.

Her deed had been dictated by her conscience, by all that her heart held to be noble and true. Therefore she repented nothing, she retracted nothing. Her one regret was that she had allowed Léon Daudet to escape!

When Daudet himself was called he showed, contrary to his custom, great restraint. The vitriolic and loud-mouthed outpourings with which he had so frequently regaled the Chambre des Députés were conspicuously absent. He even refrained from the slightest suggestion of heated oratory. The evident hostility of public opinion had undoubtedly depressed him; and perhaps he felt that the death of his son had been in the nature of a terrible retribution.

It may be that he feared the outcome of the trial and looked ahead to a day when this fiery nemesis of a slim girl again might seek to carry out her plan to kill him. Or was his attitude dictated by a shrewd idea that his quiet humility would prejudice the jurors against the defendant?

But no legalistic tactics or personal posing could have averted the storm that was gathering about him. As he left the witness-stand, Germaine turned on him with all the ferocious loathing of her passionate nature, and cried out:

"Monsieur Léon Daudet, I wanted to kill you because you are responsible for the murder of Jean Jaurès. It was *you* who killed him!

We loved Jaurès—even we anarchists. Jaurès meant for us a symbol—the soul of a noble France Monsieur Daudet, I bitterly regret having shot Marius Plateau and not you!"

Jean Jaurès! The name had an instantaneous and magical effect. Jaurès! He had now become Germaine's defender. His spirit had risen and it dominated that tense tribunal. Its power acted like a spell. And in that moment Léon Daudet was convicted and sentenced by the girl who was on trial for a murder of which he was to have been the victim!

In the great court-room strange and startling things took place. The representatives of the radical and socialist parties continued the attack so spectacularly begun by the prisoner.

Famous men and women, whose oratory recalled the old days of Hugo and Zola, came forward as witnesses. It was like another Dreyfus trial. One and all testified eloquently to—nothing relevant to the issue. Only one name was heard—Jean Jaurès!— whose murder they had come there to avenge. Augustin Hamon, the famous Shaw translator; Marius Moutet, the defender of Madame Caillaux; Léon Blum, the eminent critic and deputy; Marcel Cachin, director of *L'Humanité* and former council general of the Seine; Ferdinand Brisson, the dramatic historian, director of the *Annales,* and Commander of the *Légion d'Honneur;* Jean Longuet; Georges Pioche—men of all creeds and political opinions were united by the magic of that one name: Jean Jaurès.

André Lefèvre, the Minister of War, and General Sarrail, the defender of Saloniki, took the stand in behalf of the defiant girl who had gone forth, a solitary crusader, against the powers of militarism. Pierre Hamp, the poet, showered the court with impassioned rhapsodies in the defense of a second Charlotte Corday. Madame Séverine, the noted philanthropist and writer, appeared for the prisoner. All these, and many others of national and world distinction, were there to turn the tribunal into a second *Académie Française.*

And through it all Germaine sat with philosophic unconcern, her large beige-colored cape thrown carelessly back from her slender shoulders, tidying her hair with the aid of a small pocket-mirror.

On December twenty-fourth, six days after the opening of the trial, Monsieur Torrès rose and, drawing his black robe about him dramatically, summed up for his client. His *plaidoyer* was at once great oratory and great literature. It was conceived and executed as only an inspired French advocate could have done it; and it ranks among the most stirring summations in legal history. It was a masterpiece of pleading, crowded with references to religion, art, science, philosophy, history— in fact, to almost everything in the world except the unimportant issue before the court.

In a final burst of eloquence Monsieur Torrès invoked the deep and sacred sentiment of the season. It was Christmas Eve, the anniversary of that night nearly two thousand years ago, when the mother of the world's greatest apostle of peace, the world's greatest-hater of war, came to the little inn in Bethlehem…

The jurors, almost without leaving the box, voted a verdict of acquittal. Germaine Breton was free, her crime condoned and forgiven! That night Paris held a *réveillon* second only to the wild celebration on Armistice night in 1918. And Germaine was its patron saint.

Thus the curtain fell on one of the most spectacular criminal cases of our day.

But this is not quite the end. There is another picture to be added— an epilog poignant with wistful tragedy. In this picture we glimpse the unrequited sorrow and the thwarted romance of a heart too tender, too idealistic for the harsh realities of this life… A year later, on November first, 1924—All Saints' Day—Germaine was found unconscious on Philippe Daudet's grave in the cemetery of *Père Lachaise.*

# A Murder in a Witches' Caldron

IN 1924 and 1925, Vienna was the scene of two sensational and nationally famous murder trials which are still the subject of heated discussions, learned and otherwise, in the daily press, in conversation, and even in standard works on criminal psychology.

The Vienna that we encounter here is not the romantic *Kaiserstadt* of Johann Strauss and Schnitzler, of *süsse Madel* and *Schlagobers*, but a post-war milieu of sordid and almost grotesque ugliness—a veritable witches' caldron—worthy of the brush of a Goya or the pen of a Gorki.

The three chief actors in the melodrama are two old charwomen and a worthless youth of nineteen; and the supernumeraries comprise an almost endless procession of caretakers, dogcatchers, scavengers, midwives, peddlers, fortunetellers, scullions, house-maids and loafers. But, withal, few murder cases in criminal history have contained so many diverse and amazing elements.

Marie Eberl, the victim of the tragedy, was born in the old Austrian province of Bohemia in 1857. After the death of her husband, a postman, she received a small pension to which she added, from time to time, by working as a charwoman. In 1922 she was employed at the Rudolfsspital, a state hospital, where she met a compatriot, Franziska Pruscha, born in Lassenitz, in Bohemia, in 1870. The two at once became boon companions. When both were discharged at the end of the year, Pruscha helped her friend secure a small indemnity and also obtained for herself 1,500,000 kronen (about $22). Being a war widow, Pruscha received a small army pension which she, like Eberl, eked out with occasional odd jobs.

Eberl, at the time our chronicle opens, occupied a small apartment at 26 Kölblgasse, consisting of a bedroom and a kitchen, and she followed the thrifty habit of taking in boarders who slept on the two spare beds in her room.

Early in 1923 we find two rascally youths from Thuringia, one of whom was named Bachmann, partaking of her meager hospitality. The old woman, who was a pronounced nymphomaniac, was being systematically robbed by these young scoundrels; and a few months later they disappeared with her jewelry and all the money they could lay their hands on.

On December thirty-first, 1923, a young man named Ernst Meiche called on Eberl. He introduced himself as a friend of Bachmann, who, he said, had given him the key to the apartment and advised him to seek lodgings there. Eberl was not at first enthusiastic—her memories of Bachmann were far from roseate—but at length she agreed to accommodate the stranger for 30,000 kronen (about forty-five cents) a week.

Meiche, who was nineteen years old, was the son of a small butcher in Rudolstadt, Bavaria, and, as developed later, had run away from home. He described himself to all interested parties as a student, though he was noticeably reticent on the exact details of his academic pursuits. But, whatever his studious hobbies, he very soon proved himself a worthy successor to his absent friend Bachmann.

His room rent was never paid, and he contented himself with living on his landlady's bounty, which transcended mere food and shelter and extended to actual monetary donations. A month after his installation Eberl received a back pension of 4,800,000 kronen (about $70); and Meiche "borrowed" 1,100,000 kronen of it, for which he signed an iou for 1,500,000 kronen, the difference being, as he magnanimously explained, for unpaid board and lodging.

At about this time Pruscha, who lived a few blocks away at 22A Klimschgasse, became a daily caller at Eberl's modest establishment. Often she spent the night there—a social practice in which she had not heretofore indulged. The cynic might have concluded that these protracted nocturnal visits were not entirely attributable to Eberl's attractions; and there can be little doubt that she had begun to fancy herself a rival for Meiche's affections.

Subsequently, however, she indignantly repudiated any such disloyal attitude. Indeed, she virtuously declared that on more than one occasion she had reproached the young scala wag for his shocking illtreatment of Eberl. But she did admit, under pressure, that she took certain steps—wholly in the spirit of charity— to test the youth's fidelity to her dear friend

How far she went in these altruistic endeavors is not definitely known but the inescapable inference is that she considerably overstepped the bounds of mid-Victorian propriety.

But Eberl, it seems, was unappreciative of Pruscha's sacrifices, for the neighbors were frequently disturbed by violent quarrels between the two. Unfortunately, the quarrels were couched in Czech, and their spicy details were lost to the listeners. On March third, 1924, Meiche—who, it appears, was something of a gay dog—bade his landlady good evening at about six-forty-five P.M., and fared forth to indulge his spirits at a masked ball in the company of a young married woman, Hildegard Traunfellner.

Eberl and Pruscha were left alone in the apartment. Possibly they condoled with each other on the fickleness of man. Or it may be they locked horns over the departed object of their joint affections. Several neighbors testified later that the two old cronies had a violent fracas— again unfortunately in Czech. Pruscha, however, insisted that she took leave of Eberl a few minutes after Meiche's departure. Also she denied having quarreled with Eberl either in Czech or any other language. And two trials failed to disprove these assertions.

The next authentic development bore the hour of three-thirty A.M. At this time Meiche, in a state of great excitement, roused Ustochal, the caretaker, and various tenants of the house, with the startling news that Eberl was dead.

HE HAD, HE SAID, just returned from the ball, and had found his landlady in bed, lying flat on her back, her face covered with blood. The caretaker, after verifying the body's condition, straightway sent him to notify the police, who, incidentally, took no cognizance of the case until twelve hours later.

Meiche then went post-haste to a Doctor Eduard Dubsky, who previously had attended Eberl, and informed him of his patient's demise. But Doctor Dubsky did not arrive on the scene until seven A.M.

After notifying the doctor, Meiche spent two hours in slumber on the couch of a neighbor named Emilie Bezniak, and returned to the Eberl apartment at six A.M. Various quidnuncs were gathered gloatingly in the death room, and two of them subsequently testified that Meiche "did something at the head of the bed," but admitted they did not observe what it was.

At six-thirty A.M., Meiche went to Pruscha with his grim information. His report to her is not without interest. He told her that Eberl had died of an apoplectic stroke and had bled profusely from the nose and mouth. Pruscha, according to Meiche, was not exactly stunned by the news. Indeed, he said, she took it with marked philosophic calm, almost as if she had been expecting it. But whatever her true emotions may have been, her first reaction was a highly practical one, for she at once advised Meiche to destroy his IOU, and told him where he could find it in Eberl's sideboard.

A little later the two of them betook themselves to Eberl's niece, Marie Sikora, and broke the sad news to her. Meiche then went for a stroll in the Stadt-Park with the fair Hildegard of the ball; and Pruscha, having fulfilled her mission of informing Sikora of her aunt's death, sought out one of her old cronies, Gabriele Dunst, and had a long discussion, the details of which are still wrapped in obscurity.

IN THE meantime Doctor Dubsky arrived at the scene of the tragedy. He found the door open and the apartment deserted. For months he had treated Eberl. For a slight fatty degeneration of the heart, and when he beheld her dead in bed he saw no good reason to inspect the body. It seemed to him quite obvious that she had died of dilatation of the heart.

Whether this casual decision was due to an overconfidence in his diagnostic ability or to the fact that he was still slightly hazy with sleep, was not brought out at the trial. The fact remains that, with a cursory and somewhat distant glance at the corpse, he returned to his office—or perhaps his bedroom—and issued a death certificate giving apoplexy as the cause of dissolution.

Between Doctor Dubsky's fleeting visit at seven A.M. and two P.M. of the same day nothing apparently happened. A few morbid neighbors may have peeped in at the dead woman; but the official records are blank for these seven hours. Then Marie Sikora, the niece, came to call.

Her visit, I regret to state, was not one of mourning nor yet of mortuary propriety. A less commendable motive steered her footsteps to the dead woman's quarters. She came to make a search for the 4.800,000 kronen her aunt had recently received. But though she ransacked the apartment thoroughly she failed to find any trace of her expected inheritance.

Meiche showed up during Sikora's operations, but exhibited a noticeably bored attitude toward what was taking place. The only object that held any interest for him was the sideboard; and it was at this time that, following Pruscha's suggestion, he retrieved his IOU. A few minutes later Pruscha herself, accompanied by her friend Dunst, called at the apartment and stood looking on, with a kind of jealous curiosity, while Sikora pushed her search for the elusive legacy.

At about four-thirty P.M., before the hunt was over, another relative appeared on the scene, who, it must reluctantly be admitted, had come on an errand similar to Sikora's. The new would-be heir was Karl Taschner, a distant nephew of the dead woman. But however mercenary he may have been, to his credit let it be recorded that he was the first person to pay any particular attention to the corpse.

While in the act of covering the body with a sheet he discovered that round the throat was wound a tightly drawn lamp-wick. Sikora immediately identified the wick as one that had belonged to her aunt, who had kept it in a tin box on the sideboard.

It now appeared evident that Eberl had been murdered, and that she had met her end at the hands of someone familiar with the apartment and its appointments. Meiche, according to Taschner, showed considerable nervousness at the discovery of the wick; and so agitated did Pruscha become that she fled the scene and poured out her misgivings and apprehensions to several of her friends.

It was at about this time that the police decided to bestir themselves. They put in an impressive, if belated appearance while Sikora and Meiche were still on hand, and expressed surprise and annoyance at finding that Eberl had been the victim of foul play.

Immediately, however, they developed an almost frantic activity. They went over the entire apartment in the meticulous manner laid down by the late Doctor Hans Gross, searching for whatever clews might have survived the influx of neighbors, sightseers and avaricious relatives.

They found on the kitchen stove three *Knödeln* and a piece of *Schweinsbraten*, cooked but untouched, and therefore indicating that the murder had been committed before suppertime. Several woman's hairs were clutched in Eberl's left hand; but these were never identified.

Just before locking up the apartment the police discovered a bunch of keys in one of the dead woman's slippers. These keys were regarded as of paramount importance, for they had evidently been dropped by the murderer. But after months of systematic investigation the authorities were unable to trace them.

Though they had been found hidden in a slipper, Meiche testified at the trial that he had seen them at the foot of the bed when he returned from the ball; whereas other witnesses denied that any keys had been visible.

Unquestionably a knowledge of their ownership and peregrinations would have solved the problem of the murder without further ado; but to this day the keys lie in the archives of the Vienna police, unclaimed and unexplained.

Another astonishing and almost incredible piece of laxity on the part of the officials developed in connection with the postmortem. During the autopsy the stomach was lost. Nor was any trace of it ever found. And since the contents of the stomach had disappeared along with that vital organ, it was impossible to establish the exact time of death by determining the victim's state of digestion.

There were two immediate suspects from the point of view of the police: Meiche and Pruscha, but before many hours had passed Pruscha became the chief object of their attentions.

She always had complained of extreme poverty and was without visible means of support except for her meager dole and her more meager pension; but on the day after the murder she gave 500,000 kronen to Meiche and a like amount to Gabriele Dunst. Furthermore, she had shown unaccountable signs of nervousness and fright after the murder, and had twice voiced a fear of becoming unpleasantly involved. On the night of the fourth she was arrested; and automatically another bit of suspicious evidence came to light: 3,300,000 kronen were found in her possession.

Half an hour later, Meiche was also placed under arrest, although there was no evidence against him. But as he was able to establish an alibi—having been at the masked ball with friends—he was released from custody seven weeks later; and Pruscha was held for trial.

The trial, which opened on November twenty-sixth of the same year, created enormous interest. The sordid and scandalous circumstances surrounding the crime attracted all strata of society; and when the doors of the *Landesgericht* were thrown open there was an undignified scramble for seats. The presiding judge was Imperial Councilor Doctor Hotter; Doctor Franz Wagner appeared as prosecuting attorney, and Doctor Hugo Sperber acted as defense counsel.

Pruscha presented a commonplace appearance. She was of middle height, slightly stout, with sharp energetic features, small restless eyes and large bony hands.

She constantly interrupted the proceedings: she berated the judge, reviled the lawyers, abused the witnesses, called names and indulged generally in vituperation, invective and billingsgate. Several times the taking of testimony had to be halted until she could be quieted.

Doctor Hotter carried out, according to Austrian criminal procedure, the examination of the witnesses. The defendant, as is customary, was the first to be questioned. She testified that Ebert always had maintained improper relations with her boarders and had even admitted her delinquencies in the case of Meiche. Otherwise, she said, Eberl had been a harmless, good-natured old woman with whom she always had been on the best of terms. She indignantly denied that she herself had ever had amatory dealings with Meiche and emphasized her avowal with such frank and picturesque comments that the court had to curb her rhetoric.

She gave an account of her movements preceding and following the murder. She had left Eberl a few minutes after Meiche's departure—about six-forty-five—and gone directly home, where she had remained until the staggering and shattering news of her old friend's death was brought to her by Meiche.

After notifying Sikora, she had sought consolation in the company of Gabriele Dunst, who voiced the suspicion that Eberl's death had not been due to natural causes and that Bachmann, the departed's erstwhile boarder, might have returned surreptitiously and murdered her. Dunst immediately and indignantly denied expressing such an opinion, whereupon Pruscha called her a liar with several modifying adjectives of a vivid and forceful nature. The judge admonished her to tone down her language and to refrain from insulting witnesses; to which Pruscha retorted that her language was sufficiently refined for her needs, and that, anyway, no question of insult was involved, as Dunst was her bosom friend.

The next witness was the casual and easy—going Doctor Dubsky. He sought eloquently, but alas! vainly, to extenuate his having signed a death certificate without examining the body, and was forced to listen to some barbed remarks from the bench regarding the solemn duties of the medical profession. Ernst Meiche—the Lothario of the unromantic triangle—then entered the witness-box. He was a tall blond youth, with hard vicious eyes and a cynical sneer, carefully and immaculately dressed. From his manner it was obvious he regarded himself as an irresistible Beau Brummell.

He contemptuously admitted that Eberl had been rather fond of him and said that Pruscha, too, was by no means impervious to his fascinations. The latter, he said, often had invited him to visit her and had shown a growing jealousy because of his attentions to Eberl; in fact, the women had often quarreled over him.

He explained that on his return from the ball at three-thirty A.M. he had found Eberl dead and had at once notified the caretaker, the neighbors and the doctor. He had seen the bunch of keys near the bed, but had paid scant attention to them. He admitted destroying the IOU, and boasted that later in the day Pruscha had given him 500,000 kronen and had remarked fearfully that she was being accused of stealing Eberl's money. At the same time she had asked him to come and live with her—an invitation he had not accepted.

On cross-examination he acknowledged that he had made no effort to earn money while in Vienna, but had lived on his landlady's generosity.

Professor Doctor Albin Haberda, author of one of the great standard works on forensic medicine and an internationally recognized authority on medical jurisprudence, who had carried out the postmortem examination with Doctor Meixner of the *Forensische Institut*, testified that Eberl's death had been due to strangulation. He also stated that, despite the position of the body when found, the cadaveric discoloration showed that it had lain on its side for hours following death.

Emilie Bezniak, the wife of an accordion player, who had quarters next to Eberl's, then took the stand and stated that, at seven P.M. on the night of the murder, she had heard violent quarreling in the dead woman's apartment. She had recognized the voices of Eberl and Pruscha speaking in Czech, but had distinguished no male voice. The next morning Meiche, elegantly dressed but very pale, had roused her with the report of Eberl's death and remarked that his two ancient inamoratas had fought over him the day before.

Bezniak also stated that the defendant had visited her the following afternoon and, when told of the keys, had exhibited signs of fright. At this point Pruscha broke forth in a screeching, incoherent tirade against the witness, and the trial had to be halted.

Marie Fiirnkranz (who lived below Eberl), Bezniak's musical husband, and Ludmilla and Stephanie Mathé (next-door neighbors) took the stand and corroborated this testimony regarding the quarrel. All of them stated that the brawl had broken off suddenly at about seven-fifteen. Gabriele Dunst deposed that, at the end of February, Eberl had lent her 1,500,000 kronen, and that Pruscha had come to her at eleven-thirty on the morning after the murder and advised her to tell Sikora, the rapacious and thwarted heir, that the amount was only 500,000 kronen.

Pruscha, she amplified, had forthwith lent her this amount with which to liquidate the claims of Eberl's niece, and had at the same time shown her a large sum of money, explaining that it had been realized from the sale of some furniture.

And now came the alienists, so familiar to our own criminal trials. They were unanimous in declaring that the defendant was sane and responsible for her conduct; but they added that her "moral repressions" were very low. Pruscha's attorney at once objected to the introduction of testimony other than that affecting his client's sanity, but was overruled.

When the learned experts had departed, Karl Jirku, a twenty-eight-year-old illegitimate son of Pruscha, took the stand and told a rambling story of a mysterious Mr. Nitsch who, when Meiche was still under arrest, had approached him as a representative of Meiche's father and offered to pay the attorney's fees provided the defendants would engage the legal services of a Doctor Reiss. Nothing definite could be got from Jirku's confused tale; and he was peremptorily dismissed. But later, his recital was to take on a queer and sordid significance.

Josefine Kallinger, a toothless old odd-job woman and one of the star witnesses of the prosecution, followed Jirku. She stated that she and Pruscha had waited together at the government bureau for their doles on the morning of March 4th, and that Pruscha had told her of Eberl's death and expressed the fear that she might be suspected of murder because a lamp-wick had disappeared from the victim's sideboard. She further stated that Pruscha had told her she left Eberl's apartment at seven-thirty on the night of the third instead of at six-forty-five.

This was too much for Pruscha. She leaped to her feet and gave the court another spectacular exhibition of indignant protestation. The gist of her highly colored remarks was that she had not spoken to Kallinger on that morning or any other morning—that, in fact, the *verdammte* old hag was an utter stranger to her. This passionate disavowal led to the swearing in of four doddering crones—all unemployed dole recipients—who testified to having seen the two in conversation.

The trial then became a mere parade of garrulous neighbors, relatives, friends, acquaintances and tradesmen. One by one they retailed the gossip of the quarter and swelled the already bulging records of the court with racy and irrelevant tidbits of scandal.

During the second day of this testimony Pruscha rose spiritedly, said good-bye to the judge and started for the door. She was, she explained with admirable control, thoroughly disgusted with the whole proceedings and had no intention of remaining.

Though she was unfeelingly brought back by the bailiff, she later made two other attempts to leave the courtroom, saying that she was fed up with the trial and that if the judge insisted upon continuing it he must do so without her. She declared that it was asking too much of a respectable charlady to listen to any more such foolishness—thereby putting herself on record as one of the most astute critics of the modern judicial procedure.

On November twentieth the trial came to an end. The summing up by the judge was clearly in Pruscha's favor; but to the amazement of everyone the jury, by a vote of ten to two, rendered a verdict of "guilty of murder and robbery."

The prosecuting attorney himself appealed to the court to allow the defendant mitigating circumstances when fixing sentence. After a consultation with the assisting judges, Doctor Hotter sentenced Pruscha to fifteen years' hard labor. And in due course the Supreme Court confirmed the sentence. But the affaire Pruscha was not yet over. A leading Vienna newspaper, *Der Tag*, immediately launched a skilful and persistent campaign to have the case reopened on the grounds that the condemned woman's guilt had not been legally established. The advocates of a new trial held, not without justification, that, though the presumption of her guilt had been strong, a number of her circumstances had remained unexplained and several promising lines of investigation had been insufficiently gone into—in short, that the indictment had not been proved.

A special judicial committee was finally appointed to reconsider the entire case. The committee was presided over by Doctor Ludwig Altmann, Chief Justice of the Central Criminal Court, and one of the foremost jurists in Austria.

After reviewing the records he expressed his dissatisfaction with Pruscha's conviction; and on June fifth, 1925, he ordered a retrial.

The second trial, which opened on October twelfth, 1925, under Imperial Councilor Doctor Schaupp, aroused even greater interest than the first.

Pruscha had not altered since her earlier appearance in court, though now she was calm and without any trace of hysteria. She added little to her previous testimony. She insisted that Eberl could not have had any money at the time of her murder, as she had lent 1,100,000 kronen to Meiche and 1,500,000 to Gabriele Dunst, and had squandered the remainder (about $32) of the 4,800,000 kronen on extravagant living.

She stated that at the time she had informed Marie Sikora of her aunt's death, Mrs. Karl Tascher told her that Eberl had been strangled with a lamp-wick. When the count called her attention to the fact that the wick had not been discovered until several hours after her talk with Sikora, she violently accused the judge and the police of a base conspiracy to convict her and refused to discuss the subject.

The same long procession of gossiping witnesses appeared and testified. But now, after a year of soul-searching and stocktaking, their evidence was far less definite and positive than formerly.

They were especially vague on the important matter of the quarrel between Eberl and Pruscha after Meiche's departure for the ball. This famous dispute had evidently faded from the memories of those very scandalmongers who had been most emphatic regarding it at the first trial.

Bezniak and her accordion-playing husband markedly revised the hour of the set-to; and Ludmilla Mathé contradicted her former testimony to the extent of saying that she had heard three voices participating in the debate, and that Meiche himself had been present.

Meiche had returned to Germany after the trial and refused to come to Vienna to testify. Thus the most important witness for prosecution was missing. However, his alibi on the night of the murder came in for a searching investigation by the defense; and brought out that, though he unquestionably had attended the ball, he had absented himself from the other members of his party for periods ranging from half an hour to an hour in length. Doctor Richard Pressburger, Pruscha's attorney, was therefore able to stress the point that Meiche easily could have gone to Eberl's apartment and returned to the ball without having attracted attention.

Hildegard Traunfellner, Meiche's *pierrette* of the ball, spent an uncomfortable and unconvincing half-hour in the box endeavoring to shield her cavalier and to explain her interest in him on purely platonic lines. During her testimony, a Mr. Pines, occupation and status unknown, rose in the audience and excitedly demanded to give evidence; but he was summarily ejected, and so his revelations were lost to the world.

It was clearly the strategy of the defense to make no attempt to prove Pruscha's innocence but to create an atmosphere of doubt by showing that other persons had had both a motive and opportunity to commit the murder. In this Doctor Pressburger was aided by the vague and unsatisfactory evidence of almost every witness produced by the prosecution, all of whom seemed to be suffering from an epic of forgetfulness.

Furthermore, the ownership of the keys found in Eberl's slipper had not been determined; nor had the astounding fact been explained that, though the postmortem report stated that the corpse had lain on its side for several hours after death, five witnesses testified that the body, when seen, was flat on its back—-the only piece of unanimous evidence, by the way, produced in either of the trials.

Following its red-herring tactics, the defense suggested an entirely new suspect—a vagrant named Oscar Geyer and a friend of Bachmann's and Meiche's. Not only had Geyer been heard talking boastfully about the crime, but he had lost a bunch of keys at the refugee home where he had slept, and had mysteriously vanished on the morning after the murder. The defense, however, was unable to bring its suspect into court.

Karl Jirku, again taking the stand, repeated his incomprehensible interview with the mysterious Nitsch, and added the startling *bonne bouche* that shortly after the first trial he bad been the victim of an assault engineered by Nitsch. A deposition by Agnes Bobaty, a chamber maid, which was then read, involved Nitsch still further by stating that a bunch of keys had disappeared from his room at about the time of the murder.

The Nitsch episode was becoming altogether too tangled, and

finally the gentleman himself was hauled into court and put in the witness box. It turned out that his given name was Hubert, and that his vocation was that of pastry cook. He reluctantly testified that he had met Meiche senior in 1916 on a pleasure boat somewhere off the coast of Australia and had, as a result, become interested in his son.

That a penniless Bavarian butcher had been sailing the far Pacific seas for recreation during the World War and, while on this extraordinary jaunt, had casually met a globetrotting pastry cook who was to assist his son in a murder trial eight years later, was perhaps the most grotesque bit of testimony offered in this fantastic trial. There were, however, good grounds for the suspicion that Nitsch's interest in young Meiche was of a far less innocent and philanthropic nature than he pretended; and the court dispensed somewhat brusquely with his testimonial services.

With Meiche unavailable, the prosecution's chief hope for securing a conviction lay in the testimony of Josefine Kallinger who, at the first trial, had told of Pruscha's reference to the missing lamp-wick and of her fears of arrest hours before the wick had been discovered or there had been any suspicion of foul play. Kallinger, when called, repeated with suspicious accuracy the full tale of her conversation with Pruscha.

On cross-examination, however, her evidence lost much of its impressiveness. She was trapped into the admission that she had read in the newspaper of the finding of the lampwick before telling her damaging story to the police; and she was compelled to admit that she had completely reversed her testimony when later questioned by the examining magistrate.

Doctor Pressburger then called the four old crones who had formerly sworn they had seen Kallinger and Pruscha in conversation at the government bureau. But the intervening year had worked havoc with their memories, and they now stated that Kallinger and Pruscha not only were total strangers but had, as far as they were aware, indulged in no discussion whatever on the morning in question.

In an effort further to disqualify Kallinger's testimony the thorough-going Doctor Pressburger called a large number of witnesses who informed the court, with venomous delectation, that Kallinger was a notorious gossip and mischief maker and had been jailed several times for petty thefts and frauds. Anna Karasek, a sour-faced, righteous-looking owner of a small grog-shop, added several rakish details detrimental to the witness' character; whereupon Kallinger gave vent to her outraged feelings by punching Karasek's nose and was arrested for disorderly conduct. The defense, however, did not rest content with these character witnesses and as nothing is dearer to an attorney's heart than expert testimony, Doctor Pressburger produced a well-known psychologist who proceeded to devour what few shreds were left of Kallinger's reputation. He declared that the prosecution's star witness was suffering from pseudologia phantastica—a malady, by the way, which not only had never before appeared in a court of justice, but added a new decimal point to the already hopelessly complicated equation of modern psychopathology, But the twelve good men and true no doubt rightly interpreted the doctor's Ciceronian flight to mean that the lady was a chronic liar.

The defense followed up this coup by calling, as witness, a former crony of the murdered woman, a graphologist and charm-worker named Marie Wilfert, who took oath that Eberl had come to her three months before her death for medical and spiritual advice, and that she had sold her client a magic stone (a specimen of which she proudly produced in court) and advised her to put hot compresses on her throat. This external medication had been prescribed because Eberl was suffering from hardening of the arteries—a pathological condition which Wilfert had miraculously diagnosed by reading the patient's palm.

Wilfert stated that Eberl never slept thereafter without a hot compress about her throat; and Doctor Pressburger argued that Eberl's death might easily have been the result of —accidental strangulation. But this theory was somewhat weakened by the observations of the next witness. Marie Tuschek, a midwife, said that she had been present when Taschner had discovered the wick about Eberl's neck (though at the first trial she had failed to record her proximity to the corpse on that momentous occasion), and that it had been loosely tied—too loosely, in fact, to cause discomfiture, let alone surcease from all earthly cares.

Then Professor Doctor Haberda, the co-mortician, again took the stand and iterated his former assertion that the body had lain on its side for hours before having been turned on its back. He added the emphatic dictum: that it was a case of murder and that two persons had been involved in it.

When asked if there could be any possibility of doubt regarding his conclusions, he replied grandiloquently that he was the oldest medicolegal expert in Germany and Austria and therefore could not be mistaken! But his aplomb was visibly shaken when Doctor Pressburger dulcetly requested him to state the exact time of Eberl's passing. The oldest medicolegal expert in Germany and Austria, who was beyond the pale of ordinary human error, was forced to confess that the hour could not be stated, as the contents of the deceased's stomach had been spirited away during the autopsy practically from under his infallible nose.

Numerous other witnesses were called, but even when their testimony was pertinent, only tended to confuse and bedevil the issue.

A piquant, even though irrelevant, item added to the records by the irrepressible Gabriele Dunst. When asked regarding the domestic atmosphere in Eberl's apartment prior to the crime, she stated that it was a bit lax and occasionally livened by a touch of downright ribald gaiety, as Eberl was given at times to indulging in the shimmy!

In all, seventy-six witnesses were heard, and nearly as many more remained who were to face the limelight and give their personal recollections and opinions of the two old women and their nineteen-year-old lover. But the seemingly inexhaustible patience of the court had its limits; and, to their consternation and chagrin, they were denied their glorious chance of immortality. One of them became so incensed at the court's heartlessness that he started a riot.

The jury voted unanimously against the verdict of murder, and eleven to one against manslaughter. The court decided that of the original sentence of fifteen years fourteen and a half were to be apportioned to the murder and six months to the robbery of which Pruscha still stood convicted. As she had been in prison for almost twenty months, she was at once liberated.

The pro-Pruscha press hailed the verdict a glorious triumph of right, justice, and truth. It may have been all of that —and more. But I cannot help feeling that the interest of the case lay in its unsolved mystery. If Pruscha was not guilty, then who murdered the old charwoman?

# The Man in the
# Blue Overcoat

## Foreword:

THE story of "The Man in the Blue Overcoat" was related to Markham and me by Mr. Philo Vance recently as we sat together in a corner of the lounge-room of the old Stuyvesant Club. Pursuing the subject of actual police detection versus the deductions of fictional sleuths, Vance cited this famous Austrian case by way of proving that *truth is stranger and often times more incredible than fiction.*

In my notebook I wrote down (as nearly as I could remember) Vance's exact introductory words to his recital of the "blue-overcoat" case; and I append them here.

"Y'know, Markham, actual criminological history beggars the loftiest flights of the fiction writer's imagination. Not only do we possess, in the police records of Europe, criminal plots that outstrip the ingenuity of the master criminals of fiction, but in the matter of actual police detection we find instances that rank with the greatest feats of the most famous fictional detectives.

"Regard, for example, the case of the man in the blue overcoat, which occurred in Vienna in the early part of the nineteenth century. It is one of the great cases of classic detection in police history. With a single slender clue the police ran to earth one of the most vicious and brutal murderers in Europe.

"Heinrich Jünemann, who solved the case, carved for himself a conspicuous niche in the Hall of Detectival Fame. No sleuth of fiction—from the romantic Monsieur Lecoq to the scientific Doctor Thorndyke—has surpassed the analytic and painstaking deductions of this famous Austrian detective."

I have not attempted here to tell the story as Vance recounted it, but have sought merely to set down the facts—which, in themselves, it seems to me, are sufficiently remarkable to justify reportorial presentation.

S. S. VAN DINE

IN THE EARLY part of the nineteenth century Abbé Johann Konrad Blank, Imperial Councilor, was the professor of mathematics in the class of architecture at the Imperial Academy of Fine Arts in Vienna. He was a man of seventy years, a well-known figure in Austria's gay capital, loved and respected by pupils and teachers alike.

He had formerly been an instructor at the famous Pleban Institute, and this fact was one day to assist the Austrian police in bringing justice home to a particularly brutal murderer; for in the Abbé's class had been a young nobleman who later played a conspicuous and bloody role in the criminal history of the dual monarchy.

At eight o'clock on the morning of February fourteenth, 1827, the class of architecture had assembled at the academy for their daily lecture; but though the Abbé was a man of clocklike punctuality he failed to put in an appearance. At half past eight two of the students, worried by the absence of their beloved old teacher, went to his home at 978 Johannesgasse—a flat dwelling named "*zur eisernen Birn.*" Mounting directly to the fourth floor, where he had his quarters, they knocked. There was no response, and they knocked again. Still no answer; and now they opened the door, which was unlocked, and stepped inside.

The curtains were drawn, but enough daylight filtered in to reveal the Abbé's body lying on the floor of the living-room, viciously murdered. He had received fourteen wounds from a sharp, doubled-edged instrument—seven in the head, two in the breast, and five in the lower part of the body.

The crime created a tremendous sensation in Vienna Superintendent of Police von Persa, in his report to Count Sedlnitzky, the head of the Imperial Police, waxed unusually eloquent.

"Whereas," he wrote, "after the above-mentioned findings, the Criminal Courts Commission having gone their country way with zeal, the police are leaving no stone unturned in order to discover the tracks of the perpetrator of this abominable deed, which has filled the entire public with the utmost horror and aversion."

But in accord with the customs of the time, the newspapers printed nothing beyond a bare statement of the fact that Abbé Blank had been found dead and that the authorities were investigating. Indeed, the Wiener Zeitung, the leading Vienna journal, took no public cognizance of the murder until nine days had elapsed, and then, under the heading of "Deaths" we find merely:

"Herr Johann Konrad Blank, Abbé, Councilor. and Professor at the Imperial Academy of Fine Arts *(k. k, Akademie der bildenden Kiinste),* seventy year old, was found dead in his fiat In the city on the fourteenth instant, and his body was examined by the authorities on the fifteenth instant at the City Hospital *(Allgemeines Krankenhaus).*

Europe in those days evidently lacked the beneficent blessings of the tabloid press, and even murders were committed with reticence and dignity. But if Vienna in 1827 was ultra-conservative journalistically, it possessed a police department that functioned with a zest and up-to-dateness which would have put to shame the sluggish and ponderous methods of our modern procedure. The manner in which the Blank murder was dealt with constitutes one of the outstanding epics in criminological history.

THE MOMENT the police had been notified the investigation was placed in the hands of Criminal Councilor *(Kriminalrat)* Heinrich Jünemann, whose admirable and efficient work places him among the great detectives of all time—Vidocq Gustave Macé Froest, Arthur Ward, Melville, Cappa and Breitenfeld.

Arriving at the apartment at nine A.M., he was comforted by the difficulty that Abbé Blank, being of a retiring and somewhat morbid disposition, had always lived alone and had had few intimates—a fact he ascertained from the students who had discovered the body. After weighing the situation Jünemann adopted the tentative hypothesis of murder for robbery, and pursued his investigation from this standpoint.

Inquiries on the spot failed to elicit any information as to the Abbé's means. Blank had been particularly reticent about his financial affairs, and Jünemann straightaway made a detailed search of the apartment in the hope of turning up some clue. In an old envelope he found a will dated November twelfth, 1826, together with a letter addressed to the Imperial Court Valet *(Kaiserlicher Kammerdiener)* Kaspar Kalb, who had been named as the Abbé's executor. Among the assets mentioned in the will were seven five-percent Métallique bonds—five of them (numbers 14145, 25760, 89135, 191148, and 192511) of a par value of 1000 florins each; and two (numbers 225 and 3475) of a par value of 500 florins each—a total par value of 6000 florins (about $2400).

These securities were nowhere to be found in the apartment.

However, the coupon of bond number 89135 (due on April first, 1827) was discovered in a small dispatch-box. and Jünemann concluded that this box had also been the repository of the bonds themselves. He thereupon communicated to all the public and private bankers of Vienna a list of the missing bonds, with instructions that he be notified the moment any one of them appeared.

Within a few hours a private banker named August Wedl reported that, on the day before—February thirteenth—about three P.M., he had bought from a stranger five of the stolen bonds, and that, a little later in the afternoon, a jeweler named Wenzel Johann Swoboda had sold him the other two bonds in the series. The bill of sale for the first five bonds had been signed, "Joha Hose," and the address appended was the "Weinhaus." Wedl, however, was unable to give a satisfactory description of the man. This information not only confirmed Jünemann's robbery theory, but helped to establish the time of the crime. Obviously Abbé Blank had been murdered before three P.M. of the preceding day. Further investigation among the inmates of the house where the Abbé lived established the time as one-fifteen P.M..

Ludwig Raby, who for twenty-three years had cleaned the Blank apartment daily between ten and eleven-thirty a.m., testified that the Abbé had returned from the academy just before eleven-thirty and had settled himself comfortably in the living-room with a book.

On the third floor of the building, directly under the Blank apartment, lived a Professor Riepl. Jünemann, interrogating the Riepl cook, learned that, about one o'clock, a man had knocked on the door and had made inquiries as to the whereabouts of the Blank apartment. She had directed the stranger to the flat above. and had thought no more of the episode until about twenty minutes later, when she heard a noise on the stairway.

Looking out into the hall she had seen the same man pick up his hat and stick from the steps, where he had evidently dropped them, and then rush precipitately from the house.

Pushed for a description of the man, she was unable to recall any detail with the exception of the fact that he was wearing a blue overcoat.

Professor Riepl, who was next questioned by Jünemann, said that at one-fifteen P.M. he and his wife, who were having their dinner, had heard a loud hammering noise in the flat above, as if someone were knocking on the floor with a wooden mallet. He had remarked to his wife, "What the devil is the Abbé doing?"

Two stepsisters, Franziska Renaty and Anna Heyder, who lived on the fourth floor, told Jünemann that they had seen a man in a blue overcoat knock on Abbé Blank's door at one P.M. and had also seen him leave the apartment in a more or less disheveled condition twenty minutes later, and dash down the stairs. He had slipped, dropped his hat and stick, retrieved them and continued his flight.

Jünemann made inquiries at the restaurant where Blank ate his dinner, and learned that the Abbé had not put in an appearance that day. Thus it was conclusively established that the crime had occurred almost exactly at one-fifteen P.M. on the thirteenth, and that a man in a blue overcoat was the murderer.

WEDL, THE BANKER, under Jünemann's cross-examination recalled that the seller of the stolen bonds had been attired in a blue overcoat.

The detailed testimony of the jeweler Swoboda was also significant. He explained that, about four P.M. on the afternoon of the thirteenth, a man had come to his shop and bought a diamond ring for ninety florins, offering two bonds (totaling 1500 florins) in payment and requesting that the change of 1410 florins be given him in cash. Swoboda had refused, but the stranger had suggested that he take the bonds to Wedl—a suggestion which had been followed. Swoboda also described the purchaser as wearing a blue overcoat.

It should be noted here that these blue overcoats were at that time the latest fashion in Vienna. They were cut to about the. wearer's knees and bore a long cape with several superimposed smaller capes, or collars. They were affected by the dandies of the period, and were regarded as a hall-mark of wealth and elegance. But after the trial of Abbé Blank's murderer they became known as "gallows-cloaks" (*Galgenmäntel*), and instantly lost their vogue.

Jünemann's task, with this slender clue, was not an easy one, for there were hundreds of owners of similar blue -overcoats in Vienna; and his problem was rendered even more difficult by the fact that Abbé Blank had lived a secluded life and had had almost no acquaintances or friends. Yet Jünemann turned this very obstacle to advantage.

Because of the Abbé's morbid and suspicious nature it was reasonable to assume that he would not readily have admitted a stranger to his apartment. The door of the flat had not been forced, and Jünemann rightly concluded that only an acquaintance could have committed the crime. Moreover, the two stepsisters had seen the man in the blue overcoat knock on the door—a fact which revealed the caller's assurance that he would be received.

Careful inquiries, however, failed to reveal a single known acquaintance of the Abbé belonging to the fashionable social class. who would have been likely to own one of the modish new overcoats. The name "Joha Hose" signed to the sales note of the bonds was obviously a false one.

That night Jünemann visited the Imperial Court Valet Kalb, who had been named as executor in Blank's will. And here he came into possession of another slender clue. Kalb was the same age as Blank. and the two had. been friends for forty years. But despite this fact they seldom visited each other. A recent exception had been the day preceding the murder, when the Abbé had driven to Kalb's home to request the return ·of a dispatch-box which he had placed in his friend's care.

Kalb had never known what the box contained. but on this occasion the Abbé had explained that an acquaintance of his—a count—wanted to inspect some Austrian bonds. and through this remark Kalb had surmised that the case actually contained bonds.

It could now be assumed that the man in the blue overcoat was a count, especially as a count would be the kind of person who might dress in this fashion. But there were many counts in Vienna; and although Jünemann put his subordinates to work checking up the Abbé's acquaintances, no member of the nobility was unearthed.

The next noon Jünemann began questioning all the cabmen of the district, on the theory that a count, even though bent on murder and robbery, would ride in a fiacre. After hours of interviewing, a cabman was found, who about one P.M. on February thirteenth, had driven a man in a blue overcoat to a point near where the Abbé lived.

The cabman stated that the man, from his appearance and accent, was a Polish nobleman.

This testimony added another item of characterization to the hypothetical murderer. Not only was he presumably a count. but also perhaps a Polish count. Jünemann's search was thus somewhat narrowed although no evidence whatever had been adduced to fasten the crime on this elusive person.

But with this start Jünemann continued his questioning of Vienna's cabmen, now asking them specifically if they had recently driven a man in a blue overcoat who might possibly qualify as a Polish count.

The following morning a cabman was found who stated that the day before—February fifteenth—he had driven a man in a blue overcoat with a slight Polish accent, to a saddler named Mayenberger.

Seizing upon this evidence, Jünemann hastened to Mayenberger. After a brief interrogation he learned that the name of the blue-coated customer was Count Séverin von Jaroszynski, and that he lived in the Trattnerhof. Not only was Count Jaroszynski's name Polish, but his reputation in Vienna was far from savory. Jünemann felt that in all likelihood he had run his culprit to earth.

BUT ONE GRAVE obstacle stood in the way of his making an immediate arrest. How was it possible that a man of the type of Abbé Blank would know the flamboyant Count Jaroszynski sufficiently well to admit him to his apartment? In looking into the life of the Abbé, Jünemann remembered that before taking the chair of mathematics at the Imperial Academy of Fine Arts Blank had taught at the Pleban Institute, which was one of the most exclusive private schools in Austria attended only by the sons of the aristocracy. On further investigation he discovered that among the Abbé's pupils had been a lad named Séverin von Jaroszynski, the son of a wealthy Polish nobleman.

This fact established the welding link in Jünemann's chain of evidence, for it explained the acquaintanceship between the murdered man and his assassin. On the night of February sixteenth—the second day after the crime had been discovered—Jünemann went to Jaroszynski's apartment with a warrant for his arrest.

Of the many picturesque characters in Vienna at the beginning of the nineteenth century none was more widely known and spectacular than Count Jaroszynski. Young Séverin was born on December twentieth 1789, in Poland. His father intended him for the government service and sent him to the Nikolaus Kaiser school in Warsaw and later to the Pleban Institute in Vienna. On his return to Poland he joined the army and was made a Knight of the Order of St. Anne. At the death of his father in 1817 he inherited large estates which brought him an annual revenue of 50,000 florins (about $20,000); and he at once quitted the army and entered the civil service, where, in 1820, he was appointed Lieutenant-Governor of Mohilev and made a Knight of the Maltese Order.

His riotous extravagance, so common among the Polish aristocracy, soon plunged him into debt, from which he was temporarily relieved by a rich marriage with Theophila Scalacola, who had an independent yearly income of 150,000 lorins (about $60,000). But his extravagance, combined with an almost insane passion for gambling, soon brought him again into tight financial straits.

His wife's fortune having been dissipated and his own estates being hopelessly mortgaged, he diverted some government property to his own use, and found it safer to flee Russia. He prudently took with him all the money he could lay his hands on, consisting largely of government taxes; and in June, 1826, he established himself in Vienna.

Here he lived the life of a *Grand Seigneur*, representing himself to society "*Le Comte Séverin de Jaroschinski, Maréchal de Mohilev.*" At first he found no difficulty in borrowing large sums of money in Vienna, where a title, however spurious, never failed to impress. His chief creditors were tradespeople, innkeepers and even waiters. To his borrowings he added substantial winnings at cards, and for a time he was in no immediate financial need, but soon ugly rumors of sharp practise began to circulate; and he was soon without victims. His creditors began to grow restless, and threats of court action were made against him. In the early days of February, 1827, he became desperate.

Women were not the least of Jaroszynski's items of expense, and particularly was the famous and beautiful comedy star Therese Krones, a heavy drain on his uncertain resources. Indeed, one cannot help wondering to just what extent her demands were responsible for Abbé Blank's death. Perhaps it is significant that Jaroszynski was in her company when the inexorable arm of the law reached out for him.

At eight o'clock on the night of February sixteenth, Jünemann, accompanied by Swoboda and Wedl, presented himself at the address in the Trattnerhof given by the saddler Mayenberger. Jaroszynski was in the midst of a dinner party. Besides Fraülein Krones there were present another famous stage beauty—Antonie Jager—and a Major Lebreux, a well-known figure in Vienna.

For an hour before Jünemann's arrival the murder of Abbé Blank, which had roused public interest to an extraordinary degree, had been under discussion, and the fair Therese had expressed an impassioned hope that the criminal would be apprehended. Jaroszynski had taken but small part in the conversation.

In an effort to cheer him, Therese rose and began to sing a song which she had made the rage of the city:

Brother of mine, brother of mine,<br>Friendly must our parting be…

It was at this moment that Jünemann grimly appeared at the door with his witnesses. Swoboda and Wedl identified Jaroszynski; and the arrest was made.

A search of Jaroszynski's apartment immediately following his arrest brought to light a new carving-knife containing blood stains, the ring purchased from Swoboda for ninety florins, the famous blue overcoat, and a walking-stick which, when microscopically examined, revealed several blood spots on the ferrule. Furthermore, 2,865 florins were found in the possession of Jaroszynski's valet. Michael Sinion, who declared that his master had given him the money that day for safekeeping

Jünemann began an investigation in connection with the carving-knife; by noon the next day he discovered a shop on the Graben where the weapon had been purchased. Tobias Stubek, the salesman, stated that a man in a blue overcoat had bought it on February 5, choosing the largest knife in stock.

Considering that only two days had elapsed since the discovery of the Abbé's murdered body and that the police not only had found and arrested the criminal but also had built up a complete case to place before the courts, one can understand that Jünemann looked with satisfaction on his handling of the case.

But the task of the police was far from completed. In those days no conviction involving capital punishment was permissible without either the confession of the defendant or the direct testimony of two eyewitnesses to the crime. Jaroszynski, despite the powerful circumstantial evidence against him, continued to deny his guilt—he had, he stated, bought the bonds several months previously from an acquaintance whose name he did not know; and the money which he had given his valet had been won at cards—and the investigation soon reached an impasse.

Now, Jünemann was an efficient, energetic police official—indeed, one of the greatest evidential detectives in the history of criminology—but he lacked psychological insight into the workings of the criminal mind; and at this stage of the proceedings the authorities saw fit to call in Councilor Edmund Karhan, a man of great human sympathy and deep understanding. To this latter officer is due the credit for penetrating Jaroszynski's stubborn defense—a feat he accomplished by playing sagaciously on the other's colossal vanity and arrogance.

Karhan first acquainted himself with Jaroszynski's antecedents and psychology. He studied his actions and his traits of character; and at the very first interview succeeded in inveigling the prisoner into several damaging admissions.

One of the interesting psychological points brought out in the battle of wits between Karhan and Jaroszynski hung on the fact that the prisoner would not mention the name of his victim.

Karhan seized upon this reticence and taunted the prisoner with it. He called Jaroszynski's attention to the name on the bill of sale for the bonds, pointing out that the signer had started to write the first name of his victim—to wit, Johann—but had halted that terrifying signature after "Joha" had been penned, as if he could not bear to complete the name.

Much of the interrogation naturally centered round the financial affairs of the accused. Jaroszynski asserted that he had received sufficient money for his needs from his brother, and that he had augmented this allowance by his winnings at cards. But Karhan confronted him with the testimony of numerous persons from whom he had borrowed sums of various amounts. The tailor Missgrill had lent him 12,000 florins in cash, and also held a heavy bill against him. Valets, waiters, and innkeepers were brought forward to testify to smaller loans made to the prisoner.

Karhan then pointed out that on the evening of February four-teenth—the day after the crime had been committed—Jaroszynski had paid most of his smaller debts, besides giving the sum of 2865 florins—to his valet.

But even when faced with this mass of evidence Jaroszynski persisted in denial. He worked himself into a state of exalted and almost hysterical pride, and scoffed at the idea of having stooped to borrow money from menials. Karhan, quickly taking advantage of this mood of superior arrogance, ordered him taken to his cell and placed in irons. Immediately Jaroszynski pleaded for a rescinding the order, and when Karhan reluctantly gave in, he admitted his need for money and the loans.

On April twenty-first, Jaroszynski was on the brink of confessing, but was withheld by the idea of a possible death on the gallows. Karhan continued to prod the weak spots in his victim's armor.

For another week this psychological game went on. Karhan did all in his power to enhance Jaroszynski's self-pride and social vanity, in order to render him more vulnerable to the treatment he had outlined. Then, on April twenty-sixth, after the prisoner had haughtily refused answer any further questions, Karhan signed an order that he be given twelve strokes of the rod and placed in irons. The humiliation contained in this threat was so great that Jaroszynski broke down and confessed.

He had, he stated, decided on the murder on February 5, and had bought the carving-knife for the purpose; but twice the Abbé had produced bonds of small denominations, and the murder had been postponed. On February thirteenth the Abbé had produced the Métallique bonds, and it was then that Jaroszynski had stabbed him in the neck and had belabored the body, fearing an outcry.

We have only one portrait of Jaroszynski—a sketch made by the Viennese painter, Karl Agricola, It reveals a stout, broad-shouldered man, about five feet and four inches in height, with brown curly hair, a high intellectual forehead, a broad energetic chin framed by side whiskers, and small deep-set eyes. The sale of this sketch, as well as that of a portrait of Abbé Blank (now in the Historical Museum of Vienna), was prohibited by order of the Austrian Prime Minister. Prince Metternich feared the public effect of such a sale because of the severe criticism that had been aroused by rumors that the prisoner was receiving pref erential treatment on account of his distinguished rank. The bloody storm which was to break over Europe in March, 1848, was evidently foreseen by this great statesman.

Anna Pleban, the widow of Jaroszynski's old teacher, has given us some interesting sidelights on the character of the young man who had been a student of the Pleban Institute from his eighteenth to his twenty-second year. He was an indifferent scholar in all subjects except mathematics, and of all his teachers, Professor Blank was the only one to express satisfaction with him. His most striking trait was his colossal vanity. He was impulsive and hot-tempered but always ready to ask forgiveness, and showed a kindly disposition toward the other boys in the school.

This estimate of the man who was to shock Vienna to its very foundation with a brutal premeditated murder was borne out by the testimony of his colleagues in the Russian government service, who described him as pleasant, well-mannered, full of sympathy and always ready to help the poor with liberal gifts.

Jaroszynski was, however, boastful and vainglorious; and it is characteristic of him that, at a dinner following the murder, he told of his enormous estates in Poland and displayed a large sum of money—undoubtedly the proceeds of the crime he had just committed.

In Vienna, Jaroszynski bore himself proudly and commandingly. He had charming manners, a boundless optimism and a total lack of scruples. At his trial, Therese Krones testified to his great generosity. Incidentally, she was compelled to retire from the stage because of her liaison with him. The Viennese public regarded her extravagance as a contributory factor in the murder.

When the confession had finally been forced, Jaroszynski was given three days in which to submit any reasons why the death penalty should not be pronounced against him; for under the existing law no further trial was necessary. But he replied that he could offer no mitigating circumstances, adding, however, that he relied on the clemency of Emperor Franz. The accused was then found guilty of premeditated murder and robbery, and was condemned to death—a sentence which was duly confirmed by the Supreme Court. On August twenty-seventh, Jaroszynski was informed that the emperor had refused to intercede, and that his execution would take place on the morning of August 30.

In accord with the legal requirements of the day the verdict was publicly read in the presence of the condemned and a crowd numbering many thousands.

Jaroszynski enjoyed many privileges during the latter days of his incarceration; and among the official documents of the case we find receipted bills for food and delicacies, ordered by the prisoner for himself and his guests. We also find receipted bills for the erection of the scaffold, the executioner's fee, and the cost of the cortège to the gallows, all of which had to be paid for by the condemned—a delightful if grim touch of fitting justice. On the night before the execution Jaroszynski, with but a few hours to live, expressed a desire for a game of whist; and a rubber was arranged with Father Munich, Doctor Kölbinger— the police surgeon—and the poet Ignaz Franz Castelli, who described the episode in his famous memoirs. Jaroszynski played with no outward trace of emotion, and to his great satisfaction won two rubbers.

At dawn the next morning the prison procession started to the place of execution, arriving at the scaffold at half past eight, where a multitude estimated at more than 20,000 had collected. Jaroszynski had hoped to the last moment that the emperor would not permit a member of the aristocracy to undergo a felon's death, and suffered a complete collapse when he realized that his doom was inevitable.

At eight-forty-five the noose was adjusted; and one of the historic criminals of Austria paid the price for a brutal and sordid murder.

# Poison

AFTER *The Bishop Murder Case* had been terminated Philo Vance had fallen into the habit of dining with Markham every Sunday night at the old Stuyvesant Club. As Vance's constant companion and legal adviser, I was always present; and often after dinner Sergeant Heath would join us in the lounge-room.

The conversation turned naturally to criminology. and scarcely a Sunday night passed that Vance did not outline to us, apropos of some legal or psychological point in our discussions, a famous case—generally one of European setting; for Vance was well versed in these matters. The criminological archives of Europe were at that time a fad with him; and his library was cluttered with the official documents of many of the Continental police departments.

On previous Sunday nights he had related to us the famous Germaine Berton case in Paris (which I have already set down in "The Scarlet Nemesis"); the incredible and almost burlesque Pruscha case (recorded by me under the title of "A Murder in a Witches' Caldron,") and the astonishing and spectacular Jaroszynski case (which I have described, calling it "The Man in the Blue Overcoat.")

On the particular Sunday night of which I now write the psychology of the feminine criminal had been broached by Markham (as I remember, it had started with some reference to the Greene murder case); and Vance, maintaining that the most resourceful and most daring of all criminals were women, outlined for us the notorious Chorinsky murder case which, in the latter half of the nineteenth century, created one of Europe's criminological sensations.

Y' KNOW, MARKHAM (Vance began, in his emotionless drawl), for calculating, cold-blooded murder, women more than hold their own with men. And their most ruthless, cerebral crimes are generally the result of some powerful emotional impetus—a curious paradox. Regard the amazin' Chorinsky case. What a record of passion, illicit love, mental degeneracy and murderous mathematical precision! No fiction writer would dare use it—he wouldn't be believed. The critics would say "far-fetched," "impossible," "unconvincing," and "absurd psychology." And yet, there are the records, duly set forth with Teutonic meticulousness—an actual page in the archives of Austrian crime.

Count Gustav Chorinsky was the scion of an old feudal family in Moravia. He was born in 1832, I believe, and at the age of seventeen entered the Austrian army. In 1858 he was garrisoned in Linz, the capital of Upper Austria; and it was here he met, as we euphemistically say, his fate. And what a fate!

He fell in love with a talented young actress named Mathilde Ruef. Mathilde was then twenty-five years of age—a lovely creature possessed of rare charm, He wooed her passionately, and soon their engagement was announced. But the elder Chorinsky, old-fashioned and proud, who was at that time the lieutenant-governor of Lower Austria, frowned upon the marriage—no son of his should marry a mummer!

But did that deter the lovers? Not for a moment Mathilde and her dashing young officer simply set up housekeeping as man and wife without benefit of clergy.

Chorinsky was a rotter and a waster: his financial position soon became seriously involved, and in 1859 he was forced to resign his commission in the army.

For a time he and Mathilde lived near Salzburg, but owing to the pressure brought to bear by his outraged father, the police intervened: Mathilde went to Bavaria and Chorinsky returned to Vienna. His father arranged for his reentry into the army, and at the end of the same year he was stationed with his regiment in Italy. Here his illicit relations with Mathilde were secretly reestablished.

In March, 1860, he entered the armies of the Papal States as captain; and four months later Chorinsky senior, despairing of separating the lovers, gave his consent to the marriage, which took place at Foligno on July seventeenth.

(Vance lighted one of his *Régie* cigarettes and smiled.)

A curious incident happened at the ceremony. Chorinsky forgot the wedding ring, and being of an almost pathologically superstitious nature, he brooded over the fact for days, declaring to his bride and to his father that something tragic was inevitable. Silly, what? But in view of the horrors of what actually followed—horrors that were to add a new and terrible chapter to the criminal annals of Europe—one almost wonders if, in the weak mind of this young militarist, some shadow of the future had not already fallen. I'm not psychic, don't y' know, but my word, Markham!—such coincidences are deuced disconcertin'.

The battle of Castelfidardo on September eighteenth, 1860, in which the papal troops were completely routed, put an end to the temporal power of the Holy See; and in May of the following year, when the papal army was finally disbanded, the young couple established themselves in Nancy.

Their domestic and amat'ry relations had by now, because of their dissimilar and incompatible temperaments, grown irremediably strained. Chorinsky's ardor had cooled—it had become gelid, in fact; and in 1861 he left his wife and returned to Brünn, where he attempted to reenlist in the Austrian army. Failing in this, he lived for two years on the family estates at Wessely, with occasional visits to Vienna and Laibach—now absurdly called Ljubljana.

A most interestin' side light is thrown on Chorinsky's erratic and susceptible nature during these two years by his brief but violent infatuation for the daughter of a Colonel Miltitsch in Laibach.

For hours at a time the enamored swain would promenade before her window crying, "Marie, do you love me?"— "Marie, liebst du mich?"—until he collapsed in utter exhaustion. He sent her a locket containing a paring of his fingernail instead of the conventional hirsute clipping—an original idea, but one hardly indicative of amorous normality. He constantly threatened to commit suicide, and grew so morbidly superstitious that whenever he passed over a bridge he would drop a silver coin into the water as a means of fending off the doom that he imagined hung over him. When Colonel Miltitsch finally forbade him the house, he sought forgetfulness by returning to the army. The Danish war had just broken out, and his reinstatement was facilitated.

His infatuation for Marie Miltitsch had affected him to such a degree that his feeling for his wife underwent a complete revulsion. His indifference developed into a violent hatred, and when she refused, on religious grounds, to consent to a divorce, he left her destitute, advising her brutally to commit suicide or become a prostitute. Not a nice man, Markham.

In her despondency the young countess appealed to his parents. So captivated were they by her that they took her into their home.

In 1866, Chorinsky was severely wounded at the battle of Königgrätz, but on learning that his wife was living with his parents, he refused to be taken home.

Mathilde, remorsefully conscious that her presence in the house made impossible a reconciliation between her husband and his parents, took her departure and settled in Munich, the city of her birth. Chorinsky senior allowed her an annuity of 960 florins and also gave her the interest of her husband's marriage bond of 12,000 florins.

Although Marie Miltitsch was the primary cause of Chorinsky's fanatical hatred of his wife, this sinister passion was kept alive and later intensified by Julie Ebergényi, under whose spell he had fallen on his return to Vienna after the Prussian war.

The lady's full name was Julie Malvine Gabriele Ebergényi von Telekes, and she was born in 1842, on her father's estate, Szécsény, in Hungary. She was a fascinatin' brunette.

In 1867, after the death of her mother, Julie left home as a protest against her father's intended remarriage to a commoner. High-spirited and that sort of thing. A few months later we find her installed in luxury in Vienna, leading the life of a demi-mondaine, and on the alert lookout for a titled husband. It was no doubt with this matrimonial ambition in view that she persuaded one of her paramours to arrange financially for her being made a canoness of the aristocratic Maria Schul Chapter at Brünn.

Chorinsky, who soon after his arrival in Vienna had become one of her lovers, was not content to share her favors—exclusive fella!— and offered to marry her. Julie's father was overjoyed and was willing to make any financial sacrifice to bring about the marriage. But alas! There remained the insurmountable obstacle of Chorinsky's existing marriage in the Catholic Church. As long as the Countess Chorinsky was alive nothing could be done to remedy the situation. Very distressin'.

During the summer of 1867, Mathilde was living near Reichenhall, a famous Bavarian spa, and one day she received in the mail a box of candied fruit from Brünn, accompanied by a note which read: "An old friend who has just learned your address sends you this little gift. He is still thinking of you with undiminished affection and he hopes to see you before long"—or words to that effect. The note was signed "Wammer."

This box of candied fruit was to be heard of again under the most sinister circumstances. Incidentally, Markham, it marked a milestone in the history of the technique of crime, for though the fact was never legally proved, there can be little doubt that those sweets contained cyanide; and the episode established the first modern record of poisoned candy being sent through the mails for the purpose of murder.

Mathilde, however, was not destined for this particular variety of death. She became highly indignant at what she regarded as an unseemly joke, and after some weeks gave the candy away to a peasant family. who ate it without any disastrous results.

It is very possible. d'ye see, that the cyanide had been decomposed in the presence of sugar, liberating the hydrocyanic acid with the formation of harmless potassium sugar compounds. Or it may be that to the stomachs of these sturdy Bavarian peasants cyanide was a mere condiment which they relished.

On October fourth of the same year, Mathilde returned to Munich.

Under the name of Mathilde von Ledske—the secondary title of her husband—she took furnished lodgings with a woman named Elise Hartmann, at 12 Amalien-Strasse, where she lived a quiet and retired life. Thus matters stood on the morning of November twenty-third, 1867, when Frau Hartmann went to the local police station and asked for advice regarding her lodger.

She informed the inspector that on November twentieth a woman had visited Mathilde and that on the next afternoon the same woman had called again. At six-thirty P.M. that day Mathilde had asked Frau Hartmann for the loan of a pair of opera glasses, explaining that she had been invited by her caller to attend the Aktientheater. She had also asked her landlady to call a cab for her. But when the obliging Frau Hartmann had arrived with the cab the door of her tenant's room had been locked and no one had answered her knocking. She had concluded that Mathilde had gone to the theater without waiting for the conveyance.

Frau Hartmann had noted that her lodger remained invisible the next day—the twenty-second—but had thought nothing of it. On the twenty-third, however, she had grown anxious and had gone to the Hôtel Vier Jahreszeiten, where Mathilde had told her the woman was staying, and made inquiries. Mathilde's visitor, it turned out, had registered as the Baroness Marie von Vay, but had returned to Vienna on the evening of November twenty-first.

The police inspector now authorized Frau Hartmann to force the door of her lodger's room—which she did. On the floor she found the corpse of Mathilde von Ledske, and hastened to the police station with the tale of her discovery.

Inspector Hütter proceeded immediately to the house. Police Surgeon Doctor Wensauer, who accompanied him, announced that death had occurred about two days previously. There were no signs of violence. The body was taken to the morgue and the room locked for inspection.

The examining magistrate, Doctor Geiger, who made the first official examination of the room, found the table laid with a cold supper consisting of ham, sausage, black radishes, fruit, and cakes—not an epicurean meal; but then, gastronomic taste in Germany has never accorded with the gustat'ry principles of the late Brillat-Savarin.

On the table also stood a jug of beer, a small bottle of rum, and three glasses—one empty and two containing water. There were also two cups—one, which was at the place where, according to Frau Hartmann, the mysterious visitor had sat, was half-full of tea; the other cup contained some tea with milk.

The teakettle, however, was nowhere in the apartment. The keys to the hall door and to the door of the clothes-closet were also missing. The kerosene lamp had not been lighted, but there was a candle on the table. The fact that it had not burnt down, but had been extinguished, practically eliminated suicide.

The dead woman's jewelry and money had been untouched, with the exception that a heavy seal ring was missing; and Frau Hartmann stated that several packages of letters had disappeared.

Karl Struwe, a student who occupied the room next door, stated that on the evening of the twenty-first he had heard an animated conversation between two women which had lasted until after six P.M. when the hall door had slammed. Quiet had reigned thereafter.

The postmortem showed that Mathilde had been poisoned by hydrocyanic acid, which she had probably taken in the form of potassium cyanide in tea or some other liquid. Death had probably been instantaneous.

From letters and documents found in the apartment it was at once established that the dead woman was none other than the Countess Chorinsky, and Chief of Police Karl von Burchtorff himself undertook the investigation of the crime.

At the Hotel Vier Jahreszeiten it was learned that the woman who had registered under the name of the Baroness von Vay had arrived on the Vienna express on the morning of November twentieth, and had departed for Vienna at eight-thirty P.M., November twenty-first.

A traveling salesman, Heinrich Umlauf had arrived on the same train with the baroness and had accompanied her that same evening to the theater. Later, on reading of the murder of the Countess Chorinsky, he went to the police authorities and explained that he had met the woman for the first time on the Vienna express, and that on the evening of November twenty-first he had accompanied her to the railway station and seen her aboard the train for Vienna.

Umlauf, as well as other witnesses of the hotel, described the woman as young and attractive, and flamboyantly dressed in a black-and-white silk gown and a black Persian-lamb fur coat fastened with an enamel brooch bearing two death's-heads. She smoked cigars incessantly, making use of a meerschaum cigar holder bearing a count's coronet.

Cigar-smoking among the women of the Austrian aristocracy was at that time quite common. Thank heaven, Markham, the practice has not spread! Imagine wooing a lady who would first remove a cigar from her mouth to ask you if your intentions were honorable!

The chambermaid at the hotel testified that on November twenty-first the "Baroness von Vay" had dressed nervously and had sat at the window, preoccupied and sullen, until two-thirty P.M. At that time she had ordered a bottle of muscat and half a bottle of red wine, which she had poured into two smaller bottles, asking the porter to cork them for her.

Later in the afternoon she went shopping in the company of the Countess Chorinsky, having first ordered the hotel porter to buy her two theater tickets and to deliver them to Frau Hartmann's house in the Amalien-Strasse. The porter arrived there about six-thirty P.M., just as she was emerging from the front door, and gave her the tickets. At seven P.M. she returned to the hotel, apparently excited and much exhausted, and asked for her bill, explaining that she had just received a wire from her husband asking her to join him in Paris. No telegram, however, had been received for her at the hotel, and the porter noted that she boarded train for Vienna.

Among the papers found by Chief of Police Burchtorff in the dead woman's room was a will in which Mathilde stated that she had been abused and forsaken by her husband. Letters were also found that showed that her address and the name under which she lived were well-known to her father-in-law. That same day Doctor Burchtorff was informed that the secretary of the Austrian Legation, Herr Zwerschina, had. at the request of Count Gustav Chorinsky, endeavored to obtain information from the Munich police about Mathilde von Ledske.

These facts immediately created in Burchtorff a keen desire to have polite converse with this estranged husband of the murdered woman. He accordingly telegraphed to the Vienna police, asking them to inform Count Gustav Chorinsky of the death of his wife and to request his presence at the funeral.

On the twenty-fifth, Chorinsky arrived in Munich with his father. The elder Chorinsky at once applied to the Chief of Police for further details about his daughter-in-law's death. The younger Chorinsky, pleading fatigue from the trip, remained at the Hôtel Bayrlscher Hof. After the interview, Chorinsky senior declined to see the body and declared that he was returning to Vienna with his son the same evening, without waiting for the inquest.

Burchtorff was somewhat puzzled by this decision and insisted upon accompanying Chorinsky back to the hotel.

Near the hotel they encountered the younger Chorinsky, who was formally introduced to Burchtorff by his father. Gustav Chorinsky also declined to view his wife's body. And Burchtorff noticed that the young man was nervous and showed a marked reluctance to pass the uniformed police patrolling the streets.

Chorinsky senior expressed a desire to visit Count Trauttmannsdorf, the Austrian Ambassador, and Burchtorff politely insisted on keeping Gustav company until his father's return.

During a short stroll Gustav was unable to cloak his hatred of his murdered wife, and Burchtorff, seeing in his attitude a possible motive for the crime, decided to take immediate action.

He excused himself and after arranging to have Chorinsky kept under strict surveillance, hastened to the examining magistrate, who immediately telegraphed to Vienna for further particulars regarding Chorinsky's marital affairs.

In the afternoon Burchtorff paid the Chorinskys a visit at the hotel and requested them to call upon him at police headquarters at six P.M.. When they arrived the desired information from Vienna had been received, and the examining magistrate issued a warrant for the younger Chorinsky's arrest. He gave his word of honor as an officer that he was innocent, and protested vigorously against the custom'ry examination and the confiscation of his property.

His personal effects included a rosary, several talismans and prayers, and five photographs which he stated were pictures of his fiancée, Julie von Ebergényi. The shrewd Burchtorff at once took the photographs to the Hôtel Vier Jahreszeiten, and there several employees promptly identified them as pictures of the mysterious Baroness von Vay.

When told of this identification Chorinsky stated excitedly that Julie had been in Vienna on November seventeenth and eighteenth. On November nineteenth she had departed for Szécsény, and therefore could not have been in Munich on the twentieth and twenty-first. He also insisted that he had kept her in ignorance of his previous marriage and that she was unaware of Mathilde's existence.

That same day Chorinsky was taken to the morgue, where he formally identified the body of his wife.

In the meantime at the request of Burchtorff, the Vienna Police Inspector Karl Brettenfeld paid an official visit to Julie von Ebergé-nyi. She protested indignantly at the outrage of being crossexamined. Eventually, though, she agreed to accompany him to police headquarters

Here she was questioned by Examining Magistrate Doctor Max Fischer, and after several hours confessed to having administered the cyanide to Mathilde in a cup of tea.

The magistrate's clerk, however, had barely finished writing down this confession when she suddenly retracted it, supplanting it with the story that Mathilde had committed suicide in her presence. As nothing could persuade her to alter this second statement, she was remanded to jail to await further examination.

A search of her apartment brought to light a meerschaum cigar holder bearing a coronet, a bottle partly filled with red wine and another containing muscat wine—both of which, according to the testimony of her maid, she had brought back with her from her recent trip. The dress she had worn in Munich was also found, as well as the fur coat with the death's-heads brooch.

The following day the maid testified voluntarily to the examining magistrate that on November twenty-fourth her mistress had given her a *Maschine* and a small parcel, requesting her under no circumstances to let them out of her possession. In view of what had happened, the maid thought it advisable to turn the two packages over to the magistrate.

The "Maschine" proved to be the missing teakettle; and the parcel contained the missing seal ring, several letters from Chorinsky, and a bottle half-filled with white powder, which later, under analysis, turned out to be pure cyanide of potassium. The teakettle bore an incrustation of carbonate of potash, and the theory of the prosecution at the trial was that the incrustation was the result of the cyanide of potash having decomposed under the influence of the carbon dioxide in the atmosphere, with formation of the carbonate—a somewhat doubtful chemical hypothesis.

On November twenty-eighth a retired customs officer, Theodor Rampacher, appeared before the examining magistrate and stated that, notwithstanding Chorinsky's many kindnesses to him, his conscience forced him to make a confession.

His story amounted briefly to this: Chorinsky had repeatedly endeavored to find suitable employment for him; and in September, 1867, Rampacher had gone to Brünn to visit his family. Chorinsky had supplied the necessary money for the trip, and at the same time had given him a small wooden box to be mailed in Brünn. The box had been addressed to Mathilde von Ledske. The handwriting on the box, according to Rampacher, had been disguised, and the sender's name was given as "Wammer." Chorinsky had asked Rampacher to make no mention of the box to anyone.

During the weeks of her incarceration Julie changed her testimony almost daily. Following: her story of Mathilde's suicide, she invented a fictitious Baroness von Vay who closely resembled her. She even suggested that this inconnue had dressed herself so as to look exactly like her, and had gone so far as to provide herself with a cigar holder bearing a coronet. This hypothetical baroness had subsequently sent her a package, asking her to keep it secret, and she had given it to her maid without being aware of its contents.

A week later, when questioned about the box of candied fruits,

Julie altered the circumstances concerning her mysterious alter ego to include this new discovery.

When confronted by Frau Hartmann, who unhesitatingly identified her as Mathilde's visitor on the fatal afternoon, Julie accused the landlady of having been bribed by her terrible *Doppelgänger*; and when Inspector Breitenfeld showed her the similarity between her own handwriting and that which appeared on the register of the Hôtel Vier Jahreszeiten, she accused her mythical twin of having forged her chirography.

The most convincing evidence against the two prisoners was the numerous letters which they had carefully preserved. Particularly damaging were two letters written by Julie to Chorinsky on November twentieth and twenty-first. In one of these letters she asked her lover to pray for the success of her enterprise as it meant all their future happiness; and in the other she expressed the hope that the "white powders" were of good quality.

Chorinsky in one of his letters to her advised her to throw away anything that she might have in her possession as soon as the "sale" was concluded... Fancy preservin' epistles of that nature, Markham! *O sancta simplicitas!*

For several weeks after the arrest of the two prisoners some secret form of communication between them was evidently in operation, for the ever-changing testimony of each prisoner showed a remarkable tendency to corroborate the other's. Breitenfeld, suspicious of this subterranean collaboration, placed a stool pigeon named Amalie Drexler in Julie's cell. Among the letters which she succeeded in bringing to the attention of the authorities was one written by Julie, signed "Marie von Vay," in which this legendary lady confessed to the murder of Mathilde and apparently gave the true details of the crime!

But Julie, despite the attentiveness of Amalie, must have succeeded in smuggling several similar letters out of the prison; for during the trial no less than three duplicates of this confession were delivered to the presiding judge, each signed by a different person! Julie's astuteness was obviously not on a par with her imagination.

It is interesting to note that, according to these spurious letters of confession, the poison was administered in a glass of muscat wine, the remainder having been emptied into the teakettle and the glass carefully washed. This detail would, of course, explain the absence of any traces of poison either in the glasses or in the bottles, and would also account for the incrustation in the teakettle.

Inspector Breitenfeld, in his search for direct evidence against Julie, turned up a leading Viennese photographer, August Angerer, from whom

Julie had purchased a complete outfit of chemicals for photographer work, which had included four ounces of potassium cyanide. Confronted by Angerer's testimony, Julie admitted the fact but declared she had purchased the outfit for a friend in Hungary.

Not satisfied with this overwhelming mass of evidence, Breitenfeld succeeded in finding a messenger who, at Julie's behest, had gone to the well-known stationery firm of Theyer and Hardmuth and ordered a dozen visiting cards bearing the name of Baroness von Vay. Breitenfeld was also able to produce letters from Julie to her sister asking the latter to testify that she had been in Scézsény from November nineteenth to the twenty-second—a request her sister had refused.

As long as Chorinsky was able to communicate with Julie after their arrest, he continued to do all in his power to exculpate her. But after their secret correspondence had been stopped he suffered a complete mental collapse, and in a frantic endeavor to save himself accused his beloved of having committed the murder alone and without his assistance. His mad and abnormal infatuation suddenly turned to vicious, vindictive hatred —a psychological reversal of emotions which is to be found in many similar cases in criminal history.

On April sixth, 1868, the investigation in Vienna was completed, and on April twenty-second Julie was placed on trial before Supreme Court Justice Giuliani. The public prosecutor was Doctor Shmeidl, and Julie's attorney was Doctor Max Neuda, the most celebrated of all Austrian jurists. Doctor Neuda requested that the trial be held in camera, as, he naively explained, the defendant was too innocent to discuss her private life in public! Touchin', what?

At the trial, which created a tremendous sensation, no new evidence was adduced. Julie's ever-fertile brain, however, invented several new versions of the crime, one of them that she had fought an "American duel" with Mathilde and that, in choosing from the two cups. Mathilde had been so unfortunate as to select the one containing the poison.

On the twenty-fifth of April, Giuliani and his four assisting judges handed down a verdict of guilty. Quite correct. Julie was sentenced to twenty years of hard labor instead of being given the death penalty, notwithstanding her first confession. The court took the view that this initial confession was   evidence on the grounds it had started with the words: "I have relieved my conscience this day by confessing in the next room..." The court held that this document was the narrative of a confession and not the confession itself —a technical nicety worthy, Markham, of your own sweet judicial procedure. On May eighteenth of the same year the Supreme Court confirmed the sentence, and Julie was sent to the woman's penitentiary in Neudorf. In solitary confinement her mentality, always unstable and unbalanced, rapidly deteriorated; and in May, 1872, she was transferred to the asylum for the criminally insane, where she died a year later.

The trial of Chorinsky took place in Munich in June, 1868, and ended with his conviction as an accessory to the murder. He, too, was sentenced to twenty years of hard labor, and on July tenth was sent to the Rosenberg Fortress. *Le pauvre Gustav!* He loved not wisely but too well. I fear he was not fashioned for a criminal career. In a few months he became a hopeless lunatic and was transferred to the asylum in Erlangen. He died three years later.

VANCE LAY BACK in his chair and sighed lugubriously. "The crime was frightfully bungled, don't y' know. Most distressin'."

Markham nodded. "It was far from the perfect crime."

"The perfect crime!" Vance permitted himself a mildly sarcastic snort. "We never hear of the perfect crime, because it succeeds … Still. there are crimes that are almost perfect—they fail only because of untoward circumstances over which the plotter has no control... It's very sad. I like to see genius succeed, whether it is in crime or art."

Two weeks later the subject of the perfect crime again came up for discussion, and Vance recounted for us a most amazing case which took place in Chile in 1909—a case which had every earmark of the perfect crime but which failed because a common Spanish word was misunderstood by one of the subsidiary characters. It was the astonishing murder known as the Beckert case, and it set two countries into diplomatic convulsions.

# The Almost
# Perfect Crime

PHILO VANCE lay back in his chair and smiled sardonically "You're much too trustin' for this wicked world, Markham," he said. "There are any number of perfect crimes. Only, because they are perfect the world doesn't hear of them. It's the failures that come to our attention.

"And it's not always the murderer's fault that he is caught. Fortuitous circumstances often counteract the best laid plans. Very sad..."

Vance and John F. X. Markham—New York's district attorney—and I were seated in the lounge-room of the old Stuyvesant Club. We had fallen into the habit, after the solution of the Bishop murder case, of coming together on Sunday nights; and Vance, who at the time was deeply interested in criminology, often discussed famous cases with us.

He had already related on previous Sunday nights the Germaine Berton case, the Pruscha case, the Jaroszynski case and the Ebergényi case —all of which I have set down in these columns—and tonight, apropos of Markham's comments on "the perfect crime," he told us of the Wilhelm Beckert murder which took place in Chile in 1909 — an almost incredible record of a carefully plotted crime, the detection of which hinged on a mere misunderstood connotation of a simple Spanish word.

"I like to see genius succeed, don't y'know," Vance remarked lazily, lighting one of his adored *Régie* cigarettes; "whether it be in art or commerce or crime. And somehow, I'll always feel that the murderer in the Beckert case was, as the doughty Sergeant Heath would say, given the needle by an unkind fate."

Early in 1909 (Vance began, settling himself luxuriously in his chair), the town of Santiago de Chile was the scene of a crime which, for various reasons, holds unusual interest, both psychological and criminological.

*Imprimis*, the crime was committed on the premises of the Imperial German Legation. Not only did it give rise to many absurd and fascinatin' complications, legal and otherwise, involving the exchange of letters, notes and memoranda, such as only the ponderous punditic minds of diplomats could have conceived, but the circumstances in themselves were such that, under ordin'ry conditions, the criminal would probably never have been apprehended.

Its chief interest, however, lies in the astonishing foresight and uncanny powers of minute scheming developed by the perpetrator—qualities which stamp him as one of the world's most distinguished murderers, despite the paltry motivation of the act. Moreover, only an almost infinitesimal oversight prevented the success of his plot. It was almost a perfect crime. Eheu!...

The German Legation in Santiago was situated on the ground floor of a two-story building in the *Via Nataniel* near the *Avenida de las Delicias.* The premises consisted of two rooms—a front office and a rear room used for the storage of the diplomatic archives. The staff was composed of the minister, Baron von Boodmann, the secretary, Baron von Welseck, and a clerk named Wilhelm Beckert.

In addition, there was a messenger, porter and general factotum, Exequiel Tapia, who was an ex-sergeant of the Chilean army.

The duties of this little staff were not arduous; they consisted mainly, I imagine, of friendly luncheons and dinners with various government officials.

In 1907 this *dolce-far-niente* life was temporarily disturbed by an incident which, though rather unimportant in itself, was to have the most astonishin' consequences.

In the little village of Caleu the native peasants had attacked a party of German settlers, who indignantly appealed to the Legation for redress. The matter was investigated with that charmin' leisure so characteristic of diplomatic affairs; but nothing much came of it.

The next year, however, members of the German Legation began to receive sinister letters signed "Various Chileans"—*varios chilenos.* In these letters the minister was accused of having unjustly prosecuted innocent peasants who had acted in ignorance rather than malice. The letters warned Baron von Boodmann against continuing the suit, and threatened the lives of the members of his staff. Black Hand letters, in fact.

A little later—September of the same year, to be exact—a similar letter was sent to the minister himself, who straightaway turned it over to the Chilean police authorities. These noble upholders of the law, anxious to avoid any unpleasantness with the representatives of a foreign government, made a valiant though futile effort to find the author of the sanguinary epistles.

Neither the minister nor Baron von Welseck paid much attention to these threats. But Beckert, who was rather a timid, good-natured soul, was torn asunder. His anxiety mounted by leaps and bounds: repeatedly he expressed his conviction that he was a doomed man. His state of nerves, to judge from the records, was rather pitiful. He was thoroughly convinced that the *varios chilenos* were thirsting for his blood and would some day swoop down on him and end his earthly career.

BECKERT WAS THEN in his thirty-ninth year. He was a Bavarian by birth, the son of a well-to-do merchant. In 1889 he had emigrated to the New World and entered a Jesuit monastery in Santiago. Two years later, however, he decided that what we euphemistically call marital bliss was more to his liking than a career of pious meditation, and leaving the order, he turned Protestant. In 1899 he married the daughter of a Chilean merchant—a lady named Natalie Lopez—and entered the diplomatic service of his native country as clerk of the Legation.

A few months after the receipt of the threatening letters Beckert dashed excitedly into the office of Baron von Boodmann and reported that three suspicious-looking Chileans had, on the preceding night, chased him for several hours through Santiago's deserted streets. The minister thereupon insisted that this timorous and terrified clerk carry a revolver—much to that gentleman's distress; for Beckert had an instinctive horror of all death-dealing devices.

At this time Beckert developed an almost morbid anxiety for his wife, and at the end of October, 1908, he entrusted to a friend in a letter addressed to the German Minister, with instructions that it be delivered after his death, which he believed imminent. In it he thanked his chief profusely for the many considerations shown him, and asked that an enclosed communication be forwarded to Señor Pedro Montt, who was then the President of the Chilean Republic.

In this communication to President Montt, Beckert requested that his murder be not avenged, giving as his reason the fact that, above everything else, he was desirous of avoiding any animosity between his native and his adopted country: He stated that he was convinced that the *varios chilenos* had acted from a mistaken sense of patriotism. His one concern was for his wife, and he asked that she be provided for. In all, the letter was a rather pathetic outpouring of a man who, as he worded it, considered himself a *reo en capilla*—to wit: a man under sentence of death. (Vance sighed lugubriously and crushed out his cigarette.)

On Friday, February fifth, 1909, about eleven forty-five A.M., the minister and the secretary appeared at the Legation, where they found Beckert at work as usual. The legationary messenger, Exequiel Tapia, had, at half past ten, gone to the residence of Baron von Boodmann and had departed therefrom a quarter of an hour later, ostensibly to return to the Legation. The minister was therefore surprised not to find Tapia at the office. Beckert, in fact, said he had not seen Tapia that morning.

At a quarter of one Baron von Boodmann and Baron von Welseck departed from the Legation, leaving Beckert behind.

Half an hour later several neighbors saw smoke issuing from the windows of the Legation, and instantly turned in a fire alarm. But the apparatus arrived too late—the roof had already collapsed and the entire building was tottering. The minister himself was informed of the fire about three P.M., and when he arrived it was impossible to save anything. The building had been destroyed.

Baron von Boodmann was naturally anxious about Beckert, especially as the chap was known to have suffered from fainting spells. He feared the worst, and at nine o'clock that night his fears became a certainty when, in the ruins of the rear office, under a stack of office files, a body was discovered totally carbonized. Near the body were found Beckert's silver cigarette case, a nickel watch with fragments of a chain, and a pince-nez.

In view of the threatening letters which had been received, of Beckert's morbid fears, and of the fact that Tapia still remained perdu, Baron von Boodmann requested a judicial investigation and demanded that a postmortem be performed by the Chilean police surgeon.

On the fingers of the charred body were found Beckert's diamond and sapphire ring and his wedding ring bearing the initials "N. L." (Natalie Lopez) and the wedding date: 13.3.99. In the ruins of the building a number of telltale articles were unearthed: fragments of clothing, a bloodstained handkerchief, a dagger which had been used as a paper cutter, a blackjack, and a blowlamp.

The result of the postmortem was far from satisfactory. The official surgeon declared that the state of the body made it impossible to ascertain the cause of death. There was apparently little mystery about the fire, for it was Beckert's habit to burn all office memoranda each day after answering the Legation's correspondence; and it seemed obvious that the fire had started in this manner and that Beckert had been stunned by a falling filing cabinet, as the top of his head was badly battered. On February seventh, Baron von Boodmann received another letter from the *varios chilenos*, which had been posted in Santiago on the morning of the tragedy. In this letter the murder of Beckert and the burning of the Legation were mentioned and held up as a warning against further prosecution of the peasants in Caleu.

As it was known that a few days before the fire Beckert had received a similar communication, the minister felt that further instigation was called for. Moreover, Tapia had not yet put in an appearance. He was known to have left his home at ten on the morning of the tragedy, and had stated that he had to leave the city that afternoon on official business—a statement which turned out to be untrue. After his visit to the residence of Baron von Boodmann at ten-thirty A.M., he had disappeared. The minister, in order to quiet persistent rumors that Beckert had been assassinated, requested two German members of the faculty of the university to repeat the postmortem.

Their report was a model of Teutonic thoroughness and brought to light several important bits of evidence. A piece of the left tibia, about three inches long was missing; it appeared to have been burned off, probably with a blow-lamp. Also the bone of the left elbow was missing. The skin and the flesh of the skull had been completely destroyed, and the crowns of all incisors and canines in the upper jaw were missing, as well as the crowns of the left incisors and the left canine in the lower jaw. All the other teeth were in perfect condition, with the exception of a small caries in the upper right wisdom tooth.

There was an oval wound about one inch long in the chest, and it was now plain that the dead man had been the victim of foul play. Since the examination was only of a semi-official character, the minister requested that a new and official investigation be undertaken by a mixed body of physicians.

The Chilean authorities, however, anxious to avoid even a suspicion of partisanship in so delicate a matter, entrusted the examination to Doctor Westenhoffer and Doctor Aichel, and merely appointed as an assistant the Chilean physician Doctor Carlos Oyarzún.

The result of the postmortem was this: the aorta had been severed, and the heart had been penetrated. In the thorax a metal splinter, evidently from a dagger or knife, was found. The injury to the skull had preceded the stabbing. There was a strong probability that the dead man had been struck over the head with a blunt instrument and subsequently stabbed to death. The lower part of the body had lain under some damp office files and had therefore escaped complete destruction; and there remained fragments of a green and a white-striped shirt bearing the initials "G. B."—to wit: Guillermo, or Wilhelm, Beckert.

Mrs. Beckert unhesitatingly identified the shirt as her husband's. She was questioned in regard to her husband's teeth, and stated that they had been in perfect condition with the exception of some gold inlays in the upper incisors.

THE FOLLOWING DAY, February ninth, a medical-legal-diplomatic meeting was held to discuss the findings. The Chilean police surgeon, who performed the first autopsy, spent a most uncomfortable half-hour, and finally admitted that he himself had not carried out the autopsy, but had turned over the uncongenial task to a servant at the morgue.

The testimony of Mrs. Beckert referring to her husband's clothes and teeth was read, and it agreed in every particular with the findings of the second autopsy. Beckert had, years before, suffered from a fracture of the left tibia and was known to have had a conspicuous scar on his left elbow. It was obvious that these parts of the murdered body had been destroyed in order to make the identification impossible. The conclusion of the conference, therefore, was that the charred body was that of Beckert, and that he had been stabbed and destroyed by fire in order to hide all traces of the crime.

Well, well. It was a most unpleasant situation for the Chilean authorities. Not only had the victim been a member of a foreign government, but the police surgeon had been lax in his examination.

At once there was a feverish activity on the part of the various Chilean government departments. Every possible effort was made to lay hands on the missing messenger Tapia, whose guilt now appeared conclusive.

But there was one cynical gentleman who was unimpressed. He was the Examining Magistrate Manuel Bianchi. He passionately resented the slur cast upon the Chilean judicial procedure, and. proceeded to con all the reports with a suspicious and eagle eye. After hours of intensive study he discovered one item which seemed to hold out some hope of turning the tables on the gringos. And to this doubting magistrate must be given the credit for solving this most amazin' crime.

On the afternoon of February ninth, half an hour before the funeral was to take place, he sent Doctor Germán Valenzuela, the director of the Santiago School of Dentistry, to make a final examination of the teeth of the deceased. The German Minister magnanimously permitted the coffin to be reopened. But nothing was found that disagreed in any particular with the postmortem findings and the casket was then resealed.

It was a most touchin' funeral, Markham. At five o'clock in the afternoon the cortège set out for the cemetery. President Montt sent his personal adjutant to attend the obsequies. The coffin was lowered into the grave by eminent Chileans, who had acted as pallbearers by way of showing their sorrow and esteem. Baron von Boodmann emitted various winged words of eloquent eulogy. And to confer upon the occasion an aesthetic atmosphere, the German Liederbund gave musical voice to several mournful dirges.

The same day the Chilean Cabinet called a special meeting, and after the reading of Beckert's letter addressed to President Montt, those assembled in solemn conclave voted unanimously to petition Congress for a grant of twenty thousand pesos for the bereaved widow.

It was most impressive and quite correct. But there was one skeptical gentleman who took the episode with tongue in cheek—to wit: the cynical Magistrate Bianchi. Shrewd fella! While the Liederbund were speeding their departed *Landsmann* into the Beyond with vocal harmony, this Bianchi and his friend, Doctor Valenzuela, were discussing a most startling discovery!

When the erstwhile Natalie López had been questioned regarding her husband's teeth, the two German professors had employed a Spanish-speaking German as interpreter; and this Teuton linguist had made use of the word *dientes* for teeth—a word which, in common Chilean usage, connotes only the incisors, or the teeth that are visible when one laughs. Molars, in Chilean usage, are called *muelas*; and the human teeth in their totality are referred to as *dentadura*.

Now, Mrs. Beckert had truthfully answered that her husband's *dientes*— namely, his visible incisors—had been perfect, and since she had not been asked about his muelas, she had volunteered no information on the subject...

Forgive me this little linguistic interlude, Markham old dear. The whole case hangs on it; and it simply goes to show that even "the perfect crime" is, after all, a matter of chance.

The Chilean members of the commission had apparently overlooked this little difference between dientes and dentadura; but the perspicacious Bianchi had thought it worth a bit of scrutiny. Doctor Valenzuela, at Bianchi's suggestion, now asked Mrs. Beckert to describe her husband's dentadura; and she gave him the satisfyin' information that several of his molars had been missing. Whereupon Bianchi went to Doctor Juan Denis Lay; the dentist who had attended Beckert, and, with the help of the latter's records, ascertained beyond any doubt that five of Beckert's molars had been extracted only a few months previous.

(Vance grinned a bit sadly.)

Because of a philological nuance (he sighed) a lovely crime went to pot. It's most discouragin'. Since the charred body in the burned Legation possessed a complete set of molars, it now became obvious that the corpse was not that of Beckert. Furthermore, it became increasingly evident that the victim was none other than Tapia; for Madame Tapia informed Bianchi that all of her husband's molars had been intact with the exception of a small caries in the upper right wisdom tooth! In addition, Bianchi recalled, with chauvinistic delight, that Beckert and Tapia had been of similar physical build.

On February tenth, the day after the funeral, the morning papers of Chile published these disclosures. Baron von Boodmann promptly admitted to the Department of Justice that the body of the deceased could no longer be regarded as that of Beckert, and was in all probability, none other than Exequiel Tapia's.

It was now recalled that on February sixth a johnny named Otto—I forget his last name—had come to the police with the information that he had seen and spoken to Beckert between midnight and one A.M.—ten hours after the fire. But as Otto had an unsavory reputation and was known to have been on bad terms with Beckert, he was not believed and was told to run along and mind his own business.

The German Minister and Baron von Welseck now remembered that, when they visited the Legation offices on the morning of February fifth, the floor had been newly washed, and that Beckert was not wearing his custom'ry pince-nez. The deduction appears inevitable that at that time the unlucky Tapia had already passed to his Maker and that his mortal remains lay hidden behind the office files—a supposition which agreed with the result of the postmortem. It had been ascertained that death could not have been later than eleven-thirty A.M.

There was no longer any question that the charred body was that of Tapia; and the inescapable corollary was that Beckert had been the murderer, for the latter's belongings found by the body could have been placed there only by Beckert himself.

The German government immediately waived all diplomatic immunity for Beckert, and thus turned the case over to the jurisdiction of the Chilean authorities, who at once launched forth on the man-hunt with great gusto.

The body, which had been buried amid the inspirin' vocal strains of the German Liederbund, was now disinterred, and a third autopsy was performed. A microscopic examination of the skin and hair proved that the dead man was of swarthy complexion and had dark hair, whereas Beckert was conspicuously blond.

Immediately following the fire, a general alarm had been sent out for Tapia; and on February tenth, simultaneously with the discovery of the true identity of the corpse, a report arrived from the Chief of Police of Chillan, a little town on the Southern Railroad about two hundred miles south of Santiago.

The report stated that a traveler had appeared before the Chillan police with the information that on February seventh he had met a man on the train who, though representing himself as wealthy, had traveled second-class.

The chief of police had regarded this information as suspicious and had sent an inspector to Victoria, the train's destination. The inspector found and talked to a man bearing a passport made out in the name of Ciro Lava Motte, which had been issued by the State Department the preceding January for a voyage to the Argentine. But as the passport seemed to be in order, the inspector had returned to Chillan.

HOWEVER, ON THE arrival of the news about Tapia the chief of police, thinking that the mysterious Señor Motte might be the missing messenger, telegraphed to Santiago for Tapia's description.

In Santiago the police immediately checked up on Señor Motte and discovered that in January Beckert had applied to the Foreign Office for a passport for his brother-in-law, giving as that mythical gentleman's name Ciro Lava Motte.

But even this was not sufficient evidence for the Santiago police. They were most careful and thorough. Within a few hours they had discovered that on the day in January when Beckert had applied for the passport he had also bought a blackjack at a local hardware store, had ordered three false beards and a brunette wig, and had bought a traveling suit, leather puttees, a trunk, and a rifle with a leather case—all of which he had had inscribed with the initials "C. L. M." Beckert had also bought a revolver and cartridges and twenty yards of lamp wick.

While the police were thus engaged in checking up on the preparations of Beckert's perfect crime, the German Minister was endeavoring to find a motive for the murder. It didn't take long, for in going over the missing man's accounts, it was discovered that for more than a year Beckert had been forging drafts and discounting them at the bank. It was estimated that he had diverted to his own pocket nearly 50,000 marks ($12,000).

But even this mass of corroboratory evidence did not entirely satisfy the Santiago police. They were treading on delicate ground—the honor of their fair nation was at stake—and so they turned their suspicious eyes upon Beckert's private life. They discovered that he had not been the virtuous family man and model husband that everyone had thought him. He was, indeed, a gay dog, and had spent many leisure hours in the company of charming but fragile señoritas.

To one of these light-o'-loves he had written several letters in a disguised hand, signed "Tito Bera." He had later confessed to his dulcinea the authorship of these amat'ry epistles. The lady produced the letters, and the chirography proved to be the same as that of the author of the letters signed by *varios chilenos*.

In fact, all these threatening letters had been part of the preparation of Beckert's astoundin' plot. With them he had prepared everyone for his approaching murder. So well had he planted the whole idea that after the crime the identity of the body was hardly questioned.

There was now enough evidence even for the squeamish Santiago police, and a telegraph order for Beckert's arrest was sent to all stations along the Southern Railroad. Beckert had by this time quitted Chillan and was proceeding toward the Argentine border. But on February thirteenth, barely six miles from the frontier, the *carabinieri* overtook their quarry; and on February sixteenth the author of the almost perfect crime was safely lodged in the bastille at Santiago. The preparation for Beckert's trial took over six months—the Chilean authorities wished to have an absolutely clear case to present to the court. Also, the legal aspects of the case had to be gone into with great care, for the question of extraterritorial immunity was raised by the defense.

The trial, however, took place on September second, 1909, and ended with Beckert's conviction on all counts. He was not only sentenced to death but given thirty-eight years' penal servitude and fined sixteen hundred pesos—a sweet bit of legal inconsistency, but quite characteristic of legal procedure, don't y' know.

Beckert naturally appealed. Even in Chile such processes are part of the noble game of jurisprudence. But the Supreme Court denied the appeal; and after several stays of execution—so reminiscent of our own legal procedure—the unfortunate gentleman faced a firing squad on the fifth of July, 1910.

(Vance lighted another *Régie*.)

Y' know, Markham, my sympathies are all with Beckert. He did a noble and thorough piece of work. He spent almost two years concocting a perfect crime. Really, he should have succeeded ... No, I fear that I shall never go in for murder. The fickle goddess of chance...

The perfect crime! Yes, yes. The cards were stacked against the unfortunate Wilhelm. Most distressin', eh what?

"Yes, very distressin'," mocked Markham. Then: "There have been curious parallels of the Beckert case in America. There was the H. H. Holmes case, for instance, and the Udderzook case—both attempted insurance swindles."

"Oh, quite," Vance returned indolently. "Criminals are not original. Circumstances, don't y' know. There are parallelisms in most crimes, human nature bein' what it is. Especially is this true of *crimes passionnels*. They're based on the caressin' theory that one woman differs from another. Silly notion, what?

"Regard our own Snyder-Gray case. Lovers eliminatin' a husband.

Very sad. And yet, lovers have been eliminatin' husbands since time immemorial. I shall never be a husband, Markham. Much too dangerous.

TWO WEEKS later, when we were again gathered together in the lounge room of the old Stuyvesant Club, some mention was made of the Snyder-Gray case; and Vance dismissed it with a wave of the hand.

Reproached by Markham for his effete attitude, Vance told us of the famous Hilde Hanika case in Czechoslovakia in 1923—a case which had many amazing parallels with the Snyder-Gray case.

In my next report I shall try to set forth—as nearly as possible in Vance's own words—the record of this astounding *passionel* murder.

# The Inconvenient Husband

"I SEE WHERE Doctor N. L. Lederer, the amateur criminologist, has spoken somewhat disparagingly of the Snyder–Gray case, saying it was commonplace and hackneyed."

John F. X. Markham, New York's district attorney, leaned forward and lighted a perfecto.

He, Philo Vance, and I were seated in the lounge-room of the old Stuyvesant Club, where we had been in the habit of forgathering every Sunday night.

"Quite—quite." Vance yawned and settled himself more deeply in his chair. "Lederer is too well versed in the history of crime to have his hormones agitated by so unoriginal a murder, don't y' know.

"Every country and age has had its Snyder–Gray case. It's amazin' how seriously our great moral dailies took that saturnalia. It was a mere repetition of history— wives eggin' on lovers to dispose of inconvenient husbands. Very annoyin' for husbands, but—*voila l'affaire.*"

Vance sniffed and shrugged his shoulders; then he took out his cigarette case and deliberately selected one of his *Régies*. Both Markham and I understood the symptoms—he was about to elaborate his point.

The most famous case of the kind in recent years (he began, indolently blowing a ribbon of blue smoke toward the ceiling) was the Hanika murder in the old Austrian province of Moravia—now Czechoslovakia—in 1923.

My word, what a sensation it created in Europe! If it had occurred here in these fair states, our tabloid-editors would have gone stark mad with ecstasy. It was a greater sensation even than the Bywaters–Thompson case in England the year before—which case, by the by, constituted another almost perfect parallel with the Snyder–Gray affair. But neither Thompson's stabbing nor Snyder's brutal annihilation contained the racy and astonishin' elements of the Hanika murder.

Aside from its spectacularism, its abnormal pathology and its fascinatin' sex ramifications, there were in it some most illuminatin' psychological factors.

Captain Karl Hanika had served in France with the Czechoslovakian troops. After the armistice he met a gel named Hilde Charvat. She was not a nice person, Markham—decidedly she was not a nice person. But she had qualities. She was the daughter of a shady midwife in Brünn. Her father had died in an asylum in 1914. Not exactly an upliftin' background.

Hilde was then nineteen. From all accounts she was a great beauty—very cold, very blond, extremely self-possessed—the type that has so often been at the bottom of crimes of passion.

Hilde at the time was living with her mother; and Mama's reputation was none too good. In fact, there can be little doubt that the old lady's profession of *sage femme* was but a cloak for her real business.

Hilde, after trying her hand at various occupations, became a salesgirl in a phonograph shop—a vocation that offered glowin' opportunities for making male acquaintances. Which she did, I regret to say, with the connivance and even under the guidance of Mama.

Things were going along nicely in the summer of 1921 when Hilde, much against her mother's wishes, married Captain Hanika. Yes! Amazin' as it may seem, Hanika, an officer in the old Imperial Army, with all its prejudice of caste, wed the daughter of a dubious midwife— and this on a salary of 1400 kronen (about $42) a month. What could be hoped from such a marriage, even by the most incorrigible optimist?

Frau Charvat from the first was her son-in-law's bitter enemy, principally, I imagine, because the impecunious young man had been forced upon her by her recalcitrant daughter, who no doubt saw some sort of social stability for herself as the wife of an army officer. Moreover, Frau Charvat had to bear all the costs of the wedding and the honeymoon. Also, she had to pay the captain's debts, and she was forced to supply the money for the furnishings and the upkeep of the newlyweds' household. Hanika's salary was, of course, wholly insufficient.

It was not until after the marriage that he learned of his mama-in-law's subterranean means of livelihood. But there was little that he could do about it in the circumstances. He was willing to endure anything—want, degradation, abuse, shame—rather than suffer the supreme humiliation which a divorce would entail.

You must understand this thing, Markham; the public scandal and the publicity would have been unbearable to a man in Hanika's position. In this country, on the other hand—but let's not become sociological.

Suffice it to say the relationship between Hanika and Frau Charvat was quite comprehensible. He had made her daughter his wife, but he had only contempt for the old lady and her illicit trade. Still, he was forced to live on the proceeds of that trade.

Frau Charvat told Hilde constantly that Hanika was without a sense of obligation or duty toward her, and the old woman's continuous urgings and reproaches did not fail to bear fruit.

After a time Hilde began to grow tired of her husband. He attempted to overcome her indifference by making contributions to the household expenses—which he was invariably forced to reclaim shortly afterwards. Failing in his efforts, he reproached his wife bitterly with her mother's occupation; and she—not being entirely unintelligent— replied that they were both living on its proceeds. *Pauvre* Karl! Not a stout fella. He could find no escape, even if he had wanted one. (Vance shook his head dolorously, and permitted himself a theatrical sigh. I knew perfectly well he had no sympathy for Hanika.)

HILDE NOW BEGAN frequenting teas, theaters and cafés in her mother's company, and it was not long before she was indulging in "affairs" with her husband's friends. Hanika made many violent scenes—he was constitutionally jealous—and at last, driven almost to desperation, seriously discussed divorce proceedings; and Hilde, at Mama's suggestion, sought to egg him on to a separation by openly flaunting another man in his face. This ruse failing, she went to Prague with her mother and for a while deliberately lived the life of a *demi-mondaine*.

But Hanika, notwithstanding the unbearable conditions of his life, could not bring himself to face a divorce. He dreaded a scandal, which would have meant social ostracism; and above all he dreaded the publicity he would receive as a result of his relationship to his mother-in-law and her illegal trade.

Such was the sweet and caressin' state of affairs when Johann Vesely, a nineteen-year-old draftsman, entered the tableau. Johann was Hilde's second cousin, a Bohemian from Nosakov. Just how long this youth had been the lady's lover we don't know; but we do know that he was a weak character and that the strong-willed girl had exercised a dominating influence on him from early childhood.

And so the stage was set for a nice morbid crime.

On September third, in a field near Skalice-Boskovic, Captain Hanika's body was found. Death had resulted from a pistol bullet entering the skull behind the left ear. A second bullet, also fired from behind, had pierced the right shoulder.

Hanika had been stationed with his regiment in the little village of Ujezd, where the fall maneuvers were being held, and according to the testimony of his orderly, the preceding evening he had quitted his quarters in the company of an unknown civilian for the purpose of spending the night with his family in Brünn.

The corpse had been dragged from the pathway into an adjacent field. A state trooper had heard the two shots and had made a search of the neighborhood, but it was not until six o'clock in the morning that the body was discovered.

As Hanika had been well-liked by his men the police at once eliminated the possibility of his having been murdered by any member of his company, and concentrated their efforts on unearthing the civilian who had been seen leaving camp with the victim.

It did not take them long to acquire enough data to lead them to the guilty person. They learned that Hanika's wife, for several days before the murder, had been seen in the company of her cousin Johann Vesely who had disappeared on the morning of September fourth. It was also ascertained that Vesely had been Hilde's lover, and that the marital relationship between Hilde and Hanika had long been violently strained.

Acting on the supposition that Hilde and her mother could give vital information about the crime and the causes lead in gup to it, the police arrested the two women.

During the preliminary examination little was learned from them. They were a shrewd pair. But several remarks which they let drop led, a few days later, to the arrest of Vesely, who was hiding in his cousin's house in Selze, Slovakia. The next day it was discovered that on August twenty-eighth he and Hilde had purchased a 6.36 millimeter automatic pistol, and when young Vesely was confronted with this evidence he immediately broke down and confessed to the crime.

He stated that he had intended to commit suicide but had been surprised by the police. Even after the pistol had been found in a barn in Selze he passionately denied that either Hilde or her mother had had any knowledge of the crime. He maintained stoutly that he had intended doing away with himself but had decided first to free his lovely cousin from her brutal husband.

So far so good. The story was wholly consistent with a young lover's pathology. Though a weakling, his amorous impulse was powerful, and his one obsessing idea was to protect the object of his erotic visions. However—and here again we have a consistent psychological manifestation of this neurotic type—the moment the examining magistrate snowed him evidence of his *inamorata*'s "affairs" with other men and suggested to him that he had been used as a cat's-paw, he changed his story. You recall, of course, a similar reversal of sentiment on the part of the corset salesman Gray when he came to the realization that Mrs. Snyder had been using him for her own selfish ends.

Another interestin' parallel between the two cases lies in the fact that in both affairs there was a considerable sum of insurance money involved. A weak man will commit a crime for a woman provided she convinces him that he is the sole object of her affections; but even the weakest of men will balk at taking tremendous risks merely for a lady's pecuniary aggrandizement.

And thus it was with young Vesely. The disillusioned youth now affirmed that both his cousin and her mother had repeatedly urged him to kill Hanika, and that, during his last visit to Nosakov on August twenty-fifth, Hilde had inflamed his mind with a recital of Hanika's iniquities, at the same time pleading with him to rid her of her intolerable spouse.

FURTHERMORE, Vesely asserted that Hilde had suggested the *modus operandi* of the crime and had assured him that the murder would be regarded as an act of revenge by one of the captain's soldiers.

This second confession of Vesely's probably came near being the truth. In brief it was this:

On August twenty-seventh he went with Hilde to Prague and thence back to Brünn. Hanika had already departed for the maneuvers; and when the projected murder was discussed with Mama Charvat she approved heartily of the plan and persuaded him to lose no time in its execution.

The next morning the pistol was bought. Considerable difficulty had attached to the purchase because neither he nor his cousin had a gun license. But the resourceful Hilde had succeeded in borrowing a license from one of her friends.

On their return home Hilde, who was evidently a lady of parts, instructed her doting Johann in the handling and the use of the pistol and, when she considered him sufficiently adept, urged him to proceed at once to Ujezd.

Vesely set forth but immediately returned to Hilde, being unable to muster enough courage for the deed. But as the lady finally threatened to shoot herself if he did not go through with the business, he braced himself and promised to proceed to the act.

ON AUGUST THIRTIETH Hanika returned to Brünn; Hilde spent the night with friends and Vesely slept in the waiting room of the railway station. On September first, Hanika returned to the maneuvers, and Vesely again pledged himself to commit the murder without further ado. Once more, however, he vacillated, his excuse being that when he had sought out his victim Hanika had not been alone.

Hanika again came to Brünn for the night, and Hilde decided

that the time had come to work Johann into a frenzy. Accordingly, she locked herself in the bathroom, telling her cousin that she feared her husband would kill her, and Mama Charvat added her quota to the melodrama by informing Vesely that she had heard Hanika cock his revolver.

This wild tale had its effect on the young man, and he set forth upon his *jihad*, arriving at Ujezd on the morning of September third.

The doomed captain was absent for the day, but at six o'clock that evening he returned to camp. Here Vesely confronted him with the news that Hilde was ill. Whereupon they set out on foot for the station at Skalice-Boskovic.

The path to the station was narrow, and the women had to walk in single file. Vesely fell behind and permitted Hanika to lead the way. When a convenient spot was reached Vesely drew out his pistol and, at a distance of about four feet, shot the unhappy husband through the head. The second shot, which had lodged in Hanika's shoulder, had been fired accidentally.

Vesely then dragged the body into a field and proceeded alone to the station. He arrived in Brünn at eleven o'clock that night. He told the waiting Hilde and her mama what had occurred; but they did not believe him, for he had promised them—a most considerate young man!—to commit suicide immediately upon Hanika's demise. Eventually, though, he convinced the ladies that he had freed the world of the monster who had wrecked their lives; and finally they gave him a hundred kronen for his fare to Selze.

This, then, was the lad's confession, and it formed the basis of the indictment against the two women.

Snyder-Gray, Bywaters-Thompson, Hanika-Vesely—all alike. In each case the murderer was under the domination of a woman.

One of the most interesting points in the Hanika case is the character of Hanika himself. There was an amazin' creature, Markham. Numerous letters to his wife were read at the trial, and in addition we have a record of his diary—a sniveling but perfectly sincere document entitled: "My Marriage, Its Beginning and Its Curse, Written as Information and as a Warning for Others."

Hanika appears as a sentimental weakling, full of trite phrases and platitudes concerning his honor as an officer. Withal, he was physically brutal: he states that, at an early age, he broke off all communication with his own mother because, in his absence, she had given away some of his old clothes!

In his diary he tells of pleading with his wife and abasing himself before her. And yet one feels that it was not his heart that was pleading but his erotic desires.

In this lugubrious outpouring of his life Hanika accuses various of his friends of carrying on flirtations with his wife: he reproaches her bitterly for her frivolity.

Hilde's attorney, sensing the various prejudices which were aligned against her, asked for a change of venue. But this was denied, and a jury consisting of local tradesmen was impaneled.

There can be little doubt that public opinion was strongly biased against the young lady. The good men and true who sat in the jury box had little sympathy for the lax moral ideas by which she lived. They were a bit horrified at her admitted feeling of dislike for her husband. The press reflected, as always, the temper of public opinion.

At the same time it must be admitted that the evidence against her was rather black, don't y' know. The purchase of the gun, which was proved independently of Vesely's confession; the strong motive for her wishing her husband out of the way; the monetary advantage which would accrue to her through the insurance policy—all these things made her conviction a foregone conclusion.

Hilde testified that Hanika had finally agreed to a divorce, and that therefore she had no motive for his death. But this point was contradicted by several witnesses, mostly friends and comrades of Hanika.

Failing in this line of argument, Hilde averred that she had been forced into submission by Hanika's threat of exposing her mother's trade. But in view of his dread of notoriety, this statement did not seem particularly credible.

It was, of course, not to be expected that the practical, hard-headed jurymen would give any weight to the psychological considerations arising out of Hilde's upbringing and premarital life. And still, such consideration might have had a definite influence on their decision.

The evidence against Frau Charvat was much weaker than that against Hilde. It depended almost entirely on Vesely's confession and testimony.

Vesely appeared guilty chiefly through the brutality and premeditation of the crime, which, after all, was committed whilst removed from his cousin's influence. But it cannot be denied that there were several mitigating circumstances in his favor. His extreme youth, the general weakness of his character, the girl's complete domination over him and the total absence of any plausible motive— these things had their influence on the court.

Vesely's obvious jealous frenzy should have led the jury to scrutinize his accusations against Hilde with the greatest care. But this does not seem to have been done. Throughout the trial the tendency was to believe Vesely and to disbelieve the two women.

As is custom'ry in Continental criminal proceedings, the trial brought about several dramatic confrontations between the lovers, with their accompanying accusations and counter-accusations.

The result of the trial was that Vesely and Hilde were found guilty of premeditated murder, and that Frau Charvat was found guilty as an accessory before the fact. All three defendants had, according to the jury's findings, acted from base and dishonorable motives—a supplementary finding peculiar to Continental procedure.

The judges—in Europe judges have a very wide discretion in determining punishments—sentenced Hilde to death, Frau Charvat to twenty years of hard labor, and Vesely to three years of hard labor. In the case of Vesely the judges allowed him the lowest legal limit.

Both Hilde and her mother appealed the sentence; and, in the case of Vesely, the State itself questioned the judge's leniency. The Court of Appeals confirmed the sentences of the two women and raised Vesely's sentence to six years.

Immediately following the trial Hilde confessed to having been privy to the murder, but now she turned upon her mother and accused the old lady of having been the sole instigator. of the crime.

On the strength of this confession— which was, by the by, as intrinsically consistent as the confession of her paramour—Masaryk, the President of the Republic, commuted Hilde's sentence to fifteen years of hard labor...

A depressin' case, but not original. And *nota bene*, Markham: Hilde, like Mrs. Thompson and Mrs. Snyder, was convicted largely because she had used her influence to turn a lover into a murderer. And it was on the strength of this influence that all three women were convicted. Moreover, in all three of these famous cases the defendants were tried simultaneously, and all were convicted.

No, no. The crime of passion is never original.

VANCE SIGHED regretfully, and shifted lazily in his chair. "Most unfortunate," Markham commented with a trace of sarcasm. "As a connoisseur of crime you must suffer abominably."

"It's my aesthetic sensitivities, old dear," Vance drawled. " However, I must admit, don't y' know, that the simplest and most rudiment'ry crimes sometimes have the most entrancin' ramifications. You recall, of course, the amazin' Murri-Bonmartini case—in Bologna in 1902?"

"Vaguely," admitted Markham, glancing at his watch. "You'll forgive me if I run along. I have several transcripts of testimony to go
over tonight."

"And I have a Mozart quartet to attend at ten." Vance rose and
gave the district attorney a waggish look. "Don't sequester any of the
documents after the manner of Stanzani, or you may have a committee of righteous celebrities on your heels..."

Vance was referring to the judge of the Murri–Bonmartini affair—
the judge whose prejudiced investigations created a great legal sensation
in Europe and brought many of the leading men of literature, science
and politics to the defense of the victims.

The following Sunday night when the three of us met again at the
Stuyvesant Club, Vance, at Markham's suggestion, told us the details of
the case; and in my next article I shall try to retell the story as nearly
as possible in his own words.

Of all modern murder cases the Murri–Bonmartini affair was perhaps the most celebrated; and its influence extended over two continents.

# The Bonmartini Murder Case

LAST Sunday evening," said John F. X. Markham, New York's district attorney, when he and Mr. Philo Vance and I had settled ourselves in the loungeroom of the Stuyvesant Club, "you mentioned the Murri-Bonmartini case.

"A curious thing, but the case was mentioned in court last Thursday — the defending attorney for Freeman waxed rather eloquent over the affair, and I have a feeling he was using it as a club with which to batter me over the head." The district attorney smiled ironically. "I've forgotten the details of the case."

Vance lighted one of his *Régie* cigarettes and smoked a while in silence, his dolichocephalic brow puckered as if he were making an effort to adjust his memory.

The Murri-Bonmartini tragedy had come up in conversation at the club the preceding Sunday, but the hour had grown late and Markham had had work to do. Tonight Vance told us the story of that astounding crime and its more astounding consequences.

THE MURRI-Bonmartini case (said Vance, with an animation that startled me) was one of the greatest miscarriages of justice in modern times. It was a *cause célébre* comparable only with the Dreyfus affair.

No more sensational trial was ever held in Europe, and surely no more violent prejudice was ever shown against any defendants than was exhibited in this trial.

As you remember, the trial aroused a storm of indignation that swept over all Europe.

The most glitterin' lights in literature, science and politics leaped to the defense of the victims. Karl Federn, the great German essayist, wrote an entire book on the proceedings, which has been translated into practically every European language; and it contains introductions by such men as Bjornstjerne Bjornson, Guglielmo Ferrero, and Gabriel Séailles.

You may recall that Mark Twain and William Dean Howells planned an American and English edition of the book; and the French Law Society—-the *Jeuné Barreau*—held various meetings of protest at which

Anatole France, Charles Gide, Louis Havet, and similar luminaries exuded eloquent parts of speech.

A whole literature has sprung up around this famous case, the results of which have brought about many changes in the criminal procedure of various nations.

The crime itself was a most morbidly fascinatin' one. And I must say that the victim was rather in need of killin', don't y' know. Few women ever have suffered at a husband's hands as intolerably as the young and talented Countess Bonmartini suffered at the hands of her indecent spouse. Her life was a most distressin' martyrdom; and when the swaggering and wholly vicious Count Bonmartini was found stabbed to death in his apartment it appeared to be a blessing to the world in general and to the young countess in particular.

But alas! it was no blessing—it was a kind of augmented tragedy. For not only was the countess herself accused of the crime, but her brother, her lover, her maid, her uncle and three friends were all dragged to the Bastille. Eight arrests for one murder! A bit thick, what?

Not that any one of them wasn't morally justified in translating the count into the Beyond; but really, y' know, eight people can't wield one dagger. The astoundin' part of it was that five of 'em were convicted—four of whom were obviously innocent. And the actual perpetrator of the deed should have been placed in an asylum. It was all very sad and very terrible. But criminal and legal history was in the making...

The circumstances leading up to the Bonmartini crime were both tragic and remarkable. Augusto Murri was a well-known physician and the professor of anatomy at the famous old University of Bologna. His daughter Theodolinda—the cause of all the trouble—was born in 1871; and her brother, Tullio, put in an appearance on this earth three years later.

They were both brought up according to the strict tenets of Catholicism by their mother, but, in pursuance of the wishes of the father, Linda was given a far more liberal education than is usual in such families. She became well versed in Latin and Greek; she spoke several languages, and for many years was a keen student of the great classical writers.

When Linda was still a young girl she met one of her father's pupils and assistants, a Doctor Carlo Secchi, for whom she developed, as the saying goes, a deep and lasting passion. But her parents frowned upon a marriage between them because of the great disparity in their ages; and Doctor Secchi was politely but firmly requested to discontinue his wooing.

Linda was broken-hearted, but in 1892 she met the young Count Francesco Bonmartini, and Doctor Secchi was temporarily shelved. In June, 1892, her engagement to the young nobleman was announced, and a few months later he led her triumphantly to the hymeneal altar.

The marriage from the start was, I weep to say, a failure. Bonmartini was decidedly not a nice man, Markham. He was crude and vulgar—a boaster and a cad, possessed of an inordinate vanity, and a dashing Don Juan in the demimonde. Moreover, he was addicted to telling flowery and amorous tales of conquests which, as you may imagine, shocked his young wife.

The marriage would have gone on the rocks at an early date had it not been for the birth of two children —a daughter, named Maria, in 1894, and a son, Ninetto, two years later.

After the birth of the second child, Linda's health went to pieces. She was a sensitive and delicate woman, and her weakened physical condition accentuated her already strong repugnance toward her philanderin' spouse. Against her doctor's orders she insisted upon nursing Ninetto, and in 1897 she went through a severe attack of typhoid fever followed by pneumonia.

THE FOLLOWING year there was a complete estrangement between her and her husband; and from certain passages in Bonmartini's diary, as well as from letters which she wrote to Doctor Negri, the gynecologist who attended her, we learn that she was—as our grandparents would say—a wife in name only.

In 1898 Linda again met Doctor Secchi, at the house of the Marchesa Rusconi, and while there may have been certain flutterings in her heart at the sight of the object of her girlish passion, she maintained a discreet and uncorrupted matronhood. However, in December of the same year she suggested a divorce to her husband, but got nowhere with him. He was as stubborn as he was indecent... Most distressin'.

Entries in Bonmartini's diary give us a vivid picture of the inferno in which this unhappy woman was living. The young count, who, notwithstanding his great wealth, was extremely penurious, began to reproach Linda for her extravagances. He even objected to her doctor's bills, and criticized her severely for taking a trip to the Riviera—which, by the bye, was paid for by her father.

At the same time Bonmartini developed a deep-seated bitterness for Professor Murri. He resented his father-in-law's intellectual superiority, and, after expressing a wish to study medicine, asked the old professor to assist him in obtaining the necessary permission for entry at the university without a *Gymnasium* degree.

But the elder Murri declined the request—and rightly. Nevertheless, Bonmartini succeeded in his ambition through the influence of friends, and studied first in Camerino and then at Bologna. But he never forgave his father-in-law.

IN 1899 A JUDICIAL separation was agreed upon between him and Linda. She was to receive each year for herself and her children five thousand lire—a thousand dollars—in addition to the interest on her marriage dowry.

Bonmartini swelled out his chest for what he regarded as an act of great generosity on his part, and consoled himself for his marital misfortunes by a series of sordid amatory affairs.

Linda—poor gal—had, in the meantime, again met Doctor Secchi at the house of the Marchesa Rusconi. She then began to realize that her sentiments for Doctor Secchi were not entirely platonic; and there can be little doubt that in 1900 the doctor became her lover.

Later in the same year the lady's health again declined, and a carbon particle, which had lodged in her eye, made necessary several surgical operations.

During the trial, the prosecution stated that Linda constantly complained about her health and posed as a martyr. But this is certainly not borne out by her letters, which reveal a most exemplary patience and fortitude of character...Y'know, Markham, even an incorrigible cynic like myself cannot help sympathizin' with her.

In the meantime, Bonmartini, having taken his M. D. degree, importuned his father-in-law to appoint him his chief assistant. Naturally, the old professor refused this preposterous request; and there came a final break between him and his son-in-law.

Bonmartini had constantly pleaded for a reconciliation with his wife, and took advantage of her devotion to her children to force her to resume the marital relationship.

In 1902, when Linda had to undergo another operation on her eye in Zurich, the young *coureur des filles* made a legal demand for the custody of the children. Half-crazed with fear, and suffering agonies as the result of her operation, Linda finally agreed to a reconciliation, notwithstanding her father's protests. Curiously enough, her brother Tullio expressed himself as being in favor of her decision.

As you may recall, during the trial the prosecuting attorney declared that the only reason she desired the reconciliation was to lure her husband to his death. Ah, welladay...I have studied the case pretty carefully I have read the lady's letters and the husband's diary. and I assure you, Markham old dear, that no such sanguinary notion dictated her action. Finally, however, an agreement was reached between the two. Bonmartini—in the eyes of the world—was to live with Linda, but one of the stipulations of the pact was that he was not to enter her rooms except in case of the sickness of one of the children. It was further agreed that both parties were to maintain their complete personal freedom. This arrangement was sworn to in all solemnity in the presence of Cardinal Svampa in Bologna.

Linda enlarged her apartment at the Palazzo Bisteghi by renting an additional suite of rooms for her husband. Bonmartini insisted that she discharge her entire domestic staff—which she dutifully did. She engaged as chambermaid a seamstress named Rosina Bonetti, who had been Tullio's sweetheart.

It was quite obvious, don't y' know, that Linda's new domestic arrangements with her husband would prove neither permanent nor happy.

The diary of this strange johnny is a most amazin' document. The mentality of a man who would go to almost any lengths to force his wife to live under the same roof with him, merely so that he could vent his hatred and spite on her, furnishes enough abnormal material to equip a whole school of modern psychologists.

He gloated insanely over any little torture that he could invent; and his refined cruelty in playing upon his wife's love for her children stamped him not only as a fiend but as a lunatic whose internment in an asylum would have been the only possible solution to the appalling tragedy of Linda's life.

Bonmartini had never abandoned the idea of becoming Professor Murri's assistant, and now he threatened to put the children in a convent unless he was appointed to the post. Tullio endeavored to persuade his father to meet this demand, and Linda herself, in desperation, pleaded with him.

Finally Professor Murri decided to put an end to his daughter's unhappiness by demanding a divorce. Heaven, so to speak, knows there was enough evidence against Bonmartini.

But Tullio—now incensed beyond endurance — decided to take the whole matter into his own hands. Stout fella, but dashed misguided ... He was twenty-eight years old, an idealistic dreamer, and had made something of a reputation for himself as a political writer of advanced radical tendencies. He was hot-tempered and dangerous when aroused, but kind and generous, and devoted to his sister.

At first he had been inclined to minimize Bonmartini's vices and had been instrumental in bringing about the reconciliation between his sister and her husband. Now, however, the misery of Linda's life and her precarious state of health filled him with agonies of self-reproach. In this state of remorse and Messianic exaltation, he came to the conclusion that Bonmartini's death was the only solution of the problem. So he went to Doctor Secchi, whose relations with Linda he knew, and asked for some poison—preferably curare.

Secchi explained to him the absurdity of his plan, and pointed out the impracticability of using curare.

But Tullio was not to be pacified or put off. He made insistent demands upon the physician, and finally, to quiet the rash young man, Secchi sent him a hypodermic syringe, at the same time writing to Linda warning her against Tullio's state of mind.

He asked her to do everything in her power to prevent a meeting between Tullio and Bonmartini. Professor Murri and also Signora Murri wrote to friends requesting them to watch Tullio, although they feared nothing worse than that he would give his brother-in-law a severe thrashing.

In July, 1902, Linda had again been in Zurich for an operation. On her return she suffered a nervous prostration. The prosecution claimed that she had pretended this illness in order to inflame further her brother's murderous passion.

Bonmartini now, by threats of violence, forced Linda to spend the summer with him in Venice. Tullio learned of this move, and in August, when Bonmartini had gone away on a trip, he himself went to Venice and procured the key to the Bologna apartment from Linda's maid—his former sweetheart.

On August twenty-eighth Bonmartini came to Bologna to pay the rent of the apartment; and for several days Linda was without news of him. She suspected that her husband was merely indulging in another of his amorous adventures.

But on September second, Bonmartini's murdered body was discovered in the Bologna apartment. Several bits of dainty lingerie were found in the room, and also a *billet-doux* from a notorious *demimondaine* making an appointment for August twenty-ninth.

Soon, however, several fresh discoveries shunted the investigation to quite different lines. Moreover, on the same floor as the Bonmartini apartment was a small empty flat which had been occupied by Doctor Secchi; and the rumor spread that he had been Linda's paramour.

On hearing of her husband's death Linda returned from Venice, but her family immediately decided to send her and the children to

Switzerland; and two days after the discovery of the murder she and Tullio left for Zurich.

In the meantime, as a result of the knowledge that Linda had been guilty of breaking the Seventh Commandment, there came about a terrific revulsion of public feeling. The editor of a clerical paper, *Avvenire d'Italia*, who had always been a bitter personal enemy of Professor Murri's, at once began a campaign of persecution and slander against the entire Murri family.

The investigation into the crime was at first carried on by Judge Tinti; but because of his humane and conciliatory methods Bonmartini's family succeeded in having the case transferred to Judge Stanzani, whose fanatical hatred of the Murris was a recognized political fact.

Surely you recall, Markham, how this noble representative of law and justice collected all the documents tending to prove the innocence of some of the defendants and to mitigate the guilt of others, and sealed them in a box—that famous *Cassa Numero 4*—so that no one, not even the Appellate Court, could have access to them.

Tullio had confessed the murder to Linda while in Zurich, and when the investigation turned against Linda herself she returned to Bologna, where she was arrested on September fourteenth, 1902.

To Stanzani, Linda's guilt was a foregone conclusion, though it was not so easy to produce proof. And his treatment of the prisoners is one of the darkest blots on modern judicial procedure.

The methods employed by the Italian reincarnation of Judge Jeffreys would have been shunned by Torquemada himself. Tullio was kept in prison for thirteen months without being allowed to see or speak to a human being except the examining magistrate. He was permitted neither books nor paper and pencil. When it was discovered that he was amusing himself by feeding the sparrows from his window, the upliftin' Stanzani had his cell window boarded up.

Linda, against whom no case had yet been made out, fared even worse. For seven months she was not allowed to leave her cell, nor was she permitted to open a window.

As you know, the winter months in northern Italy are cold, and, during the entire winter, she was denied a fire or even a coat or a blanket. Only in April, when the police surgeon informed Stanzani that Linda's life was in danger, was she given an extra cover.

For eight months she was not allowed to see any member of her family, and was deprived of any news whatever of her children. When one of the prison nuns told her that her children were in good health, Stanzani had the pious woman instantly dismissed. Linda's letters to her mother begging for news of her children were not posted —they disappeared into the *Cassa Numero 4*. But a perfectly harmless letter to Doctor Secchi was added to the indictment; and at the trial the prosecutor stated that, during Linda's imprisonment, she had shown no interest in her children but only for her illicit love affair! ... A sweet state of justitia, eh, what?

Stanzani's methods during the whole investigation were a violation of the Italian Criminal Code. Not only did he put suggestive questions to the accused, but he used a threat of thirty years' imprisonment to obtain a false statement from Linda's maid, who, during the process, had a hysterical seizure.

A friend of Tullio's—a Doctor Pio Naldi—who had also been arrested, had, in a careless statement, weakened Tullio's case. Later, he tried to commit suicide by opening an artery in his wrist. Stanzani immediately instructed the prison surgeon to give the half-conscious Naldi some camphor injections, and then continued the examination until the prisoner completely collapsed.

Later in April Linda made this statement: "If I had not loved Doctor Secchi, what happened would never have taken place. It was a reawakening of my old love."

It was obvious, don't y' know, that the unhappy lady referred to her relations with Doctor Secchi—the only crime of which she felt herself guilty—and a further question would have made this point clear. But. Stanzani refused to put the question, and in his report he stated that Linda had confessed to having instigated the murder!

Stanzani had already arrested seven persons, and accused them all of the murder—Tullio, Linda, Linda's maid, Doctor Naldi, Ernesto Dalla, a friend of the Murri family, Dalla's brother, Riccardo, and Professor Murri's brother, Riccardo Murri, a well-known lawyer. And when Doctor Naldi inadvertently informed Stanzani of the episode of the curare, that sweet and humane judge added Doctor Secchi to the list.

On concluding the investigation Stanzani wrote a report of one hundred and twenty-two pages—the now famous "Résumé"—one of the most fantastic parodies ever penned. In it his imagination ran riot.

He spoke of "insane aberrations" which had taken place in Linda's room, although it had been shown that Doctor Secchi had been rather a brother and nurse to the ailing woman than a lover. He also stated that Linda had systematically slandered her husband and had taken him from his friends— statements without any basis in fact. But this was not all. In 1899 Doctor Secchi had stayed one day at San Remo, where the Murris were spending the summer, and Stanzani wrote in his report that Secchi had lived a considerable time with Linda there, despite the fact that the maid had testified that the only entrance to hermistress' room was through Bonmartini's.

Linda's letters to her husband, in which she remarked that their life together was impossible since she could not pretend to a feeling she did not possess, were called typical examples of her dissimulation. A letter from Tullio to Linda consoling her and telling her that things would be better later on, was regarded by Stanzani as an open promise to murder Bonmartini!

In 1901 Professor Murri wrote to Linda, who was then convalescing from an operation, that if she would behave herself, she would soon recover; and Stanzani deduced from this letter that the professor approved of the murder!

Stanzani concluded that Linda was the most cunning liar and hypocrite that ever lived, and that for years she had primed Tullio for the murder of her husband. He even stated that Linda's ailments were pure simulations, and that her doctors had been bribed by Professor Murri.

This astounding document was given by Stanzani to the press for publication before the trial. The papers, itching for sensation, called Linda a "monster of cruelty," and designated her a modern Lucrezia Borgia who had killed her husband merely to satisfy her sadistic impulses. Practically the only newspaper that ventured to protest against this campaign of hatred and libel was the *Corriere della Sera*, which published a series of articles by Ferrero, the famous historian. These articles endeavored to sift the mass of conflicting rumors and gossip and to arrive at a true and reasonable presentation of facts.

It must be stated, Markham old dear, to the honor of the profession which you so gracefully adorn, that the Italian law publications, without exception, condemned the proceedings and endorsed Ferrero's point of view.

Well, well! What could one expect in the way of fairness at such a trial? Even a change of venue from Bologna to Turin could not counteract the effects of Stanzani's three-year campaign of slander.

THE TRIAL OPENED in Turin in October, 1904, but was interrupted two weeks later because several of the attorneys were candidates in the elections. The trial was reopened in February of 1905 and lasted until late into the summer.

Seventeen lawyers shared in the defense of Linda, Tullio, Doctor Secchi, the maid and Doctor Naldi. The case against the other three defendants had been dropped for lack of evidence—much to Stanzani's disgust.

Stanzani, by the bye, had demanded that the defendants be tried not only for murder, but for attempted murder by curare. The court, however, decided against this further complication—thereby demonstrating that even in this infamous trial a faint ray of commonsense penetrated the judicial darkness. Incidentally, four hundred and twenty witnesses were called to testify.

The case against Tullio rested solely on his own confession: there was no corroboratory evidence. He admitted that he had gone to his brother-in-law at seven in the evening of August twenty-eighth; and that in the course of conversation Bonmartini had insulted both Linda and Professor Murri. Then, in a blind frenzy, he had attacked Bonmartini with a knife and killed him.

Later Tullio changed his confession in order to exculpate his friend, Doctor Naldi, who had confessed to going with Tullio to Bonmartini's apartment on the night of the murder. This second confession stated that the murder had taken place at midnight—which was undoubtedly correct; for Tullio, after his arrival in Bologna, had gone to the theater and had been seen there by several witnesses.

The prosecution, however, was determined that not one of the defendants should escape, and, as it was known that Doctor Naldi had left Bologna at about seven o'clock that night, it clung to the claim that the murder had taken place before that hour.

The case against the maid was equally unconvincing. She admitted she had procured the key to the Bonmartini apartment from Linda and had given it to Tullio; but no other evidence was brought against her.

Doctor Secchi was accused of having urged Tullio to poison Bonmartini; and although no evidence was adduced to bear out this accusation, his relations with Linda were sufficient to turn the jury against him.

The most astonishin' phase of the trial was the case presented against Linda. Not one scintilla of tangible evidence could be brought against her; yet the prosecution was so intent on having her condemned that it built up its case on vague suspicions and rumors.

Linda had written a letter to Tullio a few days before the murder, and, although this letter had been destroyed, the judges permitted the prosecution to state that in it she had begged Tullio to kill her husband. Also, the fact that Professor Murri was a freethinker was admitted as evidence against Linda!

Throughout the trial the Italian press continued its systematic persecution of the defendants; and the *Avvenire d'Italia* spoke with touchin' fervor of its righteous crusade against "the atheistic gang of criminals."

On the last day of the trial the newspapers, in order to make sure of a verdict against the defendants, stated that Professor Murri had cashed a check for three hundred thousand lire with which to bribe the jury. And these newspaper articles were actually read to the jury by the presiding judge in his summing-up.

Under the circumstances, the result of this tragic *opéra-bouffe* was a foregone conclusion, although the savage severity of the sentences exceeded the fondest hopes of God's good common people.

Tullio and Doctor Naldi were both found guilty of premeditated murder, and each was sentenced to thirty years of solitary confinement. The poor half-witted maid was sentenced to seven years, and Doctor Secchi to ten years.

Linda was found guilty of complicity in the murder by seven votes to five. Although the jury stated that the deed would have been committed without her participation, she received a sentence of ten years' hard labor.

Even the jury was aghast at this sentence and petitioned the judicial authorities to revise it. But nearly a year later the Appellate Court in Rome confirmed all the sentences.

With the characteristic inconsistency of the popular mind—a touchin' euphemism!—the agitation in favor of the defendants now became as strong as the previous attacks against them had been. Indignant protest arose all over Europe. Baron Sonnino, the Italian prime minister, requested the King to exert his royal privilege of pardon, stating that the trial had been a mockery.

A FEW WEEKS after the appeal in 1906 Linda was pardoned, first under condition of exile, and in 1909 unconditionally. Tullio was pardoned in 1919; and Doctor Naldi was freed the same year. Doctor Secchi died in prison; and the maid went insane a few days after her conviction and went to her Maker after her transference to an asylum. As an indication of the widespread indignation aroused by this judicial outrage, it is interestin' to note that in 1908 an open letter was sent to Linda, expressing the utmost horror of the vindictive prosecution of which she had been the victim, and assuring her of the senders belief in her innocence.

This document, which has long since become one of the most famous historical epistles of modern times, was signed by a truly amazin' array of prominent men and women. The signatures included the names of Björnstjerne Björnson, Max Burckhard, Richard Dehmel, Gerhart Hauptmann, Julia Ward Howe, Ricarda Huch, Ellen Key, Maurice

Maeterlinck, Victor Margueritte, Heinrich Mann, August Vermeylen, Auguste Wilbrandt-Baudius, Marie von Witte, and Madame Emile Zola...

Permit me, my dear Markham, to add one tidbit of gossip. Linda has married again and, I understand, is quite happy.

WHEN VANCE had finished his narrative Markham commented: "The worst of it is that a similar injustice might occur wherever a judge let his prejudices predominate."

Vance smiled sardonically. "And that would be almost anywhere—eh, what? 'The law is an ass—a idiot,' as Mr. Bumble said. I'm rather in favor of the repeal of all laws. A bit inconvenient, d' ye see; but I'm inclined to believe that more justice would result if each man were his own lawyer, judge and jury."

Markham ignored this heresy. "There's a terrible irony in the Bonmartini affair," he said meditatively. "Here was Tullio attempting to free his sister from one horror, only to plunge her and her family and friends into a greater horror."

"Irony—yes, yes." Vance puffed a moment on his cigarette. " But there can be irony in justice too... Do you recall the Otto Eissler case a few years ago? What a grim affair it was!—a truly amazin' crime. And how the ruthless gods sniggered during the whole of Bissler's life! Oh, my aunt, what irony! —the irony of consumin' weakness ..."

Vance did not tell us the story of Otto Eissler until nearly a month later, when a brief news dispatch from Europe mentioned that Eissler, a broken old man, had been discharged from prison.

And it is this story that I shall relate next month, as nearly in Vance's own words as I am able. The poetic side of Vance's cynicism came to the surface during his recital of those tragic events; and Markham and I were able to glimpse the deep humanitarianism which he so persistently kept hidden, and which only those who were close to him ever sensed.

# Fool!

"YOU mentioned the Eissler case last month, Vance," said Markham, when Philo Vance and he and I had taken our accustomed places that Sunday night in the lounge-room of the old Stuyvesant Club. "Otto Eissler, I see, has been discharged from prison and is bringing a civil suit against his former firm for money he claims he has been swindled out of."

Vance adjusted his monocle and blew a ribbon of blue smoke toward the ceiling.

"Yes, yes,' he answered, with a sigh. "Sad—sad. Poor devil! Otto was undoubtedly swindled from a purely moral point of view. But whether or not the Austrian courts will recognize his claim is highly problematic. However, there was genuine Greek irony in that astonishin' crime. You may not recall the story; but I've gone into it recently—its drama appealed to me. Most unusual, don't y' know: like an Attic tragedy."

Nearly every Sunday night since the solution of the Bishop murder case, Philo Vance and Markham—New York's district attorney—and I had met for dinner and a causerie on crime, and Vance had already told us many interesting stories of famous Continental murders. Tonight he recounted to us the details of the famous Eissler case.

IN ORDER TO understand the amazin' irony of Otto Eissler's tragic but futile crime (Vance began, regarding the tip of his Régie cigaret meditatively), it is essential that I recount a bit of commercial history. Really y' know, Markham, I don't wish to bore you unnecessarily, but the background of this grim and fascinatin' murder is most important.

(Vance lay back in his chair and passed his long tapering hand across his brow as if trying to recall certain facts that reposed in the recesses of his retentive brain. Then he spoke again in his emotionless drawl.) Among the famous industrial firms-that—had been connected with the exploitation of the wealth of the  soil in the old Austrian Empire, not one had a higher reputation for financial stability and managerial integrity than the lumber firm of J. Eissler und Brüder.

It was a very old firm. Bernhard Eissler had founded it in 1825; and when that pioneer passed to his Maker his four sons—Heinrich, Johann, Jakob, and Moritz—not only carried on the tradition, but greatly extended the scope of the enterprise. At the outbreak of the World War its ramifications covered the whole of the vast forest domains of Austria, Hungary and neighboring states.

TRUE TO THE ancient Jewish tradition that children should remain subject to their father's leadership during their lifetime, the four brothers had made an arrangement by which their sons could become members of the firm only on the death or retirement of the father.

Don't sigh so impatiently, Markham old dear, for this arrangement was, in a way, the crux of the terrible and incredible events that were to follow.

Johann and Jakob died, and their sons—Alfred and Hermann— succeeded to membership. The son of Moritz—Robert—being an ambitious and able youth, did not take kindly to his two cousins thus getting the better of him, as it were, and enlisted his uncle Heinrich's help in persuading his father to admit him to the firm before the old gentleman's death. Uncle Heinrich, who evidently had a soft spot in his heart for his nephew, interceded and managed to obtain Moritz's consent, with the latter's stipulation, however, that Robert should invest 600.000 kronen— $120,000—in the business.

Robert hadn't the money—maybe his father thought that this stipulation would keep Robert out of the firm. But Uncle Heinrich again took a hand. He turned schatchen and arranged a marriage for Robert which brought him the required capital. And then Robert's father died, and the newest member of the firm, because of his forceful personality and unquestionableability, became the manager of this vast enterprise.

Robert was not a nice man, Markham. He had qualities not dissimilar to some of our American magnates. He was hard and unscrupulous, turning everything to his own ends and showing no mercy to anyone who stood in his way. I don't say he was after personal aggrandizement—the firm of which he was now the head had become his golden calf. Scarcely had he seized the reins of management when he decided that his Uncle Heinrich—to whom he owed his position—was not the proper person to be the senior partner of the firm. Heinrich was filled with principles of integrity and exuded a charitable public spirit. He actually had refused to sign a tax return because he deemed it too low!

Such old-fashioned honesty didn't appeal to Robert's sense of commercial *Schrecklichkeit*, and he went to work to oust the older man. He submitted a contract—which the trusting Heinrich and his son Otto accepted in good faith—to the effect that, upon the retirement of a partner, the partner should not receive any share of the tremendous reserve funds but only his portion of the capital itself.

Having thus taken his first Machiavellian step, he decided to rid himself completely of the old gentleman, who was now seventy-eight. And so, after an honorable reign of forty years, Heinrich Eissler was asked to resign. When he refused, Robert took the matter into court, demanding his retirement on the grounds of general inefficiency.

The two other junior partners—Alfred and Hermann—were too much under the domineering will of their cousin to oppose him; and moreover, they had artistic rather than commercial temperaments. Alfred was a collector of miniatures and first editions; and Hermann's collection of modern French paintings is one of the finest in Europe. He owns some excellent Delacroix canvases and several notable examples of Géricault's work.

GÉRICAULT was a great realistic painter, Markham, He was not as vigorous and artistic as Courbet or Daumier, but a craftsman who deserves far more credit than he has received from the critics. Gérard and Gros loosened Ingres' drawing; and Géricault, with the help of Guérin, completed the disruption of the *méthode* David.

(Markham heaved an audible sigh, and shifted in his chair.)

Forgive me, old dear (Vance apologized without the slightest intonation of contrition); but after all, don't y' know, art is far more inveiglin' than crime. However, we will forgo aesthetics pro tempore.

Robert did not succeed in eliminating his uncle. and a sort of peace was eventuaily patched up. It lasted only a year, however, for the following summer old Heinrich died.

Otto Eisler—the tragic Don Quixote of this sardonic tale—was the son of Heinrich; and upon him Robert vented his wrath and contempt. He had consistently refused to admit Otto to partnership in the firm. but when the peace negotiations were being threshed out he permitted Otto to become a silent partner upon the payment of 750,000 Swiss francs—$150,000—-and the latter's relinquishment of all his rights in the Bosnian branch of this business, which amounted to over $1,000,000.

On the break-up of the old Austrian Empire, the Eisslers had claimed Czechoslovakian citizenship and had fortified their hold on their great lumber enterprise by forming a ring of subsidiary companies in the Succession States. The wealth of the firm was colossal.

Oh. I say! Are you awake, Markham? I'm deuced sorry and all that tohave been so soporific; but if you will go in for crime, you must force yourself to tolerate the necessary preambles. The share of this great business which old Heinrich left to Otto amounted to nearly 8.000.000 Swiss franccs, or more than $1,500,000; and Robert—with his Vergilian *auri sacra fames*—decided that the firm. rather than Otto, could use this fortune to advantage.

Consequently. he instigated one of the most astoundin' maneuvers of financial jugglery in modern history under cover of the collapse of Austrian currency. When the ledger value of the firm's capital had been reduced to a minimum, through conversion and reconversion of its assets. He paid Otto his entire share in the business with a check for 15.000 Swiss francs. Or $3,000! And this sum included not only Otto's inheritance, but the $150,000 which he had put into the firm the preceding year!

HERE WAS HIGH finance with a vengeance. One can hardly blame Ottofor being angry.

And my word! He was angry, Markham. It was the impotent and disorganized anger of the neurotic weakling—the most dangerous of all passions. But Robert, obsessed with his lust for power and contemptuous of all human inferiority. did not know it. Had he been able to look into the future he certainly would have treated his cousin differently, for when he signed that $3,000 check he also signed his own death warrant. With that stroke of the pen he turned Otto into a murderer and himself into a corpse. Very distressin'. Still. don't y' know. one can't help admiring Robert. He was so dashed consistent—a strong, domineering man with an idée fixe.

And Otto was a weakling—there can be no doubt of that. He was soft and petty—and pathetic. He was on theside of righteousness, and Robert represented the powers of darkness—as the theologians would say. But humanity, for all its caressin' platitudes, does not admire piety and weakness nearly so passionately as it admires strength.

Robert was a symbol of strength. The terrible. coruscatin' irony of the events which followed revealed the natures of these two disparate men; and even in death Robert maintained the ascendancy.

Otto. however, is a more interestin' character from a psychological point of view. Never, perhaps. in the history of crime have the gods been as cynical as they were when they manipulated the drama of Robert Eissler's murder. The thing was Sophoclean.

Otto Eissler had spent an empty and desolate childhood—among nursemaids, teachers, and sycophantic servants. His father—the soft-hearted Heinrich—had been absorbed completely by business affairs; and his mother—a cool. unloving and aloof woman—paid scant attention to him. At school he was noted for his taciturnity. his brooding seriousness, and his abnormal attitude of suspicion.

And so he grew up a stubborn, sullen, self-centered hypochondriac. who feared his family and his friends. but who still had a warm understanding for the sufferings of humanity. He worked for fifteen years in the firm of J. Eissler und Brüder, but in commerce he never felt at home. The overshadowing ability of Robert was too much for his sensitive nature. And he developed  marked inferiority complex which sought temporary relief in a desperate stubbornness.

He had scorned the age-old tradition of his race and had refused to emulate his cousin Robert contracting a marriage of convenience.

But at his father's behest, he refrained from marrying the woman who was to be the one ray of light in his drab and miserable life.

Anna Heimerle had been his companion for many years. and his love for her and their three children was all that seemed to matter to him. But even the self-sacrificing love of Anna was insufficient to banish the constantly deepening shadows of neurotic disturbance.

When the war of his tribe. headed by Robert was directed against him and his father. his vague feelings of distrust and suspicion began to reveal symptoms of paranoiac delusions. At his trial many witnesses testified to his peculiar behavior. During his visits to the various lumber camps, he would be found stark naked walking with an umbrella in one hand and a revolver in the other. At night he would barricade his bedroom door with furniture. His food had to be tasted before he would touch it. for he was obsessed with the idea that poison plots were being hatched against him.

At about this time he developed a bacteriophobia and lived in an atmosphere of disinfectants. His newspapers had to be warmed before he would touch them.

For all these eccentricities he would give glib pseudo-scientific explanations; and the very ardor with which he disclaimed anything abnormal in his behavior characterized him as a neurotic whose life-long repressions someday would bring him to the bar of justice. Robert Eissier became the center and symbol of his hatred; and this hatred was intensified by the unwilling admiration and envious love which he could not withhold from the stronger man. Robert was for him everything that he was not yet everything he wished to be. He alternated between an instinctive desire to combat the iron rule of his antagonist and an impulsive wish to submit to the other's will.

Otto's deep and overpowering desire to provide for his children made him anxious to settle financially with the firm and to come to an amicable understanding with his cousin. It was because of this desire that he agreed to accept payment for his share in the business at a time when Robert had reduced the nominal value of the firm's holdings to almost nothing.

When he had accepted the $3,000 as payment of his inheritance of nearly $2,000,000, his eyes suddenly opened. But it was too late to avoid the jaws of the trap that Robert had sprung on him. He attempted to get more money; but the courts decided in favor of the unscrupulous, iron-willed Übermensch who had trampled on the Sklave.

And then a change came over Otto Eissier. Hitherto Robert had been his private enemy; now Robert became for him an enemy of mankind, an Anti-Christ, an Attila, a Genghis Kahn. a Tchaka, a scourge, a besom of unholy destruction. And in Otto's breast there grew up a distorted sense of duty which demanded atonement for the wrongs that Robert had done to humanity.

In the summer of 1923, Otto's nervous disturbance reached a stage bordering on mania—a condition augmented by Robert's contemptuous and sneering attitude. The neurologists whom he consulted warned him of a collapse, and advised retirement and absolute quiet.

But in vain. This poor desperate creature fought on for a hopelessly lost cause. He importuned Robert constantly in the hope of obtaining redress.

And then one word began riding in on his tortured brain. That word was "Fool." Robert had called him a fool since his childhood; and now that appellation took on venom and became fraught with terrible significance. A score of times he had gone to Robert and pleaded for more money for himself and his children, and each time Robert had answered him with a sneer and that devastating epithet—"Fool."

POOR OTTO! With his permeating sense of inferiority he could not withstandthe gibe. He knew it was true. He was indeed a fool—a tragic, hopeless fool. The bulk of the $3,000 had been eaten up in litigation, and he saw only ruin ahead.

Otto had always carried a small automatic with which to protect himself from his imaginary enemies, But now he bought another larger gun. A catastrophic idea was forming in his mind. And always he could hear Robert's derisive voice calling him a fool.

On the thirtieth of August, 1923, he called on Robert. The head of Eissler und Brüder sat smugly at his desk and regarded the visitor contemptuously. Otto made his last plea for justice.

"I will carry on a suit for seven years rather than pay you a heller," Robert told him. He then leaned forward acrossthe desk at which Otto's father had sat for forty years. "For all of, me," he said, "you can rot. Fool!"

(A smile, half pathetic. half sensitive, flitted over Vance's mouth.)

"Y' know. Markham,  I've sometimes wondered whether  Otto realized what took place during those next few moments. I'm inclined to think that he only saw, as in a haze, the fire from his gun as he sent six shots into Robert's body.

There were seven bullets in the gun—the seventh was intended for his own head. But as he raised the weapon to his temple, Robert, having fallen to the floor in mortal agony, spoke. And those words stayed Otto's hand. They brought the whole of the murderer's life crashing down. They were incredible—and yet consistent. As Robert gasped at Otto's feet, a sneer passed over his face.

"How often did that fool shoot?" he asked.

Fool! Again that epithet!

Otto, for once, was to have been the master—for once he had hoped to overcome his cousin's iron will and to force him to take cognizance of a weaker kinsman.  To this end he had sacrificed everything. He had become a killer in order to have one supreme moment of domination—one supreme moment of superiority in which he could feel that he had administered a triumphant retribution to the man he hated.

But in his great moment, to which he had sacrificed everything, he had only evoked the old contemptuous taunt—"Fool."

Otto's extravagant deed of heroism was to Robert only a stupid accident, not the fiat of a stronger will.

Without resistance Otto allowed himself to be disarmed and arrested. The world had toppled about him. He had steeled himseif to a great deed which was to have given him back his self-respect—and for all his pains he had been called a fool by the dying man.

On the eighth of April, 1924, Otto Eissler stood trial before the Austrian Criminal Court.

The alienists—who, according to Austrian law, do not form a part of the defense corps, but who are appointed by the authorities to investigate and report on the responsibility of the accused—had a deuced difficult task; for Otto stubbornly repudiated any idea of insanity. They were unable to find that his phobias and hallucinatory manias were symptoms of true paranoia; but they did report that Otto represented a highly neurotic type whose lowered mental repressions caused him to succumb easily to his violent hatred. They therefore decided that he must stand trial, though they suggested that he should be accorded extenuating circumstances.

During the preliminary investigation Otio had changed attorneys several times. His mania persecutoria caused him to see enemies and spies in everyone with whom he came in contact. Even Doctor Teirich, whom he finally selected, had a most tryin' time with him. Poor Otto apparently preferred to risk the maximum sentence of life imprisonment rather than plead insanity... By the by, Markham, you know the death penalty was abolished in Austria in 1919. I'm rather inclined to believe that Otto's greatest tragedy would have been to admit his own insanity—he had fought against the idea so long, d'ye see.

He insisted upon basing his defense on the plea of extreme provocation. Furthermore, he denied that the murder had been premeditated.

But alas! his purchase of the second gun. and his waiting for the moment when Robert would be alone, told heavily against him.

Moreover, the Sophoclean irony beneath the whole affair was still working. The presiding judge, Doctor Ramsauer, was a type of jurist somewhat on the order of Robert himself, He had a Nietzschean temperament and could feel no sympathy for a man of Otto Eissler's character. He was stern and uncompromising. He had no concern save for the letter of the law and its enforcement.

As I've said, his character was similar to that of the man whose death he was avenging, and, he may have felt an understanding sympathy for Robert,

The testimony was, on the whole, favorable to the unhappy prisoner. The witnesses related in detail the many symptoms of neurotic tension which finally broke down his self-control.

UNFORTUNATELY for Otto, when the motives were discussed, when the details of the financial jugglery were presented, and when fantastic figures of depreciated currency and doubtful foreign-exchange transactions were presented, the twelve good men and true were so confused that they chose to regard the murder as an act of sordid revenge rather than retributive justice on the part of a deeply wronged man.

Even the prosecuting attorney admitted Otto's strong provocation for the deed and showed a fine humaneness. But nothing except the offended letter of the law existed for the judge, and his summing-up was against the defendant.

After a brief deliberation the jury found Otto guilty of premeditated murder, by ten votes to two. According to the Austrian law the presiding judge has a wide discretion in imposing sentence in murder cases, which varies from one-year to life imprisonment. But only if. the sentence exceeds ten years has the prisoner the right to appeal.

Judge Ramsauer, anticipating the probable result of an appeal promptly sentenced the prisoner to exactly ten years, thereby allowing him no loophole through which to escape. For a man of Otto's age and broken health those ten years were tantamount to a life sentence. Again—at the end—he had been defeated by a stronger character.

Y' know, Markham, I cannot help feeling that behind the stern face of that uncompromising judge Otto Eissler saw the face of Robert sneering at him from the grave. And when the judge passed sentence upon him I'm inclined to think that poor Otto once again heard the voice of Robert saying to him: "Fool!"

Markham was silent for some time. "An ironical tragedy," he murmured at length. "And it's hard to say just where justice lay. The law is inadequate when dealing with such cases. I'm inclined to think, however, that in this country Otto would have had a fair chance to escape. He might have been proved insane despite his protestations—especially in view of his frank, unsubtle method of murder."

"True." Vance smiled cynically. "But what would our courts have done with Grete Beier—the last woman to be publicly executed in Germany? She. I am convinced, was a genuine psychopathic case; yet she plotted her crimes with infinite skill—there was nothing frank or unsubtle about Grete: she was the apotheosis of chicanery and shrewdness. Personally, I'd have been more content to see Otto sent to the block than Grete … What an astoundin' case the Beier affair was!"

The following Sunday night Vance related the Grete Beier tragedy; and in my next article I shall try to retell it as Vance told it to us[1].

---

1 If it was ever written, no such narrative was published by *Cosmopolitan*.

# The Cinema Murder Cases

By Tony Medawar

In addition to the novels published as 'SS Van Dine', Willard Huntington Wright also provided scenarios for a series of 12 short mystery "two reel detective stories" produced by Warner Brothers at their Brooklyn Vitaphone Studio, which were developed by Burnet Hershey into scripts. These films were released between September 1931 and August 1932 and, happily, prints of several survive and one, *Wall Street Mystery*, can even be found online. All but one ran for 20 minutes; the exception - *Transatlantic Mystery* - ran for 22. While the stories are original and unrelated to Van Dine's novels, the plots are generally thin with leadenly planted clues and, from an early point in the story, there is little doubt as to the murderer's identity. Disappointingly, none features Vance instead presenting a Holmes-Lestrade pairing in the form of the bullying Inspector Carr, played by John Hamilton - Hamilton is best known for playing Perry White, editor of the Daily Planet in the television series *Adventures of Superman* (1952-1958) - and Dr Amos Crabtree, a psychology professor played by the Glaswegian actor and former acrobat Donald Meek. As the San Francisco Examiner put it: "*A criminologist and psychologist match their wits; the one jumps to conclusions, the other comes to the right conclusion through coolly calculated deduction*". The films played as a featurette supporting a major release, such as the *Sidewalks of New York* or the Marx Brothers' *Monkey Business*, alongside a newsreel, a cartoon and another short film such as 'High School Hoofer' or the doubtlessly enthralling 'Woodrow Wilson's Great Decision'.

Trumpeted in the advertising as "*the first of a new screen success*", *The Clyde Mystery*, was directed by Roy Mack and produced at Vitaphone's Brooklyn Studio. Shooting was completed on 8 August 1931 and the film was released on 27 September 1931. Some reviews were reasonably positive but *Variety* was not impressed, condemning the film as "*amusing but never thrilling nor exciting ... conventional murder and questioning, with usual answers inferring guilt. Surprise finish achieved through the solving of the mystery.*".

*The Clyde Mystery* opens with the discovery of the body of Angus Clyde by his manservant, sitting in an armchair in his bedroom dead from a shot to the head. Inspector Carr is called in and asks his old friend Dr Crabtree to assist with the investigation. The four suspects were guests for dinner the previous evening: Ann Clyde, the victim's young wife; her dissolute brother Larry Merton; her school friend and former fiancé, Captain Dick Rugg who admits to still loving Ann; and Eric Muller, who wanted to purchase a diamond belonging to Angus. While Carr is swayed by the thought of a conspiracy involving Ann Clyde, Crabtree establishes that Angus Clyde had been killed by … Angus Clyde in an attempt to frame his wife, using precisely the same trick that, seven years later, would appear in one of Agatha Christie's most successful novels.

Shooting on the second film in the series, *Wall Street Mystery* began in late September and the film was released on 4 November 1931. The film opens with the discovery by an "Oirish" cleaner of the bodies of two stockbrokers, shot dead in their Wall Street office. Carr is called in and wastes no time in summoning Dr Crabtree to join him at the scene of the crime – "*I don't need anybody's help but I kind of like the old doc. He's sort of a lucky piece to me.*" – whereupon the professor promptly discovers the brokers' secretary locked in a cupboard.

There are various suspects, including clients and colleagues, who are duly interviewed before Crabtree reveals what happened. While the solution – one broker murdered the other and then accidentally killed himself while trying to make the death look like suicide – is genuinely surprising, what is considerably more surprising is that it is not until the denouement that the audience is shown the clue that allowed Crabtree to deduce what had happened.

The film is nonetheless enjoyable, even if only for its Marxian humour – "'*Have a chair.*', '*Look here, I'm* Colonel *Pettijohn.*', '*Have* two *chairs!*'" – but its few merits are undermined by the blatantly offensive characterisation of a African American lift attendant called "Andy Amos Lindley", after the inexplicably popular radio show *Amos 'n' Andy* (1928-1960) – "*I was named Abraham Washin'ton but I done baptise' masself for somethin' more famous*". Once again, *Variety* was not impressed – "*Feeble comedy attempts don't click, with no one in the cast giving other than a perfunctory performance. Not as much for metropolitan audiences as for smaller communities*".

The next film was *The Week-End Mystery*. on which filming began in October; the film was released on 6 December 1931. During a storm there is a dinner party at a remote manor house; Carr and Crabtree are among the guests, fortunately as it turns out. At nine o'clock, the host excuses himself from the card table to take a medication with the apparent intention of returning soon. When he doesn't, his body is discovered behind a locked door. There is a second shooting and even a raid in a plot that involves "*trick placement of a revolver, an overheated room and melting candles … considerable time is spent before these occurrences at a bridge table"*.

Released on 10 January 1932, the next in the series, *Symphony Murder* was very well received by the critics. The star was Rita Lau, *"a beautiful 22 year old Russian émigré"* but, if only to modern eyes, her performance is somewhat histrionic and this appears to be her only cinematic role.

*Symphony Murder* opens with Inspector Carr receiving a warning that there will be a murder at a classical music concert that evening. Seemingly out of curiosity rather than any desire to forestall a crime, he decides to attend and invites Crabtree to join him. The concert begins and shortly afterwards one of the cellists is shot dead and then the main suspect, the manager of the concert hall, is found dead, apparently having committed suicide. Crabtree solves the mystery but *"just a bit too patly"* for Variety.

The fifth in the series, *The Studio Murder Mystery*, was released on 7 February 1932 and *Variety* felt it offered *"more melodrama than mystery and [that it was] not nearly as strong on entertainment value as most in this series"*; somewhat surprising given *Variety's* fairly lukewarm reviews of the earlier films.

As the title suggests, *The Studio Murder Mystery* is set in a film studio where the leading actress is stabbed to death on set. Carr and Crabtree arrive to interrogate the suspects, who include her main rival and also her boyfriend. Again, there is some well-judged humour – filming the actual murder under the impression it is being acted out, the director complains that it is not realistic enough – but the mystery is relatively straightforward and there is an implausible climax in which a pair of gloves is found to fit only one of the suspects. The *"production [was] poorly managed with scenes cluttered up with people and no real punch anywhere … Meek [is] less effective - because of poor story situations and dialogue - than he ordinarily is"*.

For the sixth film, production moved to Vitaphone's studio at Flatbush. In *The Skull Murder Mystery*, released on 24 February 1932, a skeleton is found in a trunk buried in an alley and a mysterious Chinese merchant and his eccentric tenants come under suspicion, leading to an exciting climax in an attic. With only the skull as a starting point, Crabtree quickly solves the murder. *Variety* was slightly more positive than usual: *"Skulls, groans, dim lighting and a laboratory provide suitable atmosphere. Some of the performances are stagey but there is enough action packed in the two reels to keep the audience interested"*.

However, *Variety's* reviewer felt that the next film in the series, *The Cole Case*, - also advertised as *The 8 O'Clock Mystery* - was a *"splendid little thriller, well developed and built up to the anti-climactic murder, with the solution making for a surprise denouement … it grips intensely … direction is expert and the casting ditto*". In the film, which was released on 3 April 1932, Crabtree is visited by a man who has been receiving notes threatening to kill him. The latest note says he will die at eight o'clock that evening so Crabtree persuades Carr to send a couple of men to the house. Unsurprisingly, the man is murdered and an obvious clue leads to the identification of his killer.

In *Murder in the Pullman*, released on 22 May 1932, a newly-wed gold-digger is murdered on a train during her honeymoon with her husband, a night club owner. She also has a boyfriend and has been "playing around" with the public prosecutor and these men are among the passengers as are Carr and Crabtree. Crabtree quickly identifies her husband as the guilty party. *Variety* was positive about this film – "*Pretty nearly the plot of a five reeler condensed into two and compelled to hustle along. Usual formula of several suspects, with the crime placed on the one least suspected, as usual. In spite of that, it holds the surprise element*".

In *Side Show Mystery*, released on 11 June 1932, a side-show manager is found stabbed in the back. A knife thrower is the obvious supect and other "acts" also come into the frame. While praising the interesting setting, the reviewer for *Variety* was not impressed – "*In spite of a skilful handling, the author is less succeessful here in preserving the mystery than in most of the others of the series*".

The next two films were released on the 2nd and 9th of July 1932. *Variety* felt the first, *The Campus Mystery*, was "*rather frothy, lacking the compactness and punch which have distinguished some of the earlier releases in the series.*". In the film, a pole vault champion misappropriates funds belonging to his athletics association. After threatening him with expulsion, the Dean of the Association is found murdered. Suspects abound including the Dean's daughter, the sympathetic manager of the track team and the team coach.

The other July release was *Crane Poison Case* and it finds Carr and Crabtree investigating the poisoning of a millionaire called Crane. Suspicion falls on his doctor - who turns out to be guilty - and also on the victim's stepson, a herpetologist freshly returned from the South American jungle. *Variety* loathed this film – "*less effective as a mystery than others in the series ... failing to attain [the] degree of suspense that's so vital to material of this kind ... action is laborious, with the machinery  of detection as to the cause of the poisoning managed in an amateurish way. Carelessness is evident throughout ...In a production way, generally, shoddy*".

The final film, *Transatlantic Mystery*, was released on 31 August 1932. The story begins in London with the robbery of the famous Stanhope diamonds. The two thieves fall out. One kills the other and boards a ship bound for New York. Then he is found dead too. Carr and Crabtree happen to be on board and quickly narrow the suspects down to the widow of the first thief to die and the valet of the second thief, who turns out to be the murderer. *Variety* considered it "*not good … it ends confusingly …although the story started off with good dialogue and action, it lapses into a hasty finish with practically no convincing action. The solution by dialogue in close up leaves customers confused as to what actually happened aboard ship*". Confused? Well, not as confused as those reading the "other" version of this particular story would be, as we shall see …

<hr>

While the original scenarios for the Amos Crabtree murder mysteries appear to be lost, three of Wright's scenarios were developed as cartoon serials for syndication in American newspapers, with the adaptation and artwork by R B S Davis. Like *The Clyde Mystery* these newly discovered adventures also feature Philo Vance in place of Crabtree and, instead of Carr, there is Vance's usual sparring partner, New York District Attorney John FX Markham. In the Vance novels the official police are represented by Sergeant Ernest Heath of the homicide department and for the cartoons, Heath takes the place of one of the police officers accompanying Carr in the films.

The first cartoon featuring Philo Vance is *The Insurance Mystery,* serialised in 25 episodes. Notwithstanding that the victim's surname is Clyde, the cartoon is based on Van Dine's scenario for the film *The Cole Case* and it has nothing to do with *The Clyde Mystery*. The second, 'The Skull Mystery', is clearly based on Van Dine's scenario for the film *The Skull Murder Mystery*.

Curiously, the third and final cartoon, *The Transatlantic Mystery,* based on Transatlantic Mystery, was discontinued without any explanation. It appears that the complete story was never published anywhere, nor were any more films in the series produced as cartoons, at least not be the same artist; for completeness, the partial cartoon of 'The Transatlantic Mystery' is included in an annex to this collection.

Despite the fate of *The Transatlantic Mystery,* a fourth cartoon did appear. A cartoon based on the scenario for *The Clyde Mystery* appeared in *Illustrated Detective Magazine* in 1932. While the approach is broadly the same - Crabtree and Carr are replaced by Vance and Markham — the style is different to the earlier newspaper cartoons and the artwork, by A E Jameson, is of a markedly higher quality. However, despite the announcement that 'The Clyde Mystery' was merely the "*first of the new Philo Vance series*", *Illustrated Detective Magazine* published no other cases nor, it would appear, did any other magazine or newspaper.

Why were the two series of cartoons ended so abruptly?

One can only speculate. One reason might be the generally poor reception that the films received. Was there concern that the cartoons could undermine the reception for SS Van Dine's sixth Vance novel, *The Kennel Murder Case*, which would begin pre-publication serialisation in November 1932.

It is also possible that the cartoons were unauthorised even though they are marked as Van Dine's copyright. It is certainly possible that he was never consulted on the idea of using the scenarios he had knocked out for a film series to create "*new adventures of* [the] *renowned detective fiction character,*" Philo Vance. After all, four Philo Vance films had already been released – three with William Powell and one with Basil Rathbone. If the scenarios had been that good surely Van Dine would have put Vance in them from the outset? *If*, that is, Van Dine *really* wrote the scenarios and did not merely lend his name to them? That *appears* to be the case with another film, *The Blue Moon Murder Mystery*, which is usually described as being based on a scenario by SS Van Dine. However, no such scenario can be found in the archives at Warner Brothers other than a 17-page treatment by Norman A Cerf. There are also at least eleven full drafts of a script based on that treatment, including one written by Willard Wright's friend Florence Ryerson and another by James Dalton Trumbo. In early December 1932 it was reported that production had begun at Warner's West Coast studios on the film, now known as *The Blue Moon Murder Case*. However, when the film was released in 1933 - as *Girl Missing* - the script was credited to Carl Erickson and Don Mullaly with additional dialogue by Ben Markson; there was no reference to Ryerson or Trumbo and it is unclear what, if any, of their work survived into the final script.

Definitive answers to at least some of the many questions above *might* lie in the archives of Warner Brothers or one of the newspapers that published the cartoons, but none have so far come to light. Either way, the published cartoons – *very* late additions to the casebook of Philo Vance - must surely be regarded as no more than a curious addendum to the bibliography of SS Van Dine.

'The Insurance Mystery'. Serialised in the *Lincoln Evening Journal*, 23 April to 6 May 1932

'The Skull Mystery'. Serialised in the *Lincoln Evening Journal*, 7 May to 2 June 1932

'The Transatlantic Mystery'. Partially serialised in the *Lincoln Evening Journal*, 3 to 6 June 1932

PHILO VANCE—The Insurance Mystery—By S. S. VAN DINE.
THE INSURANCE MYSTERY ~ CHARACTERS ~
Joseph Winter ~ Coles Butler...
Olga Olsen ~ Coles Cook...
Mr. Hoffman ~ Superintendent of Chester Cole's House...
Fred Cole ~
Ada La Tour ~ Fred's Fiancee ~
Chester Cole ~
Dist. Atty. John F. X. Markham
Philo Vance... amateur criminologist.
Sergeant Ernest Heath...

PHILO VANCE—The Insurance Mystery—By S. S. VAN DINE.
A MR. FRED COLE INSISTS UPON SEEING YOU RIGHT AWAY, MR. MARKHAM.....
I'VE GOT TO HAVE PROTECTION, MR. MARKHAM. I'VE BEEN GETTING THESE THREATENING NOTES FOR MONTHS, AND TONIGHT THEY PLAN TO KILL ME...... I DON'T KNOW WHAT TO DO. NOR CAN I IMAGINE WHO IS SENDING THEM!
JUNE 12th.
JUNE 3d
MY DEAR COLE,
JUNE 14th
MY DEAR COLE, TO NIGHT AT 8 O'CLOCK YOU SHALL DIE! BON VOYAGE.... Eva.
MAY I EXPECT YOUR HELP. SIR..?
YES. MR. COLE, I'LL COME TO YOUR APARTMENT TONIGHT WITH PLENTY OF PROTECTION AT QUARTER OF EIGHT..!
MUTT AND JEFF—A Very Snappy Idea On Jeff's Part—By BUD FISHER.

PHILO VANCE—The Insurance Mystery—By S. S. VAN DINE.
IS MR. COLE IN...? THIS IS THE DISTRICT ATTORNEY....
JA-JA-COME IN, PLEASE
THANK HEAVEN YOU'RE HERE. GENTLEMEN—IT'S QUARTER OF EIGHT!
ANYTHING HAPPEN YET..?
AND THEY'RE TO KILL YOU AT EIGHT, MR. COLE?
SERGEANT. STATION A MAN AT EVERY DOOR OF THIS PENTHOUSE—!
RING—8—0
I'M SO NERVOUS. MR. VANCE...... OH! WHO'S THAT..!

ADA, MY DEAR—! WHY DID YOU COME.....?
YOU SOUNDED SO WORRIED, FRED. WHAT IS THE MATTER...?
THIS IS MY FIANCEE. MISS LA TOUR
I THINK YOU'D BETTER GO. MISS LA YOUR..!
AH.H.H.NO, MARKHAM. YOU MUSTN'T SEPARATE THEM AT A TIME LIKE THIS...!
MISS LA TOUR. SOMEONE HAS THREATENED TO MURDER MR. COLE TONIGHT AT EIGHT O'CLOCK!
AND IT'S NOW THREE MINUTES OF...
MUTT AND JEFF—A Kind-Hearted Customer—By BUD FISHER.

ENEMIES···? I DON'T KNOOW, MR. MARKHAM····I GOT INTO A JAM IN ENGLAND, TEN YEARS AGO, WITH A WOMAN···HER FAMILY ARE THE TYPE THAT WOULD PLOT FOR YEARS FOR REVENGE····!
I CAN'T STAND THIS ANY LONGER I'M GOING TO PHONE MY BROTHER AND ASK HIM TO COME OVER····
HELLO ····CHESTER···? THIS IS FRED···I'M AFRAID SOMETHING SERIOUS IS ABOUT TO HAPPEN AND I WISH YOU'D COME OVER RIGHT AWAY····WILL YOU···? THAT'S FINE···! HURRY!
MUTT AND JEFF—Jeff Can Do a Hundred Yards In Nine Seconds Flat—By BUD FISHER.

PHILO VANCE—The Insurance Money—By S. S. VAN DINE.
WHERE IS MR. COLE ····?
HE'S IN THE DEN PHONING····· MISS LA TOUR··
FRED ···FRED DEAR ··· ! ··· I THINK I SHALL ·····
!! !!
E·E·E·E~!
HE'S DEAD ···
MUTT AND JEFF—The Little Fellow's Ignorance Is Refreshing—By BUD FISHER.

THAT'S ALL I CAN TELL YOU ABOUT CHESTER COLE ··· HE'S LIVED IN THE BUILDING ABOUT A YEAR. A QUIET, RETIRING MAN. RARELY SEEN, FOR HE GOES AWAY FOR LONG PERIODS AT A TIME ·····
QUITE
I DON'T SEE THAT WE'RE GETTING ANYWHERE, VANCE··!
HAVE PATIENCE OL' DEAR SEND FOR THE INSURANCE MAN NOW, AND LET ME HAVE A CIGAR SO I CAN ACT LIKE A BUSINESS MAN
DID YOU INSURE FRED COLE'S LIFE, MASON ···?
YUP FOR 100,000 DOLLARS CHESTER COLE IS THE BENEFICIARY
THAT'S THE WHOLE STORY, MARKHAM, AND IF YOU WILL HAVE MISS LA TOUR AND CHESTER COLE AT THE PENTHOUSE THIS AFTERNOON I'LL HAND YOU THE MURDERER····!

PHILO VANCE—The Insurance Money—By S. S. VAN DINE.
VANCE'S INVESTIGATIONS TO DATE, SHOW THAT FRED COLE'S LIFE WAS INSURED IN FAVOR OF HIS BROTHER CHESTER THAT CHESTER IS A REPUTABLE PERSON AND THAT FRED COLE INTERVIEWED THIRTY PERSONS BEFORE HE HIRED JOSEPH WINTER TO ACT AS HIS BUTLER.
ONE OF US IN THE ROOM IS A MURDERER. IT MAY BE SERGEANT HEATH, OR MISS LA TOUR, WE DON'T KNOW. AT ANY RATE, WE'LL ALL KNOW SHORTLY····· NOW. OLGA ·····
DO YOU RECOGNIZE THIS RING ····IS IT FRED COLE'S OR HIS BUTLER'S. JOSEPH WINTER ···?
JA·A ···IT BAN BE MR. WINTER'S, I SEE···!
AH, ME···HOW CONFUSIN'·····LADIES AND GENTLEMEN··· THE MAN WHO WAS MURDERED LAST NIGHT WAS NOT FRED COLE···! ···· IT WAS HIS BUTLER, JOSEP WINTER ·· ····!!
MUTT AND JEFF—The Uncrowned Champ—By BUD FISHER.

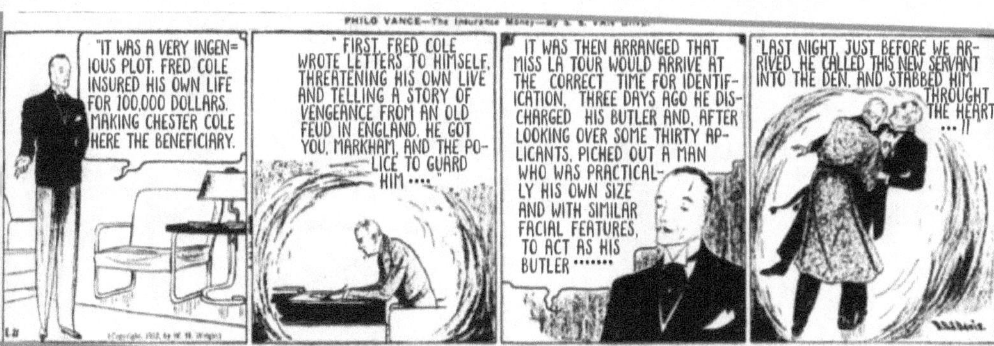
PHILO VANCE—The Insurance Money—By S. S. VAN DINE
"IT WAS A VERY INGEN=IOUS PLOT. FRED COLE INSURED HIS OWN LIFE FOR 100,000 DOLLARS, MAKING CHESTER COLE HERE THE BENEFICIARY.
"FIRST, FRED COLE WROTE LETTERS TO HIMSELF, THREATENING HIS OWN LIVE AND TELLING A STORY OF VENGEANCE FROM AN OLD FEUD IN ENGLAND. HE GOT YOU, MARKHAM, AND THE PO-LICE TO GUARD HIM ·····"
IT WAS THEN ARRANGED THAT MISS LA TOUR WOULD ARRIVE AT THE CORRECT TIME FOR IDENTIF-ICATION. THREE DAYS AGO HE DIS-CHARGED HIS BUTLER AND, AFTER LOOKING OVER SOME THIRTY AP-LICANTS, PICKED OUT A MAN WHO WAS PRACTICAL-LY HIS OWN SIZE AND WITH SIMILAR FACIAL FEATURES, TO ACT AS HIS BUTLER ·······
"LAST NIGHT, JUST BEFORE WE AR-RIVED, HE CALLED THIS NEW SERVANT INTO THE DEN, AND STABBED HIM THROUGHT THE HEART ·····!!
MUTT AND JEFF—Eggsactly Right—By BUD FISHER.

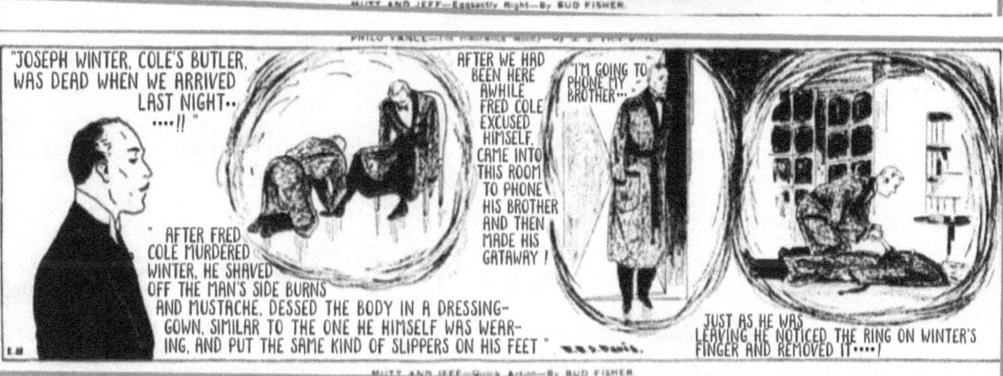
PHILO VANCE—The Insurance Money—By S. S. VAN DINE
"JOSEPH WINTER, COLE'S BUTLER, WAS DEAD WHEN WE ARRIVED LAST NIGHT·· ·····!!"
"AFTER FRED COLE MURDERED WINTER, HE SHAVED OFF THE MAN'S SIDE BURNS AND MUSTACHE, DESSED THE BODY IN A DRESSING-GOWN, SIMILAR TO THE ONE HE HIMSELF WAS WEAR-ING, AND PUT THE SAME KIND OF SLIPPERS ON HIS FEET"
AFTER WE HAD BEEN HERE AWHILE FRED COLE EXCUSED HIMSELF, CAME INTO THIS ROOM TO PHONE HIS BROTHER AND THEN MADE HIS GETAWAY !
I'M GOING TO PHONE MY BROTHER ···
JUST AS HE WAS LEAVING HE NOTICED THE RING ON WINTER'S FINGER AND REMOVED IT·····!
MUTT AND JEFF—Quick Action—By BUD FISHER

PHILO VANCE—The Insurance Money—By S. S. VAN DINE
I NEVER HEARD OF SUCH A THING·····!
LISTEN, DANDY, WHO D'YE THINK YER TRYING TO PIN SOMETHING ON··? ·····IF YOU THINK I HAD ANYTHING TO DO WITH THIS, YOU'RE NUTS !
QUITE··
BY HEAVEN, IF YOU DON'T TAKE THAT BACK ABOUT MY BROTHER ···· I'LL ···
NOW JUST A MINUTE·· FELLOW ··!
HEY··!
MAY I ···? MR. FRED COLE ···?
A Cloudburst Had Arrived—By BUD FISHER.

PHILO VANCE—The Insurance Money—By S. S. VAN DINE
GET HIM, FRED ····!
PRETTY·· MR. VANCE!
SOCK !
THERE NEVER WAS A CHESTER COLE·····FRED COLE ESTABLISHED TWO RESIDENCES ······ AFTER MAKING HIS GETAWAY IN HIS CAR, HE PUT ON HIS MAKE-UP AND RETURNED HERE AS HIS OWN BROTHER, TO FURTHER IDENTIFY THE DEAD MAN, AND COLLECT THE INSURANCE···!
A Lucky Break for the Police—By BUD FISHER.

FIN.

S. S. VAN DINE PRESENTS
THE SKULL MYSTERY
AMY & PAUL TURNER PECKS GRANDCHILDREN—
GRANDFATHER PECK—
PHILO VANCE—
WING YUN A CHINESE PHILOSOPHER—
DIST. ATTY. JOHN F.X. MARKHAM—

BEGORRA, YOU'RE A LAZY ONE ··! GIMME A HAND ON THIS OLD TRUNK·· ··!
A 'AND, H'INDEED, SOR ···!
GIMME THAT PICK-AXE, TILL I OPEN THIS ···
TSK!
OW ·w··! MAY THE DIVIL FLY AWAY WIT YOU··· ··LOOK AT THOT····!
'OW 'ORRIBLE!
SURE AN' WASN'T THOT THE FIVE O'CLOCK WHISTLE···?
INDEED IT WAS·· SOR·!

'ER, WOULD YOU AWAKEN, SIR? MR. MARKHAM IS CALL—ING····
LO, MARKHAM— TROUBLE NOW·· SOMEBODY DEAD···?
WHAT
A COUPLE OF WORKMEN, LAYING SOME PIPE ON THE EAST SIDE TODAY, UNEARTHED AN OLD TRUNK. THEY FOUND A HUMAN SKELETON IN IT···WANT TO COME UP WITH ME···?
I'D RATHER DO THAT THAN HAVE DINNER WITH MY AUNT EDNA ····!
OF COURSE NOTHING MAY COME OF IT, BUT····SWING OVER TO PARK, DRIVER ···
THIS MAN WAS MURDERED ABOUT A YEAR AGO···HIT ON THE HEAD WITH A HEAVY BLUNT OBJECT. SEE THAT FRACTURE··? HE WAS A SHORT MAN, ABOUT FIVE FEET SIX···
WHAT ARE YOU DOING ON MY PROPETY····?
GET OUT OF HERE·· ····!

JUST A MINUTE, SIR! A TRUNK HAS BEEN FOUND IN YOUR YARD HERE, WITH THE REMAINS OF A MURDERED MAN IN IT··! OF COURSE WE'LL HAVE TO QUESTION YOU····
NOW, WON'T YOU SIT DOWN, GENTLEMEN ····?
AH···YOU COLLECT CHINESE IMPLEMENTS OF WAR, MR. BECK··!
IS THERE ANY- THING WRONG, GRANDPA ·····?

···KNOW, IF ANY OF YOU KNOW ANY- THING ABOUT THIS AFFAIR IT WILL BE FAR BETTER FOR YOU TO TELL ME FRANKLY, RATHER THAN HAVE US FIND IT OUT····
WE KNOW NOTHING ABOUT THIS, SIR ····!
YOU ARE MR. BECK'S GRANCHILDREN ···· ···H··H HOUSE A ···· WHERE YOU LIVING IN THIS YEAR AGO····?
YES, SIR, WE HAVE LIVED HERE ALWAYS.
WHO LIVES NEXT DOOR, MR. BECK···?
AN OLD CHINESE PHILOSOPHER NAMED WANG YUN····

THOSE WHO HAVE BEEN INTER- VIEWED SO FAR KNOW NOTHING ABOUT THE SKELETON FOUND IN THE TRUN BURIED IN THE REAR YARD OF THE BECK HOUSE
I REGRET TO SAY THAT I KNOW MY WORTHY NEIGHBORS BUT SLIGHTLY, MR. DISTRICT ATTORNEY···A MOST MYSTERIOUS HOUSEHOLD···· ·····!
DO YOU RECALL ANY INCIDENTS OF THE PAST THAT MIGHT BE CONNECTED WITH THIS AFFAIR, MR. WANG···?
WELL, I DON'T WISH TO IMPLICATE ANYONE, BUT A YEAR OR SO AGO I WAS IN MY GARDEN WHEN I OVER- HEARD MR. BECK AND ONE OF MISS AMY'S SUITORS SAYING ······
YOU OLD BEAST ··!
GET OUT OF HERE··! AND IF YOU COME BACK I'LL KILL YOU··!

I THINK THE WHOLE FAMILY ARE A LITTLE UNBALANCED···THE HUNCHBACK BOY INDULGES IN WEIRD EXPERI- MENTS IN HIS LABORATORY A YEAR AGO HE TOLD ME THAT HE COULD COMPLETE THE EXPERIMENT HE WAS MAKING ON A NEW ELIXIR OF LIFE, IF HE HAD A HUMAN BODY TO WORK WITH····
AH-H-H-HA-A-A··!
MIND GETTING UP A MINUTE, MR. WANG··?

VANCE ... ! WHAT IN THE WORLD IS THE MEANING OF SUCH AN ACTION ... ?
A SIMPLE MATTER NOT THAT I ANTICIPATE ANY TROUBLE BUT IT'S NICE TO AVOID UNPLEASANT THINGS THAT MIGHT HAPPEN ..... PLEASE ATTEND A MINUTE ..
I'VE SEEN THIS OLD CHINESE TRICK BEFORE - YOU SEE WHEN I STEP ON THE BUTTON UNDER THE RUG, WHAT HAPPENS TO THE CHAIR I WAS SITTING IN ..... !
YOU HAVE A WEALTH OF OBSCURE KNOWLEDGE, HAVE YOU NOT, MR. VANCE ... ?
M-M-M-M ...... ! COMIN', MARKHAM ... ?

WELL, VANCE, I GUESS THE CASE IS CLOSED. WE'VE BEEN THROUGH ALL OUR RECORDS, AND HAVE FOUND THAT NO ONE DISAPPEARED A YEAR AGO THAT ANSWERS THE MEDICAL EXAMINERS DESCRIPTION OF THE SKELETON ..... !
NEVERTHELESS, THERE ARE OTHER POSSIBILITIES, MARKHAM .....
WHAT, MAY I ASK ..? WE HAVE ABSOLUTELY NOTHING AGAINST THE OCCUPANTS OF THE HOUSE ..... !
WAN YUN STRIKES ME AS A CULTURED GENTLEMAN, WHO WOULD HAVE NO MOTIVE FOR KILLING A MAN AND PLANTING HIM IN THE NEXT YARD ...
QUITE! ER - MAY I BORROW THIS CHAPPIE'S SKULL ... ?
THANKS OLD DEAR BUT DON'T BE SURPRISED TO SEE ME BACK ANON ... !

HOW'VE YOU BEEN, YOUNG FELLA ..?
OH, RIPPING ... ! SAY JAKE IS IT POSSIBLE TO RECONSTRUCT THE FACIAL CHARACTERISTICS OF THIS SKULL IN PUTTY AND PLASTER ... ?
I THINK IT MIGHT BE DONE, VANCE ..... !
LATE INTO THE NIGHT VANCE AND HIS FRIEND, THE ANTHROPOLOGIST, WORK ON THE FACE UNTIL FINALLY IT NEARS COMPLETION
VANCE, THOSE INTERPUPILARY DISTANCES ARE PERFECT ... !
TRUE, JAKE AND THOSE CEPHALIC INDEXES ARE NOTHING TO BE SNEEZED AT !
I'LL CALL A CAB FOR YOU .....
THANKS, OL' CHAP AND MANY THANKS FOR THE HEAD ...

HERE'S THE PLACE
VOT CAN I DO FOR YOU ..? HEH-HEH HEH HEH HEH
KEEP COOL, FOR THE TIME BEING .....
NOW, THIS IS WHAT I WANT YOU TO DO FOR ME .....

YOU REMEMBER MELVILLE DAVIS, DON'T YOU, PAUL...?
OH---IT'S DAVIS!!

WAIT A MINUTE...BOY...!

TRYIN' TO SLIP ME, EH ----!----
----HA!

VANCE HAS HAD THE FACIAL CHARACTERISTICS OF THE SKULL RECONSTRUCTED AND A MASK MADE, WITH WHICH HE INTENDS TO CONFRONT THE MEMBERS OF THE HOUS.
NOW YOU HAVE YOUR INSTRUCTIONS --- I FANCY THE STAGE IS SET----

AND NOW, SERGEANT. SEND FOR MR. BECK----

MELVILLE----! WHERE HAVE YOU BEEN FOR THE LAST YEAR----?

SO YOU RECOGNIZE HIM, DO YOU---? WHAT WAS HIS FULL NAME---?
MELVILLE DAVIS-

WHERE DID HE COME FROM ---?
THAT EXPLAINS YOUR NOT HAVINF ANY RECORD OF HIS DISAPPEARRANCE-
SAN FRANCISCO--

SEE HERE, BECK, YOU'D BETTER COME CLEAN ----!
YOU'RE PRETTY OLD TO GO TO JAIL-!!

I WILL NOT TOLERATE SUCH HIGH-HANDEDNESS!
THAT'S ENOUGH FOR MR. BECK, MARKHAM ---SEND FOR WANG YUN.

DO YOU KNOW THIS PERSON, WANG YUN--?
WHY, YES, MR. DISTRICT ATTOR-NEY----

THAT IS THE MAN WHO WAS COURTING MISS AMY, AND WHOSE LIFE WAS THREAT-ENED BY MR. BECK ----!

MR. WANG, WHY ARE YOU SO ANXIOUS TO PIN THIS CRIME ON MR. BECK ·····
PERHAPS YOU, YOURSELF, HAD SOME GOOD REASON FOR KILLING DAVIS AND BURYING HIM NEXT DOOR ··?
ANYWAY, RUN ALONG AND WAIT IN THE NEXT ROOM ·····
SERGEANT, BRING IN PAUL ···

AH- HA-! SO YOU DID COME BACK ·····
RIGHT-O, MARKHAM, AND I THINK WE HAVE A FAIR CHANCE OF SOLVING THIS MYSTERY NOW ···
INDEED ! AND WHAT DO YOU WANT ME TO DO ··?
GET SERGEANT HEATH AND TWO DETECTIVES. ONE MUST BE EXACTLY FIVE FEET SIX, THEN COME UP TO BECK'S HOUSE ·····
SWACKER, GET SERGEANT HEATH ON THE PHONE AND TELL HIM TO MEET ME AT BECK'S WITH A COUPLE OF HIS MEN ···
AND SOME SMELLING SALTS ···

SO HE WAS A SUITOR FOR YOUR SISTER'S HAND, EH ? AND YOU HAVEN'T SEEN HIM FOR A YEAR ·····
WHY DID YOU TRY TO RUN AWAY WHEN YOU SAW HIM?
ALL RIGHT, BOY, TELL WHAT Y KNOW!
YOU CAN'T DO ANY MORE WITH HIM NOW, MARKHAM, SEND FOR MISS AMY ·····

DO YOU KNOW THIS YOUNG MAN, MISS AMY?
HELLO, AMY ···
E-E-E-!
GOOD HEAVENS ··· SHE'S FAINTED ·····!

PUT HER ON THIS COUCH ···
GOT THOSE SMELLING SALTS, SERGEANT ···?
WHY DO WOMEN ALWAYS FAINT ···?
I'LL WAGER YOU'D HAVE FAINTED UNDER THE CIRCUMSTANCES ·· !
WELL, MARKHAM, YOUR CASE IS SOLVED ··· I MORE OR LESS SUSPECTED THE TRUTH OF THIS CASE, BUT HAD NO WAY OF VERIFYING IT EXCEPT BY HAVING THE SKULL RECONSTRUCTED AND A MASK MADE TO CONFRONT THESE PEOPLE WITH ··· NOW, HERE'S WHAT HAPPENED ····

EVERYONE HAS BEEN FOOLED BY THE MASK AND MISS AMY HAS FAINTED. VANCE MOVES TO EXPLAIN.
AMY TURNER, WHO WAS A VERY MUCH INTERESTED IN HER BROTHER'S WORK, AND WANTED TO AID HIM IN HIS EXPERIMENTS, INVEIGLED SEVERAL SUITORS TO THE HOUSE AND FINALLY, WHEN THE OPPORTUNITY CAME, KILLED ONE OF THEM SO AS TO GIVE HIS BODY TO HER BROTHER FOR HIS EXPERIMENTS ···· !
YOU SHOULD HAVE DONE EVERYTHING IN YOUR POWER TO STOP HER, PAUL ···· !
BUT I DIDN'T TOUCH THE BODY ·· ! I'VE LIVED IN HORROR EVER SINCE ·· ···· ! IT'S ALL HER FAULT ··· ! I TELL YOU ··· IT'S ALL HER FAULT ··· !

TAKE HIM OUT ··· !
I TELL YOU IT WAS ALL HER FAULT ··· !
MARKHAM, THIS WHOLE FAMILY IS MENTALLY UNBALANCED, THEY SHOULD HAVE BEEN IN AN INSTITUTION YEARS AGO ··· THIS IS NOT A CRIMINAL CASE, IT'S A CASE FOR AN ASYLUM ··· !
I'LL SEE THAT THEY ARE PLACED IN THE PROPER HANDS ···
WELL, MR. VANCE, THAT SURE WAS A SWELL IDEA OF OURS, TO RECONSTRUCT THE SKULL, EH?
STARTING TOMORROW ANOTHER PHILO VANCE STORY : THE TRANS ATLANTIC MYSTERY BY S.S. VAN DINE DON'T MISS IT !

# FIN.

ANNE CLYDE
*murder victim's young wife*

CAPTAIN TED RUGG
*aviator friend of Reggie Moncton*

JOHN F. X. MARKHAM
*district attorney*

ERNEST HEATH
*sergeant*

# S. S. VAN DINE'S *New Picture Explo*
# The CLYDE

Copyright, 1932
By W. H. Wright

### SCENE 1
*District-Attorney
Markham's Office*

Yes, this is District-At-
torney Markham. . . .
Yes, Sergeant Heath is
here. . . . What's that?
. . . Good heavens . . .

### SCENE 2
*Philo Vance's Apartment*

MARKHAM: Angus Clyde has been murdered, sergeant!
  We must go to his home at once.
HEATH: Wow! That's a knockout, chief.
MARKHAM: Swacker, get Philo Vance on the phone
  immediately!
HEATH: Huh! It's only ten o'clock! That bird ain't
  outa bed yet!

VALET: Mr. Markham on the phone, sir.
PHILO VANCE: Right-O, Currie. . . . Gree
  Markham. . . . Really! Fancy that, now! . . .
  Clyde collected rare jade, didn't he? . . . You
  me abominably, old dear. . . . Very well, I'll
  right over. . . . Currie, lay out a sedate suit
  thing suitable for a murder, y'know.

**ANGUS CLYDE**
*the murdered man*

**REGGIE MONCTON**
*Anne Clyde's ne'er-do-well brother*

**EMIL MUNTER**
*art collector*

**HANKINS**
*the Clyde butler*

# of PHILO VANCE—
# MYSTERY

**PHILO VANCE**
*amateur criminologist*

*Illustrated by A. E. Jameson*

**SCENE 3**
*Angus Clyde's Library—the Investigation Begins*

**SCENE 4**
*Philo Vance Questions the Clyde Butler*

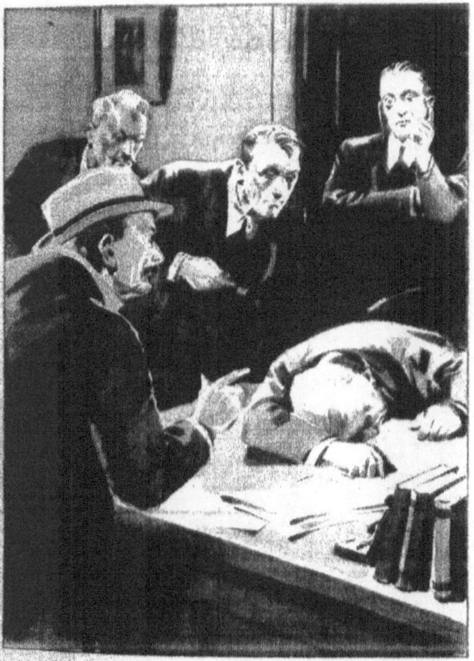

CORONER: Bullet entered behind the right ear. Contact shot. .38 caliber revolver. Clyde's been dead eight hours. Was shot about 2 A.M.
HEATH: Let's put Mrs. Clyde on the grill, Mr. Markham. *Cherchez la femme*, as Mr. Vance would say.
PHILO VANCE: Tut-tut, Monsieur Heath. Let's tackle the butler first.

HANKINS: I disliked Mr. Clyde because he was so insanely jealous of his young wife. . . . I found Mr. Clyde dead this morning about nine o'clock when I brought his breakfast to him.
PHILO VANCE: And I say, Hankins, who was in the house last night?
HANKINS: Well, sir, there was Mr. Reginald Moncton, Mrs. Clyde's younger brother; and Captain Rugg, his friend; also Herr Munter, to whom, I believe, Mr. Clyde refused to sell his collection of rare jade, and, of course, Mr. and Mrs. Clyde. . . .
PHILO VANCE: And, Hankins, what about dinner last night? Quite a jolly affair, eh, what?
HANKINS: Dinner last night, sir, was anything but jolly. Mr. Clyde, as usual, sat at the head of the table.
PHILO VANCE: Deuced grateful to you, Hankins; and, now, please, tell Mrs. Clyde that we should like to see her.

## SCENE 5
### The Young Widow Refuses to Answer

PHILO VANCE: Did you hear the shot that killed your husband, Mrs. Clyde?

MRS. CLYDE: No, I did not.

HEATH: Wait a minute. She musta heard the shot if she was in her bedroom!

PHILO VANCE: Where were you at two o'clock this morning, Mrs. Clyde, when your husband was murdered? . . . So—you prefer to keep silent? . . . Maybe we can find out if we speak to Captain Rugg!

## SCENE 6
### Markham Grills Mrs. Clyde's Admirer

CAPTAIN RUGG: Mrs. Clyde is a wonderful woman. The mere thought of such a lovely creature married to an old beast . . .

MARKHAM: Yes, yes. But where were you at two o'clock this morning?

PHILO VANCE: O toi! qu'aujourd'hui, j'adore. . . .

RUGG: I repeat, sir! I had retired to my room long before two o'clock.

PHILO VANCE: But, Captain Rugg, you're upsetting all the sergeant's pet theories, don't you know. Do tell us where you were at two o'clock.

REGGIE: Why such silly gallantry, Ted? You know jolly well you were on the balcony with my sister when old Clyde was shot!

## SCENE 7
### What Startling Information Can the Young Wife's Dissolute Brother Possess?

PHILO VANCE: You were a bit in your cups last night, Mr. Moncton, I understand. And you didn't love your sister's husband, eh, what?

REGGIE: Clyde had no business forcing my sister into a marriage just because we were poor!

PHILO VANCE: Oh, well, I'm no domestic snoop—but what about this moonlight rendezvous on the balcony?

REGGIE: Well, I'll tell you about it. And drunk or not, it's the truth! . . .

## SCENE 8
### Reggie Moncton Discloses Love Tryst Between His Sister and Captain Rugg

REGGIE: We were all in the drawing room—it was around twelve. . . . Pretty soon, Clyde says he's tired and starts for his room. A few minutes later, Herr Munter follows. It wasn't long before the decanter was empty, and I decided to go to bed myself. . . . I couldn't sleep—my head ached so. I went over to the window and stuck my head out, just as the clock on my mantle struck two . . .

. . . And I saw my friend, Ted Rugg, and sister Ann on the balcony.

## SCENE 9
*Herr Munter Volunteers Information, and a New Suspicion Is Born*

RUGG: Yes, I remember noticing the clock on the mantel just before we stepped onto the balcony; it was a few minutes to two o'clock; we were out there about twenty minutes, I should judge.

HERR MUNTER: I think there is some mistake about this, Mein Herr, for when I looked out of my window at two o'clock, the balcony was empty. . . .

PHILO VANCE: My word, Munter, I think you and I had better have a little heart-to-heart talk. . . . You say you looked out of your window last night at two, and the balcony was empty. Mind lending me your watch?

PHILO VANCE: Oh, my aunt! You're half an hour slow. How careless of you! . . . By the bye, how did you happen to be in the Clyde home?

MUNTER: I came here to buy, for my Berlin museum, the Clyde collection of rare jade. But he would not sell, Mein Herr.

PHILO VANCE: Most disappointing. You were in the war, I suppose, and know how to handle firearms?

MUNTER: *Ach, zum Henker. Ver dammter dummkopf!! Ich spreche nicht mehr mit solch ein kerl!*

PHILO VANCE: A queer Johnny!

## SCENE 10
*Sergeant Heath Takes Philo Vance and the District Attorney on a Searching Party*

HEATH: Maybe the gun that killed Clyde ain't in his wife's room, but it won't surprise me none if it is! . . . Hey! Here's the gun! And it was in that dame's room and it's a .38 and what's more, one cartridge had been fired!



MARKHAM: It looks pretty bad to me Vance.

HEATH: I told you so. . . .

PHILO VANCE: I confess, Markham, I'm positively stunned. But still, old chap, I'm unconvinced.

MARKHAM: It's direct evidence, Vance!

HEATH: And there's nothing to do but arrest her!

PHILO VANCE: Just a second! I've a brief experiment to make, and it may decide this matter one way or another. Where is Mrs. Clyde?

## SCENE 11
*Philo Vance Determines Mrs. Clyde's Guilt or Innocence*

PHILO VANCE: May I speak with you for a moment, Mrs. Clyde? . . . Lovely Hokusai print—that in the hall, Mrs. Clyde. . . . Will you have one of my cigarettes?

MRS. CLYDE: Thank you, Mr. Vance. My nerves. . . .

PHILO VANCE: The perfect lighter; it won't light. I'll always keep it. . . .

MRS. CLYDE: I have my own lighter here, Mr. Vance. . . . So you like my Hokusai? I bought it myself in Japan.

PHILO VANCE: A beautiful print. But, personally, I prefer the old Chinese prints—Ririomin, for example. . . . And now, I'm sure you did not kill your husband, Mrs. Clyde, and I shall so inform the district attorney and Sergeant Heath.

## SCENE 12
*Philo Vance Proves Mrs. Clyde's Innocence*

PHILO VANCE: So you see, Markham, Mrs. Clyde could not possibly have murdered her husband, for I have just proved that she is left-handed by offering her a cigarette and watching her light it with her left hand . . . Did you ever try to work a lighter with your left hand, sergeant? . . . The bullet being in the right side and from behind, considering the position of the desk and the body, the shot could not only have been made by a right-handed person . . . and now there is some more information which I crave. I will be gone only half an hour, but I hope to have news for you when I return.

## SCENE 13
### *Philo Vance Visits Angus Clyde's Physician*

DR. WOLFE: Yes, sir. I'm here to state that Clyde was suffering from hardening of the arteries, aneurism, leaky valve, and was not expected to live for more than three months! . . .

PHILO VANCE: I see. . . .

DR. WOLFE: And, as I say, I told him this fact only two days ago. . . .

PHILO VANCE: Quite so, doctor. . . . Thank you, Dr. Wolfe, you have given me the strongest clue to Clyde's murder.

## SCENE 14
### *Back in the Clyde Library, Philo Vance Sets To Work Again To Unravel the Mystery*

PHILO VANCE: Well, Markham, I have the key to Clyde's murder, but not the explanation. . . . Now let me see. . . . Clyde sat right here . . . when m-m-m-most interesting! . . . What do you make of that, Markham? . . . This nick in the fireplace is fresh, as you can see. It has been made recently. . . .

HEATH: Well, what of that? There are gas logs in the fireplace, and no one would hit it putting in a log of wood.

PHILO VANCE: That's just it, sergeant. They are gas logs, and therefore that nick is going to solve the murder—and now let's have Hankins up here.

## SCENE 15
### *More Mystery! What Has Philo Vance Discovered?*

PHILO VANCE: Hankins, fetch me a pair of old gloves and an old hat . . . and, er . . . tell the family to step up here, will you? And . . . I say, sergeant, have you a flashlight?

HEATH: Right here, Mr. Vance.

PHILO VANCE: And now, if you will excuse me, I am about to take a short journey . . .

## SCENE 16
### *The Discovery in the Chimney*

## SCENE 17
### *Philo Vance Clears Up the Mystery*

PHILO VANCE: I will show you how the murder wa committed.

## SCENE 18
### *Finale!*

### *The Day's Work Ended for Philo Vance*

PHILO VANCE: You see— Clyde—knowing he was going to die anyway, and being intensely jealous of his young wife, because he suspected her of being in love with Captain Rugg, planted a .38 revolver, with one cartridge missing, in her bedroom, took a long piece of elastic, attached one end to his gun and the other end up into the chimney, shot himself, and waited for the police to send his wife to the chair. . . .

. . . Truly, a diabolical trick, but one entirely consistent with the old fellow's character . . . and now, if you don't mind, I will hurry over to Carnegie Hall to hear Toscanini conduct Brahm's Second Symphony.

# The Transatlantic Mystery

# THE CASEBOOK OF ALBERT OTIS

By Brooks Hefner

In 1928, when the true identity of bestselling detective novelist S.S. Van Dine was revealed to be none other than the elite intellectual writer and editor Willard Huntington Wright, readers were likely quite surprised. How could it be possible that the author of books on Nietzsche and modernist art, a committed highbrow of the highest order, had stooped to author popular fiction catering to the masses? In 1913 after all, Wright had nearly run the magazine *The Smart Set* into the ground by jettisoning its signature society fiction for European experimentalists, and his 1916 novel *The Man of Promise* dramatized the tragic fall of an "intellectual aristocrat" (much like Wright), who gives up his intellectual ambitions to write "inconsequential" popular novels.

Wright himself sought to take control of this narrative with his self-conscious pseudo-autobiography "I Used to Be a Highbrow, but Look at Me Now," first published (under his now-famous pseudonym S.S. Van Dine) in the *American Magazine* in September 1928 and issued the following year as a pamphlet by his publisher Alfred A. Knopf. Here, Wright emphasized that his interest in detective fiction emerged only after his doctor, treating him for a "nervous breakdown" in 1923, prohibited him from reading anything more demanding than "a little light fiction." This convenient division of the writer's career—from Wright the highbrow intellectual (and "man of promise") to Van Dine the lowbrow popular novelist—remained, for a long time, the standard version of Wright's biography.

While researching Wright's career-long obsession with highbrow/lowbrow dichotomies in 2011, I came across a curious reference in a letter written by Wright to his wife in June of 1916. "I havent [sic] a cent except what Land gives me and some money from a magazine for some terrible stories which I print over another name. (*Pearsons*—Albert Otis) Dont [sic] look at them: they are not worth noticing."[1]

---

1 Willard Huntington Wright to Kathrine Boynton Wright. 8 June 1916. Willard Huntington Wright Papers. Special Collections, University of Virginia Library, Charlottesville, VA.

Wright's biographer John Loughery had already identified some of Wright's early 1920s "hack jobs," writing for pay (such as articles on motion pictures under the name Frederick Van Vranken), but these "terrible stories" were not identified there, in part because Loughery misread the name as "Albert Otis Pearsons." Still, it was clear that Wright was publishing these "terrible stories" for pay in the same year that saw his most ambitious publications: *The Man of Promise, Modern Painting: Its Intention and Meaning*, and the Nietzschean aesthetic treatise *The Creative Will: Studies in the Philosophy and Syntax of Aesthetics.* Such a juxtaposition severely complicates the notion that Wright's early career was exclusively highbrow and that his interest in crime and detective fiction emerged only in the mid-1920s as he was under doctor's orders to avoid strenuous intellectual reading.

Indeed, these Wright stories appeared in *Pearson's Magazine,* a periodical that featured a variety of writers from across the cultural sphere. Under the pseudonym "Albert Otis," Wright published eight stories between January and August 1916, each featuring the protagonist Harry Franklin, a "gentleman crook" who resembles in some respects a mildly villainous inversion of Wright's later creation Philo Vance. Although these stories took up crime from the other vantage point—that of a highbrow criminal rather than an intellectual detective—the first of these, "The Wise Guy," was advertised on the cover of the January 1916 issue of *Pearson's Magazine* as "a new kind of detective story." With their intersection of genre, crime, highbrow intellectuals, and aesthetics, Wright's "Albert Otis" stories anticipate many of the themes that would dominate the bestselling novels he later wrote under the more famous pseudonym S.S. Van Dine.

Throughout these stories, the globetrotting protagonist Harry Franklin abides by a code that is at once highly aesthetic and deeply Nietzschean. In the introduction to this character in "The Wise Guy," this is made quite clear: "From his early youth he had admired the heroes of the D'Artagnan class; and by adhering to the Nietzschean formula, 'Live dangerously!' he received that stimulation for which all healthy natures crave." His peculiar interest in criminal enterprise stems not from any moral or psychological depravity (as it often does in S.S. Van Dine's Philo Vance novels), but instead from an interest in romanticized criminal aesthetics and intellectual challenges. In "Full O'Larceny," he tells his wife and criminal partner Lilly Dinan, "I'll never take a cent from any one unless there's a mental battle involved, or unless the man is inherently dishonest. To that extent I'm an idealist. You see, I must feel I am a kind of Nemesis, a retribution, a sterilizer of men's souls." As a result, many of Franklin's operations are against other criminals, outwitting them at their own game and punishing them for a more serious breach of the moral order. In this respect Franklin is at once a criminal and a detective, uncovering the wrongdoings of womanizing rakes, collectors of stolen art, jewel-obsessed bankers, and others—and ultimately giving them a taste of their own medicine.

Franklin's other partner in most of these enterprises, Red Bernheim, finds this pursuit of intellectualized crime inexplicable, and he calls Franklin "a high-brow nut." Bernheim, however, is a more troubling figure here: a broad antisemitic caricature of Jewish criminality. Whereas Wright had used a Jewish figure in *The Man of Promise* to represent a model of idealized intellectual distance for his writer protagonist, in the Albert Otis stories Bernheim's ethnic difference and uncouth criminality stand in stark contrast to Harry Franklin's "generations of careful breeding." Wright's essentialist descriptions of Bernheim ("No one could mistake the fact that he was a Jew") are cringe-inducing but of a piece with other unflattering descriptions of ethnic difference across these stories, which see the criminal trio operate in locales as exotic as Honolulu, Nagasaki, and Constantinople. While Franklin flirts with the idea of abandoning Bernheim—not out of racial animosity but out of aesthetic differences—they remain together until the end, when the group helps Bernheim's lover escape her marriage with an unfaithful husband.

Willard Huntington Wright's Albert Otis stories represent the best-selling detective novelist's earliest sustained efforts at writing crime fiction. Offering a valuable context for Wright's better-known S.S. Van Dine novels and documenting the writer's much longer engagement with the genre, these tales show Wright working through his interests in the intersections of art, intellectual life, and racial hierarchy, a host of themes that would inform his work well into his success with the detective Philo Vance. Working with ideas like the racialized marks of "intellectual aristocracy" and the aesthetic pleasures of crime (and crime-solving), Wright would, nearly a decade later, successfully transmute these ideas into some of the most widely read novels of the 1920s.

# THE WISE GUY

WITHIN ONE OF the shadowy, ill-kempt houses of the upper Thirties, in a. heavily curtained room behind locked doors, five representatives of that stratum of society commonly referred to as crooks, reclined head to hip on a broad bed. The steady yellow flame of an opium lamp lighted their faces and accentuated the lines which years of cunning had stamped there... Three of them were powerful sluggish creatures with no traits to distinguish them from hundreds of their fellows in the same walk of life. One, Red Bernheim, was obviously Jewish. His figure, now approaching corpulency, was carefully but tastelessly clothed. In a different *milieu* he might have passed for a successful pawnbroker. His aggressive personality dominated the quintet: his was the directing genius over the conversation of his companions.

The fifth member of this synod of vice was the only one whose criminality was not congenital. He was a slender, well-built man of about thirty, blond, with frank blue eyes and the shoulders of a college athlete. In his face there were undeniable marks of refinement. His nose was straight, his mouth severe, and his hair grew away from his forehead in a manner which attested to generations of careful breeding.

Harry Franklin, in fact, was the offspring of gentle parents. Five years before he had been an honor student at Yale, and he was not unfamiliar with certain European capitals where he had spent two years after graduation. Scrutinizing him, even critically, one could discern no temperamental affinities between him and his present surroundings. On his stern, somewhat boyish, face there were no signs of meanness or underhandedness. To the contrary, one sensed in him a gay, quixotic daring—a reckless courage which, to all people good or bad, has its attraction. From his early youth he had admired heroes of the D'Artagnan class; and by adhering to the Nietzschean formula, "Live dangerously!" he received that stimulation for which all healthy natures crave.

At the death of his father (followed almost immediately by that of his mother) he found himself confronted with poverty, and with no surer weapon of combating it than an academic education. At this point, he drifted into an acquaintance with Red Bernheim. How he fell under the latter's sway and deliberately adopted the life he was now leading, is a question which would require both a psychologist and a social economist to answer. Neither of the men inquired into the event very profoundly.

FRANKLIN SAW IN the alliance an opportunity for adventure; while Bernheim, on the other hand, considered the penniless young college man purely from a practical standpoint. The latter's appearance of good breeding, coupled with his physical strength, made him desirable both as a "come-on" man and a "watch dog."

As the five men reclined about the "layout," their conversation was sporadic and desultory. From comments on the latest police regulation for closing unlicensed pool-rooms and bitter remarks on "bulls" and judges, the talk drifted to the latest gossip of the underworld and the technical methods of crook "jobs" as practiced in New York, Chicago, and San Francisco.

"The methods of crooks to-day," said Red, "are about as out-of-date as *Uncle Tom's Cabin*. Take it from me, it ain't healthy to pull anything like the match or the badger game these days. Even the long hairs know 'em by heart." He surveyed the company with a philosophical air. "If we'd gone with our Noah's Ark tactics on this last beat, we'd be getting free board on the Island by this time! It's a question of doing the wise guys with their own wisdom now. To-day's game is going to be pulled off right, believe me. Kingsley thinks he's a wisenheimer." He paused. "Why, it's like selling hymn books to Moody and Sankey."

"If I didn't know Kingsley to be a blackleg," said Franklin, "I'd wash my hands of the whole affair."

"He's no worse than the rest of 'em," remarked Red. "You're wrong," the other contradicted.

"You're a misanthrope, Red. Kingsley is a whited sepulcher. He's paid rent on two apartments for years, and his little excursion into politics netted his business a pile of money. His coming marriage to old Stamwater's daughter is only a business episode. He needs big capital, and the girl's happiness is going to purchase it. I've no respect or sympathy for a man who'd play Romeo for money. If he was straight and loved the girl you'd have to count me out."

Bernheim had tried numerous moral arguments with Franklin, but always without success. Franklin disliked blackmail and refused to swindle an honest man. He adhered to a code which, however irrational it might have been from an ethical point of view, was nevertheless consistent. He abhorred all games which did not involve a battle of wits. The sole enjoyment he wrung from life was in turning deals in which the conceit or the inherent dishonesty of the victim paid the bill. The bamboo pipe passed round again. Franklin, his slender fingers tired from rolling the needle, and slightly nauseated, as opium smokers invariably are at first, turned over silently and subsided into reverie.

SPRING HAD broken over New York. The lemon-yellow sun flecked the struggling grass in Central Park and cast deep blue shadows from the buildings along the roaring streets. The trees had taken on a vivid freshness, and the whole world seemed to have emerged once more from a long sleep to a new and finer cycle of life. The shimmering panoramas of the Hudson and East rivers were as placidly pretty as a painting by Monet. Along the avenues happy throngs passed backward and forward in an endless eddy. To the casual observer New York seemed *en fête*.

Down Sixth Avenue passed a girl. The checker-boarded sun and shadow made by the Elevated seemed to take away the last vestige of reality from her slim figure. She was simply dressed in a navy-blue tailored suit, with a white Lord Fauntleroy collar, a drooping black leghorn hat and the shoes of a shop girl worn with the distinction of a *femme entretenue* of the *Quartier de l'Etoile*. Her tight black curls formed a frame for a pale face to which two quiet brown eyes and a childish mouth gave a touch of ethereality. Hers was the face of a modern Madonna, gentle, dependent and innocent. Men looked twice before passing her by. She produced in them an emotion analogous to that of minor music, recalling to them their early loves, their ambitions, their youths. She personified romance, and they felt cleansed in spirit with the thought of her.

At Thirty-Seventh Street she rounded the corner. Crossing the street timidly, she made her way toward Eighth Avenue. About two-thirds of the way down the square she turned into a sordid doorway and rang the bell twice. There was a long wait. Then, after she had answered a raucous voice which hailed her from within, the door opened, and she was admitted into a dark hallway smelling of must. As with a creature of the night a subtle change came over her as she quitted the sunlight. Running hastily up the stairs, she knocked four times on a door.

The sound of men's voices within hushed. There was the clank of a small chain, and Lilly Dinan entered her home.

The five men on the bed turned toward her lackadaisically. Harry Franklin alone sat up—an act prompted by both deference and admiration. For several months he had taken more than a casual and "business" interest in her. And she in turn had admired him in a spontaneous and unquestioning manner.

THIS RECIPROCAL interest between the young people did not escape Bernheim. Though he used Lilly only as a wheel in the machinery of his games, he was jealous of any interference in his affairs. These visits were generally accompanied by irate fault-findings, and though Franklin refrained from interfering, he felt that Red could have accomplished more by employing less severe methods. From which it will be seen that all the sentimental juices had not been squeezed from Franklin's nature.

Today, after the acerbic greeting had been completed, Lilly dropped into a chair near the bed and rolled a cigarette.

"Why don't you open the window, Red?" she asked, coughing over the thick atmosphere.

"Since when have you been running this joint?" Red flared up. "Do you come here to get orders or to give them? You're getting too high-toned lately, and there ain't nobody round this layout that don't know it. Every time you come here you make high signs to Harry. What do you think he can do for' you?"

The girl smiled wearily, and blew some cigarette smoke in the other's face. "You're getting as peevish as a prima donna. What's the program?" was all she said.

"Now sit up and take notice," replied Bernheim, altering his voice. "Everything's framed, and no girl in the world could bungle it except you. You're such a bonehead that you're liable to forget where you live. But get this, kid: your hide depends on your doing this up neat. If you had any brains I wouldn't have to pull this John Drew stuff on you every day. Now here's the dope."

Then carefully he outlined the story, going into its minutest details. The girl sat listening intently. When he had finished she recited it after him, being coached and corrected at every point. When Bernheim felt satisfied with the rehearsal (and there was genuine histrionic ability in her actions), he said: "Now get your room in order. Make it look like a perfectly respectable hangout for an honest, take-back-your-gold, shop girl."

Lilly Dinan disappeared, only to return ten minutes later.

"Off you go now," said Bernheim, "and if you bungle this, we're done for. Even if we get away with a whole hide it'll be slim eats for some time to come. With the long-hairs closing down the lid and the hard times making all the suckers sit on their bank rolls, life ain't all beer and skittles." Then appealingly: "Lil, kid, the whole thing's up to you. It means Europe and a holiday for the bunch. Now mush, and when you pull the song and dance think of the Swanee River and the morning glories on the veranda."

LILLY DINAN'S father, a native of Provence, had come to America in his youth, and through his industry and unscrupulousness had at length become the proprietor of a down-town restaurant of evil repute. One night, just after a change in the city's administration, his establishment had been raided, and he had retired mysteriously from the world, leaving nothing behind him but an unsavory reputation and a ten-year-old daughter. Lilly mourned her father bitterly, for he had always been kind and generous to her. Never had she had to complain of his lack of lenience. Indeed, so lenient had he been, that she had escaped entirely the irksome routine of school.

Five years after his death the girl was still running errands and doing housework in the place her father had left. She developed quickly in both body and mind, as do those people of Southern blood when thrown upon their own resources. At fifteen she was an asset of no small value in the very house where she had worked so long; and when she was seventeen she knew by sight most of the fly-by-night characters of the underworld. But Lilly had never become contaminated by her environment. While participating objectively in a life which disgusted her, she had inwardly remained aloof. Many men had tried to make love to her, but she had repulsed them all, guided by an instinct which told her that some day she would find the things her heart vaguely craved. Red Bernheim was then in the heyday of his illicit career, and Lilly had attached herself to him as a business part ner for no particular reason, being convinced that the onrush of fate would carry her to her desired end.

But Bernheim's prestige had now begun to decline. More and more Franklin's ideas were insinuating themselves into the "gang's" plans: little by little he was asserting that intellectual leadership which hitherto had been Bernheim's prerogative. Consequently Lilly's attitude toward many things was also undergoing a decided metamorphosis. Heretofore she had looked upon Bernheim's whinings over bad luck as legitimate criticisms of an unjust police vigilance; but recently his complaints had come to spell weakness in her eyes. She had never had any love or even affection for him. Nor was she ashamed of the tenderness which sometimes welled up in her at the thought of Franklin, although at all times she managed to hide it well. In spite of all this, however, she feared Bernheim. And this fear was the measure of her loyalty to him.

TODAY AS LILLY seated herself in an uptown surface car and watched the thousands of people hurrying back and forth in the fresh glare of the spring sunshine, she felt in her heart a pain whose origin she could not understand and whose meaning she could not analyze. She thought of the squalid places where she had lived, and, unbidden, the visualization of a neat and cleanly flat took birth in her mind. How good it would be to return each night to a home which would not depress her with its sullenness and poverty! Would it ever be her fate to experience that miracle?

The question swept through her like a wave. Her mind which, despite her experiences, was still girlish, realized keenly what she had missed. She formulated the pleasing yet distant hope that some day this desire might be attained. Though she did not connect this novel dream with Franklin, it was he to whom her thoughts immediately turned. A longing for peace and love welled up in her as patriotism does in a soldier at the sight of banners and at the sound of fife and drums....

She alighted on upper Broadway about a hundred yards from her destination. There she waited before one of the shop windows. Presently a large touring car drew up outside the Dolores Automobile salesrooms. Every midday, at just this hour, the same car arrived in front of the salesrooms, and John Kingsley, president of the company, entered it and rode to the National Club, where he spent two hours at luncheon.

Kingsley was a pompously happy man.

He was well on the road to wealth; he enjoyed, though undeservedly, the goodwill and the respect of his fellows; his engagement to Muriel Stamwater, the daughter of the railroad magnate, was announced for the coming June; and his prospective father-in-law had promised to finance a large new manufacturing plant for the Dolores machines.

FROM THE CORNER of her eye Lilly saw Kingsley step proudly onto the pavement and walk toward the waiting car. Unhesitatingly she advanced toward him. Her slim little figure in dark blue was not unfamiliar to Kingsley. Many times at the noon hour and in the evening he had seen her pass. And to see her once was to remember her. On one or two occasions he had caught her eyes, and the manner in which they drooped under his scrutiny conveyed to him the fact that she had been conscious of his gaze. Now, as she walked by him this miraculous Spring day, something in her gait clinched his attention— something unsteady and helpless. She staggered a trifle, putting a hand before her as if groping for support. He strode toward her instinctively and reached her just in time, for her footsteps faltered and she swayed. Catching her by the arm deftly, he led her to his automobile, upon which she clung blindly. Kingsley was strong, and it was no effort for him to lift the girl and place her in the tonneau. Having done this he dispatched his chauffeur to the nearest chemist's for smelling salts.

Then suddenly—too suddenly—the girl regained consciousness and sat upright. She looked at her rescuer directly in the eyes, and began to sob.

John Kingsley was nonplussed. The fact that the girl had fainted had not surprised him. But her sudden resuscitation and sobbing puzzled him and made him suspicious. He drew a little away and asked peremptorily, "What's the meaning of this?"

The girl did not answer, and he repeated his question. "Come, come, tell me what's the trouble. If anything's really the matter, let me know. If it's just some game it won't help you to stay any longer." His suspicion increased. "Perhaps I'd better call an officer."

At this the girl looked up startled. "Oh, don't—don't do that!" she cried, brushing the tears away. "And please forgive me for what I've done. I'll tell you the truth."

The girl looked at him steadily. "Will you promise—on your word of honor—that you'll forgive me and not do anything to me?"

"I promise," said he.

"Well, listen then." She spoke calmly. "It *was* a put-up job—a game to ruin you—and they sent me here to lead you on, to get you where they could demand money from you. But I'm sick of the whole affair. Please forgive me—and try to believe me."

"BLACKMAIL, HUH?" murmured the man, looking sharply at the tear-stained face.

The girl nodded her head. "They knew you were going to be married and all about your money matters, and they thought they could get you in a position where you would pay them to shut up." She glanced up quickly. "You won't let anything happen to me, will you? It's rotten of me to tell you, but I'm sick to death of the business and want to get away."

"Nothing will happen to you," Kingsley promised, "if you tell me the truth."

"All it was," replied the girl, stifling a sob, "was to entice you to my room by pretending to faint. I've come here every day for more than a week so that you'd notice me. When you saw that I was ill, I was going to ask you to take me 'home. Then one of the five men who've been tailing you—that is, watching you—was going to come in and pretend he was my husband and get money out of you for not making a row about it. If you refused he was going to threaten to tell the world that you'd been caught in a woman's room in a rotten part of town and that you frequented opium dens—for there's one there. They knew you'd rather pay than have it known, and that's all they want. She halted. "Now I've told you all, and you've got to keep your promise not to let anything happen to me. If they found out, it would be the end of me. You will protect me, won't you?" Her tone was startled as if she were overcome by the extent of her faithlessness and the enormity of the consequences which were sure to devolve on her should Bernheim find out her infidelity.

KINGSLEY PUT his hand on the girl's arm and said almost affectionately: "Now don't you worry, my girl. I've given my word that nothing will happen to you. But it's a mighty good thing you told me all the same, for you and your friends would never have got away with so transparent a game. I'm not as easy as all that. I know a thing or two. I'm not an innocent." He emitted a low, self-contented laugh. The girl began to sob again. "I'm so frightened," she wailed. "You don't know what would happen to me if they found out I'd squealed."

"Oh, yes I do," the man returned with an air of one who did not wish to admit the extent of his experiences. "But don't let that bother you. They won't be in a position to do any one any harm when I get through with them. But look here, why didn't you go on with it? What was your idea in telling me?"

The girl replied without looking up. "I —I don't know exactly. I just didn't have the nerve, I guess. And then again, you seemed so decent and— Oh, I don't know— the thing was too rotten, and I'm sick to death of the whole outfit. I want to get away. I want to have a home—a real home. You don't know what I mean. I guess I don't know myself. You have everything you want; you're in love and are happy. But I've never had what I want. There have been times when I've almost starved to death, and I've had to do these things to keep alive. Now, I don't know what I'm going to do. I've spoiled what little chance I had of getting a living. And that isn't the worst of it. If any of them find out what I've done they wouldn't stop at anything. They'd kill me!"

John Kingsley was silent again. He was thinking fast, in terms of himself. Suddenly he turned to the girl. "Now look here," he said. "You've told me so much. I want you to tell me the rest: who are these men, and where are they?"

THE GIRL'S EYES widened in fright. "You mustn't ask me that," she said pleadingly. "It wouldn't do any good, and they'd be sure to know I'd told you. Please take my warning and let it go at that." She arose and started away, but Kingsley drew her back firmly.

"I've told you I'd protect you," he said. "And I can do it," he added boastfully. "Your friends don't know who John Kingsley is."

"I don't want to tell you," the girl replied sullenly. "You don't understand."

"I understand this much," the man replied, "that if you'll help me I'll have those men arrested. Then they won't be in a position to do you any harm."

The girl glanced up hopefully. "If I told you who they were and did all I could to help you, would you promise—*honestly*— that you'd have them arrested?"

"That's my only reason for wanting to know."

John Kingsley had not been unmoved by the girl's story. Nor had he been unsusceptible to her quiet charm. Furthermore, he felt indignant toward this unknown band of blackmailers who had planned against him, and saw honor for himself in their arrest. The two emotions had blended into a determination to turn the tables on the conspirators. With the girl's help it would be an easy matter, There would be nothing undignified in it, he mused, but, to the contrary, it would be gratifying to instigate the arrest of some notorious criminals, Such a distinction was not to be let pass. And then there was advertising in it.

"There's only one way to do it. "The girl was speaking. "If we don't show up there pretty soon, they'll get suspicious and leave. Why don't you go to the police station now and tell them? Then you and I can go around there just as if nothing had happened, and as soon as we're there the police can come in suddenly and arrest them in the act."

"That's the way I've figured it out," Kingsley said. "It's the simplest way. Now tell me where the place is."

"It's at 235 North Thirty-Seventh Street," the girl answered excitedly, "and the room is on the second floor at the rear."

KINGSLEY GAVE an order to his driver. In five minutes, he was being ushered into the little office of the police sergeant at the Sixth Avenue station.

"Now, what I want you to do," Kingsley added with an air of authority, "is to send your men round exactly five minutes after I've entered the house. Have them come up immediately and catch them red-handed."

"Did you get their names?" the sergeant asked.

Kingsley repeated two of the names he had got from the girl.

The officer jumped to his feet with a grunt of satisfaction. "We've been after those men for six months," he said, "but we've never been able to get the goods on 'em."

The sergeant pushed a bell and ordered a squad and patrol. Kingsley, chuckling to himself, walked quickly out to his car.

"Everything's arranged," he said confidently to the girl, after having told his chauffeur where to go. "You take me upstairs just as you had planned. Inside five minutes the handcuffs will be on everyone. Then I'm going to give you enough to go away and have that little home you want."

"You're very good," she replied softly. "It would have been a rotten thing to do you, and I'm so glad I didn't."

"Don't you know," Kingsley laughed easily, "that every man in the country who reads the magazines is familiar with all the details of this scheme you were trying to work on me?"

"They are?" the girl asked in astonishment. Suddenly she leaned forward to the chauffeur. "It is the eighth house from the corner," she directed. "The one just there with the broken gate."

The machine drew up in front of the designated house. Kingsley noticed that the white figures on the front door were large and conspicuous.

He jumped from the machine and assisted the girl to alight. He was a little nervous but confident. The adventure appealed to him aside from the moral gratification he was deriving from it. Chivalrous by instinct, he felt the romantic appeal in his present role of fairy god-father to an unhappy girl. And these men had underestimated him! They thought he was as pious and inexperienced as he pretended to be!


KINGSLEY swaggeringly followed his companion into the doorway. Her ring was immediately answered by a thin sallow Negro woman. Once inside, the girl led the way up two flights of stairs, and, taking a key from her worn leather bag, admitted herself and the man into a small dingy hall-bedroom. Kingsley sat down and lighted a cigar. The girl took off her hat.

At this moment Red Bernheim entered. At seeing Kingsley his expression changed. He slammed the door and, setting his teeth, stood menacingly before the visitor, He seemed too astonished and infuriated to say anything at first. But suddenly a stream of invective flowed from his thick lips.

The girl interposed, taking hold of Bernheim's arm pleadingly. "Don't carry on that way, Red, it ain't what you think it is. I almost fainted in the street and this gentleman was kind enough to bring me home."

Bernheim threw back his head and laughed derisively. "A fine story!" he said, glowering at Kingsley. "A sweet little story to tell a husband! So you fainted, did you? And your friend brought you home?"

"It's the truth," the girl wailed, as Bernheim's voice became more threatening.

"Shut up," commanded the man. "You can't fool me with any such yarn. Men of this type don't visit working girls in their rooms without a reason."

The girl fell on her knees. "Believe me, Red," she pleaded. "Believe me! It isn't true—what you say."

She was brushed aside brutally. "What have you got to say?" the man bellowed at Kingsley, drawing a Browning from his pocket and shaking it menacingly.

The girl rose suddenly; and threw herself in front of Kingsley. "Don't, for God's sake!" she cried. "Think of me; think what you're doing."

BERNHEIM'S manner suddenly changed, He returned the weapon to his pocket, and dropped into a chair. "To think that it's come to this!" he moaned, assuming an air of sorrow. "After all I've done for you! My wife!" He paused and looked down at the floor like one overcome by sudden bereavement.

During this sham melodrama Kingsley had sat smoking placidly. He thought to himself that the man's and girl's acting was sufficiently realistic to have been convincing had he not been cognizant of the true state of affairs.

The spurious husband had just begun another harangue about Kingsley's wanton breaking up of a happy married life, when hurrying footsteps were heard on the stairs, Then three uniformed officers burst into the room and without a moment's hesitation put the handcuffs on Bernheim. The manacled man sank to the floor as if paralyzed with fear, looking questioningly first at the girl and then at Kingsley. The officers had been followed by a young well-dressed man of about thirty. A flat camera was hung over his shoulder. He stood in the doorway looking about him with an interested air. Kingsley paid little heed to him.

The officer turned to Bernheim who still sat on the floor, a look of blank astonishment on his face. "Get up, you!" he ordered. "Charlie, take him downstairs and put him in the wagon. You, Jim, grab the girl."

Kingsley took a step forward to protest, and Lilly Dinan threw her arms round his neck as if for protection.

At that moment there was a blinding flash which illumined the entire room—a *click*, and the young man with the camera said, "Much obliged," and shoved his instrument back into the leather case.

"Who's that man?" demanded Kingsley.

"Only Mr. Wilkins, that Associated Press reporter," said the officer, who had paid no heed to the flashlight and was now shoving Bernheim before him out the door.

"Here, wait a minute, you fellows," Kingsley called, stepping to the door. He was thunderstruck by this new element which had entered into the preconcerted drama. "What are you going to do with that picture?" he asked the reporter.

The young man raised his eyes with an expression of boredom. "Sell it to the papers," he answered in a tone which was at once indifferent and haughty. "What do you think I'm here for? This story's worth two months' wages. 'John Kingsley, the auto king, saving the beautiful and notorious Lilly Dinan from the clutches of a blackmailing gang.' And then the picture with Miss Dinan's arms stinking lovingly around the aforementioned Mr, Kingsley's neck." He chuckled.

"I'll have that story suppressed," Kingsley blurted out. "I've got influence, and you'll lose your job in the bargain."

"Oh, say! "The reporter was thoroughly disgusted. "Have you got influence with every paper in the United States? I'm not a one-paper cub, I'm an A.P. man."

"Pardon us," interrupted the officer who had Bernheim in hand. "We've got to get down."

Now, when a man of Kingsley's type finds himself in an unpleasant situation from which he desires to be extricated, he becomes immediately conscious of the power his wealth gives him. He was not a man' who took roundabout routes, and it was not therefore incompatible. With his nature that he should have said to the young reporter before him, "See here, my boy, how much do you want for that camera and to forget what you've seen today?"

And perhaps it was not incompatible with the young reporter's nature that he should have answered, "One thousand dollars," without hesitation.

"PARDON ME, Mr. Kingsley," interrupted one of the officers, before Kingsley had time to reply, "It'll do you no good to buy this fellow off. The minute we put these men in the cooler there'll be twenty reporters on hand, and there'll be no way of keeping your name and the girl's out of it. The case is too important. This man here"—he jerked his thumb at Bernheim—"is one of the biggest catches in years. The only possible thing that would save you, provided you don't want to get mixed up in the affair, would be if the outfit got away."

"Then look here," Kingsley replied directly, "we've got to talk quick. I want you fellows to drop this business. I brought the charge, and I ought to be allowed to withdraw it. What are your jobs worth?" At length the officer named a figure which made Kingsley hesitate, but only for a moment. He took out a check book and a fountain pen. He knew that whatever he gave these men would come back a hundredfold from old Stamwater.

"We can't take a check," the officer advised him quickly.

"Do you think I carry that amount with me?" Kingsley asked petulantly.

"I'll take a chance." It was Mr. Wilkins, the reporter, who spoke. "Put it all on one check, including my thousand, and I'll go to the bank with it while you fellows"— addressing the officers—'wait here." He looked at the blank check to ascertain the name of the bank. "Then you can let Mr. Kingsley go. I'll drop in at the station and settle with you fellows later."

The plan did not appeal to the officers.

"It's your only chance," explained the reporter. "And you know me."

Kingsley waited expectantly, while the others demurred. When they at last consented, he drew a sigh of relief.

After scrutinizing the check carefully, the young man disappeared, having turned over his camera.

Presently the girl crossed to Kingsley. "What about me?" she asked. "You said you'd protect me. I'm done for now."

"Can I help it?" growled the man. "I guess you'll get along all right."

"Aren't you going to help me?"

"No," snapped Kingsley. "I've lost enough already.... And if you try anything on me you'll be sorry.... Get away while you have a chance."

The girl looked at him sorrowfully. "I can't get away. I'm done for."

"Well, don't blame me. You got me in for this."

When the five minutes were up, the officer arose and addressed Kingsley. "I'm sorry things turned out this way for you, sir," he said politely, "but I know you understand the situation. You may go now."

WITH a sigh of relief and a few half-hearted amenities, Kingsley hurried down stairs and out into the street. There was a considerable crowd gathered at the house next door, in front of which was standing a police patrolwagon. Near by it several officers were talking in low tones. Kingsley looked for standingbile, but it was nowhere to be seen. He could not understand it, and was about to call to one of the officers, when he saw the machine, driven at high speed, round the corner and come toward him.

"There's something wrong," the chauffeur exclaimed excitedly. "That note you sent your secretary was blank."

"What note?" cried Kingsley.

"Just after you went in there with the young lady," explained the driver, "a man came out and gave me a note addressed in your handwriting and said I was to take it immediately to your secretary."

One of the officers in front of the house next door had caught sight of Kingsley and came running up to him, "We've been looking for you, sir," he said, and there was anger in his tone. "We've searched that house from top to bottom and haven't found anybody. You told us we'd find you at 235, and that you had a line on some crooks we wanted."

"There's 235!" was all Kingsley could reply, pointing at the house. "Two-thirty-five!" the officer exclaimed. "That's Two-thirty-seven!" Kingsley's eyes sought the numerals which, fifteen minutes before, had stood out in such bold relief, In their place were the dim, weather-beaten figures, "2-3-7."

IN a flash he understood. So, after all, he had been played for a sucker! The girl had duped him! The pseudo-reporter now had his money! No. wonder the so-called officers whose presence he had just left were willing to trust to the "reporter's" honesty!

Kingsley was shaking with excitement.

"They're up there now!" he fairly screamed, pointing to the house which had harbored his recent undoing. "Hurry!"

And he and the officers burst in the front door and dashed up the stairs.

All they found were three empty uniforms lying in a heap before an open window which led upon a spacious fire-escape.for you, sir," he said, and there was anger in his tone. "We've searched that house from top to bottom and haven't found anybody. You told us we'd find you at 235, and that you had a line on some crooks we wanted."

"There's 235!" was all Kingsley could reply, pointing at the house.

"Two-thirty-five!" the officer exclaimed. "That's Two-thirty-seven!"

Kingsley's eyes sought the numerals which, fifteen minutes before, had stood out in such bold relief, In their place were the dim, weather-beaten figures, "2-3-7."

IN A FLASH HE understood. So, after all, he had been played for a sucker! The girl had duped him! The pseudo-reporter now had his money! No. wonder the so-called officers whose presence he had just left were willing to trust to the "reporter's" honesty!

Kingsley was shaking with excitement.

"They're up there now!" he fairly screamed, pointing to the house which had harbored his recent undoing. "Hurry!"

And he and the officers burst in the front door and dashed up the stairs.

All they found were three empty uniforms lying in a heap before an open window which led upon a spacious fire-escape.

# FULL O'LARCENY

ALTHOUGH the English merchants were the first to introduce the practice of opium-smoking into China, the Mongolians effected an adequate reprisal by teaching the habit to another branch of the white race, the Americans. California, perhaps more than any other State, has suffered from the use of the drug, for California is nearest China and is looked upon by the Chinese as their Mecca in the western world. San Francisco suffered first, but it was not long before Los Angeles, San Francisco's south-of-Tahachepi rival, became inoculated with the vice.

The evil of the opium den lies not only in the effect of the drug on habitués. Were this the case, the police might well ignore its existence, for society could easily dispense with those few individuals who prefer an induced lethargy to normal activity. The chief evil, however, of opium dens lies in their being the clearing houses for the members of the underworld. In them are hatched the plots which those persons, skilled in the ramifications of vice, carry out against the peace-loving and law-abiding majority. Opium clears the mind, sterilizes the judgment and nullifies the moral outlook. Just as many surgeons, before entering the operating room, pacify their nerves with sedatives, so does the average crook on the eve of a "job" clarify his brain with the gum of the poppy.

The establishment of Woo Ching Fang was the most popular rendezvous of criminals in the Angel City. Fang, because he enjoyed the protection of the police—paying for that privilege a sum of money which would startle the financier unversed in the profits of the underworld—could offer his customers a security not afforded by any other of his brothers.

Fang's restaurant resembled externally all of the many Chinese cafés which surrounded the famous Plaza opposite the Church of Our Lady of the Angels. But over half of Fang's customers ignored the enticing white linen of his tables in the front room, and directed themselves swiftly and surreptitiously toward a rear door which leads to the floor above. Here an alert lobby-gow, after receiving a small pourboire, unlocked a heavy door from which escaped a sweet aroma as of boiling chocolate. The moment the customer had passed beyond the door, it was again locked. Inside were many bunks built about the walls in tiers of two, like the beds in the state-rooms of ocean liners.

These bunks were nearly as wide as an ordinary double bed, and here and there scattered among them were soporific, low murmuring figures faintly illumined by the yellow light of a small lamp which sat on a tray at their side.

ON THE DAY OF which we relate, in a far corner of the room, Harry Franklin and Lilly Dinan faced each other in silence on one of the lower bunks. Between them was a lay-out whose appointments attested to their station in the underworld. The globe on their little brass lamp had been painfully cleaned. The *suey-pow* reclined in a dish of glass and brass. The *yen-hocks*, one of which the girl toyed with idly, were not of the ordinary variety: they were of the finest tempered steel, their handles wrapped with gold wire. Only the fingers of the underworld's aristocrats know the feeling of these substantial and pliable needles. Upon the lacquered tray, inlaid with gold-leaf, there was a small pair of silver manicure scissors for regulating the lamp wick, and an ivory-handled *yenshi-gow* which had been polished with oriental diligence. In addition, there were two small cloisonné ash-receivers and a hammered-brass holder full of gold-tipped cigarettes. A clean set. of gee-rags awaited at one side; and in a small ivory *toy* was a substance resembling molasses. The toy was nearly full, for Franklin and the girl were but sporadic smokers. They indulged in the drug gingerly and at intervals, and only when the exigencies of fellowship demanded it.

"It certainly feels good, Harry, to be away from New York and the gang," the girl commented contentedly. "But the best of it all is being with you. Red was always a good fellow and played square, but a girl wants little attentions that a man like him never thinks of. He didn't care anything about *me*. He never thought of anything but getting money. You don't, though, do you, Harry?"

Although Harry Franklin did not answer, it was true that he looked upon money merely as one of the results of life, not as a principal factor. He was a good-looking young man of about thirty, well-educated and possessed of a quiet refinement rarely found in the underworld. He loved danger and the excitement of uncertainty.

His nature was romantic rather than criminal. Had it not been for certain economic circumstances coming in juxtaposition with certain other psychological ones, he might have found his recreation hunting wild game in Africa or in a similar occupation where a man's fight to existence is constantly questioned.

FRANKLIN patted her affectionately on the cheek and lighted a cigarette. "Look here, Lil," he said, "now that we're married, why don't you give up Red altogether? The law is going to overtake him soon. His day has gone by. The world has changed, and Red has stood still. As a helper, he's useful; as a creative artist, he's as antedated as James Fenimore Cooper. He lacks that simplicity which comes from an understanding of men's hearts."

"Red would be willing to let you plan," said the girl. "Then we'll get along better," said Franklin. "Personally, I don't care much what happens. It's you I worry about now."

Lilly smiled happily. "The only trouble will be your—your unwillingness to 'play' anybody. Red doesn't hold your ideas."

"He'll have to," Franklin announced curtly. "I'll never take a cent from any one unless there's a mental battle involved, or unless the man is inherently dishonest. To that extent I'm an idealist. You see, I must feel I am a kind of Nemesis, a retribution, a sterilizer of men's souls."

"I don't know what you mean, Harry," the girl answered sadly, "but I wish we had enough money to drop it all. Since I've known you, I've lost my nerve. I'm always leery that you're going to get caught or that I'm going to get caught, and that we'll be separated."

"Don't worry your little head about that," Franklin consoled her.

She made a little *moue* and, drawing up her legs, settled comfortably back in the cushions while Harry Franklin, Bachelor of Arts by parental coercion and crook by personal choice, formulated and rejected a dozen plans for getting the better of his more hypocritical brothers.

THEY REMAINED in silence for some time. Then Franklin, who up to now had been indifferent to the new arrivals, instinctively, or rather in accord with that curious psychological law which informs one telepathically of things not tactically experienced, turned his gaze toward the door. A stocky, somewhat flashily dressed man entered. The new arrival exhibited a familiarity with the surroundings. Coming to the center of the room, he lighted a cigarette and looked round him. Franklin nudged Lilly and pointed to the new-comer. Then he called out in a loud tone of mock irritation: "Where's Mr. Fang? The membership here is not very exclusive."

The large man in the center of the room turned quickly toward the sound of the voice, an unpleasant look on his face.

"Well, I'll be pinched!" he exclaimed, his countenance clearing. "If there ain't a couple of crooks! I thought you'd have got sick of waiting for me and beat it. How goes it, Harry?" he asked good-naturedly, approaching the latter's bunk.

"Lethargically, as befits the climate," the other replied, while Lilly extended a delicate hand for Red Bernheim to shake.

The man took it with some hesitation. He looked first at the girl and then at 'her companion. "What—what's the meaning of this, Lil? Thought you were in Frisco." He was visibly annoyed.

"You guessed wrong, Red," the girl replied cheerily. "I'm here, and I'm here to stay as long as Harry does."

"It's the oldest story in the world," put in Franklin, taking the girl's hand. "When we left New York, we decided to be married. And here we are. Not very exciting, is it? But it has the advantage of being true."

Bernheim appeared to be too stunned to speak.

"Well, aren't we to be blessed by you, Red? Don't you wish us joy?" Franklin was laughing.

Red ignored the other's questions. "I suppose you two will be getting one of these bungalows with the built-in bookcases next and spending your evenings by the open fire."

"I wish we were," answered the girl seriously.

BERNHEIM hesitated. "Well, it's a bum trick to pull on a friend," he commented at length. "But I'm a man of my word, and if it wasn't for making Lil sore, I'd say 'to Hell with broads' anyway, But I ain't going to kick. Nobody'll ever be able to say that Red Bernheim held a grudge against a friend on a gal's account. But"—he leaned over closely to them and spoke in a voice not devoid of passion— "there's one thing I don't forget, and that's been done to me by a guy who owes to me everything he's got."

"Just as I was leading him into a good thing, he stole my money and got away with it." Bernheim snorted disgustedly. "Yes, sir, he got away with it!"

The two listeners looked at each other and laughed in mild derision. "I'd like to know the Artful Dodger that could get away with your money,' Franklin retorted.

"He'd have to be the wisest man on five continents."

"Wise!" roared Bernheim. "When you trust a guy and he beats it with your money, it ain't wisdom; it's ungratefulness."

After this comment he climbed into the bunk and settled himself comfortably. Waving away the coolie who was bringing a tray, he began expertly to roll a pill from Franklin's toy. After he had converted four of them into smoke in quick succession, amid an expectant silence, he sighed ecstatically and recounted his grievance:

"The day I was waiting for the train down at Weber's, Freddie Long drops in and tells me he managed to get a line on old Wimble's cellar where he keeps his goods. You know who Wimble is. He's the downtown clearing house for all the goods the boys can't get rid of at the hock-shops. He pays the boys about a tenth of what they ought to get and then blackmails 'em to boot; and Freddie swears he's a stool-pigeon too—sells information to the bulls."

"I know of Wimble," agreed Franklin. "He's made more money blackmailing the boys than he has cheating them on their hauls. If there was any justice in the scheme of things he'd have been up the river long since."

Bernheim nodded his head emphatically. "You know, he never banks his money and keeps his jewelry in the cellar. A lot of the boys have been drawn to his place for little visits. But it's a bad house to get mixed up in—full of burglar alarms, charged wires and watchmen."

BERNHEIM lighted a cigarette, and looked out into space. "I ain't the boy to balk at a hard job. And brains'll open a safe when jimmies won't. So I hunted up a young Englishman I knew named Carlisle, one of these swell boys, and-put it up to him. You've got to hand it to Carlisle, he's got nerve; and I hit him at just the right time. He was flat, and his working partner had got in the can a week before.

"The next A.M. I calls up old man Wimble, telling him I'm police headquarters and saying that I'll be around to see him a little later on a matter of importance. He didn't know me, so I was safe. When Carlisle and me goes up to the house he was looking for us.

"Mr. Wimble,' says I, 'we're sorry to trouble you, but this A.M. we rounded up a notorious cracksman who once made an attempt on your house.' This didn't surprise the old boy much. He was used to visits from the boys, but it gave him the opportunity to rail against the inefficiency of the police, the bum laws and the thieving qualities to be found in all human beings—the old hypocrite!

"I lets him finish, and then I goes on. 'Mr. Wimble,' I says, 'we rounded up a lot of the crook's swag at the same time, and we got a confession out of him in which he says that some of the goods belong to you—that he got 'em out of your safe in the cellar 'While I'm saying this I draws out the confession on police stationery and shows it to him, but he's too excited to look at it.

"'Impossible!' he yells; and for two minutes he raves round the room like a crazy man. Then, I says, 'I sincerely hope, sir, that it may prove incorrect... Even if it ain't,' I goes on, 'you understand if there's anything gone, the chances are we can get it back for you, provided you let us know what's missing. We can warn the pawn shops.'

"I hadn't finished my spiel when the old boy gets up excitedly and goes down cellar, us after him. For ten minutes he monkeys with the catch on his safe. It sure was complicated. At last, leaning to it like a Roman, he managed to pull a door outward. We helped him and stood respectfully behind. The old boy picks up a lot of cases and looks into 'em. At last he turns to us and says, peevish-like: 'You've made me a lot of trouble and worry for nothing. Al my property's intact.'

"The old boy starts to shut the door again, and just then Carlisle and me gets busy. I steps suddenly and puts one hand over his mouth. Carlisle kicks his feet from under him, and we wraps him up like a piece of hop gum. Then we dumps the contents of the plush boxes which held his ill-gotten jewelry into a sack, We're just beginning to go a little deeper into the safe when somebody comes walking down the stairs."

"CARLISLE pockets the swag quick, and I says something, pretending to talk to the old boy. We walks quickly out just in time to meet a guy on the first landing. Seeing us come up alone, he looks suspicious and leans over the railing, calling to the old man. Carlisle and I clears the remaining steps four at a time and gets to the front door just in time to hear the guy on the stairs shout. We're no more than on the front steps when *Bing!*—a shot goes by my ear, and Carlisle gets a piece of shattered front door glass in the ear. We covers the front lawn in nothing, and hops the machine waiting for us. There's a commotion behind us, and another taxi starts after us. Just as we turn the corner Carlisle and I jump out, going in opposite directions, while the car goes on fast.

"I goes to Weber's and waits for Carlisle who has the shiners. I waits all night. He doesn't show up. Maybe, thinks I, they've grabbed him. So I reads the morning papers. Nothing doing. Then I know I've been a sucker. Nothing to do but to come on to California as I'd planned. I puts on some bum whiskers and gets down to the Penn. station in time to get the flyer for Chicago. Then luck hits me. Carlisle didn't know I was headed for the Pacific or he wouldn't have taken a chance. But there he was, with a mustache and goatee, looking like a dude, waiting for the train to pull out. He didn't see me, and he wouldn't have known me if he had. So I keeps close the whole trip, gets sick and stays in my berth. When he hits Los Angeles I tails Mr. Carlisle to the Angelus Hotel.

"That was last Tuesday. The next day he takes the Interurban and goes to Santa Monica. I didn't say anything to him. I thought I'd do a little thinking first. Now I comes up here to Fang's just in time to meet my old friends, Harry and Lil. That's my story, as the shop girl says."


"YOU SHOWED true physical courage, Red," Franklin said at length. "It isn't the sort of adventure that would appeal to me. It lacked the essence of true romance."

"Not delicate enough—huh?" asked Bernheim sarcastically.

"Well, let us say, not subtle enough," Franklin smiled back. "It was over too suddenly, and—forgive me—it didn't require much thought. You always think of the end: I'm more interested in the means."

"You've got to live," remonstrated the other. "A guy can't negotiate excitement at the green grocer's; and love don't pay your tailor. Sometimes I think you're a nut—a high-brow nut,"

Franklin ignored Bernheim's excursion into psychiatry, and said, "Red, if any one would guarantee me a moderate living, I'd agree to return every cent I took from society... However," he added, lest Bernheim should try to open an ethical discussion, "from your viewpoint, you deserve your share of the dividends Carlisle has. And if I can help you, I'll do it."

"If you do, we'll cut 'em three ways," replied Bernheim, ignoring the other's fantastic morality.


THE Arcadia Hotel at Santa Monica occupies one of the most beautiful sites along the Pacific coast. It clings to the summit of a high cliff overlooking the ultra-blue sea, and there are violet headlands to the north and south. A few miles inland rise the majestic undulations of the Sierra Madre Mountains, whose highest peaks are white with snow throughout the entire summer.

On a typical California day in early May, when the sky was like a giant sapphire and the birds were busy building their nests along the eaves of the veranda, a large Mercedes car drew up before the hotel entrance. From it stepped a quietly dressed and well-proportioned young man of about thirty, followed by a diffident young woman many years his junior. She was a slender and delicately lovely creature, whose tight black curls set off a sensitive oval face. She was dressed in a semi-tailored broad cloth suit of blue-green, with a little hat to match trimmed with orange and purple fuchsias. Her small, but not too small, feet were shod in the latest style, and white glacé gloves snugly covered her mobile hands. Her fragile and child-like beauty immediately attracted the attention of those guests who were gathered on the veranda. The young woman took her companion's arm tentatively as he crossed to the great front door which led into the rotunda, and stood timidly behind him as he registered.

The man asked for the best apartment on the ocean side, and, after some instructions regarding his conspicuously new baggage, followed the boy who led the way to the bridal suite.

AMONG THE lookers on was Sir Rodney Beauchamp, Bart. He was leaning back rather stiffly on the window seat caressingly stroking his carefully waxed mustache. : "A charming girl," he murmured, "*chaussée et gantée avec art*. Slim and dainty as the new moon. And to think," he added, addressing himself to no one in particular, "that the inevitable ennui of marriage will so soon destroy her girlishness."

Sir Rodney was himself a new arrival at the Arcadia, but he had, by his quixotic manners and his gift of pleasing speech, quickly endeared himself, if not to the hearts, at any rate to the brains, of those moneyed ladies whom a cruel fate had deprived of physical charm. His genial gallantry together with his baronetcy, had won for him a place of high esteem among his fellow guests. He assumed an attitude of decadence when talking to ladies with marriageable daughters; and when in the company of men, he exuded a boredom which, far from being offensive, seemed to those about him the natural condition of a man who had lived life fully in the midst of unusual advantages.

Sir Rodney was at his best that evening at dinner. He was mildly delighted to find that the bride and groom who had arrived that afternoon had been given a place at his table. He had been favorably impressed by the appearance of the young woman, and, let it be known, Sir Rodney, who posed as a connoisseur of feminine pulchritude, was most exacting in his tastes. From the very first he evinced an interest in the young bride, and she, in her turn, far from resenting that interest, treated him with consideration.

The following evening at the hotel ball she danced with Sir Rodney oftener than the conventions dictated. But since the young husband showed no indication of resenting the baronet's actions, Sir Rodney felt justified in pushing his attentions as far as good taste permitted.

MRS. MARTEN—such was the bride's name—grew in popularity among the summer visitors; and Mr. Marten likewise came in for his share of notice from the feminine contingent. However, the bride and groom and Sir Rodney were much together to the exclusion of the other guests. Nearly every morning they would motor along the beautiful Ocean Avenue and disappear into the fastnesses of the rugged Santa Monica Canyon.

Perhaps if Mrs. Marten had not seemed so eager for the attention of the baronet the other guests of the hotel might not have begun to talk scandal. But whether this was the reason, or whether they saw in the young bride a serious competitor in their plans to make an advantageous marriage for their daughters, the fact remained that it was but a short time before they were breathing unpleasant remarks about the constant propinquity of Sir Rodney and Mrs. Marten. This gossip developed shortly' into a malicious wagging of tongues. Even the men were not slow in adding their disapproval to the general protests.

Mrs. Marten, however, took no heed of the social upheaval she had caused. Rather did she seem to encourage it. The result was that there came a day when she was openly cut by several of the older and more strait-laced women. But even after this the young bride, despite her apparent lack of sophistication, paid scant attention to their condemnations and acts of disapproval. Nor did her husband appear to object either. By his manner he announced his entire satisfaction with his wife's conduct. There were those who believed he was blinded to the true state of affairs, while more vicious ones suggested that he saw and did not care. Thus a difference of opinion added the elements of speculation and argument to a discussion already reaching the dimensions of a serious scandal.

ALL BLAME, however, was not affixed to Mrs. Marten and her husband. There was something in the youthful innocence of the bride as well as in the frank, open expression of the: bridegroom, which, while it did not entirely disarm criticism, nevertheless tempered that criticism with sympathy. Sir Rodney was the principal target for the abuse of the quidnuncs. His decided seniority in years led the hotel guests to lay most of the onus of the affair on his doorstep. His popularity had been the result of American snobbishness, rather than the outcome of any genuine admiration; and the reaction against such a spurious popularity proved very formidable. His attitudinizing, formerly so facinating, became the subject of bitter ridicule. It was even suggested in one or two quarters that Sir Rodney, like many other Englishmen who had settled in California, was a "pensioner"— that is, an undesirable member of a worthy family, who was allowed an income provided he absent himself permanently from the family circle. One gentleman from the middle west, who had taken no less than three Cook's tours. through Europe and felt himself qualified to speak authoritatively on the aristocracy of England, intimated that Sir Rodney was not a baronet at all, but a fortune-hunting impostor. This observation, however, was too radical for the other guests to accept with entire credence, but it led to many doubts and misgivings. And the fact that it had now become known that Mrs. Marten was enormously wealthy in her own name, lent color to the middle westerner's suppositions.

IT WAS THE night of the Arcadia's formal ball, and the hall was full to overflowing. Early in the evening Mrs. Marten entered, leaning languorously on Sir Rodney's arm. Mr. Marten was nowhere to be seen, but it soon became known that a half hour before he had suddenly been called to the city on business. The young bride, as on previous occasions, devoted her entire attentions to Sir Rodney, dancing nearly every number with him. She was in her gayest and most captivating mood, and between every dance she insisted that her companion bring her refreshments from the punch bowl and that he indulge as often as she. Several times he protested mildly, but she always overcame his objections with sweet cajolery.

"The spring is so short," she said with a trace of wistfulness in her voice. "And I shall be going away so soon. Should we not be as happy as we can?" He leaned toward her expectantly. "And tonight, with Archie away, there is no one to scold or to frown at me if I appear too happy."

"Your slightest wish," Sir Rodney said, touching her arm gently, "shall be my law— for evermore."

"Then don't moralize for just this one night, dear friend," she answered.

Before the evening was half over, certain of the guests had begun to remark the frequency with which Sir Rodney visited the punch bowl, and when a little later from a corner of the balcony an unusually loud peal of Mrs. Marten's silver laughter rang out, there were those who nodded their heads knowingly.

THE EVENING'S festivities had been over for an hour and Sir Rodney had just extinguished the lights in his room when there came a subdued knock on his door. As he arose to answer the summons, he connected this unusual event with Mrs. Marten, although there was no reason for his so doing. However, his intuition was correct, for when he opened the door a porter handed him a note which ran:

My Dear Sir Rodney:

> Please forgive me, but I feel so unwell and nervous that I must get out into the air for a little walk. Would you please be so good as to call at my room and fetch me? Otherwise I am afraid I should have to call the house physician."

It was signed merely with Mrs. Marten's initials.

Sir Rodney read it with a beating heart and was about to dismiss the porter when the latter informed him that "the lady particularly wished the note returned." She had said that he would understand. Sir Rodney understood perfectly, and handed back the note, at the same time sending word that he would be down at once.

Five minutes later, having quickly donned a lounge suit and seized his hat, he descended the stairs to the Marten apartments. The door to the drawing room was slightly ajar and there was a light within.

Sir Rodney was too discreet to knock and understood the meaning of the door having been left slightly open. He shoved it cautiously and took a step into the room....

A moment before, Mr. Marten, returning unexpectedly, had crossed the office to the elevator and spoken a friendly word to the night clerk. It happened, therefore, that before Sir Rodney had scarcely entered the Martens' drawing room he found himself caught in the vise of two powerful arms and thrown violently to the floor.

"You cur!" It was Marten's voice that assailed the startled man's ear.

SIR RODNEY was a man of considerable physical prowess, and his temperament was such that he would not submit passively to a trouncing from another, especially with his reputation at stake. He began to give battle valiantly; and the two men rolled over and over in the doorway, groaning and breathing heavily. Although, like a man having much to lose, the Englishman fought desperately, he was unable to cope with the superior tactics of his opponent. Chairs were upset; a vase was swept off a table by the door; and the two men finally lay panting in the hallway, the young husband in a position of superiority. The baronet's arms were pinioned against his side, and he was unable to move.

Along the hallways many doors had been opened slightly, and

the occupants of the rooms, attracted by the unusual noise, were peering out. Mr. Marten at that moment  raised his voice in a cry for help, which made the empty corridors of the old hotel. Echo resoundingly, The night clerk and his assistant, as well as other employees of the house, rushed to the scene of the disorder; and many guests, donning temporary attire, crowded round the excited throng in front of the Marten apartments.

The house detective soon made his appearance, and on being informed by Mr. Marten of what had happened, helped the two antagonists to their feet, keeping hold of Sir Rodney's arm with a grip of iron.

"I returned unexpectedly from the city," Mr. Marten explained, "and just as I entered my room I found this gentleman slinking out of it."

Several of the guests passed remarks in low tones and nodded their heads like wiseacres. They had lost all sympathy for the baronet, and his conduct that evening during the ball had completed the alienation.

They were now prepared to believe the worst.

"It's a put-up job! It's a plant!" stormed Sir Rodney excitedly, giving vent to an argot which seemed strangely incompatible with that gentleman's culture.

Mr. Marten paid no heed, but rushing into the drawing room and through the open door into the boudoir, flooded the apartment with light. Many of the spectators, including the hotel servants, followed him expectantly.

AT THE SIGHT which met their gaze they gave vent to a low exclamation of mingled astonishment and anger. On the bed, gagged and tied, lay the prostrate figure of the young bride, like a heap of silk lace and warm ivory.

Mr. Marten halted, and there was terror written on his face. The next instant he had caught his young wife in his power ful embrace. Tearing off the gag, he covered her inert face with kisses.

"Send for the house physician—quick!" he commanded, as he severed with his pocket-knife the bonds about Mrs. Marten's wrists and ankles.

But the doctor was already there, his nose professionally snuffing the slight odor of chloroform which hung like a light haze over the room. One of the women guests, her eyes streaming with tears, hurriedly came forward with smelling salts and, lifting the cameo-like head, set herself the task of bringing the prostrate young woman back to consciousness.

During these few minutes no one had spoken. Everyone had

crowded into the room, including the house detective, who still clung to Sir Rodney's arm. For the moment Mr. Marten had remained oblivious to all save his wife, but when she began to move uneasily and the doctor had said she was not injured, he turned savagely to Sir Rodney, who seemed overcome by astonishment.

"So, you're a thief, are you?" he began angrily. "Under the guise of friendship you come here to my wife's rooms when you thought I was safely away—"

He would have said more but the distracted wail from Mrs. Marten interrupted him.

"Oh, Archie, what has happened?" she exclaimed in a broken voice. "That's for you to say," he answered tenderly. "Try to think hard and let me know."

"It's a put-up job, I tell you!" bellowed Sir Rodney. But he was silenced by the house detective.

Every one was waiting for Mrs. Marten to speak.

"Oh, yes, I remember now," she began in a terrified voice. "It was all so dreadful. I had just fallen asleep when I woke with a start— you know the feeling you have that some one is near you. I thought it was my husband and called him; but just as I spoke a horrible wet rag smelling of chloroform was crushed over my mouth, I heard an awful hammering sound in my ears—and then I woke up with all you people here. . . . Oh, Archie," she hurried on, "what has happened? And who's the thief?"

THE young husband laughed ironically. "There's your thief," he said bitterly, pointing at Sir Rodney.

Mrs. Marten was too astonished to reply at once. "Sir Rodney!" she exclaimed, unbelieving. "It can't be. Why, he was with me all the evening. There's some mistake."

"Say, look here," began Sir Rodney. "I tell you this is a hoax. It's a put-up job." Again the house detective silenced him, adding some unpleasant threat.

Mr, Marten looked at Sir Rodney sneeringly. "A put-up job, is it? I remember now how confoundedly interested you were when my wife was telling you once about her jewels" He crossed quickly to the dresser and, opening the top drawer, took out several plush boxes and opened them. They were empty.

The young woman jumped up terrified. "Where have my jewels gone?" she cried. "All mother's presents—and yours, too." She looked round her distractedly. "Oh, Archie, will we ever get them back?"

There was a tense silence. Then Mr. Marten turned to the house detective. "Search him," he ordered peremptorily.

Sir Rodney tried to jerk himself free from the officer's grip, but the night clerk and two porters seized him from behind.

"This farce has lasted long enough," the prisoner bellowed, losing all control of himself, "She sent me a note and asked me to come down here. As soon as I got here this man knocked me down."

The house detective was going through Sir Rodney's pockets, and: before the other had finished speaking he drew out a handful of jewels—diamond pendants, ruby and emerald rings, two sets of pearl earrings and an exquisite set of brilliant sapphires.

"There they are!" exclaimed Mrs. Marten. "Oh, Archie, thank God!"

Mr. Marten stepped up to Sir Rodney. "A put-up job, was it? Now what about this note my wife sent you? Let's see it"

"I returned it," stammered Sir Rodney. A murmur of disbelief greeted his words. "I tell you the porter brought it to me."

At this point the clerk pushed forward two men in uniform. "Which one of these men," he demanded, "brought you the note?"

"Neither," replied Sir Rodney.

"Then no porter brought you the note," chuckled the clerk, feeling keenly his importance in having cleared up a valuable point.

SIR RODNEY was now gaining control of himself. "I tell you," he remarked calmly, "that you people are being victimized. I begin to see light on this whole thing, and I'll tell you something—"

Mr. Marten interrupted: he had evidently been expecting this moment. "I've got something to say to Sir Rodney, and Sir Rodney has something to say to me. He has insulted and compromised my wife, and there is a personal factor here which has to be settled." He turned to the crowd. "Will you kindly wait in the next room a moment? Surely you understand—the situation is so intimate and delicate a one."

His request was in the nature of a command, and they turned and departed.

"It's all right," added Mr. Marten to the house detective who had hesitated.. "I'll take care of the affair. Only wait in there a minute. This is a personal thing."

The house detective went reluctantly, leaving Mr. and Mrs. Marten and Sir Rodney alone. His duty was to stay, but he sensed a subtle finesse of social usage in the request, which he thought advisable to recognize.

"Now look here, Carlisle," the husband began, "there's no advantage to be gained in giving this affair away. "I'm Harry Franklin: you've heard of me, no doubt; through Bernheim. You didn't play a straight game with Red, and while you deserve punishment, you're going to be allowed to go free. All that these people can do to you is to arrest you tonight. There'll be no one to appear against you tomorrow. Tell them then you've been victimized. They'll believe it because they'll find we've disappeared and. left all our new baggage. You'll be discharged then with apologies." He paused. "If you can't see the advisability of that course, Red's determined to tell the police who you "are and how you got the jewelry. State's evidence. He'll go free; and you'll serve time."

Carlisle smiled faintly. "Yes, I've heard of you, Franklin" he said resignedly. "You've beat me to it. I wish I had, you for a partner. Your methods are A1."

Franklin overlooked the compliment. "You have courage, Carlisle. If it wasn't for your—well, ethical weaknesses, I'd be glad to work with you, but temperamentally, I'm afraid we'd clash."

FRANKLIN made a gesture of finality as the other was about to speak. Then he continued: "Now listen. To-morrow call at Woo Ching Fang's. I'll leave five hundred for you there. You're a long way from home, and after all, your courage deserves some compensation. Only, after this, play the game according to the rules. There's such a thing as honor everywhere."

Before the other could answer, Franklin went to the door and opened it.

"Sir Rodney has made a full apology to my wife for his extraordinary behavior and his insults," he announced, "He's ready to give himself up now."

Just then a heavy-set chauffeur, with his cap visor pulled well down over his eyes, appeared at the edge of the crowd.

"Is Mr. Beauchamp here?" he inquired. He caught sight of Sir Rodney and came forward. "The taxi is waiting, sir. You'll have to hurry if you want to make that train. I've been waiting for you, but there wasn't nobody in the lobby, so I came up."

Sir Rodney peered speechless at the newcomer and said nothing.

"Going to take a train, were you?" the house detective said, and chuckled. He led his victim downstairs.

The guests, after offering their congratulations and condolences, dispersed.

"I feel so nervous," Mrs. Marten said. "Let's keep that taxi and go for a ride. I need a little fresh air."

"The very thing, dearest," the fond husband answered.

FIFTEEN minutes later they were speeding along in the moonlight on the road to Hollywood.

"I take it all back, Lil," good-naturedly called the chauffeur, leaning back. "You broads are still there with the goods… Did you have any trouble, Harry?"

"Not a bit, Red," answered Franklin. "I took the jewels from his trunk while he was dancing and slipped them into his pocket during our little struggle. I took off my porter's costume while he was dressing to go to Lil, vanished out the rear way and entered from the front as if I had just returned from the city. He saw the wisdom of keeping quiet at the close of the game…My only complaint is that there wasn't enough opposition. The affair was only mildly exciting."

"Just as I said," Bernheim commented with unfeigned satisfaction, "the guy that's full o' larceny falls the easiest."

# THE KING'S COUP

THE little church bells sent forth their deep tones along the roadway of grim and ancient Kilauea. Their monotonous music raced along up the precipitous green slopes, leaping into the crisp diamond air above and on into the far blue sky. A sun, whose brilliance seemed lost in a sky almost as bright as itself, transformed the countryside into an unreal land of lemon-yellow, rose-madder and blue—a land like a painting by 'Turner, devoid of everything heavy and gross. The few tourists who hurried by from the Volcano House seemed out of place in this land of mirage. Their talk was too loud, their laughter too harsh, their reality was like a blasphemy.

As the figure of a young woman drove past them toward the chapel further on, an involuntary hush passed over them. They looked at her with a touch of wonder, as though realizing their isolation and ashamed of their desecration of so holy a day. The girl seemed to personify the day's calm spirit. Her face was pale and thoughtful; her eyes reflected the vastness of the hills and air; and her jet-black curls symbolized the shadowy mystery of this southern land which the white man has forever profaned. She was youthful, as is the spirit of the island people, yet she exhaled that subtle sadness which one feels in their music and language. Hers was the youth which has had more than its share of those sorrows which, instead of making old, only make beautiful. Her beauty was not alone superficial; there was an added intangibility, as with the beauty of an exotic flower or with the serenity of a south sea island twilight. She went by silently, her head bent a little forward as if in meditation. At the sight of her, those in the roadway, both men and women, felt more alive to the still glory about them, more inclined to silence and meditation.

"So," said one man to his companion, "in spite of our experience there are after all some lovely island girls left." He was a poet, and added: "That one seemed like a moonlight night."

"Did you see her mouth?" the other asked enthusiastically. He, too, was a poet. "It was like a poinsettia. And her face was that of a sensuous nun, unawakened as yet, but like smoldering Mokuaweoweo, only waiting until the right combination of events, and then—you can guess the results."

ALTHOUGH the speaker had a reputation as a man who knows women, he was far afield in his present estimate. In the first place Lilly Dinan was not a native of the islands. Neither was she an unawakened child. Nor yet did she even remotely resemble a nun. To the contrary, she belonged to a class which modern ethical culturists designate as "outcasts." But, like many species of flowers, Lilly had retained her pristine loveliness in the most adverse surroundings. It was true she was on her way to church, But it was not altogether her instincts that led her to sanctuary. She was acting under orders from her husband; and orders from him were to be obeyed while life remained.

For three months she had been weary of the life from which she had sprung. She desired to leave it, to embrace an existence which held only simple joys without dangers or surprises. 'The woman in Lilly Dinan had awakened' at the warmth of a genuine love. She had had many suitors, but until she met Harry Franklin, no one had aroused in her a constant desire for their presence. Not one had been able to make himself necessary, to inspire in her both confidence and fear.

But with Franklin it was different. She feared him; yet she wanted nothing more than to forego the fierce excitements of a life lived beyond the pale of the law, with its consequent rewards and risks—a life which she realized held a deep and fundamental joy and a challenge to all who followed it. She had been forced into the life as a child, but she had never complained. She lived it objectively: spiritually she had remained aloof. True, she had felt the lure of its wildness, its romantic outlawry, its dangers; and she had-no grudge against the law-abiding. classes out of whose stupidity she made capital.

NOW MORE THAN ever, her past actions seemed to belong to another existence, to another: Lilly Dinan. The conservatism which hides in the depths of all women's hearts was slowly asserting itself, bringing with it the consciousness of a long dormant, protective instinct. She feared to look frankly into the future, knowing that the majority of those who gained sustenance by the means she and Franklin employed were sooner or later broken by the law they held so lightly. This fact meant more to her now than formerly, for separation from Franklin spelled tragedy, and she shrank from it. She had resolved several times to try to persuade him to give up the game before it was too late, though she knew it would be no easy matter. He had not been born to it, and experienced no intimate fear of its consequences. But she knew fear, and had always known it. And to-day that fear gripped her heart with unusual tenacity as she traversed the path that led to the bungalow-like villa where she was temporarily diving.

Harry Franklin sat on the big veranda awaiting her.' He was in earnest conversation with a wizened, wrinkled man prematurely old from long years spent in the pounding tropical sun. Franklin was a clean-cut young man scarcely out of his twenties, lithe, athletic and with the undeniable marks of gentle breeding—a striking contrast to his carelessly clad, heavy featured companion.

As Lilly mounted the steps both men rose to greet her. A Japanese servant rushed forward to take charge of her horse. Stiffly the older man came forward and led her to a chair with a chivalry which, though affable, had grown awkward through desuetude. Franklin sat down without a word.

At Woo Ching Fang's, overlooking the historic old Plaza of Los Angeles, Lilly Dinan and Franklin had foregathered five weeks ago to discuss future plans with their old friend and "business partner," Red Bernheim. A change of *venue* was imperative, for, since their Arcadia adventure, the City of Our Lady of the Angels had become untenable. San Francisco also was unavailable, being too busy rebuilding after— the earthquake to pay much heed to sensational methods of amassing easy fortunes. Seattle, now that the spring freshet had again opened the Yukon, was divested of miners, and the regular inhabitants were more than taken care of by a large and competent brigade of light-fingered gentry, Portland was too new and offered few advantages. Chicago and New York and the other eastern cities, besides being dangerous, had already sent forth their moneyed population into the capitals of Europe.

They had about decided to rest until the autumn, when Mr. Fang himself came over to them and sat smilingly on the edge of their bunk. Unlike the great majority of Chinese in California, Mr. Fang was a gentleman of culture. No I's and ah's garnished his conversation. He spoke fluent English with that fine modulation of which only high caste Chinese are capable.

"Well, gentlemen," he began (a woman is taken for granted in such circles), "why not Honolulu? A virginal pearl in a setting of purple sea,' as the steamship prospectus puts it. An ideal place for gentlemen of your avocation. The islands are, full of pioneers who have made fortunes without realizing it. There are small settlers and farmers avid for gain who will lend their assistance to certain paying enterprises, as well as men along the beaches ready for anything from pineapple stealing to a coup d'état. An ideal spot," he smiled complacently, "the halting place for all trans-Pacific travel to and from San Francisco and Seattle, Batavia, Hong Kong and Sydney. A rich harvest, gentlemen,. And not alone in fruit gathering.' He beamed beneficently, like a father upon his children.

Franklin sat up admiringly. "Your advice is admirable," he said. "Perhaps you know of some spot in the islands where congenial friends may foregather occasionally?"

"Perhaps so," said Mr. Fang. "I shall consult my desk." He glided away through the heavy odorous smoke, and the only sound of his going was the faint click of a door.

THE NEXT DAY Woo Ching Fang handed Franklin a folded sheet of paper. On it were written the address of a rich friend in Honolulu and the names and where abouts of several Hawaiians and Chinese, who might prove serviceable.

Those who were careful in their attire and above suspicion were designated with a cross. Those who came in the category of beach combers (because they are washed up like waves on all sea ports) were left *au nature*. A brief list of rich natives and native-born American planters followed, together with the names of docks where boats could be rented in case of hurried departure—boats which would take one to neighboring groups of islands without the customary clearance papers or asking of indiscreet questions.

Such a memorandum in the possession of a less scrupulous man than Franklin might have led to a political upheaval of considerable extent. But Woo Ching Fang knew that with its present owner the paper, as well as the knowledge which went with it, was safe. There is but one law in the underworld; to remain true to a trust; and its transgressors are dealt with in a manner so summary and efficacious that, for expedition and justice, it leaves the military court martial far behind. And another thing, Harry Franklin enjoyed the reputation as the "squarest" man in his profession. To most of his associates he was an enigma. In many of their safest enterprises he refused to participate on moral grounds. His victim, he had always said, must be inherently guilty. An honest man, no matter how gullible, was safe it his hands. This eccentricity in temperament was laid to his college training, for it was known that Franklin was once an honor student at Yale. And his refinement (called "class") was put forward as a mysterious condition which, in some recondite manner, was supposed to explain away his vagaries of action and ideation in a wholly satisfactory way.

THE DAY AFTER Franklin had received Mr. Fang's memoranda, he and Bernheim and the girl were heading westward through the Golden Gate in one of the big Jim Hill boats which touch at Honolulu, Tutuila and Australia enroute for Nagasaki. A week later at twilight, when the shore lights were just beginning to send their glinting spears over the shadowy water, Oahu was sighted. The island was a low, rolling handful of land, the green of whose slopes was now turning to violet along the horizon. As the steamer rounded the point of Diamond Head and nosed its way into Pearl Harbor, above which the giant palm trees jabbed their feathery tops into the graying sky, a boatload of dark, sweet-voiced natives, with multi-colored flowers draped round their necks and in their dark hair, rowed alongside and began singing the minor strains of *"Aloha-Oe"*—the "welcome" song of the island— accompanied by *ukeleles* and guitars.

The next morning, after a night spent at the Royal Hawaiian Hotel, Franklin and his two companions wandered about the beaches near the town and along the countryside. They visited the native quarters and indulged themselves in the sights tourists know so well. Franklin and Lilly were radiantly happy and played in the low surf like two children.

The experience which pleased them the most, however, was the witnessing of a shark hunt, a sport widely indulged in by the Hawaiians. In return for a gratuity, they saw in the mist of early morning, a great brown fisherman in a small boat leap into the sea directly in front of an oncoming black fin. With a loud laugh he plunged his long knife into a white belly just as the great man-eater rolled over and charged. Then the man arose to the surface, knife in air, and was dragged breathless back into the boat.

The days went swiftly with no thought on the part of Franklin or the girl but to enjoy to the full the novel wonder of the tropics. But there was work to be done. Bernheim was becoming impatient. Franklin as yet had formulated no plan, and he knew the responsibility for its creation would devolve on him. He scoured Honolulu for suggestions, and visited Woo Ching Fang's friends. But he learned nothing.

ONE DAY, HOWEVER, while reading casually a short history of the Islands, which embraced the Hawaiian, Society, Friendly, Navigator and Fiji groups, he noted with some surprise that the original native rulers of them were treated with all consideration by the great white men's government, that they received every courtesy due to royal personages. There was one account of a certain Monalukki, former sire of Payata Island in the Fiji group, who insisted on keeping his harem, continued his depredations at the head of his tribe into neighboring islands, and stole from, cheated, and lied to the English officials at every opportunity. He had been educated at Stanford University, and his suave manners had for many years deceived his conquerors and the men he hated. When officials were sent to criticize his conduct he received them with quixotic civility, repudiated their charges so far as he was personally concerned, indignantly accused one of his henchmen, and straightway ordered the of fender's severed head to be brought before the complaining official, who, at the sight, was glad to accept any excuses and retire. Old Monalukki had received many; warnings, but never a punitive expedition.

This account, written with a touch of sarcasm, interested Franklin in no casual and superficial way. And it came about that Mr. Samuel Saunders received a visit which, though he knew it not, was a direct result of Franklin's discovery of this bit of history.

SAUNDERS WAS one of the checked names on Woo Ching Fang's list. An American citizen, although half Kanaka, he was born in the islands forty-eight years before of a Yankee father and a native girl, ,hrough some service to the native government (at that time controlled by the famous and. lovely Queen Liliuokalani), Saunders, Sr., had received vast grants of land on the Island of Hawaii, about thirty miles from Hilo, between the craters of Kilauea and Mokuaweoweo. In 1894, a year after the American occupation, he had died, only to be followed a few months later by his native wife. Samuel Saunders, the only son, had continued his father's work. He lived the life of a bachelor hermit, driven to such an existence largely because of the unsociable attitude of unmixed Americans who shrank instinctively from Saunders's Maori blood. Isolation had engendered defiance in him. Brooding over real or imagined wrongs committed by the white man against those he called his own people, had made him cruel to all pale-faced intruders.

He had amassed a considerable fortune from his vast pineapple and cane ranches in Hawaii and Moki, and, being able to spend but little of it, had come to look upon the amassing of money as a fetish.' Franklin had settled on Saunders as a man worth knowing. Touching at Hilo to verify his information, he had gone inland to the Volcano House, posing as a farmer desirous of settling in the neighborhood. In his search for land he had been directed to Saunders, and had driven with Lilly to the old man's house ostensibly to invest in real estate. Saunders had asked them to dinner, and so pleased had he 'been with his guests that a week-end in the old planter's house had followed. At length an invitation hat been extended to them to remain in Saunders villa until they had found a location.

In the outposts of civilization many conventional rules are suspended; and it had created no comment that the lonely Saunders had offered indefinite hospitality to the young couple. Nor were there comments when Franklin absented himself for days at a time for business trips to Hilo and Honolulu, leaving Lilly to the fatherly care of the old man. No one knew, however, that when Franklin's back was turned. Saunders invariably launched out upon a comic courtship of Lilly.

Her beauty, coupled with the fact that Franklin treated her with scant courtesy, led Saunders into the most grotesque avowals. The young woman pretended to take them seriously but always kept herself at arm's length. Saunders, never more earnest in his life, received his rebuffs in a way that made his servants suffer. He justified himself in his advances by Franklin's brutal attitude toward his wife, and used it as a basis for his amatory appeals. Lilly would meet his asseverations with platitudes concerning her wifehood and the duty she owed her child which at present was in the States. She must start this, child honorably, she explained. She must suffer in silence the indifference of her husband. She must set an example of uprightness. At these remarks Saunders would groan and pace the floor, as if confronted by the most colossal problem man has yet had to solve. But he was not ready to forego his wooing. His desire was only enhanced by this temporary ethical defeat, and he told himself, and Lilly, too, that time would surely bring about, an honorable solution.

One morning after a three days' absence, Franklin returned bringing news that he had met an old friend he had known in San Francisco five years before—Mona-lukki, the King of Payata.

"We shall have to entertain him," he informed Lilly in Saunders's presence. "To morrow we must go to Hilo to the hotel and get rooms." Lilly protested, suggesting that he go alone.

At this Franklin became angry. "Is it demanding too much to ask you to help entertain one of my friends? It's his first visit here, and he's traveling as a private citizen. Otherwise he would have all the attention he wanted. You're going—and you're going pleasantly; and that's the end of it" he added with finality. Then he turned to Saunders. "I should like very much to have you join us. It would be a pleasure to be able to return at least a part of your hospitality."

Saunders muttered some thanks without committing himself. That night, however, Lilly spoke to him alone, and the conversation resulted in Saunders's insisting upon Franklin foregoing his trip to Hilo and bringing the monarch to his own house for a visit. After mild protestations, Franklin consented to the arrangements.

KING MONALUKKI was a large man, uncommonly brown and with a Mongolian cast of features. His cheek bones were high, his nose flat, and his forehead low and sloping. He spoke excellent English, and his conversation at first had to do mostly with sports both in the Western States and in the islands. On the second day of his visit, however, his talk became more intimate. He had a violent hatred for the English and referred to them as dogs and thieves. Saunders agreed heartily, adding that the white man blasted like a pest, all places he touched. The king and Saunders seemed to like each other. For hours at a time they discussed the superiority of the old system of government, 'and denounced the stupidities and injustices of the white men's régime.

On the third night, when Lilly had retired and the men sat drinking and smoking, the king began a recital of his own grievances. The white man, it seemed, had practiced all manner of inhuman schemes upon him, leaving him practically bankrupt. But he had a way of getting even, and he informed his listeners that it would be only a short time before he would have deserted his throne for a life in Paris befitting his position.

Franklin, interested, asked him for particulars. The king was reluctant to tell; but later that evening Franklin was so persistent and the wine flowed so freely that the scheme was related.

The next day Franklin talked earnestly with Saunders, and it came about that the two men offered their services and their financial help to the wronged monarch in his plan for avenging himself. If the plan succeeded—and there was every reason why it should—Saunders would be able to make in one coup as much as he earned in a year. He trusted Franklin, and had a genuine liking for the king. Furthermore, there was no danger in the plan.

BRIEFLY THE adventure was this: In a little island about 1800 miles south of Hawaii lived a friend of King Monalukki, a high-caste Chinese who for years had been a dealer in prepared opium. This Oriental, who used the island as a depot, smuggled his product into Mexico, from where it was rushed across the border into the United States. At the fall of the old Mexican republic under Diaz, which had resulted in a tightening up of the customs supervisions both in Mexico and the States, this illicit dealer suddenly found himself unable to dispose of his treasure. He was now anxious to sell it for next to nothing.

He had in his possession on this island thousands of pounds of Li-un, the finest brand of *shandoo*, or pure opium. King Monalukki, as a royal personage, was exempt from all custom inspection of baggage, and was therefore able to bring into the United States as much secret luggage as he desired. His plan was to buy up this Li-un, fill his trunks with it, and walk into San Francisco, where he would have no difficulty in disposing of it at twenty dollars a pound. The part in the affair to be played by Saunders was the furnishing of an adequate boat. For this he was to receive fifty per cent of the profits. Franklin was to manage the expedition, for which the king had agreed to pay him liberally out of his own share. It was agreed that Lilly was to know nothing of the transaction. The affair was not mentioned in her presence, and she continued her Sunday excursions to the little church on the slopes of grim and ancient Kilauea.

THEN CAME THE days of boat hunting. Saunders suggested renting one, but the King and Franklin were so emphatic on the necessity of buying outright that the old. planter had to conform. The critical and enthusiastic trio searched the ports (of Mahukona, Hoopuloa and Hilo, but without success. In Makena on Maui, however, they discovered what they were seeking. The boat, like a great prehistoric white bird, lay at rest on-the still waters of the harbor. She was a three-masted schooner, neither too large nor too small, and being fore and aft rigged, without steam, was more likely to escape suspicion on the high seas than a more ambitious craft.

The three men stood admiring it from the wharf when they were accosted by a man who vouchsafed them the information that it was the property of a Captain Dunn now in the "Good Nuns" Hospital. They found the sick skipper a little unwilling to make a sale. But he was persuaded to set a. price, and the men went out in a small dinghy to inspect her. The king, a connoisseur of everything that could float, scoured every part of her with an eagle eye and even went overboard, much to the admiration of the A. B., to see what she had picked up from standing about. His report to Saunders and Franklin was laudatory, but in the presence of the skipper he showed little enthusiasm. His *marchandage* saved the planter nearly a thousand dollars when the sale was consummated.

Saunders was willing to have the papers made out in Franklin's name, for, in case of: any mishap, this meant absolute exoneration for himself. He had secretly planned to pose as an innocent passenger. In order to secure him, Franklin gave him his private note for the full amount. Then, with great care, the crew was picked. The captain and mates, while being honest, must not be too curious.

The day of departure arrived, and Lilly was informed that she was to be left alone for several weeks in the care of the motherly old housekeeper. Her curiosity became very pronounced. She insisted that Franklin tell her the whole truth. It was evident that she suspected something. But Franklin was more vicious than heretofore, and answered her curtly, resorting to insults when she persisted in her questioning. Saunders, whose solicitude for the, young woman had, during the last week, increased a *coup d'oeil,* took Franklin aside. "Look here, Harry," he said with an apologetic smile, "what makes you treat the little woman with such indifference?"

Franklin's reply was such that when the planter repeated it to Lilly an hour later, she broke down and sobbed on the old man's shoulder. Saunders was tempted to suggest that he stay behind, but he was afraid: Franklin might suspect and make things unpleasant. for him. Instead, he merely comforted Lilly and expressed the hope that matters might turn out favorably for them. Lilly did not answer, but looked into the old 'man's eyes in such a way that he carried her tear-stained image with him throughout 'the entire voyage.

THE BOAT WAS to steer a direct course south by south-west to Phoenix Island, and from there east by south-east to an uncharted island south of Dudoza; thence, via the Walker Islands, to San Francisco. This route was well off the beaten path of regular steamer traffic, and the danger of being—overhauled in the high seas was thus minimized.

On the evening of the fifth day, after a voyage of perfect weather in which every sail was crowded on, land was sighted off the beam, and Phoenix-land hove purpling into the horizon. On the seventh day, to the cracking of the cross-jacks, Dudoza was passed; and four hours later the boat came to anchor off a tall bluff covered with palms and stubble. This was the little island of Susiva where lived the friend of King Monalukki with his precious caches of contraband.

Franklin and Saunders were to remain aboard while the king went ashore to make arrangements about the cargo. This merchant, he explained, might refuse to do business in the presence of persons with whom he was not personally acquainted. The skipper had merely been informed that they were to take on a passenger for San Francisco.

THE NEXT DAY the king returned to the boat with his guest. He was a large, flashily dressed man with an unmistakable Jewish cast of features and a crop of closely-cut red hair. He was introduced to Franklin and Saunders as Mr. Bernheim, the Chinese merchant's trusted manager and representative who would accompany them to San Francisco. The skipper was informed that it would require the whole crew to get Mr. Bernheim's luggage aboard, as there were nine trunks, five packing cases, and a number of valises.

It was twilight when the boat once more got under way. "That's the finest hop ever brewed," remarked Mr. Bernheim that night, rubbing his hands together and beaming upon the assembly. "In the old days we used to get twenty dollars a pound for it, and then it was resold for a higher price."

"Why not have a look at it?" suggested Saunders. "I never saw any prepared opium."

"By all means," Mr. Bernheim agreed.

The four men went below, and one of the packing cases was opened. Within was a tin receptacle full of a dark brown, sticky fluid, sweet to the smell.

"It looks like treacle," laughed Saunders.

"A trifle more dangerous," supplied Franklin.

The king took a little on his finger and sniffed it. "The genuine article," he murmured, with the air of an expert, winking surreptitiously at Franklin.

"I hope," Saunders remarked a bit nervously, "that there'll be no trouble about passing it in San Francisco."

The king laughed heartily. "I've been to San Francisco fifty times," he assured his listeners, "and they've never questioned my bags yet. Why should they begin now?"

"It'll serve 'em right," chuckled Saunders. "The swine! I always believed in free trade anyway."

TWO DAYS LATER in the early afternoon they made an anchorage in the little harbor of Walker Island... Every one went ashore. At the post office Franklin and Saunders found a letter awaiting them. Lilly had promised to write here and to San Francisco to let them know how things were going with her. The fast mail boats in both instances, though leaving later, would arrive before the little sailing vessel.

Franklin's letter ran:

> At last things have come to a climax. Every one here seems to know what you are doing. Some one who knows Monalukki has told everything. As is always the case, the woman is the last to learn. No wonder you wouldn't tell me. But I have found out and you cannot blame me for what I'm going to say. I write this with many tears, for I have always hoped that you could be led to love me again, as you did when we were first married. If it was for myself alone I might go on bearing my sorrow as I've done for three years.
>
> But I must think of our boy. When his father is

found out to be a criminal, as will inevitably happen, he will be disgraced for life. You know, Harry, that I have always been a good wife to you, although from the first you have treated me like a slave and a chattel. Well, I cannot stand it any longer. You have broken my heart, and this letter is simply to tell you that if you wish to disgrace yourself I will not be a par ty to it. When y ou receive this I shall already have started proceedings for a divorce .

Lilly.

FRANKLIN passed the letter with trembling hand to Saunders. When the old planter read it he blanched. He feared for his legal safety; and suddenly desired to be free of the whole expedition. If he could escape he realized that he might go to Lilly and make her his wife as he so desired. With a puzzled and averted mind he opened his own letter which was directed in the handwriting of his old housekeeper. Franklin, with bowed head, left him. The letter was from Lilly and its faint perfume set his blood thumping. He read it eagerly.

My dear Mr. Saunders:

I am writing you because I am in a most terrible predicament. I have decided to separate from my husband. One of Monalukki's men knows and has told all about your expedition and its purpose. If you could only get away before it's too late, for the boat was bought in Harry's name and the guilt would all fall on him. Please, by some pretext, leave them at Walker Island and take the steamer back. Do this for my sake. I deeply fear something may happen to you.

Most sincerely, Lilly Franklin

When old Saunders finished the letter he was filled with a great joy. After a moment's reflection, he hurried up to Franklin excitedly. "Look here," he said in a perturbed voice. "I've just got a letter which makes it necessary for me to get back immediately. I'm sorry, but it's absolutely imperative. Everything's going wrong on the plantation. I don't like the looks of this business anyway, after that letter from your wife."

Franklin laughed easily. "Don't be afraid," he said. "There's no danger. Even if the authorities in San Francisco were informed by  wire they wouldn't interfere with the king. They'd wink at the whole thing— diplomacy, you understand. Anyway, it's worth chancing."

But Saunders was immovable. He refused point-blank to continue.

"If you want to go ahead, Harry—all luck and good," he answered. "You don't need me anyway; and I've got to get back on the nex steamer. There's one to-morrow."

"Sorry," answered Franklin. "But I see argument is futile. Anyway, we'll see you in a few weeks… Do what you can for Lilly. She's terribly upset."

THAT evening at dusk, just as Saunders pushed away in a dinghy from-the schooner where he had gone to fetch his baggage, another small boat, rowed by two lusty natives and containing a slim dark youth, put out from the shore. This second boat made straight for the schooner, and when it came alongside the youth leaped out and threw himself into Franklin's arms.

"Hello, Lil," called Bernheim, lounging forward and shaking the newcomer's hand, "That get-up's bcoming."

"I thought you boys would never come," said Lilly, breaking down and crying.

The skipper and the crew were astonished, but they had been chosen because they lacked curiosity, and they said nothing.

"When did you get here, dearest?" asked Franklin, comfortingly, with his arm about her.

"Yesterday morning," the girl replied, trying to stifle her happy sobs…"I came on the same boat as the letters."

"If we hadn't had fine weather my little sailor girl would have had to 'wait even longer." Franklin kissed her tenderly.

"Say, Lil, it went off like clock-work," put in Bernheim proudly. "By the way,"—he turned eagerly to Franklin—"this is a swell vessel, what'll we get for her?"

The other smiled, and when he spoke it was with that playfulness of tone which irritated Bernheim. "Ah, Shylock," he responded in pseudo-anger. "It's the money you think of first. Here we have had at, ideal adventure in the tropics—an adventure full of that romantic essence which, from the beginning of time has sent men out into the waste places of the earth, and you see only the monetary climax. Suppose we never sell the boat—what matter? We have taught a lesson to an unscrupulous and avaricious old man who has stooped to smuggling, who is willing to disseminate great quantities of poison to a lot of unfortunates, and who has tried to steal my wife from me. We have lived for weeks here amid the magic of the South Sea islands. We have played a perilous game with our wits for weapons. We have tapped the fountainhead of true romance—and you are wondering how much you are going to be paid for a life that Gauguin was willing to live in poverty for!"

"Romance is all right, Harry," argued Bernheim seriously. "But you can't eat it,—I suppose if Saunders had been honest you wouldn't have done him. And I suppose that if the smuggling story had been straight, you'd have passed it up."

"You understand me better every day, Red," Franklin replied, smiling. "I even have hopes of proselytizing you some day."

"Why don't you start a mission here among the heathens?" Bernheim retorted disgustedly, as he went aft.

AT NIGHTFALL they put out on a new course. When they were well out of sight of land the crew received orders to heave overboard all the trunks, packing cases, and valises which they had so laboriously shipped at Susiva.

"Save a little of that molasses," Lilly put in laughing, "and I'll make you boys and the crew a good old-fashioned cake." Smilingly the captain and Franklin complied.

"And that's darn good molasses, too," commented Red, lighting a long black cigar.

"I couldn't get a cheap brand. Why, that cost me sixty cents a gallon. And it took me three days to find it all, and it had to be taken to Susiva by canoes. Romance?— I've lost ten pounds doing manual labor." He puffed contentedly at his cigar.

In due time they arrived at Wellington and sold the boat in one of those great clearance houses for marine furniture at the gratifying price of £3.200,

The king's share was such that he lay drunk for months at a waterside resort in Honolulu Bay, and anyone who wishes to talk to him may do so, for they will always find him in that vicinity. For a small gratuity he will give a skillful exhibition of shark killing, or for an even smaller gratuity he will start a quarter of a mile from shore on the swell of a breaker and ride on a slender board through the shallows to the dry sand, poised upright, like a bronze God. But one should address him as Azoona and not king Monalukki. The real king, who has not left Payato for fourteen years, bears no resemblance to this humble Hawaiian.

# Chivalry

IN THE glass-enclosed deck of the *Neptuna*, one of the I and O's biggest liners sailing from Adelaide to Nagasaki *via* Guam, Harry Franklin, alias Archie Martin, alias Samuel Wilkins, and alias other *noms de guerre* too numerous to be recorded .here, sat buried in the pages of *The Conservative Monthly*, He was young, broad-shouldered, tastefully dressed.in gray tweed, and shod with the care which only educated men give their feet. He had a high, well-shaped forehead, a stern, studious mouth and a straight, liberal nose. No one would have taken him for a member of the profession against which laws are passed and upon which modern moralists heap anathemas. He had the air and appearance of an Englishman of the better class, though when he spoke it was with a slight nasal drawl which marked him as an American.

Franklin was not going to Nagasaki haphazardly, nor, yet merely to visit that ancient city. There was method in his direction. At Honolulu he had been undecided as to his next residence, but he had received a cablegram from Woo Ching Fang, which determined him. The message had been brief and to the outsider would have meant little. It said: "Mackinlay. Rich father. Ruined girl. Year's absence in Europe Cook's tour. Nagasaki August."

To Franklin its meaning was clear. Mr. Mackinlay, whose. father was rich, had compromised a girl, and, either through personal initiative or by the advice of his father, had gone abroad on a Cook's tour, to be gone a year, while the affair should blow over. He was due at Nagasaki sometime in August. These details had come to Mr. Fang through one of those thousand underground channels, most of which led sooner or later to that shrewd Chinaman's establishment in Los Angeles; and Mr. Fang, knowing Franklin's code of ethics, had cabled him the particulars, thinking they might inspire him to action.

HARRY FRANKLIN, though legally a crook, had a quixotic strain in his nature, which withheld him from using his talents on any one inherently honorable.

Only those members of society who deserved retribution or were dishonest had aught to fear from his machinations. The young man had embraced a criminal life as one embraces romance—for the adventure and danger and excitement attached there to. The game, and not the results, appealed to him.

Now a man like Mackinlay, who would desert a girl to escape the consequences of his own act, was no better in Franklin's eyes than any criminal escaping from justice Mr. Fang knew this before he cabled and so Franklin, who had been in Honolulu, determined to seek this Mr. Mackinlay's acquaintance, and to administer a justice which a busy and whimsical fate might have overlooked.

This midsummer day, as he sat studiously plowing through his magazine, he was unaware that a girl was approaching him from behind. Playfully she placed her small conical hands over his eyes and whispered something trivial in his ear. Franklin removed her hands firmly and then kissed them: She was young—to be exact, only nineteen; but her simple, girlish manner of dressing made her appear even less. She was small and slender; and her delicate face was marked with unusual beauty. Her features were at once tender and exotic, this latter characteristic being emphasized by the thick, black curls which seemed to swathe her face like a heavy oval frame.

"Why don't you put down your book Harry," she remonstrated gently, "and play quoits with me, or deck hockey? You've done nothing but read ever since we've been together, but like an old married woman." She looked at his magazine. I wouldn't feel so bad if you read something interesting. You know, I have some of those novels and plays you made me study."

I'm reading this for a purpose just now," the man answered kindly. "I'd explain it to you, but I don't think you'd understand it."

The girl took a chair by his side and said nothing. Presently Franklin leaned forward and touched the shoulder of a man sitting near him.

"Listen to this, Red," he remarked.

The man addressed turned round, was stocky and had the appearance of having just come into a fortune. His rings were large; his cravat pin was conspicuous; and his clothes proclaimed his primitive delight in the colorful and outlandish."

FRANKLIN pointed, to the article he was reading—"The Fetish of Chivalry in America." Here's a bit of genuine social criticism," he announced. Then he read aloud: "This spurious and extravagant chivalry resolves itself upon inspection into temperamental weakness. It could only exist in a country where abnormal conditions have brought about a misconception of the functioning elements of, women. However, American chivalry, despite its manifest hypocrisy, constitutes that nation's chief point of vulnerability."

"That's worth thinking about," Franklin commented, noticing the puzzled look in his listener's face. "Do you realize," he went on, " that nearly every law is built on chivalry? That's: why a woman always has the advantage in court. That's the reason she never gets the death sentence. It accounts for nine-tenths of all alimony. That's what makes men get up in street cars, and work all day in offices to furnish women with luxuries. The American, more than any one else, has chivalry drummed in him from the day he's born. There's no kid in America who hasn't been thrashed some time or another for not being chivalrous. He's educated along with girls, and has women for teachers. The American man is little more than a slave to women. But that's not all. Women are taught how to use this weapon of chivalry. They're schooled in its psychology from infancy. With it they obtain luxuries and all kinds of privileges because of it, and take everything he has with it afterwards. If he momentarily refuses to be victimized, there's your breach of promise award—another act of chivalry."

Franklin looked at the man opposite and laughed ironically. "We are called crooks," he scoffed finally "We make a profession of getting other people's money. We're supposed to be shrewd. But, Red, there isn't a good looking *débutante* seventeen years old that couldn't teach us wisdom. Chivalry! That's their open sesame"

"Well, what are you going to do about it, Harry?" the other man asked.

"I'm going to study the habits of the *débutante*" Franklin informed him." Now you take Lil into the smoking-room and give her a lemonade with a cherry in it, while I meditate a little on the eternal feminine."

A YOUNG COUPLE sat in the little palm-shaded room which led into the main sun parlor of the Grand Komura Hotel at Nagasaki. From the distance the hum of the docks and the whine of the steam cranes on the *hotaba* drifted faintly through the heat that danced and shivered outside the closed amada. Beyond, the door passed long-robed servitors on noiseless feet, fetching and carrying trays through the cool shadows of the great hallways.

The girl was speaking, and her voice was soft and caressing. Now and again the sound of it would die away as if she were too timid to continue. Finally she looked up into the tense face oi the young man at her side.

"And what will Auntie say when she hears that I've —" She halted confused, and a faint flush passed over her delicate face encircled by close black curls.

"That you," the young man supplemented, taking her hand tentatively, "have made me the happiest and proudest man in the world?"

"But," admonished the girl. "I haven't given my promise yet. "The young man's face fell, and because he looked so crushed she hastened to add "It isn't—because I don't like you very much. It's such a big thing though. It would be such a change for me."

Of course," replied the young man sympathetically, "it means a great deal for you to give up your old life. There are years of hard work ahead of me before I can give you everything I'd like to. But after all," he went on, "the glamour of the stage has a lot to do with these other men's interest in you. Even though they can give you everything in the way of luxury, I'm not so sure they'd go on loving and respecting you as I would."

The girl turned her head away stiffly, as if offended.

"Forgive me," he pleaded, seeing her displeasure, "but sometimes I feel that your whole heart is wrapped up in your stage work and that it blinds you to the true state of things."

THE GIRL softened again. "You should learn to hold your temper a little; don't you think so, dear?" she asked him. "Doesn't it mean anything to you that I've given you every minute of my time since I arrived here?"

"It means everything," he hastened to assure her.

Then why are you so unfair?" There, was a note of injury in her tone. "Why do people think that an actress is different from other women—that they're not quite as good perhaps—that they can be treated with less courtesy? I liked you because I thought you were different, but lately you've said things that make me wonder whether you aren't like the others."

"How can you say that, Aileen?" the young man protested earnestly. "You are all the world to me, and you know it. Would I want you for my wife if I thought you were the kind of woman that people imagine all actresses are? I know what you've suffered from managers and others of their breed. That's why I want to protect you from them. I want to take you away from it all. Aileen, say you'll marry me."

The girl hesitated a fraction of a minute, and then slipped her hand in his...

The young man was Percival Mackinlay, the junior partner in the Mackinlay-Thompson Dry Goods Company of Clinton, Ohio In appearance he was not unlike many prosperous middle-west youths He had an aggressive bearing, a swagger that Was not genuine, and though his manner was indicative of a profound and overbearing conceit, his gaze lacked frankness and directness. His mouth was small and his lips were thin and compressed. His chin was broad and his hair was closely cropped.

"I know that type well," Franklin had remarked to Bernheim.

"America has produced many of his sort…When he's older he'll grind his employees down, and contribute ostentatiously to charities. He's reliable only in so far as it answers his purpose. Already he has run away and left a girl in the lurch, yet I'd warrant he'd be the first one to condemn an unfortunate woman. He's the arch-hypocrite, and he's all the more despicable because he's the kind that convinces himself that he's right

"No scruples about him, then?" Red had asked. Bernheim always half expected some fantastic and incomprehensible quirk on Franklin's part to upset their plans.

"No, Red," Franklin had laughed. "Mr. Mackinlay needs chastisement, and if we give it to him my conscience will be clear.

IT HAD BEEN three weeks since Mackinlay had met Miss Aileen Aerschotte at the Grand Komura Hotel. During all that time he had been ardently attentive to her. There had been others at the hotel who solicitously tried to win favor from this beautifully modeled girl who had come to Japan for the summer. Most conspicuous among them was a Mr. Greenbaum, an aggressive and somewhat vulgar man. For Mr. Greenbaum Mackinlay had an instinctive aversion. This man with his flashy clothes, his liberal paunch and his heavy features, rep resented to the young Ohioan the sort of man he always imagined hovering obnoxiously around pretty actresses.

But the girl on all occasions had given preference to Mackinlay. He had been a member of a large touring party, but his; ticket was sufficiently liberal to allow him any personal alterations he wished to make in his schedule. Since meeting Miss Aerschotte he had chosen to remain behind that he might be with her. Already they had visited all the places in and about Nagasaki to which the tourist invariably goes They had drunk tea in a score of the little houses whose names had appealed to their sense of romance The Rising Moon," "A Thousand Cherry Trees," "The Magic Goldfish," and the much frequented "Old Nippon' with its burning *senko* and its delicious *teriyaki*. They had spent many afternoons in the shade of the *Daibutsa Kamakura*, and sipped *saki* in the exquisite lantern-hung gardens along the beach. They had ridden in rickshaws through the less frequented parts of the town and bought curios in the old Honchodori. The romance of the East had thrown its magic mantle around them.

ON THE afternoon of his first day at Nagasaki, Mackinlay had met a young man of about his own age, a companionable and pleasant

American also on his way round the world. He and his new companion, Harry Driscoll, had liked each other from the first. It had been Driscoll who had introduced Mackinlay to the beautiful Miss Aerschotte, and for a time the three young people were much together. But it soon became apparent that Mackinlay's interest in Miss Aerschotte was such that the position of Driscoll as a member of the party became untenable. He absented himself diplomatically, and it was only late at night, after Miss Aerschotte had retired, that the young men came together steadily, and' Driscoll never, once intimated that he resented the intrusion of Miss Aerschotte upon their plans for seeing the sights together.

As the two sat together on the evening when the young woman had agreed to accept Mackinlay's proposal, talk drifted naturally to her.

"You know, Mac," said Driscoll, "you don't find many girls like her on the stage. As a rule they're a bad lot. I could tell right away that she's an exception. I've heard a great deal of her both in England and America, but never has there been a scandal breathed against her. They say she's conscientiously chaperoned by an old maiden aunt who brings her to the theatre every night and calls for her after every performance.

"She is different," agreed Mackinlay. "It's remarkable, too, when you think of all a girl has to go through on the stage, and of the rough class of people she has to associate with.

"It certainly is," responded Driscoll ."And it's all the more to her credit too. It shows what stuff she's made of. I'd bank my last dollar on the girl."

Mackinlay smiled. "That's what I've already done, he confessed boastingly, throwing out his chest a little. "Miss Aerschotte is going to marry me."

DRISCOLL jumped from the chair and grasped the other man by the hand. "You don't say!" he exclaimed warmly. "Congratulations " Then after a pause: "I hope your father hasn't any of the conventional prejudices against people on the stage."

He won't have them long," replied the other confidential. "I plan to marry her first and discuss it afterward." He laughed. "I've been through the mill."

"A girl like that," remarked Driscoll later in the evening, "deserves all the chivalry and respect a man can give her—and even more than other women. She's always conscious of the onus attaching to her profession and is apt to take any lapse of chivalry more keenly than she might otherwise."

You're right," assented Mackinlay thoughtfully.

Although, as has been said, Mr. Greenbaum was. Mackinlay's particular aversion during the latter's courtship, the surrender of Aileen had smoothed over the relationship between the two. He would even permit Greenbaum and Aileen to sit together for short intervals. Now that his suit had proved successful, he considered his fiancée impregnable to the blandishments of others. It even turned out that Mackinlay's leniency permitted him to accept an invitation for himself and Miss Aerschotte to accompany Greenbaum the following evening on a visit to one of the famous Japanese Monte Carlos, an establishment which, like the "Moulin Rouge" and the "Lapin Agile" in Paris, are supported almost exclusively by the English and Americans.

"You may want to try your luck," suggested Greenbaum to Mackinlay, "so don't forget to take a little money. They say beginners always break the bank."

"Do they?" exclaimed little Miss Aerschotte. "Won't that be sport!" She looked smilingly at Mackinlay. "Are you lucky?"

"I'm the luckiest man in the world," quoth Mackinlay

"Then bring a bunch of money," laughed Greenbaum, pretending not to understand the significance of the other's remark.

"How much shall we take?" Mackinlay asked the girl.

"Well," put in Greenbaum, "I'm taking what in Christian money amounts to about three thousand dollars. You know these are no tin-horn joints, and things come high." He excused himself pleasantly, and walked away.

When they were alone, the girl said, "I wouldn't take as much as that—not over half that amount. It's foolish, for you might lose it."

MACKINLAY'S vanity was touched by the girl's interest and solicitude, but he had no intention of appearing small in her eyes. "I'll take enough, don't worry," he said swaggeringly.

The next day being Saturday, Mackinlay went early to the bank and fortified himself well against any adverse fate which might await him. That evening was no time for economy. Too much was at stake; and he thought of the rich men—even of Greenbaum, in fact—who were eager to supplant him in the affections of Miss Aerschotte.

That evening on the stroke of ten Greenbaum's large green and orange touring car drew up in front of the hotel. Miss Aerschotte and Mackinlay, followed by Harry Driscoll and their host, arranged themselves in the spacious tonneau. The professional guide, hired for the evening; sat in the front with the driver.

The party drove down the main streets of Nagasaki and out through its suburbs. Then, after a five-mile stretch of moon-illumined country-side there appeared ahead of them a large pavilion, brilliant with, electric lights of many colors, set back in one of those luxurious gardens which the Japanese, better than any other people, know how to organize.

As they left their cloaks and hats at the door they noticed about them many of their own countrymen; and they discovered that the employees spoke English. Greenbaum there up on dismissed his guide, as his chief duties were to have been those of interpreter and the four pleasure seekers moved forward into the gaming room. They stood around the roulette table for a while, and Greenbaum explained to Miss Aerschotte and Mackinlay the rules of the games and the methods for placing their money. They noticed, however, that wherever they went, either in the faro room or the baccarat room or to the fan-tan or dice tables, the visitors were losing heavily.

GREENBAUM drew his three guests to one side and said to them in a low voice: "Don't play, not for a while anyway. I want to try something. I think these tables are crooked."

The three young people watched Greenbaum lay small wagers on each of the different games. In every instance they saw Greenbaum's money go into the coffers of the management.

"It's just as I thought," he said, surreptitiously to his companions. "You haven't a look-in here. Every game is fixed. It's an outrage in Europe they close a joint like this in ten minutes. My advice to you fellows is not to play."

Driscoll and Mackinlay looked disappointed.

"Furthermore," he went on, "this place is full of dips—that is, pick pockets. I've put every bit of jewelry I've got in my pocket where I can keep my hand on it." He touched his outside coat pocket, and his listeners noticed that his diamond scarf pin, his rings and his jeweled watch chain, heretofore so conspicuous, had now disappeared.

"But I want to play something, just for the fun of it," pleaded Miss Aerschotte, pouting. Greenbaum, shrugged his shoulders, but Mackinlay and Driscoll humored her. They stood by the roulette table for a few minutes selecting the numbers and watching the ball spin. But they lost regularly, and the girl took them by the arm, saying, "Come, let's go; Mr. Greenbaum's right."

Their host then suggested supper, and they were soon seated in the garden beneath the roseate glow of the lanterns, drinking merrily and sampling appetizing oriental dishes.

Despite the disappointment of the early part of the evening it was a happy party which, two hours later, when the *kodzukai* had commenced to extinguish the twinkling lanterns, started homeward in the moonlight.

"What a glorious night for driving," exclaimed Miss Aerschotte ecstatically, when the little squat flower-covered houses of the city's suburbs were looming ahead of them,

THE WORDS WERE scarcely out of her mouth when the machine sputtered, gave a few jerks, and came to an abrupt standstill. An oath escaped Greenbaum who immediately apologized profusely. The chauffeur leaped out and began prying into the engine.

What's, the trouble?" demanded Greenbaum irritably, coming alongside of the driver I can't tell yet," responded the other bringing out a box of tools.

Greenbaum returned to the tonneau and began offering his apologies for the delay. He intimated that the evening had been a failure all round. He was volubly contrite.

In a few minutes the chauffeur looked up hopelessly. "It's no use," he remarked. "The machine'll have to go to a garage. I'm very sorry, but it's not my fault."

Greenbaum stormed furiously and threatened the driver until he was interrupted by Driscoll.

"It's all right, Greenbaum," the young man said palliatingly. "We can get a couple of rickshaws to take us to the hotel."

Greenbaum quieted down and ordered the chauffeur to go for assistance.

It was half an hour later when the chauffeur returned with one rickshaw. He explained that it was all he could find at that hour of the night. His sincerity of tone was only matched by his humility.

"Well, we'll have to make the best of it," Driscoll commented pleasantly.

"Miss Aerschotte can ride home," he said to Greenbaum. "Mackinlay and I'll walk. It's not far, and the weather's tip-top."

"I wouldn't think of it," Greenbaum protested. "I'm to blame, and I should be the one to walk."

But the two younger men would not listen to him, and he was finally persuaded to abide by Driscoll's original suggestion.

An hour later the two pedestrians arrived at the hotel, the chauffeur having remained behind to look after the machine till morning Greenbaum and Aileen were waiting in the deserted sun parlor. The four sat and talked for a while. Then Greenbaum with renewed apologies retired. Driscoll immediately branched out on romantic tales of globetrotting, and the girl persuaded one of the night porters to make them some tea.

They were on the point of retiring when heavy footsteps were heard descending the stairs, and the excited voice of Greenbaum echoed through the silent halls. "Where are they? "He was demanding of the dazed night clerk. "Have they gone?"

WITHOUT waiting to give an explanation or for a reply even, he half-ran to the sun parlor. When he caught sight of the three young people he sputtered something, but seemed unable to speak. His face was red, and he was choking with anger "So! There you are!" he managed to roar at length, shaking his fist. "You thought I was a sucker, did you?" He beckoned frantically to the night clerk, a young Englishman of impeccable manners, who came forward hesitatingly as if he scented disaster.

"Look here, young man," Greenbaum continued excitedly, "that woman, there," he pointed to Aileen—"has stolen all my jewelry. Now I want you to get the police and to be quick about it."

Mackinlay had now arisen. He was in an ungovernable temper, and he strode forward and faced Greenbaum. "Take back what you said, or I'll wring your neck." His voice was trembling.

Greenbaum was not to be frightened. "Don't try anything on me, young man," he responded in a tone of complete self-possession. "I feel sorry for you. I guess you've been taken in too."

Mackinlay clenched his fist blusteringly, but Driscoll interfered. "Don't make matters any worse" he said to Mackinlay. "Wait till we find out something more about it. There'll be time."

"There may be some mistake," the night clerk was saying to Greenbaum. He was endeavoring to pursue a diplomatic course.

His diplomacy, however, did not appeal to Greenbaum. "You English," Greenbaum sneered, "make me tired. A mistake? Listen. I'll explain something to you. I take these people here out for a pleasant evening. I put all my jewelry into my coat pocket for safety. They know it. On the way home my machine breaks down. We can't find but one rickshaw. I get in it and. ride home alone with that woman there. I get to the hotel and she excuses herself a minute—"

"It was only to take my wraps off," interposed the girl.

"As I was saying," went on Greenbaum,,"she excuses herself. Then later, when I go to bed, my pocket's empty. Now, does that sound like any mistake? You get the police, like I told you, sonny, and if there is any mistake, it won't be your fault."

The clerk turned to the others. "I'm very sorry," he said apologetically, "but there's evidently an error. Perhaps the police will be able to straighten it out. I sincerely hope so." He left the room, and in a moment the tinkle of the telephone bel was heard.

"I'll get even with you for this, Greenbaum," Mackinlay threatened indignantly. "You're dealing with the wrong man when you deal with me."

Greenbaum appeared not to notice him. He walked deliberately to the girl, now pale and speechless. She shrank from him in terror.

"Now look here, young woman," he said patronizingly, "in a few minutes the police'll be here. But if you want to turn over the stuff to me, I'll tell 'em it's all a mistake. I'm wise to your little game, so talk quick."

Mackinlay, unable to restrain himself longer, aimed a blow at the girl's tormentor.

But Greenbaum dodged agilely and Driscoll caught the infuriated young man in a grip of steel.

"You're just making matters worse," Driscoll admonished. "Hold your temper a minute. I want to speak to you."

Mackinlay subsided, and the two stepped into an anteroom.

I think this man's a crook," Driscoll confided. "And it's no good taking this thing too seriously. His jewels are probably hidden somewhere, and if we lie low we'll get the goods on him. He's up to some game, and if we keep our heads we'll get him."

Mackinlay acquiesced sullenly. The girl had begun to sob hysterically, and going over he knelt down at her side.

"DON'T cry," murmured Mackinlay, feeling like a knight of old. "There is someone to help you. I'm going to stand by you.

As he was comforting her and promising to do all in his power to help her, two bowing and smiling Japanese police officials were led in by the clerk stepping forward, One asked of what service he could be. Then he caught sight of the weeping girl.

"Ah," he exclaimed. "The lady has had something stolen from her. It often happens here. Low people, bad people—the thieves in Japan."

"Just a minute," interrupted Greenbaum. "I'm the one who's been robbed, and that young woman did it."

"Quite so, quite so," replied the still smiling official, making a grandiloquent gesture. "The young lady, you say? She has, taken something from you? Very unfortunate."

He would have continued his comments proud of his English, had not the clerk in the official's own tongue explained the situation, The Japanese listened attentively, looking first to one and then to the other of the principals, smiling politely at each.

When the clerk had finished, Greenbaum interposed. "They all saw me put my jewelry in my coat pocket when I went into the pavilion. Then I drove home alone with this woman in a rickshaw. That's when she did the job."

"It's a lie," Mackinlay broke in. "He's taking advantage of this girl. The man's a crook."

The official stepped forward, still smiling. "I'm very sorry," he said, "but, if this gentleman insists, I shall have to take the lady away. No doubt it will all be arranged—"

"It's an outrage," whispered Mackinlay.

Driscoll stepped to his side. "It's easy enough to arrange bail," he said. "Then we'll have a chance to run the thing down. I introduced you to Greenbaum, and I feel responsible, for what's happened. I'll go Miss Aerschotte's bail, and we'll be back here at the hotel in half an hour." Mackinlay hesitated. "I guess you're right, Driscoll," he agreed. "But as far as you're going bail. I wouldn't think of it. It's really my affair, you know."

The officials, with many bows, were now advancing on the weeping girl ho had arisen and was clinging helplessly to her fiancé's arm. Ten minutes later they were standing before a sleepy magistrate.

Greenbaum made a formal charge, and left immediately. Bail was demanded and fixed at what was equivalent to two thousand dollars. Driscoll immediately came forward, and taking out his money began counting it.

"I only have about a thousand," he said to Mackinlay. "But if you'll cash my check I 'll straighten out the balance. My uncle is a merchant at Canton and has orders to pay me my next allowance. He can send the check off tomorrow and have the money cabled back,"

Don't worry about the check," put in Mackinlay. "Here's the money."

"But I insist," the other replied. "I'm to blame for this," and he wrote out a check and handed it over.

"It isn't really necessary," Mackinlay assured him again, although he took the small folded paper proffered him.

Driscoll registered the bail in his own name, and the three returned to the hotel.

AFTER the private detective hired by Mackinlay had surreptitiously searched Greenbaum's baggage and found nothing, and had with the assistance of the police made careful inquiry of the attendants at the pavilion without result, things began to appear hopeless. He was sure the girl was innocent; and Driscoll was equally emphatic in his expressions of faith in her. But having exhausted every effort to clear her, their plans became hazy. The time set for the hearing was but two days of, and Mackinlay was becoming panic stricken. They had consulted a lawyer who encouraged them to the extent of saying that there was little chance of the girl's conviction because of the lack of material evidence. The girl's room and belongings had been carefully searched by the police, but nothing incriminating had come to light. But Mackinlay was far from satisfied. He wanted more than a mere discharge on lack of evidence. The affair, even if the case were dismissed, would, he considered, be injurious to him. Above all things he desired positive proof of her innocence and. an apology from the instigator of the proceedings. Sunday was at hand and he became despondent, for only one day intervened before the hearing on Tuesday. Furthermore, he had given his promise to the girl that he would prevent her suffering the ignominy of being put on trial. Every evening after the day's fruitless endeavor to exonerate her, he' renewed this promise, although of late he had but little faith in his own words.

As he and Driscoll sat gloomily waiting for the dinner hour Sunday night, however, the unexpected happened. A Japanese boy approached them, and with a deep bow handed Mackinlay a letter addressed in meticulous copy-book handwriting. The boy immediately departed and Mackinlay read the letter curiously. With an exclamation of joy he turned to Driscoll and handed it to him. "Here's luck!" he announced excitedly, as the other read:

> Most honored Sir :
>
> I think that should y our honorable self go to the trouble to visit the Komatzu Dori, numeral 16, this night after dinner, I could inform your honor as to the whereabouts of the other honorable American's jewelry. But should your honorable self feel a desire for police help Komatzu Dori house will be dark and untenant. Hence please to come alone Ho ever, if you have fear, you may bring Four mast honorable frend.

AN HOUR LATER found the two men knocking at the door of a small house set back in a little garden where fountains played and lanterns swayed gently in the breeze. The shojis were tightly closed, and it was some time before they were ushered into the narrow hall by a wrinkled little old man whose dark face and stooped back gave him a sinister appearance. Without a word their host led them through the house to a small rear veranda where they were given seats.

In the ensuing conversation, carried on principally by the little old man, it developed that he had seen a friend of his—a constant frequenter of the pavilion—deftly extract the jewels from Greenbaum's pocket. He had taken his friend to task for treating so distinguished a visitor in such a manner, and the friend had told him that the jewels had not been stolen for himself but for his employer, a man well known in Nagasaki life and one who had great influence with the police. The little old man had tried to ascertain this other gentleman's name, but had failed. However, this friend had given him the information that if he should receive a recompense which warranted it, he would return the jewels. It was a difficult feat, though, and one in which great personal risk would have to be taken. Therefore, if the two gentlemen wanted the jewels sufficiently to pay a large price, they would be returned. Otherwise nothing would be done.

Mackinlay and his friend listened to the story in astonishment. So startling and in credible was it that Driscoll, taking the other aside, advised him to pay no attention to it.

"It's obviously a hold-up game," he said, "and I, for one, don't believe a word of it. Let's think it over anyway. "turning, they thanked their host for his interest in the affair and informed him they would let him know later.

"To-morrow night," warned the old man, "will be the last evening. If you decide to take his offer you will find me here again at this hour with the property. But no police." He shook a wrinkled finger. "You will be watched. And should any intercourse between you and them be discovered, that will end the matter."

It was late when they returned to the hotel, but they decided to have one more talk with Greenbaum. He was in an unpleasant mood and laughed at Mackinlay's offer of compromise. "What do I care for money?" he asked.

"I have plenty of money, and the jewelry's. nothing to me either. But,—" he brought his fist down on the table—"I refuse to be played for a sucker. Nothing makes me so sore as to have a woman do it."

"I've made you an offer," Mackinlay persisted, "to reimburse you for everything you've lost. But if you insist on going ahead with the case, it'll be thrown out of court anyway, and you'll lose everything.

I've offered you more than bail. What's to hinder Miss Aerschotte from simply jumping bail?"

Greenbaum laughed craftily. "You thought of that, did you?" he asked. "Let her try to jump it, and see what happens."

It was plain there was nothing to be done, so the two, men left him.

"Greenbaum evidently isn't a crook," commented Driscoll, "but something worse and harder to reach—an honest man who is playing in a modern way what his famous ancestor did in *The Merchant of Venice*. The only thing to be done is to meet. The official's terms or to take our chances in court. My advice is to fight it out."

"Perhaps you're right," replied the other. "I'll save a lot of money, and maybe, after all the affair won't hurt Aileen much. Only" he added, "if my old man hears of it, he'll make it deuced unpleasant for me. You know, I've had one pretty serious affair with a girl back home. She was crazy about me—couldn't get rid of her."

Driscoll thought of Woo Ching Fang's cablegram which he had in his pocket, and said nothing.

MACKINLAY SPENT a restless night. The next morning he called on Aileen. She was pale and nervous from her week's worry and suspense. He told her of his experience of the night before and watched its effect on her. When he had finished she looked to him hopefully.

"I knew something would happen to save me," she said. "And you will advance me the money to get them back, won't you, dear? It will only be until I can communicate with my aunt. My whole happiness depends on it."

That afternoon found him in the private office of a large Nagasaki bank. Letters of credit, travelers' checks and passports were inspected. There was even an exchange of cable messages with Clinton, Ohio. And shortly before the bank closed for the afternoon, Mackinlay emerged with the largest sum of money he had ever before carried on his person.

That night he went alone to the little house in the Komatzu Dori. He did not ask Driscoll to go with him. He wanted all the credit for himself. In the dimly lighted hallway the wrinkled old man handed him a little packet of jewelry.

The next morning Greenbaum withdrew his charge against Miss Aerschotte and apologized humbly and profusely to everyone. The same, afternoon, Mackinlay, Driscoll and the girl set sail for Canton. Two hours before boat time Driscoll had gone to the police station to recover the bail, but on returning had announced that it was necessary for three days to elapse before the reimbursement could be made—

a formality of Japanese law. He had, he explained, left instructions to have it sent on to the American consul at Canton.

At Canton bad news awaited them. Aileen's aunt was ill in San Francisco. It was necessary for the girl to go there at once. Mackinlay engaged her ticket and passage and would have accompanied her by train to Hong Kong from where the boat sailed, but she was frantic with grief and insisted on going alone. She'd cable him from San Francisco, and he was to follow later. That evening when he returned to the hotel from the station he found a note from Driscoll stating that the latter had received a call from his uncle and had gone to Chaoking for a few days.

Mackinlay awaited his return. Five days in all he waited. Then, in need of money, he decided to take Driscoll's check to the bank. He was astonished to find, at the address which had been given him a small tea house whose proprietor ceremoniously assured him there was no bank in the neighborhood. Then, after consulting the American consul and finding that no bail money had arrived, he cabled to Nagasaki only to learn that it had been paid to Driscoll on the date of sailing

The same day he received a cable from Constantinople, It was signed "Driscoll" and read:

> A deserter should expect to be deserted. Aileen was my
> wife, and Greenbaum our closest friend.

A week later Percival Mackinlay rejoined the original party of Cook's tourists at Manila.

# THE MOON OF THE EAST

IN A LARGE, heavily curtained bay window of the Palace Hotel, Constantinople, looking over the writhing street which led to the Mosque of St. Sophia, stood the heavy figure of a man. He was large and aggressive, and his clothes proclaimed him to be an idle tourist. No one could mistake the fact that he was Jewish. His nose was round and flat; his eyes were small, and his lips thick. His pudgy hands were adorned with expensive and garish rings, and a huge diamond scarf pin glistened in his shirt bosom.

Sitting behind him in the comforting—folds of a sprawling chair, was his companion, buried in thought. The appearance of these two men offered a striking contrast of temperament and breeding. The sitting man was slim and quietly garbed in a suit which would have been equally fashionable in Berlin, London and New York; and his delicately chiseled features and slender fingers proclaimed his inherent refinement. His forehead was high, and as he now sat in the strong reflected light, he did not look unlike the portraits of Byron and Shelley which one occasionally sees.

A girl completed the party. She was a perfect brunette. Her hair had those peculiar bluish lights one seldom sees outside of Latin countries; and her eyes shone with a depth of expression as she occasionally glanced proudly toward the man seated near her,

This: man was her husband, and they had been married but a few months. About the girl hovered that indescribable something we call charm—a thing which existed apart from her beauty.

SHE WAS DRESSED like an English lady of station, simply, quietly and richly. No one would have imagined that she had not come from a family of culture and that every social advantage had not been hers. One would hardly have believed that only for a few months had she associated with educated people, and that before this time she had consorted only with the outcasts of New York's underworld. But such was the case. She was no other than the notorious

Lilly Dinan, unpleasantly known to the American police. Her parents had been French criminals who had hastened to America when she was very young to escape arrest in their own country. Lilly was left an orphan at a tender age and had drifted into a life of crime; but she was impressionable and intelligent, and when she met Harry Franklin, a college man who had chosen the adventures of lawlessness in preference to any other career, she had fallen in love with him and later married him. He took it upon himself to educate and train her, and now she could appear anywhere, for she possessed all the external traits of culture.

The trio had been silent for perhaps half an hour, when Red Bernheim, the man at the window, unable to contain himself longer, gave vent to his anger.

"A great lay, Harry!" he burst forth.

"A real Coney Island without the amusements! And not a saloon in sight—only coffee, coffee, coffee everywhere. Me, I'm melting away and getting rusty from overwork doing nothing. Staying here is like doing a three days' yawn. Besides that, it's all going out, and pretty soon I'll be spending the last sawbuck in my kick for a rope to hang my Adonis-like form on, I warned you in Japan not to get among these heathens. We'd gone far enough away from the U.S.A. then. I'm for kicking out."

Harry Franklin raised his head and folded his arms.

"I fear, Red, you'll never understand the exigencies of the artistic temperament," he remarked. "Strange lands and people! To see them has been a dream of mine. But your observation that the place bores you goes as well for me. Lil here is the only one even a little at home. Luckily she speaks French. But for us, my friend, the trip has been only a panorama, whereas I counted on an experience. By the way, what shall we do this afternoon?"

"Do? Do? That's the rub!" Bernheim ejaculated angrily. "There ain't nothin' or nobody to do. As Patrick Henry said, 'Give me a sucker, or give me death!' Do? Why, to have something to do I'd split a jimmy over a yellow dog's head to steal his collar; only the dogs here ain't got no collars."

HE GRUNTED and turned to Lily, who throughout the conversation had ceased reading to listen,

"Say, Lil, read us something outa that paper," he asked. "What's Tammany doing? Have any of the boys been pinched? How's the hop market in little old New York?"

"Hold on," hastily interrupted the girl, "here's J. H. Hilliard, the steel millionaire, just arrived in port on his yacht, *Gayety Girl.*"

At her words Harry Franklin looked up quickly.

"J. H. Hilliard? Humph! That's interesting," he commented.

"Maybe you can get excited over it, but not me," said Red. "Do you happen to number him among your close personal pals?"

"No, but I know a little something about him. If you, Red, took more interest in the social and political betterment of your native land, you too would have heard of him as a man who epitomizes the repugnant hypocrite posing as a benefactor of mankind. Twice divorced by fine women, called by his first name by second-story belles all along Broadway, having bought his way out of many a scandal that should have made his name anathema among decent and even honest people, he is the veritable wolf in sheep's clothing. Why, he's on tour now to escape the onus of the bankruptcy proceedings: of the Merchants and Trades mans Bank of which he is the president, He's a thoroughly dishonest, sly, graspingfellow and has a habit of avoiding the consequences of his acts by shifting the blame onto the shoulders of his cat's-paws. Let us commend him, however, for one trait that he has in common with many better men, He has a passion for collecting rare jewels and of paying enormous prices to enhance his large collection."

Red turned hopefully. "Well, he's just the kind of a guy you wait for. Why don't you get him?" he asked.

"Perhaps, perhaps," droned the younger man. "Take Lil out for a walk along the harbor front; and, by the way, find out what you can about Hilliard's movements since he has been here. I'm interested in him more than he knows."

J. H. Hilliard sat in the spacious deck garden on the after part of his million-dollar yacht, the *Gayety Girl*, He was coatless and hatless, and his thin legs were swathed in the ample folds of a pair of pongee silk trousers. He was fanning himself vigorously, sipping Tortino, and cracking risqué jokes to his two companions about the object his eyes were fixed upon—the austere walls of what the Turkish guides invariably point out as the sultan's harem.

Hilliard was about fifty, smooth shaven and with dyed hair which he always wore long over his forehead. A hard line of mouth bespoke his domineering instincts, and his flabby cheeks and pouched eyes attested to his irregular habits and dissipations. American papers three weeks old lay about him on the richly carpeted deck, and there were exotic flowers in stationary vases on the wicker tables.

Every afternoon since his arrival he had come and sat here in the same seat to watch the last rays of the sun strike fire from the domes and minarets of the mosques and palaces, and to watch the ever-moving dark crowds—from such a distance resembling serpents—wend their way up the shore of the Golden Horn. As he looked now across the bay, the great city rose before him like a fairy dream, the huge swelling structures made transparent by the hot reddish light and cold shadows. Like bubbles upon bubbles shot with all the colors of the rainbow, they would disappear one by one and blur in the gathering dusk, one by one becoming a cold and brooding silhouette against the flames of the sky about Bab Humayun. The ships rocked rhythmically; and from seemingly great distances one could hear the calls to prayer and see the trembling lights burst into being, like glow-worms over the fading city of enchantment. Seen from this point and at this time of day, Constantinople has not changed for a thousand years. It lies on its hills like a spilled basket of pearls, and one can picture the stories of the Arabian Nights just beginning' over again under the first stars.

Hilliard by his silence appeared to have absorbed some of the romance about him, and his friends kept silent, expecting some human or kindly word from him as a result of the spell which the dark waters of the Bosphorus throws over every traveler on its bosom. But Hilliard's romantic nature took a different turn.

"Say," he began, "I bet there's some fine looking dames in this burg. They tell me that here when a man gets tired of his wife he can take her out and bowstring her, whatever that is ... But I'm too soft for that ... and it's not so bad to be known as a good alimonist. It makes you more desirable in the eyes of many more."

A HALF-hour later there came a sound of creaking oarlocks away off on the port beam. The three men on the yacht paid little attention to the noise at first, but when the sound became more distinct and seemed to be approaching them, they sat up a little straighter.

"Wonder what's coming off?" Hilliard asked, as he rose and went to the rail.

The other men followed him. Then for the first time they could distinguish another splashing still further away. Excitement now grasped the men on the yacht, and they looked at each other inquisitively.

As they were about to speak the darkness opened suddenly, like a curtain, and below them they could see a small boat speeding, as if for life, directly toward them. A huge black figure was at the oars, and a second dark figure was huddled in the stern. The boat dashed on into plain view and made straight for the yacht's overboard launching steps which had been left lowered to the very water's edge. As if guided by a sixth sense, the panting Negro came straight on; and in another moment his boat grated the yacht's side. Letting his oars slide overboard, he grasped the step with one huge hand, and with the other he caught hold of the slight figure of his companion. Then, exhibiting great strength, he strode up the steps with his charge hung limply under one arm.

He was not a moment too soon. The second boat crashed into the abandoned one, and a white man stood up in the darkness and fell to cursing in broken English. The new arrival then began to ascend the steps. The Negro saw him and, gently depositing his burden on the deck, drew a long waving knife from his belt and started to go down again.

Hilliard, who, when this strange and terrifying visitor had first come aboard, had impulsively stepped back into the shadow, now came forward excitedly. He did not want to see murder done on his yacht. His interference was not needed, however, for when the man in the boat below saw the light shining on the other's knife, he tactfully sat down in his boat again and shoved off a little.

"THE SLENDER figure which had been carried aboard by the Negro, though silent and immovable up to now, suddenly precipitated itself across the deck toward the master of the yacht. Half way toward him the fez fell off its head, unloosing a great wave of black glistening hair; and a cape slipped to the ground disclosing the baggy silk trousers of the Turkish woman and the full silk waist and coat which could not hide the grace and beauty of the perfectly controlled body of a girl.

"*A moi, à moi!*" she sobbed. "*Oh, M'sieu Eelyer, M'sieu Eelyer, aidez moi!*" Burying her face in the astonished millionaire's arm, she grasped his sleeve convulsively and sobbed.

Hilliard had traveled much and as a consequence had a good working knowledge of the French language. He stroked the girl's head as a father would, and assured her that she was safe with him.

At the sight of Hilliard the man in the boat calmed down and told the owner of the yacht to get the negro away so that he could come aboard and explain. Hilliard made an effort to persuade the Negro to forego his murderous intention for a moment, but the great black giant remained immovable until the girl had spoken a few words to him in a strange mellow language. The man below then came aboard, but when his head emerged over the rail, fear again seized the girl and she clutched Hilliard's coat and endeavored to hide behind him.

"Don't let him have me!" she cried. "Oh, *m'sieu*, if you only knew!"

The newcomer now stood before Hilliard. He was a tall, well-built man with black whiskers and a black bristling moustache. He wore a dark slouch hat pulled well down over his eyes. His clothes were loose and his shoes heavy and unpolished. Both in appearance and in accent he gave the impression of being a German.

"My name's Franklin," he said in broken English, giving a peremptory and officious gesture.

But at this point the girl broke in.

"Oh, listen to me first!" she cried to Hilliard. "You don't understand…If you only knew…"

Hilliard ignored the German and turned to the girl. "Knew what?" he asked tenderly.

"Oh, if you only knew why I came to you, how I knew who you were and where your boat was! Don't believe anything that man tells you. Hear me first. Oh, *m'sieu*, take me away from the sight of him. He is a terrible man—terrible!"

The German was about to speak again, but Hilliard cried suddenly: "Wait a minute!" He turned to several sailors who had now appeared, "Keep that man here for a minute," he ordered, pointing to the German. "I want to find out what's the matter." Then he took the girl by the arm.

"Come inside with me," he said; and he beckoned also to his companions.

The four moved toward the salon, the girl walking backward and gazing, terror-stricken, at the German who was now being held between two sailors. The big Negro followed at their heels.

AT THE END OF fifteen minutes, Hilliard was in possession of the facts concerning her life. It appeared that she was half Armenian and half French, hence a Christian, living, as she thought, in perfect security in her own country on her father's large estate, when the Turks, in one of their uprisings against the "infidel," came down upon her family, murdered her father, mother and elder sister before her eyes, burned their home and took everything of value in the house. She herself was dragged away to confront one of the commanding officers of the expedition, and because of her youth and beauty, he decided; to carry her away with him and place her in his harem. She was taken to Constantinople, along with nearly two hundred other women, all of whom were allotted to different officers. From the very first she planned to escape, and to get back to the sunny France which her mother had never tired of telling her about.

In order to accomplish this there was no sacrifice she was not willing to make, and gradually, by stifling all her hatred for her possessor, she became his favorite wife and won his confidence. Now, three years later, she had managed to escape with the help of a devoted slave, and hoped to reach what she considered her native land, France, and to start life anew. Achou(who now stood at the door watching the proceedings with lowering brows) had at first taken her to the house of a friend where she was to stay until the excitement following her escape had somewhat died out. Then she was going to try to board a train and slip out of the country. In order to defray her expenses *en route* she had taken with her a great jewel which belonged to her husband; and she intended to sell it on arriving at her destination,

Then she had heard of Hilliard. The man brought her papers to vary the monotony of her hiding. In them she had read of Hilliard and his yacht, and by means of a glass she had been able to see from her seclusion the white boat and figures moving about on it. It was then she had decided to throw herself on the mercy of its owner and to appeal to him to take her away. She had heard so much of American chivalry and of the women's freedom in the United States.

"Never for a minute did I fear that you would harm me or give me up to the authorities. I thought I was safe at last from pursuit, when that man"—she pointed toward the deck—"saw us at the boat landing and followed....Achou there will kill him if you will only give me permission to command him," she added frantically.

Hilliard shook his head quickly. "No, you mustn't do that," he said. "Maybe there is some other way out."

"Here is the jewel." The girl broke the silence after a minute. "I will give it to you gladly if you will only save me from that man. Once I get to France I can live somehow. I have relatives there."

She drew from her bosom a large parcel and, handing it to Hilliard, said, "Keep it. Keep it. It's yours—only save me! Don't let him touch me!"

Hilliard gazed at the girl wistfully, and a wave of tender sympathy for her surged over him. He opened the parcel abstractedly and shook the contents out on the table—

The Moon of the East! Hilliard promptly forgot the girl in his breathless amazement at the gem. It was at least seven inches across, four of which were occupied by a crescent emerald of immense proportions. About the emerald, shading from light to dark, like a spectrum, were diamonds, pearls, opals, rubies, amethysts and sapphires, set solidly together, making a six-pointed star in imitation of the Seal of Solomon.

MY GOD!" he breathed excitedly. "One of the great jewels of the world!"

He raised his head quickly. His two friends were bending over him, their eyes bulging.

"Well?" snapped Hilliard. "What are you looking at?"

He immediately thrust the jewel in his coat pocket and turned to the girl.

"Wait here and tell that Negro not to let anyone in," he said.

The girl spoke to the slave, who at once drew his knife and stood menacingly in the doorway. Hilliard went out to where the German was waiting.

"Now I will talk to you," he said. "What's the matter, and what do you want?" He was a little frightened, not for the girl or for himself, but for fear that something might arise which would force him to give up that gem in his pocket.

"I don't want anything," the other man answered peremptorily, "except a piece of jewelry this woman, in company with her slave, stole from her husband and brought to your boat. I was one of the secret agents employed to find her and to return the jewel."

"Well, suppose I tell you to get out that the jewel is not here?" Hilliard was testing the man. The other laughed scornfully and unpleasantly.

"Perhaps you don't know who my employer is." And leaning closer he mentioned a name high in the political history of the East, the name of a man reputed to be the chief advisor of the Crown and one who was virtually ruler of a great number of the Turkish provinces.

Hilliard was taken aback at this revelation. He could see that there was only trouble ahead for him if he assumed too high-handed an attitude.

"Is there no other way out?" he asked.

"None," the other replied roughly. "The girl and the slave are here on your yacht, and I propose to take them back with me. I give you fair warning that if you attempt to thwart me things will go hard with you. Another thing; I am not rich and there is a reward of 50,000 francs which goes with the return of the gem, so don't think for one minute that I am not prepared to push this thing relentlessly."

Hilliard made a very quick mental calculation. He thought of the possibility of giving the girl up and of escaping in his yacht with the jewel before being caught.

But after a moment's reflection he realized that this would be too hazardous for a man of his standing. He would surely be caught. He then estimated the value of the jewel and decided that his safest course lay in bribery.

"This young lady," he began, "has made me promise that I will take her to France. I have given my word, and therefore I feel under obligation."

As a matter of fact, Hilliard had little, interest in the girl. He knew, however, that if he did not return her to France she would probably give the information as to who had the Moon of the East.

"Now look here, my man," he went on; "you say you are not rich and that you would get fifty-thousand francs if you returned the girl and the jewel. What do you say to forgetting the whole incident for one-hundred thousand francs? I can take you to Italy at once, and from there you can return, via Switzerland, to your home and live well until this thing has well blown over, say for five years, At Naples I will pay you the entire sum. How does that strike you?"

THE GERMAN hesitated. "What assurance have I that you will pay me when we reach Naples? I don't doubt your word, Mr. Hilliard, but you must remember that I do not know you. At Naples you will be out of danger, and it would be quite possible for you to put me off the boat without giving me the money."

Hilliard laughed. "Very clever of you," he commented. He sobered and thought for a moment. "Still," he said gravely, after a pause, "if I pay you now you could easily go ashore and turn the tables on me; and I would be out the money and—everything."

"The thing can be managed satisfactorily for both of us," the German replied. "We can go-ashore at once. You can make out a sight check to me for one-hundred thousand  francs. The money can be given to a friend of mine whom I can trust; and then I will be only too delighted to return with you and take a trip to Naples. When I reach Germany my friend can send me the money."

"That suits me." Hilliard called to the second mate and had a boat made ready to go ashore. He congratulated himself on his astonishing bargain. The jewel intrinsically was worth half a million dollars, and he had bought it for twenty thousand.

Hilliard and the German went ashore. The German's servant, a young Turk who had rowed the other out to the yacht, was left on board. The financial arrangements were soon disposed of. Hilliard gave the German the check, who handed it over to another man with instructions to hold it and await advices. Then he and his companion returned to the yacht.

Hilliard gave instructions to the Captain that steam should be gotten up at once, for they were sailing for Naples early the following morning.

The German paid and dismissed his personal boatsman who at once began rowing toward shore in the little boat in which he had given chase to the fleeing girl earlier in the evening. Then the secret agent pleaded weariness and retired to his cabin.

Two hours later Hilliard was on deck. Due to the excitement he had been unable to sleep. He was standing by the rail looking out over the black bay when a small launch whisked alongside. A much excited and very nervous young man, tall, well built and hatless, called from the steps, demanding the owner of the yacht and saying that he was on business of the American government. Hilliard, with misgivings, beckoned him aboard.

"Are you Mr. Hilliard?" the newcomer asked. Receiving an affirmative nod, he added hastily: "I must see you alone. My name is Johnson. I am an attaché from the American Embassy here."

Hilliard, frightened, led him into his palatial cabin.

THE ATTACHÉ plunged at once into the reasons for his visit at such an hour. "I was working late to-night alone at the embassy. Everyone had gone when I heard the bell ringing. At first I paid no attention, but it was so insistent that I at last went down and opened the door. A man, among the highest in this country, complained that a woman of his harem, and also a thief, was aboard the yacht of an American now lying at anchor in the Bay, where the owner also held captive a detective he had sent to bring her back. He cared nothing except for a priceless jewel which had disappeared with the woman, and argued, with some show of logic, that where she was the jewel would also be. He de manded the instant delivery of the gem, the woman and the detective. It seemed that the Turkish boatsman who had rowed the detective out to the yacht had suspected some double-dealing and had come to the official and had told the story to him. The official was angry—terribly enraged (you know how the Turks scorn white men's religion) and threatened the government with international complications if his property was not immediately forthcoming,

I prevailed upon him to wait—that I would go personally and ascertain if there was any truth in the thing. He said he would wait at the embassy for my return...

"Now, for Heaven's sake, if you have had anything to do with this— well, you know what position you are placing both yourself and the government in. What about it, Mr. Hilliard?"

Hilliard was on the point of emphatically denying everything. But the young man added, "If I come back with a denial he'll never believe it, and Heaven knows what will happen to you and our prestige at the Court."

Hilliard believed in personal safety first, and had never felt exactly at home among a people all of whom carried knives and of whom such cruelties and weird disappearances were recounted. He sized up the young man before him, and decided that the safest course lay in telling the truth.

"My God! This is serious!" Johnson exclaimed at length. "And now that you have taken me into your confidence that makes the embassy a party to the intrigue. I see nothing for me to do but to get into touch with the ambassador himself and tell him all the circumstances. Of course, if you turned the jewel and the woman over to me at once, nothing would be done. You would have lost twenty-thousand dollars, however."

HILLIARD hesitated. This, of course, was the safe thing to do. He did not mind the twenty-thousand dollars so much, but he did hate to lose the jewel. "Can't you go back to this official," he suggested, "and tell him that there is no one on the boat; that he has made a mistake? He would certainly take your word for it, and this German secret service agent of his would be willing to swear to the same story."

"But supposing the official refuses to take my word and had your boat searched? It would mean your arrest and imprisonment, my job, the American ambassador's recall, and maybe more serious diplomatic complications ... No, there is nothing to be done but to return the jewel and the woman, and to let me return them at once. Then the safest thing for you to do is to sail as quickly as possible. If you stay, the official may take it into his head to prosecute you and to call me as a witness. You would have no chance. Once you are away, however, they would not go to the trouble of extraditing you...Now, take my advice, Mr. Hilliard. This is a damnably serious affair. I tell you there is nothing else to be done. If you don't do as I say I shall have to make a clean breast of the whole matter."

Hilliard looked at the young man and saw that he was in earnest. He shrugged his shoulders hopelessly. The jig was up, that was certain. Too many risks were involved to carry the game further.

Reaching in his pocket he took out the jewel and handed it to the other man,

Then he sent for the woman and her slave and told her that she must go back. There was a bitter and sorrowful scene, but at length she stepped into the government launch and gave orders to Achou to follow her.

"Now, Mr. Hilliard," the attaché called, "I want you to sail away from here at once —as fast as you can. I will take as long as I can in returning to the embassy, so as to give you a chance to get away."

Hilliard turned excitedly and gave orders to the captain to weigh anchor and speed out to sea immediately. Then he went below to the cabin of the German agent to tell him of what had happened.

The cabin was empty,

THE NEXT DAY Lily Dinan, Harry Franklin and Red Bernheim sat in the bay window of the Palace Hotel, sipping Turkish coffee.

"You don't look so down-hearted to-day, Red," smiled Franklin.

"No," the other replied jovially. "I've got to hand it to you, Harry. You can find joy everywhere. Did you have any trouble getting the check cashed?"

"Trouble? How trouble?" The other lighted a *Régie* cigarette and sniffed the smoke approvingly. "I had old Hilliard make out the check to H. Franklin and my passport identified me and the money was handed me without any question."

"I wonder," mused Red aloud, "if old Hilliard will ever wake up to the fact that the harem queen was a Broadway flapper"—at this Lily pouted—"and that her slave was a Jewish actor on Broadway."

Harry Frankin laughed quietly, "What I was afraid of was that he might have suspected me when I took off my German whiskers and mustache and reappeared as the embassy attaché."

"He never would have known it in the world," Lily put in admiringly, taking her husband's hand. "Your German make-up was immense."

"There were several times, however," Franklin said, "when I thought everything was lost. I had paid the hotel porter to meet me at a certain café and to pretend to be my friend and to receive and hold a check I would give him. When Hilliard and I arrived, and the old boy had made out the check, the porter hadn't shown up. There was no time to rustle up another friend, and I felt shaky; but the porter came at last.... Then again, when I had to swim away from the yacht, after having pretended to retire, one of the deck hands came to the rail and leaned over, before I had swum a dozen strokes, And to make it worse, that numbskull of a Turkish fisherman who had rowed me out in the first place and was to pick me up as I swam away, began to yell his head off to attract my attention as soon as he caught sight of me in the water."

"Well, don't worry about the close shaves," Red advised philosophically. "It's all over now but the spending."

"Only," Lily remarked a little sadly, "I do wish that old fool Hilliard could know that it was all a game."

Franklin laughed and patted her hand.

"That's the feminine point of view, I guess," he said smilingly…"I'll tell you what I'll do, Lil," he added. "If we hear where Hilliard lands next I'll send him the Moon of the East and write him that, since he is out twenty-thousand dollars, he is entitled to it."

"If I could only be there," Lily chuckled, "when he finds out that it is paste!"

# THE SCANDAL OF THE LOUVRE

ONE SOFT SUMMER day, when the walnuts were casting fluttering embroideries of light and shadow over the parks and streets of the French capital, and the rich green grass had reached its height of vividness in the lawn stretches of the *Cour Carrousel* of the ancient palace of the Louvre, a trio of what appeared to be tourists alighted from a swaying fiacre before the entrance to the great picture museum. Two of them seemed more than eager to proceed to the Salon Carré where hung the masterpieces of Veronese, da Vinci, Titian, and many other world-renowned masters. But the third lagged behind muttering and grumbling as though performing a most unpleasant duty.

He was a large, florid man of about forty-five. His clothes were baggy and of a loud check, his cravat was of a lurid blue-green with red stripes; and his hands were adorned with expensive but ill-chosen rings. A large diamond shone aggressively from his shirt front, and there was a feather—an adornment in-vogue at the time —protruding from the ribbon of his hat. All in all, he looked the part of a sluggish German of the working class, who had lately come into a fortune, and was "doing" Europe.

His companions' looks served to accentuate the eccentricities of the other. There was a quietness and good taste displayed in their well-fitting and simple garments, and they possessed an undeniable air of good-breeding. One was a man of about thirty, whose every movement betrayed his social culture, and whose restraint and delicacy of feature showed the man of inherent refinement.

His companion was a girl, eight or ten years his junior. About her hung a sense of appealing and happy melancholy—a something from which emanated affection and tenderness, a potent charm of both appearance and character. Her hair was as black and alive as a starling's wing; and her eyes, bright from beneath long lashes, had a vitality and alertness seldom seen in brunettes.

THIS GIRL WAS Lilly Franklin, née Dinan, wife of Harry Franklin, who was one of the cleverest, "squarest" and most intelligent crooks then operating. The heavy man of German appearance was Red: Bernheim, a Jewish man from New York, erstwhile leader of a band of organized crooks, but now the devoted and ardent admirer of Harry Franklin, as well as his absolutely reliable henchman.

The three went slowly through the long gallery, down the short flight of steps into the Rubens rooms, then back through the galleries of the French school, and at last stood once again in the Salon Carré, tired and satiated with art for the day,

There were few visitors about at the time, it being an admission day, and the trio strolled about looking at the copies of the hung work being made by the students. They were astonished at the exactitude of the imitative work and watched the busy students with intense interest. They were particularly wonder-struck when they stopped in front of da Vinci's *Gioconda* and saw a picture, nearly finished, which in every detail, down to the very cracks in the paint, the tint and drawing, was a perfect duplicate of the original. In silence they marveled for some time at the closeness of the work and at the infinite patience with which the student laid in the details. Then Red, bursting forth at last, fairly cried:

"There you are! D'you see? Do you fine art lovers think you could tell one from the other? If not, which is the best? I'm asking you: which is the best—the work of the old gink what made that one?"—pointing to the wall—"or the guy what's putting the finishing strokes on this one?"—indicating the one on the easel.

Red laughed triumphantly and turned away while Harry Franklin stood in deep thought. Lilly looked up anxiously into his eyes, her arm through his. His mind was not altogether on art, however. He was thinking of a subject more relative to his wife's and his own welfare. He stood perhaps five minutes thus, unseeing. Then he turned to Red Bernheim.

DO YOU KNOW," he commented, "that picture of Leonardo's is one of the most talked-of paintings in the world? It is probably one of the most valuable works of art in existence, for it has a tremendous sentimental interest, as well as an artistic one. There isn't a great collector in the world who wouldn't give his last dollar for it. If we owned that, Red, we could live in luxury for the rest of our lives."

"Sure!" agreed the other. "The same goes about Brooklyn Bridge. Let's slip up New York Harbor some night and run away with it."

Franklin ignored his partner's good-natured sarcasm, and hurried out of the Louvre without a word, Lilly and Red following him. He called a taxicab, and the three climbed in and were driven to their apartments in the Hotel. Lutetia on the *boulevard raspail*.

For a while Harry sat in thought. Then he turned to Lilly. "How's your French, kid?" he asked. "Do you find you still remember your native tongue after all your years in America?"

"Oh, I get along like a Parisienne," the girl replied proudly.'Mother and Father always used to make me talk in French. My accent's fine. All I need is to pick up some of the current slang—then no one would know I'd ever left France."

"Good!" commented Harry, kissing her. "Now brush up on your slang. You'll need it."

Red rubbed his hands together He scented a new adventure.

A WEEK LATER Henry E. Ostrander was surprised from a sound slumber at eleven o'clock in the morning by an urgent call on the telephone in his luxurious rooms at the Grand Hotel. At first he was for letting it ring. His head still ached from the champagne and dancing of the night before when, in company of two friends and a guide, he had attempted to exhaust the ribald pleasures of Montmartre. But the ringing was so persistent that at last he arose to stop it. He jerked down the receiver angrily and grunted "Hello." A voice, vibrant and masculine, asked if he were the Mr. Ostrander whose fame was worldwide as a picture collector. He answered affirmatively in a curt voice, and was about to cut off his unknown inquisitor when what he heard made him change his mind. His tone altered and he consented to a rendezvous with the stranger for twelve o'clock.

At the appointed hour, he met Harry Franklin on the enclosed-veranda at the rear of the hotel. The two men shook hands and sat down. No time was lost in preliminaries. Franklin told him immediately and in a business-like way that he could secure the greatest picture in Paris for the other's collection if he, Ostrander, would pay the price and see to its shipment out of the country. The millionaire was eager to know what work it was, hoping it might be some small canvas from a private collection. He was ready to pay liberally for such a work. He was in Europe at the time hoping to pick up something valuable.

In his collection were many ill-gotten works. There was a Gothic angel from the cathedral at Rouen, an altarpiece from Notre Dame, a very old *prie-dieu* from Milan, and many smaller works, each representing a sacrilege committed by one of those bands of thieves who are organized for the one purpose of stealing *objets d'art* from public and private collections, only to sell them to avid and unscrupulous collectors who care more for the object than for a clear conscience. Ostrander was acquainted with the leaders of several such bands, and had made purchases through them. He knew they were fearless and daring, but he was carried wholly off his feet when Franklin announced his intention.

"I shall steal the *Mona Lisa* of da Vinci and sell it to the highest bidder!"

If Franklin had said he was to steal the *Venus de Milo* or Napoleon's tomb itself, he would scarcely have made more of an impression,

Ostrander nearly fell from his chair; his eyes bulged from his head. The enormity of the deed!

"Man, you're raving crazy!" he managed to say at last. "What kind of a fool are you, anyway? Don't you know that, besides being priceless, that work stands supreme as the best 'preserved example of Italian art?" Then he smiled. The thing was preposterous. "Say, don't joke about such things. Come down to earth." Then he asked more calmly, "What's your proposition?"

"I have told you, Mr. Ostrander," Franklin returned quietly, "I intend to steal the *Mona Lisa*, and if you don't care to make a bid, I shall say good-day."

Ostrander raised his hand.

"Wait!" he said. "Let me think a minute." Franklin resumed his seat. The great collector was trembling slightly,

"My God!" he exclaimed, as if to himself. "If I really thought I could get the *Mona Lisa*—to have it for my own, personally, privately!" He gloated over the thought. "But it's incredible—utterly preposterous! It can't be done." He looked at Franklin sharply. He suspected some hoax,

The other defined his suspicions, and smiled. : .

"You need not pay one cent till you are satisfied—till the picture is in your hands," he said. "You will know it has been stolen sometime before I will present you with it."

"You fellows are slick," Ostrander admitted. "You've gotten me things before I didn't think possible. But this—" He whistled, and strode up and down excitedly. "It would be the great scandal of the century!"

"Do you want the picture?" the younger man asked, rising and putting on his hat.

"Sit down—sit down!' Ostrander urged. "Let's talk the matter over."

THE CONVERSATION was resumed on a business basis. Fifteen minutes later Franklin departed after having secured an offer which meant riches if he would deliver the picture to Ostrander before a certain date. Ostrander, however, did not expect to get it. The idea was too fantastic. Steal the *Mona Lisa*! Impossible! The dream of a crazy man!

The man must be drunk to hold the belief that he could outwit the police of the world.

"Well, anyway," he mused, "the picture is priceless, worth millions, ungettable; and the sum I offered would be indeed small if I really got possession of this famous masterpiece."

Chuckling, he strolled out upon the boulevard and took a seat on the terrace of the *Café de la Paix*.

Every one interested in art who has been to Paris knows that the picture museum of the Louvre is closed every Monday and Thursday morning for the purpose of cleaning and dusting the statuary, pictures, frames, cases and floors. Early on these two mornings are to be seen groups of men and women going into the small entrances which lead, by devious and dark, narrow stone stairways, to the big, light galleries above.

The Monday after Franklin's talk with Ostrander, Lilly, dressed in the manner of the other workers and carrying a bundle in which were threads, fine wire, *savon noir*, and rags (all for cleaning) entered the Louvre with the others. It had not been an easy task for her to secure employment. It had first been necessary to find out who was the head of the cleaning squad, Later Lilly was brought to his notice; and then, by her charming ways and intimate beauty, she ingratiated herself in his good graces in a manner he could not resist. She had taken a room in the boarding house where he lived, and had made it a point to be constantly passing him in the hall with a smile. After he had spoken to her once she felt assured of obtaining her end.

TODAY WAS HER first chance; and the man who employed her, himself a workman and one of the museum guards, was on the point of acknowledging to himself that she was a very desirable and charming young woman to know. But on this particular day she kept him at a distance and worked hard—so hard, in fact, that her heretofore well-kept and dainty hands became red and blistered. The man, however, hovered about her, joking and laughing; but she, though seeming to enter whole-heartedly into the innocent fun, was, in reality, making mental notes of the conditions which obtained in the gallery on closed days.

She noted that there was no formality necessary to go in and out of the many rooms. The restorers and workmen were continually coming and going unchallenged through this storehouse of treasures, as freely as if there was not a thing: of value to tempt them. Often whole rooms were left entirely unguarded for as long as ten minutes at a time. At noon, she departed, happy in her knowledge, to report to

Harry every detail of what she had seen. He was greatly pleased. He gave her some further instructions, and sent her back to her lodgings.

The following Monday was the day fixed upon for the coup. The magnitude of the undertaking appalled Red Bernheim. And Lilly. Though outwardly calm, Lilly at heart was in a terrible panic of fear, not so much for herself, as for Harry, whose love and companionship had made of her an ideal wife and had raised her from the dregs of the underworld to what seemed to her a paradise.

Harry himself was not so easy in his mind as he had been on other occasions. A certain restlessness could be noted in his actions. The worry he was undergoing showed in an occasional slight drawing of his features. It was to be the big "job" of his life. Indeed, he was half inclined to promise himself he would settle down and live quietly if he carried it through successfully.

TO Red, Harry seemed to have gone back on his original ideas of taking money only from those who richly deserved a lesson.

"What do you call this?" he would ask sarcastically. "Is there some ethical reason for lifting the dame from this here nation to America? Don't tell me you're as patriotic as that! It's just what I told you before: when the big money calls, those who can, goes! But I'm fer letting it slip by. It's too much chance. It can't be done; and you know what these here wrist-watch frog-eaters'll do to us if we're caught. Stealin' the *Monny Lisy*! Gosh! I'd rather rob the Turks or the Japanese than these boys. They're small, but they're cute. You never know what they've got up their sleeve. What do you say?"

"You know I never give up a thing I have started to do, Red," Franklin would answer. "And as for your jibes about my waning principles—well, I shall answer for them later. Besides, there is a very good reason why France should lose many of her treasures. You are, perhaps, not aware that the great Napoleon carried about in the wake of his armies art experts who saw to the selecting and shipment to Paris of the great artworks of his conquered territories…

"This was eminently evil—not morally, understand, but artistically. Those countries that can produce no art, deserve none. Napoleon had a right to despoil his enemies of money and goods; but the thought and flower of a nation should be inviolate. His divinity I could question on many points. At present, I must ask you, for your own good, to be patient. Mourn my loss of self-respect if you will, but never believe that any one can make of me a man who gives up the fight."

And this was all Red could extract from the admired partner who had made him rich through the play of his nimble wit.

"As I have told you before, Red," Franklin philosophized, "men who can swindle and steal in such a way that the law is powerless to punish them, deserve punishment even more than smaller and less subtle offenders. The judges on the bench receive a salary for dealing out justice, do they not? Very well. I have appointed myself a judge superior to the men of the Supreme Court. I handle cases beyond their scope—insidious and dastardly cases whose gangrene honeycombs the social fabric. Why should I not receive a living?

"My efforts are bent to punish the guilty and to attain happiness at one and the same time. Would that I could train others to the task!" The time passed more than slowly, but finally the great day arrived.

There was little sleep in that household the night before, but early Lilly was on her way across the river from the *Rive Gauche*, on the top of the omnibus. With her was her ardent admirer—the Louvre guard— who had gone so far as to pinch her cheek while she was looking the other way.

As she began her duties she thought once more carefully over her plans. The minutes dragged while she had to conjole the workman and keep him about her. As the clock neared eleven, she let him become more familiar. She brushed against him coquettishly, put her face close to his, and playfully pushed him about. All the time her heart was beating like a trip hammer. As the minutes rolled by she began to loathe this creature whom she had to deceive. All her love for Harry came up to choke her and to moisten her eyes; and it was an herculean task to laugh and sing under the circumstances.

At five minutes of the hour she stopped, and said with an exaggerated seriousness which made her companion thrill:

"You say you love me, don't you? How do I know if you tell the truth? You've never even kissed me."

Then springing lightly to her feet, she tripped across the room, laughing aloud. The man sprang to his feet, a large smile on his heavy face, and ran after her,

"If that's all the proof you want," he exclaimed, "you shall have it now, *petite môme*."

She easily eluded his arms until her watch pointed to one minute of the hour. When the great clock outside sounded eleven, she ran between two long curtains in a passage that led to another gallery. This passage was where old frames and students' easels and copies were kept, and it was always empty. Here she led him a merry chase about the table until she was out of breath. At last he caught her and put his arms about her, she struggling and on the point of tears all the time. The tears he took for surrender, little dreaming they were for worry for another man to whom her very life would have been willingly given. She was very tired now, and putting on a serious face, she pushed him away, saying:

"Listen, Auguste, they'll miss us out here, and you see you can't get a kiss unless I want you to. So promise me only to take one—and it's yours. But lie to me, and I swear I'll never speak to you again."

The man laughed and promised, for a given kiss in France would mean that she loved him. She patted his cheek tenderly, and at last let him lean down and kiss her forehead…

In the meantime much had happened. As these two left the room, a small door at the rear had been noiselessly opened and a workman, with the blouse of a plasterer, a dark head of long hair and a black mustache, had come in quickly. With him he carried a large cloth and a screwdriver. Hastening across the room he quickly jerked the frame of the *Mona Lisa* from the wall. Next, he loosened the nails which held it in place, and, covering it with the cloth, ran out of the same little door through which he had come, and disappeared, He jumped into a waiting machine, which straightaway sped from the grounds and across the bridge. At last it stopped, and its occupant alighted and was soon lost in the crowd of the *Rue du Bac.*

The machine had already left the museum door with its sacred prize before Lilly let her pretended admirer come back, and it was ten minutes before they were back in the *Salon Carré.* The *Mona Lisa* is not a large picture, and its absence was not discovered. The workmen and guards were all too busy in their preparations for going home,

LILLY WAS trembling violently as she walked out of the door with the other cleaners. Her knees were shaking so that she could scarcely stand; and her face was very pale. She had eluded her would-be lover: when he had gone to secure his hat and coat, she had hurried away. Once in the street, she almost ran to the Metro station. When she was seated, she burst out crying from sheer reaction, and the subway guard took it upon himself to comfort her,

Lilly alighted at the *Gare Montparnasse.* There Red awaited her. She quickly changed her clothes, which were awaiting her under the seat, and was driven to the hotel. She found Harry indolently smoking a cigarette with a sage smile on his face, and threw herself, sobbing, into his ready arms.

"When do we leave, Harry?" she asked. "Soon?…When will you see Ostrander? Is everything all right? What will happen when they discover that the picture's gone? They're sure to notice it tomorrow… Oh, Harry, I was so afraid you'd get caught. Tell me how you did it."

Franklin answered all her questions and soothed her as best he could, admonishing her that all was not over yet and that some still very risky work was still to be accomplished.

Red strolled in and grasped Harry's hand. "I'll hand it to you again, Harry. You're there! Where's the money? Have you got the cash?"

"No." Franklin smiled. "I have neither the picture nor the cash. We'll have to give Ostrander a day or two to be sufficiently pleased with the excitement which will start to-morrow. We must make him feel that he is getting his money's worth. It's a big price he's paying, and he could hold me up easily if he wanted to lose the picture. The picture, by the way, I left in the tool box of the machine, under the circumstances that is about the safest place. An auto is also about the safest place for a money transaction when you want to be sure nobody is listening. It is also a good trunk for the smuggling of contraband goods to a foreign country… Let me see, we rented the machine by the week. I'm afraid we're going to be obliged to pay a large price for it, because to all intents and purposes it will have to be wrecked."

THE NEXT morning, August the twenty-second, 1911, the storm broke forth.

The theft of daVinci's great masterpiece was discovered by one of the guards. In an hour the newsboys were dashing up the boulevards crying the extras at the top of their voices, "Paris went nearly insane. Every one ceased their duties to discuss the great tragedy. The city was hysterical with excitement. All the officials were blaming the curator, Dujardin Beaumetz, who, in turn, was blaming the administration for not supplying him with sufficient guards. Investigations were called. Recriminations were hurled back and forth. The police announced clues, and the papers teemed with interviews and explanations. But despite the uproar and confusion of the entire capital, every one felt that the picture would be returned or found very soon. One impression which gained considerable headway was that some accident had befallen it, which the government was endeavoring to hush up by saying it was lost.

The next morning—Wednesday—Ostrander did not keep the telephone ringing so long as on the first occasion, when Franklin called up. A proud and self-satisfied smile lit up his features as' Harry's name was announced. He hurried down 'stairs immediately…

The two men shook hands and retired to a secluded corner of the American bar,

"You did it, man!" exclaimed the collector in an awed voice. "By God, you're a wonder! Left no clue, and fooled 'em all!  Well, I'm

ready with my end. When can I get hold of it?"

"Mr. Ostrander, here is my advice," Harry answered. "You know the difficulty of the American port authorities. The best thing to do is to buy the machine which I'l] point out to you; then ship it at once to your home in New York. The picture will be in the toolbox carefully wrapped up and concealed. In order to buy the machine without the painting being discovered, we'll pretend to wreck it, and I'll go and pay the claim. You know, if you purchased it in the ordinary way some salesman might open the tool box by way of demonstration; and again, suspicion might be aroused… The car is below. If you'll come for a ride, we'll have a look."

THAT NIGHT Franklin took the machine out by himself, and early in the morning returned with it to the hotel. He left his car at the door, went to the owner's and, after telling of the imaginative accident, bought the car and brought away a bill of sale.

He lost no time in going to Ostrander to collect. That man, still suspicious, demanded to see that the picture was still in the car before paying. After another long drive and a careful scrutiny of the master. piece in the early light of dawn, they returned in time for the bank opening, A half hour later Franklin and Red were traversing the Pont St. Michel with over $150,000 in American bank-notes safely tucked away in their wallets. Ostrander was elated over his possession of the stolen picture and the bill of sale of the automobile. He kept his eye on the machine until it was safely under way for Calais, from where it would be put aboard a fast boat for America.

That night Franklin, Lilly, and Red took the train for Florence by way of Marseilles and Milan—happy to be free of the encumbrance of the dangerous art treasure and rejoicing in their possession of a new fortune.

Once in. Florence the warm and balmy air of the most beautiful city in the world made dreamers of them all. They settled down for a well-deserved rest on a high hill overlooking the Arno in a villa surrounded by flowers and tall cypress trees. There the days flew by as though on magic wings. Even Red forgot his lust for gold and seemed to become part of that wonderful southland.

Every day or so they would hear echoes of that famous theft, and at sight of these bits of news or new clues Franklin would smile, and Red would gloat over the fact that the largest amount they had ever made was a downright steal and not an idealized lesson in decency for the benefit of some erring brother. He had always: scoffed at Franklin's idealism; and now he felt that in some way he had won a sort of immoral victory over his partner.

NEARLY THREE YEARS of pure happiness passed thus, and the memory of that thrilling day in Paris had nearly faded from their minds when one day a bellowing and stamping was heard on the walk leading to their little house. Red Bernheim, scarlet in the face, rushed in, waving a paper.

"Look here!" he cried angrily. "What in hell does this mean? ... Read! 'The *Mona Lisa* restored to its place on the walls of the Louvre. Thief a patriotic madman, caught at Milan. His name is Vincenzia Perugia. Says he stole it to restore it to the Italian Government,"

And Red went on to tell how this Italian, imbued with zeal, becoming depressed over the thought of the great Napoleon's vandalism while in Italy, walked into the gallery one day, took the masterpiece and escaped.

"Well, Red, what's the matter?" he asked pleasantly. "All is well; the picture has been restored to its rightful owners."

"What's that!" shrieked Red. "How about Ostrander? Did he give it back again?...Say, Harry, let's have the dope."

"Sit down, Red, and I'll give you the story." Franklin was grinning, "Ostrander had the picture. He only saw it once in his life, and that was the day you drove us to Robeson. The next drive was, if you remember, made in the early morning, and his view was not as microscopic as it might have been. You may well wonder how I avoided giving it to him. Well, you remember the day we arrived in Paris and saw that poor fellow copying the picture? You tried to kid me about the duplicate's perfection. Well, I bought that finished copy, and: it was that copy, which cost me three hundred francs, which I sold to Ostrander for $150,000. I did leave it in the tool box until the old scoundrel had seen it. But when I took out the car the same night I changed the copy for the original, bought a trunk on my way home, nailed the original in the bottom, and checked it at the *Gare de Lyons*. Ostrander bought a machine in which to smuggle a copy to America!" Harry laughed.

I BROUGHT the original here to Florence. As you see, I could have deprived the French nation—the most capable of appreciating and loving art—of that picture.

But I didn't want to. Six weeks ago I hired a reliable Milanese to take the picture back and clumsily expose the shape and size to some custom house man so he would be detected. Of course, I paid the man well for taking the chances. Just as I thought, the *beau geste* is highly appreciated by the French; and this man's story of taking the work as an act of patriotism will set him free in Italy and be indulgently regarded by the French. He has done his work well."

He paused a moment. Then he went on:

"Everyone, I believe, is happy. We ourselves have no complaint to make, nor has M. Dujardin Beaumetz, the curator of the Louvre. My man will be well paid, and, as I see it, every one but Ostrander has been squarely treated. For him, I have little sympathy. He is a thief by nature. He would hide a transcendent piece of art from the eyes of the deserving in order to gratify his own vanity by hanging it in a dark gallery. The lesson I have given him is—"

"Oh, Hell!" growled Red, casting an indignant look over his shoulder, and stamping out of the room,

Lilly snuggled close to her husband, and Franklin looked after the retreating form of Bernheim with a facial expression somewhat akin to the *Mona Lisa*'s enigmatic smile.

# A DEAL IN CONTRABAND

A LONG A SHADY street in Tampa one September day two years ago a trio of companions walked leisurely toward the water front. Only a month previous they had arrived from Florence, Italy, where they had almost forgotten the outside world in the perfect happiness they had found in the exquisite old city of Michelangelo. But indications of the outbreak of the Great War had come to disturb their peace of mind, and they had hastened back to their native land.

The years they had spent in so quiet a place had worked many changes in the outlook of them all. Lilly Franklin had almost wooed her husband, Harry, from his adopted life of hazardous undertakings and brought about in him a conventional satisfaction with what the world calls an honest career.

Harry Franklin had not been born a crook. Indeed, he had had educational advantages far above the average; but he had chosen what to him was a romantic life in order to assuage the latent wanderlust which possessed him. His attitude toward crime was an unusual one. He had a strict, if fantastic, moral code; and liked to believe that he was the personification of retributory justice, whose mission it was to seek out and punish all arch-hypocrites and within-the-law criminals. Perhaps his extraordinary success was attributable to the fact that he brought to. outlawry many novel ideas and conceits, a different angle of vision, a certain quixotic fastidious-ness which denied him spoils from honest men and prohibited him from playing those games in which so many conscienceless men profit.

LILLY'S LONG vacation had made her more lovely and girlish than ever. Her eyes saw only Harry, and she was so utterly his that his plans for future "jobs" horrified and frightened her. As a result she implored him constantly to mend his ways and live as other people lived, in safety and peace, pointing out to him they had no need of money now. She appeared to make some headway, for Harry had been idle for over two years, and had turned his energies to literature with a view of becoming a writer.

Throughout the halt in his activities Red Bernheim, the third member of this strange party, was somewhat restless. Older than the other two, he had never before known the meaning of a quiet or sequestered life.

He had been born to crime and could not appreciate Lilly's desire to leave it all behind. In fact, he dreaded the day when Harry would say definitely that he was through forever, for on that day the big, loyal and kind-hearted Jewish man, wholly devoted to Harry and Lilly, would have to hunt another "pal" with whom to work and Red knew there was not another pardner of Harry's caliber to be had. That he himself had ample money for all his needs mattered little. It was impossible for him to be idle, and he knew of no other method of killing time save in the pursuance of his illegal profession.

Consequently he was far from happy, especially as their visit to this southern city had been dictated by purely legitimate reasons. A month before the war Harry had been told, by a friend high in maritime circles, that there would be an inevitable shortage of bottoms should the war actually come, and had been advised to charter several ships for rechartering purposes as a sure and lucrative investment. Harry, with money to spare, had acted on this advice. He had found the Black Cross Steamship Company of Tampa possessed of two sister ships which he obtained at a very low figure for delivery the first of September. As everyone knows, in the first days of August there was a frantic demand for every type of ship available, from the old square-rigged windjammer to the fancy yacht-like steamers of large tonnage.

Transatlantic trade needed them; and, in consequence, the prices of all concessions went up enormously. Harry found he had on hand a large fortune, and now he was on his way to see what could be turned over by their transfer to a marine agent who was going crazy at the thought of them.

As they neared their objective, Red suddenly veered about without a word and disappeared up a side street, making a well-known sign which meant that he was "tailing" someone. Harry and Lilly kept on, heard a highly flattering proposition, and later returned to the hotel. There they found Red waiting for them.

"Why the sudden interest in the man who swung out of the saloon?" Harry asked.

Red was ready to burst with rage, and his story flowed from him without a halt. He had recognized an old acquaintance by the name of Carter, despite the fact that the latter had grown a beard and wore double heels. Harry also remembered Carter.

"Say, Harry," Red went on excitedly, "this guy is worse than Carlisle who bilked me and who you backed to get my stones, back in California. This guy makes his wad after fixin' a Florida town six seasons runnin'. The boys always was good to him, and he always took all the money he could get. At last he sold out to Jacobs for about twenty thousand, sayin' he's had enough. Well, about three years later—he can't stay away from the 'racket'—he comes into it again. But this time he comes in as a sucker. Having been there himself, he knew where the boys would see him and how to get himself rapped to. So, one day this wise sucker shows up, having effected some changes in his face and make-up, and acts the innocent so well that he's marked for the pay-off and led along. In the meantime he flashes a roll and talks about how much he's got at home.

"WELL, THE BOYS rig up a *deluxe* pool room in Albany for his special benefit. He sure does look like ripe and easy pickin'. The big day comes. All the preliminaries are done; the readyin' up is finished, and they lead him into the pool parlor. He bets and of course they let him win at first. He acts almost like a kid over it, and bets a little more. Again the boys let him win so as to get his confidence. Understand, there's some big money back of this game, because two of the boys just finished a tip-top season in California. Then came the big blow-off to do him out of his entire wad, which amounted to over forty-five thousand! Suddenly he says, as if he ain't quite convinced: 'Listen, boys: you say this is a sure thing, and I believe you. But you never can tell with these slick racin' people. I'm goin' to lay one more small bet to make sure before I risk my pile. The horse is a long shot, and I'll I put up the thousand I've won and two thousand more. Then if I win I'll lay my whole pocketbook on the next roany.

"Some of the boys was for kickin' him out, not wantin' to take such a big chance; but the others was for lettin' him win and cleanin' him out right the next day. So they went ahead and played him. He laid three thousand at ten to one, and naturally he won. Thirty thousand bucks he carried away in his jeans that night in company with the boy who was doin' the friendly act. ' He was so anxious to come back the next day that it was all they could do to get him started for his hotel. That night he showed that he was no coward. He started a fight with the boys in the room over some little card game, and a couple of gorillas -he'd hired steps out and taps the boys on the head.

WELL, THE SUCKER had won out. He was about twenty thousand to the good, for not all the money was negotiable. He left town and never since has anybody been able to locate him. Carter was the guy I tailed today; and now there's going to be some real sport. He don't know it, but some of my money left with him. He owes me three 'grand,' with interest that'd make the three-ball uncles of twenty years ago look like philanthropists. Carter's going to pay me all he's got, plus his jewels, good looks and health. So help me Gawd, I wasn't born for giving away money."

And Red reached round unconsciously and felt a large lump in his hip pocket. Here was something more ominous than determination in his eyes.

Harry had listened sympathetically through the story. A great disgust for so mean and contemptible an act as Carter's was written on his face.

"Red, I'm with you," he said. "If the truth be known, Mr. Carter and I once had a little deal on together, and he didn't play square. But without your grievance I should never have bothered with him, considering any contact with him degrading. Now, however—well, he hates me because the outcome of our incident was unpleasant for him. So, in anything you have to say to him, steer clear of me. Hatred in such creatures is even more potent than gold. Don't do anything tonight. Give me time to do a little thinking. There is always a quiet way of murdering a man financially without putting his body in the morgue."

Lilly looked at him with a sigh and sank dejectedly into a chair to await the inevitable work ahead of her.

THREE days later many things had happened. Harry Franklin was suing Lilly Franklin for a divorce, and their pictures had appeared in the papers more for the beauty of the lady and the spicy details of the case than for the importance of the persons concerned. On the night after the publication of these articles Red and Lilly strolled into a restaurant and sat down at a table close to one occupied by a bearded man of good appearance. They began deprecatingly to discuss Harry Franklin, and ridiculed his ideas of right and wrong in voices just loud enough to reach the man nearby. Red pretended to comfort Lilly as best he could. He painted a picture of a rosy future and admonished her not to be too resentful, occasionally looking about as if to make sure that no one could hear him.

In one of these uneasy scrutinies of the other guests his eyes fell on Carter. A light of recognition flashed over his countenance, and he rose and went over to the other's table. After greetings, hearty on Red's part, rather nervous in the case of Carter, he began to relate to Carter the latest news of the underworld. He told of Franklin's turning straight, of his cutting all his old friends and trying to trump up a game on his wife to get rid of her of his despicable actions in throwing him, Red, out because the latter's grammar grated on his nerves. The listener laughed at the other's narrative, and soon the two became at ease. Carter was led back to Lilly's table, and the three put in an hour severely criticizing their erstwhile friend. Carter still harbored a great hatred for Franklin, and everything vicious and mean which was said concerning Harry pleased him greatly. At length, they separated in high spirits, agreeing to meet again the next night.

ON THE OCCASION of their second meeting hints were thrown out that something should be done to this despised man; and on the third night the flame of enmity, burned so high in Carter and Lilly that a plan was decided on whereby they all could be revenged and at the same time make a small fortune. Happily, the circumstances were just right for a coup, for, according to Lilly's explanation, Harry was entering upon an undertaking of some magnitude—an enterprise in which they could beat him.

It was Red who framed the plans.

"You see, it's this way," he said. "Harry has got next to some ginks here that wants Pajara to be president of Mexico. Pajara's got the backin' in men, but since Wilson closed the border to guns, he can't do a thing. These Pajara henchmen are willin' to pay, but being in the public eye, they don't dare make a move. So Harry's to be the goat. Well, a Pajara official comes here with some cash as security and turns it over to Harry. Harry charters two sister boats in the Black Cross Company which has four boats all alike; only the two Harry gets are slow, while the other two like 'em, which the Company holds on to, are fast. Item one: Harry was bunked on his boats. Harry's game is to load one boat, the *Alice*, with coal, and the other, the *Edith*, with guns. Then he's goin' to substitute the *Edith* for the *Alice* after the clearance papers for the *Alice* are gotten, change the names on the ships at night, and sail the ammunition ship for the west coast of South America through the canal. But when he gets into the Pacific he's goin' to jump up the coast, dock in Porto Vieja, get his big war money, and live a straight and happy life ever after. There's his game.

"Now, here's what we can do. We can either tip off the government and get him cooped with a long stretch here, or we can double-cross him, get him cooped in Mexico, where he'll never get out, and beat him out of the price of his boat and cargo as well." Red then unrolled his scheme.

LILLY was strongly for telling the government at once. She wanted revenge, she said, and nearly carried her point when the avarice of Bernheim and Carter overthrew her hatred. At length they decided to take the latter course: to make money while getting even was more in their line. The idea of it brought added color to the pasty face of their new companion.

Red's plan was, easy of accomplishment if Carter had any .money to start it going. Red assured him that he knew the Pajara official, and could "fix" him easily if Carter would say the word. Their scheme was practically the same as Harry's. They were to charter the other two boats of the Black Cross Company, load one with coal, the other with arms and ammunition, effect the change at night as Harry had done, and, by reason of their superior speed, beat Harry's boats to the coast.

After passing Harry's boat they were to change their boat's name to that of Harry's—namely, to *Alice*—so as to deceive the Pajara hench-men atVieja into believing their boat was the one expected. then they were to have Pajara arrest Harry as an impostor. Pajara could do this, as he held and controlled the district aroundVieja, and by so doing he could confiscate Harry's cargo of ammunition, thereby acquiring two cargoes for the price of one. Red assured him that Pajara's henchmen, then in Tampa, had sufficient influence with the would-be president to have the arrest ordered and the confiscation made without legal formalities. Harry, of course, could not appeal to the United States for help as he was confessedly a smuggler.

"But why," asked Carter, "wouldn't Pajara have us arrested, too, and confiscate our cargo without paying for it? Your friend, Mr. Hench-man, might take it into his head to double-cross us."

"Nothin' doin'!" chirped Red. "The Pajara guy don't get his hand-out until Pajara pays us. See? We'll get ours, or Mr. Henchman won't get his. He'll see to it we're paid, and paid quick."

Carter was satisfied, and left the details in Red's hands. It was nec-essary for them to wait three days to see if Harry succeeded in his subterfuge with the clearance papers. In the meantime, Red, with Carter's money, secured an option on the two Black Cross boats for immediate delivery. Three days later they read in the maritime news that the *Alice* had put to sea for Guayaquil, laden with a cargo of soft coal. There was great rejoicing; and the Pajara official was immediately got hold of. He proved himself an easy tool, apparently being ready to betray anybody on earth for a little *dinero*.

Naturally some one would have to go to Mexico to be the con-signee and take the name of Franklin, for Franklin was the name the official had already telegraphed to Pajara. Red was willing either to stay in Tampa and see to the loading, or to go and look after the reception of the cargo.

But Carter, having paid an enormous sum for the chartering and advanced a large amount to the head of the ammunition and coal companies, and feeling that this money was safely tied up in Tampa, decided that he would like to be the recipient of the check when the ship arrived in port. He had been led deeply into the game by his desire for Harry's downfall, and by the sly looks of Lilly, of whom he had heard much, as well as by his greed, and he had no intention of foregoing the pleasure of seeing Harry put safely away in a Mexican jail or of receiving personally the amount of his enemy's betrayal. The Mexican official was to accompany Carter to see that things went smoothly in Vieja, and Lilly and Red were to come on the ammunition boat.

When they had seen the loading of coal underway, the two men left for Porto Vieja. On their arrival, Carter received in the little office a telegram from Red saying that his ship had cleared without any trouble, that the transfer had been made, and that the coal-laden boat had been sent to Pernambuco, where a fair profit could be expected on its cargo.

PORTO VIEJA was something less than a village, situated on a rocky and difficult coast, due west of San Jose del Cabo, in Lower California. It enjoyed an unsavory reputation as a center of opium smuggling in the old days, and constituted the general headquarters for all the banditti of illicit sea-trading and contrabanding on the entire west coast. In it there were no telephones, and the mail service was desultory. There was little necessity, however, for any mail service, for most of the inhabitants had no addresses, and the transient visitors who filled the old saloon, called the Cafe Maximilian, had no desire to communicate with the outside world.

Carter spent an insufferable two weeks of fan-tan playing and drinking in the huts that passed for "Palaces," cursing the necessity which made a consignee necessary, and keeping steadily on the lookout to dodge Franklin, who had also come to Porto Vieja to await his shipment. Franklin, however, was not to be found. He had been there and established an address, and had even hung out a sign as agent for the Black Cross Steamship Company, in order to answer the requirements of the law; but he had ostensibly left again, not to return until the arrival of his ship.

At the end of a fortnight Carter received another telegram from

Red, advising him that Franklin's ship had been passed at Mindi, in the canal, and that already the name of the boat had been changed. This varied somewhat the monotony of Carter's laborious sojourn, and that night he lost a large sum of money to the Pajara official, who seemed to have astonishing luck and a sharp eye to tricks as the two played *stuss* in the dingy hotel room.

Two days later a newspaper arrived, and Carter was horrified to read that the *Alice* had been brought into the port of Manzanillo on suspicion and was being held. The same night he received a telegram from Red asking immediately for five thousand dollars to "ready up" the port authorities of Manzanillo. The money was wired without delay, and Carter fell again to cursing his luck and his impetuosity for entering the game that had given him a stretch of such discomfiture,

Four days more dragged by; but on the fifth he had the great joy of seeing his long-awaited boat sail into the port. The captain, Red, and Lilly made their way to the hotel to turn over the papers and make their reports. Carter almost wept at the sight of a familiar face, and after an evening of news and conversation he went with the Pajara official to the telegraph office to announce to the would–be president the arrival of the boat. In the telegram Pajara was reminded of his agreement to arrest Franklin on the arrival of the second boat, which was due in two days. Carter rubbed his hands in satisfaction. Was not the answer of this message to.be a large check? His walk back to the hotel, arm in arm with Miguel—by which name the Pajara official was called—was the most joyful he had yet had in this country the poets write about. He laughed aloud as he stepped into the big room which served as café and lobby, thinking of how well things had turned out. He caught sight of Franklin standing at the bar, but the latter did not see him; and Carter stole upstairs to tell in gleeful whispers of how the "straight guy" had come back "to get laid away."

THAT NIGHT and the next morning he kept under cover until, about noon, he and Red were interrupted by a knock on the door. At last! Here was the telegram! They sent for Miguel, who came and read the message first to himself. On being pressed for an answer the Mexican, with a great deal of blasphemy, translated it aloud. It said:

> Don't understand this message of ship. Destination of
> cargo was changed from Porto Vieja to Banderas Bay,
> one hundred eighty miles south. Cargo arrived five
> days ago. Your men, no doubt, plotters or impostors.

Order immediate arrest. Have sent orders that no ship
be permitted to leave Porto Vieja. Investigate at once.

The message was signed "Pajara."

There was immediate rage and consternation in that trio. Somebody had betrayed them; and, with one look at each other, Carter
and Red turned with fury on Miguel. They were too late, however.
Miguel had them covered with the largest revolver they had ever seen.
Then he spoke:

"Now, see here. I don't want to arrest you people. I'm an honest
man, and never play double-cross games. I don't understand myself
why *el presidente* changed the ship's destination. I'm in the same trouble
as you. So, we'd better vamoose together. There are horses outside…
Come along."

THE OTHER TWO were speechless for a moment.

Red was the first to answer. "The game's up. Harry's gotten wise,
somehow; he's beat us to it. We gambled on a horse, but something
has slipped, and if we don't beat it, we'll be covered with flies. I'm for
the vamoose. Do as you want, Carter, but if you value your hide, you'll
skin out with us, and pronto. Well?"

"What about the woman?" Carter asked.

"Oh, forget her!" Red replied.

Together the three left the house, mounted the horses and rode
away. Three days later they were in Tucson, Arizona, safely away from
the vengeance of Mexican justice.

Franklin watched them until they were only a cloud of wavering
dust across the cactus-studded desert. His arm was about Lilly, who
was sitting close to him on the arm of his chair.

"Oh, Harry, you don't know how I hated myself when I was saying such nasty things about the dearest husband in the world," she said,
her eyes filling with tears, "How I longed to kill that vile Carter when
he raved about you. And I know Red felt the same way. He told me
it was all he could do to keep his: hooks off that sneak's throat. And
didn't Chihuahua Johnny act the part of Miguel well? Say, if Carter had
known who he was playing cards with—well. And they both laughed.

Business held Harry and Lilly more than a week on the coast of
the southern republic. Then they met Red at Coronado Beach, where
they had agreed to pass the early autumn.

SOME TWO WEEKS later Carter received the following letter in Florida, where he had gone to recoup in a small way what he had made and lost in a large way:

"Dear Carter: Before the war broke out I was advised to charter and hold two ships for the inevitable rise in transportations which the conditions would bring about. I obtained the *Alice* and the *Edith*, two sister ships, from the Black Cross Steam Ship Company, of Tampa, and was on the point of rechartering them when my friend, Red Bernheim, saw you and acquainted me with your despicable trick on your former associates and friends. Feeling called upon to take the punishment of so outrageous an action upon myself, I evolved the scheme to which you so easily fell a willing victim. I wanted to catch you on the old wire-tapping game you have so profitably played for twelve years, but knew that beating you with horses was out of the question. Having two ships at my disposal, I naturally thought of them. I made you play one against the other, even as you have made suckers play horses to their sorrow. The story of Pajara and his American backers, and of the change of cargoes at the docks, was, of course, a canard. The ships you chartered and paid good money for were the boats I already had chartered: you merely rechartered them from me. By this transaction I turned over eighteen thousand dollars!' The arms and ammunition money was paid to one of the boys whom you once bilked out of three thousand, and whose brother is managing the Associated Turbine Company, of Tampa, which, since the war, has been making weapons for the Allies.

"The boat that sailed into Porto Vieja was the one you loaded with coal, and since you billed the cargo in my name, I collected on it after you had fled. The other boat of yours I loaded with food-stuffs and sent it to Mazatlan. This I collected a fair profit on also. Besides my expenses personal and commercial, and after paying back to the boys what you stole from them, I still have a neat little pile. The two boats were turned over

again to me since you defaulted in your second payment, and I have again rechartered them at a profit.
Now, I am through with maritime speculation.

"BY the way, the telegraph office at Porto Vieja was
my own— just like a little pool room, eh? And all the
messages you or 'Miguel' received I wrote myself! Also,
I paid to have the account of the *Alice*'s attempted confiscation inserted into the Mexican paper which jnter
ested you so much when you read it.

"Undoubtedly you will be even more angry with me
than heretofore, but let me add that had I not taken
this method of satisfying Red, your health would have
suffered more at his hands than I care to think of. He
was for personal violence, Mrs. Franklin sends greetings
and encloses that ring your enthusiasm and intoxication
prompted you to give her on the evening your boat
sailed so majestically into Vieja harbor. Such easy trim-
mings of an old-timer, by the game he has played all
his life, leads one to believe that, when a man's passions
lead him, he moves too fast to carry his money.—Harty
Franklin."


"What's the idea of sending back that 'Simple Simon,' Harry? That's
a good stone," growled Red, who liked good stones and disapproved
of such generosity to the defeated.

"Ah, Red, the exigencies of good taste demand these little sacrifices at times, especially where the ladies are concerned," answered
Harry, smiling.

"Whatever that means!" snorted Red, adjusting a large four-carat
diamond in his red necktie. "Anyway, Miguel and I certainly cold-
decked him enough on the road to Tucson to make up for it and
another one like it."

# AN EYE FOR
# AN EYE

ALONG THE moonlit paths, bordered by great hedges of geraniums, in the grounds of the old Coronado Hotel at. San Diego, walked two young people. Their arms were about each other, and on their faces was that happiness which comes only with great affection and after many vicissitudes. The girl was several years the young man's junior, slight, and dark as the night itself; and she was as beautiful and dainty as a piece of Sèvres china. In her eyes was a hint of sadness which her red lips belied, and about her there clung a cloak of feminine mystery, making her seem like some shade that had stepped from the frame of a picture by Greuze. Her name was Lilly Franklin, née Dinan, and she was the wife of the man at her side.

Harry Franklin, one of the cleverest and most resourceful crooks in the business, was as handsome as Lilly was beautiful. He had the bearing of a man of the world, and his sensitive hands and mouth, his wide-set eyes and high, wide forehead attested to a genuine innate refinement.

Harry was the type of the much-written about and seldom-seen "gentleman crook," with this difference: the gentleman crook of the magazines takes all things with a suave and deferential air, and thinks little of his victims' feelings; whereas Harry stole only from those who were by nature thieves themselves, and who, by their exalted social or financial position in an unjust world, were out of the reach of the courts. Indeed, Harry would never have called himself a crook. He looked upon his operations as the acts of an incorruptible destiny which never permitted a malefactor a chance to buy himself out, and which took upon itself the supreme duty and pleasure of punishing the moral lapses in those whose lives should be an example to others by reason of their high position in the public gaze.

LILLY HAD always been his greatest help in his nefarious adventuring, and had now impressed upon him the necessity of giving it all up and living a normal life where danger was little known, and where one could mingle with people unhypocritically. He had promised her after his last adventures of the two ammunition boats that he was through pursuing his victims either for the purpose of awakening their consciences, or of adding dollars from their ill-gotten wealth to his own credit. Consequently she was happy.

Even Red Bernheim, their partner, seemed less desirous of money-getting during these last few weeks. As Lilly and Harry walked in and out of the shadows cast by the date—and monkey-palms, they real-ized why the big-hearted Jewish man, whose loyalty to them in all things was incorruptible, had become contented with a quiet life. On a bench near a cypress nook they saw him ardently making love to a woman about his own size and weight, whose long-lidded eyes were cast down and whose two hands reposed in one of Red's, while he used the other as an aid to expression. A moment they stood watching, long enough to see the woman wipe a tear from her eye and begin a long protestation. Then they continued their strolling, happier them-selves because of Red's happiness and elated to feel that even their practical confrere had succumbed to the little hunter.

When they returned to their rooms Red was waiting, deep in thought.

"Look here, Harry!" he began. "What are you goin' to do to a trum-pernick like that, huh? Got a poke of half a million or more, and gives her just enough to squeeze along on. Chicken-chaser, too. Has fought three divorce suits. She knows he's a bad egg, but can't get the goods on him; and he hasn't seen her for two years! ... Say, we've trimmed some bad lobs in our day, but we never had the chance to fix a hard-boiled egg like this one! I've played the lemon, badger, pay-off and, when I was a kid, I even done some moll-buzzing and heel jobs. But I've a soul like the driven snow beside this guy. He's what you'd call a white-washed tomb, eh? But me, I'd have to go away off to say what I think of him, down to the 'blue grotto' in Kentucky where the color of my language wouldn't be noticed!"

He jumped up and paced the floor excitedly, muttering:

"Well, well, Red! What's the matter?" Harry asked amusedly. "I don't know who you're thinking about or what this person has done to you or to her. Let's have the dope calmly, and from the start. Sit down and compose yourself."

"Sure, you're right, Harry," the other answered, quieting himself. "Here it is.

You've seen the little lady, Mrs. Levinson, around the place? Well, the minute I laid my lamps on her, it was open and shut with me. I felt myself slippin' right then and there, and as the days went by, I gathered speed. Last night I decided I'd had enough stretches and near-stretches. Also my poke was well lined, enough for an old man like me anyway, and I come to the conclusion I'd danced enough and that I was gettin' too old to skip around the world. In other words, all I could think of was some little Ikeys and Rachels tuggin' at my coat-tails, an open fire and the Rabbi's blessin'. The rosary kept runnin' through my head, and although I felt hungry, I didn't feel like eatin' at all. So, knowin' what's up, I put it up to her straight, for I could see that, although I ain't no Narcissus, I'm a charmer here; and she tells me the story."

Red turned a deep crimson and took off his coat —for greater comfort and freedom.

"We've all seen the old boob, Levinson, hangin' round Zincand's in Frisco with a table full of chickens, buyin' them flowers and throwin' the eye to the singers and ponies. Well, he's her husband, or rather, he's the guy her parents insisted on her marryin', although he's thirty years older than her. She had a dowry of just a hundred quid, and after he got that added to as much his self, and had started in big makin' a wad, he  gets cold and never comes home more than once a month. She's tickled because she could never stand him anyway, and she's been all right and waitin' for a chance to give him the gate. She tried three times, but each time he got in his dirty work and it failed; and each time she tried he'd sneer and cut down her allowance. Once he had her shut up in a private asylum for six weeks merely to show her what he could do and what he would do if she persisted in her manoeuvers."

Red exploded.

"Can you beat it?... Well, the whole size of it is we want to get our beads strung on the same string. Get me? But what's, to be done? Oh, you can smile, you happy guy! You're hitched up—but look at me! Laugh, why don't you?" roared Red."Laugh! You're a great help to a partner."

Red was blushing furiously and trying to hide his high color under the sound of his booming voice. But Harry made no reply to him.

"Red," interposed Lilly, "I don't believe in coming between a man and his wife," and she looked lovingly at Harry, who was now apparently studying the pattern in the carpet.

Red grunted and angered Lilly by muttering something about not giving a whoop what went on in a broad's mind. Lilly left the room pouting, followed by Red already sorry for what he had said; and Harry was left to his own thoughts.

Lilly sent a long letter that night to J.F. Levinson, San Francisco, in which she introduced herself as Mrs. Levinson's friend. She said that a trick was being put up on him that would cost him much worry and trouble, that he had better come at once, and that he and she together could defeat the aims of the conspirators.


WHEN LEVINSON received the message he was at a loss to

decipher its meaning, but at last construed it as a betrayal, on the part of one of his wife's friends, of some plan to obtain a divorce and alimony. He came to the conclusion that Lilly hoped, by thus winning his gratitude, to share in his fortune. He laughed to himself, and as it was a slack season in his business, he decided to go at once to Coronado. He left his office hurriedly, after telling his manager he had suddenly been called south, and left his address as the Coronado Hotel. Four hours later he was on the Owl Flyer bound for Los Angeles.

The next afternoon he registered at the resort hotel, and the same night had his card sent up to the suite occupied by Miss Franklin. Lilly spent much time on her toilet that evening, and when she appeared Levinson saw a -vision of loveliness such as he could not behold every day in San Francisco.

She was dressed in a ruffled, sleeveless gown of some shimmering and diaphanous red material. Her raven black hair glowed like onyx, and her flesh, warm and rose of tint, reflected the red of the dress so that her body seemed like a vase of rare and delicate workmanship through which the light transpersed.

She gave him her most gracious smile, and after apologizing for the unconventionality of her action on the grounds of its importance to him, she went on to hint that Mrs. Levinson might be in great danger as she had disappeared two days before, leaving her baggage and personal effects, and had not been heard from since. Lilly said she feared that something might have happened, and she, as. Mrs. Levinson's best friend, felt it incumbent upon her to break the news to him.

Mr. Levinson was duly alarmed. He had always trusted his wife not to disgrace him, and indeed her strictly honorable character had not permitted her to think of such a thing. But here -was a serious situation.

Could it be possible that he had goaded her too far? Had she in self-defense at last taken the step which was the only one she knew would hurt him? A certain bitterness crept into his rather crafty expression, an, uneasiness which told Lilly more plainly than words that she had made an impression on him in his one vulnerable spot. When she saw this, she made him still more uncomfortable by hinting desperate things and piling up the evidence, even going so far as to tell him that a man had been seen in Mrs. Levinson's company of late, and that he too had left the hotel rather suddenly, Levinson at once forgot all his little poses and tricks of conversation, and set to work planning what was to be done.

LILLY LET HIM ponder in silence for some time, and then announced that she was holding back an important piece of information that she could not divulge just then, not being sure of its truth, but that she could know for a certainty in several days. At this Levinson cheered up. As the night was warm and balmy, Lilly told him she always took a walk in the evening, and asked him if he would be so good as to accompany her. He was more than willing, and almost immediately she had opportunity of seeing what manner of man she was dealing with. All his former self-possession had returned now. He capered about boyishly in the way old men will when wishing to appear young, and talked with his little pouched eyes half closed to achieve some effect he considered youthful. He was slightly bald, and the hair was white about his temples. His nose was large, and his lips were thick. He wore dancing pumps with his evening clothes, and across his pleated shirt front hung the wide black ribbon of a monocle which he never tired of adjusting. He smoked monogrammed cigarettes, and altogether was the type of *roué* of the French capital without the cosmopolitan *roué's* knowledge of life and women.

Lilly found it hard to keep from laughing when he was in the midst of one of his pretty speeches. But, despite her self-enforced seriousness, she managed to keep him at a respectful distance. This surprised and piqued Levinson, because in the last five years he had chosen to associate only with that class, of women who felt flattered by his attentions. By the end of the evening, however, he began to feel himself softened by a tender feeling not uncommon to old men when they have basked for hours in the smile and loveliness of what they consider a "good" woman. He said nothing to betray himself, having decided to play the game deferentially. Lilly noticed a different and more natural look in his eyes as he bade her good-night. When they had first met, he had frankly appraised her charms, and had evinced a pleased surprise. When he parted from her there was something almost canine in his admiration with which was mingled perhaps a bit of adoration as well.

The next day, although he pressed Lilly for the information she had spoken of, she skilfully held him off; and they went automobiling in her car. Steadily his charmed gaze grew more and more servile. By the end of this second day he would have done any bidding of hers. On the third day she confessed that she had only come to the hotel to meet him—that, not knowing what manner of man he was, she thought it wiser. The truth was she lived out of town a few miles in her own house, and rarely came to the hotel or mingled with the beach society. Now that they knew each other, he could come the next day and visit her at her home. She emphasized the "knew each other," and he imagined he saw in this somewhat prudish remark an indication of genuine affection. He thrilled at the thought, and only at rare intervals thought of his wife, and then only as an unpleasant obstacle. Why had he not let Mrs. Levinson obtain a divorce?

Lilly had promised to call for him at the hotel directly after luncheon the next day.

The morning dragged itself along inter minably; but at eleven o'clock he was approached by a man in chauffeur's livery, who presented him a note.

> Dear Mr. Levinson: Let the chauffeur bring you to me. We will lunch under the palm trees out here. That will be more pleasant than the hotel dining-room, I'm sure.
>
> Lilly Franklin

HE SPRANG up happily. She had not, he told himself, been able to wait! He took his hat and thin rhinoceros-hide cane, and 4 sprang into the machine. In another moment he was shooting away from Coronado at break-neck speed. The ride was much longer than he had expected, and it was not until a half-hour later that they drew up at a high door way set deep in tall cypress trees and tall flower beds. The chauffeur sounded his horn, and a servant in livery opened the heavy door.

Levinson alighted, twirling his cane and humming, and lightly danced up the stone steps. The machine sped away as he entered the hall. The door swung shut suddenly, and all at once he felt strong arms crushing his arms to his body while others applied a gag over his mouth. Before he had time to scream he was picked up, weak with fright and carried up two long flights of stairs and deposited in a room smelling of dust and age.

He lay still, expecting some terrible thing to happen to him, but, save for some whispering, he heard nothing. Then footsteps walked quickly from the room, the door banked, a key turned in the lock, the hall echoed retreating footsteps and all was still except for the warbling of a bird outside the window.

He sat up and removed his gag, inwardly cursing everything and feeling himself over to see if any bones were broken. Then he looked round. He was in a large room, sitting on a deep double bed with a canopy, there was a wash-stand in the corner, and near it, a large commode. A pile of books on mental diseases lay in one corner, and a heavy carpet completely covered the floor. Two great windows, barred strongly, gave on lovely grounds that gardeners had deserted for several years, and, sparkling over long stretches of hills and plains, could be seen the dancing noon-day sea. He walked cautiously to the door and tried it. Locked!

The windows could be raised, but the bars were immovable. A blind rage seized him, and he thrashed around like a wild man, throwing the chairs and books about, and cursing in a high hysterical voice. He rushed for the tenth time to the heavy door, trying to kick it down; but it did not give in the slightest.

SUDDENLY HE heard a blood-curdling scream, prolonged and shrill, which brought him up short with his eyes bulging. It sounded as if some poor creature was being tortured hideously, and the noise scattered his thoughts as wind dispels smoke. Louder and louder it grew, and then to Levinson's abject horror it ended in a peal of cackling, maniacal laughter. Where could he be? Was he awake? He pinched himself, but the scene did not change. Again that horrible cry started, only to end abruptly in laughter. This was repeated a dozen times. At last there was a crash which shook the house and, closely fol- lowing it, a noise of falling iron. Levinson shook the bars and screamed for help; he was panic-stricken. But only that shrill laughter answered him. The birds had stopped singing, and the ensuing silence was more hideous than the noise. It was as though the living world had died on that last peal of mirth. Levinson threw himself down on the bed and tried to think, but fear was on him too greatly.

At that instant 'the door opened silently, and a figure filled the opening. The newcomer was tall and black-garbed and wore a long professional-looking beard. The man advanced into the room, speaking in a monotonous and subdued voice to another figure in the rear. The second man was stout and also possessed a heavy well-trimmed beard. There was something both stern and scholarly about the two. The taller of the men surveyed the upturned furniture and shook his head. "I did not understand that Mr. Levinson was violent," he remarked quietly. "I understood that his dementia was of a more physic nature phobias, perhaps. From what I heard, I should have diagnosed his case as dementia praecox."

"And I also, Doctor," the other answered. "The case is more interesting than I imagined."

For a moment Levinson was too astonished to speak. At last he jumped from the bed.

"You blithering idiots," he exclaimed.

"I'm no more crazy than the president! Let me out of this or there'll be trouble. This isn't the Middle Ages. What do you mean? How dare you keep me here against my will? Let me out, I tell you!" and he rushed at them, waving his white, soft fists.

"Do you see, Doctor?" said the first, catching Levinson's two hands in one of his and holding him as one would a baby. "Do you see?"

The stout man nodded professionally. "Let me go, I tell you!" cried Levinson.

"Who said I was crazy?"

The "doctor" spoke conciliatingly. "Mrs. Levinson had you brought here... You should try to be calm. We will do all we can for you."

Levinson fell back dumbstruck. Here was a turn of the wheel! Locked up by his wife whom he had once locked up himself? He could not deny to himself that she had been clever about it. So Miss Franklin had been only a decoy! Why couldn't he have seen that a woman like her could not care for an old fool like him? Again anger surged over him to think that he had been such a dupe.

"Look here," he demanded, "what place is this, and what has Miss Franklin to do with it?"

THE TALL MAN answered with great dignity: "This place, my dear sir, is Dr. Josephus Dane's Private Sanatorium. I know nothing of a Miss Franklin, having received all my instructions from Mrs. Levinson who, by the way, will return in about a week... Also, let me add that, unless you are able to control yourself, it may be necessary to resort to a straight jacket. Everything will be done to make you comfortable. The treatment will be most careful. Your meals will be sent to you, and although the fare is not elaborate, it is wholesome and nourishing."

He bowed and was about to go out when a feminine voice was heard, and Lilly Franklin pushed her way into the room.

"Why, what are you doing here, Mr. Levinson?" she asked in surprise. "And why did you break our engagement? It is by the merest chance that I have found you. When I went to the hotel for you," she hurried on, not giving the astounded man a second to reply, "they told me you had hurriedly left at about eleven, and gave me a description of the car you left in. As luck would have it, I have often seen that car coming from this house (I live only ten minutes down this road), and I hurried here for an apology and because—because—I was afraid— well, I wanted to see what had happened to you. We can't let an old friend get away as easily as that, can we?" she ended lamely.

Levinson was speechless. He drew forth the note he had received, and showed it to her, explaining the whole affair rapidly and nervously. "Why, I never wrote that note, Mr. Levinson. My hand-writing is entirely different from that. Oh, I begin to see a light!" She glanced shrewdly about her and at the silent doctors standing in the doorway. Levinson scrutinized the note carefully. Suddenly a great light dawned on him. The writing was that of his wife! He clapped his hand to his forehead and sank limply into a chair.

Lilly came close to him.

"Tell me, won't they let you out? …This is the scheme I heard a rumor of and was going to tell you— oh, why," she almost sobbed, "didn't I do it before?" She glared at Dr. Dane. "But to make up for it. I'll see about this place; I'll have the police here. How dare they sequester a man of your standing and prominence!"

HER EYES flashed and she made quickly for the door. But Dr. Dane gathered her, shrieking and kicking, into his arms, backed quickly out, and locked the door.

Levinson heard the doctor depositing her in the room next his own. What daring these pirates had! He marveled at their colossal effrontery in kidnapping two adults for the sake of a little money that his wife was paying them. They couldn't be getting much, he thought, for he did not give his wife enough to permit her any extravagant fees. What would it all lead to? he wondered.

He had fully decided to try to bribe his way out when he heard a rapping on the wall. Eagerly he answered, and then began to bore a hole through the plaster with his pen-knife. Once it was finished he and the girl could talk in whispers and make plans for their escape. As he finished he saw Miss Franklin's desirable young lips whisper- ing to him: "A door leads into here. It must be behind the canopy of your bed. Look and see."

He hurriedly pushed aside his bed. Sure enough, there was the door. He shot back the bolt and, to his inexpressible joy, found it opened. The girl came to meet him, one pink finger across her mouth to enjoin silence. And until the last orange light of day they sat together, undisturbed.

But they could arrive at no conclusion.

In truth, Levinson was no longer loath to stay here with so charm- ing a companion. She subtly flattered him and awoke the hope that ever lies even in the most repugnant of men—namely, that a beauti- ful woman will some day find their good qualities and love them for themselves. Why should she take such an interest and seem so little perturbed if she did not enjoy his company? After all, it was not her duty to have foie lowed him up after he had apparently broke en their rendezvous. With such thoughts he lulled himself into a beatific state of emotion which so consumed him that foot-steps in the hail were almost at the door before he hurried to his own room and shoved back the bed, avoiding discovery.

Dr. Dane had come to take Miss Franklin away and to bring Levinson his supper two great disappointments in one. The next room was silent now, and as the San Franciscan epicure uncovered his tray he saw the truth of the doctor's description of the fare for the inmates. There was beef broth, very weak tea, some mashed potatoes with gravy, a small slice of cold ham, and rice pudding. Levinson almost wept at the sight of this unappetizing spread, and at first refused to touch it. But later, over—I come by hunger, he ate what had been I brought him. He had scarcely finished when Dr. Dane came in, rubbing his hands.

"I see you liked your meal," he said "You see, this being Friday, we have a little extra. Sundays we have only tea and cold supper." Levinson groaned.

"Lights out at ten o'clock," continued the doctor. "And I might add that any attempt to escape will be seen by our night watchman. Good-night. Breakfast at six."

The unhappy victim was on the point of crying out in anger, but controlling himself, he called Dr. Dane back.

"See here, how much do you want to let Miss Franklin and me out of here?" he asked in business-like tones.

The doctor smiled. "When you are cured you will be permitted to go." With that he went out.

THERE WAS just enough uncanny noise to keep Levinson awake and trembling most of the night. He was up walking the floor when his breakfast arrived, consisting of mush, hot milk, and cold bread and butter, His nerves were on the breaking point, and he sent for Dr. Dane. When that gentle-man appeared, Levinson acted his calmest and asked if it were possible to communicate with Mrs. Levinson. He was willing to pay well if he could see his wife. He realized he had to get this business settled at once no matter what price. The suspense was too trying. And there was Miss Franklin to be considered.

The doctor, after much persuasion, agreed to telegraph to Los Angeles for Mrs. Levinson.

All that morning the room next to his had been empty, but directly after luncheon he heard Miss Franklin being returned to it. He lost no time in getting in communication with her and in going into her room. She appeared hysterical and frightened, and Levinson did his best to comfort her, telling her he had, sent for his wife, and that before long he would be free and would see that no harm came to her. All his wife wanted was a divorce, and he believed that if he let her obtain it, everything would be well.

Lilly calmed down, and Levinson took her hand in his. Adversity had brought them close together.

The next afternoon he proposed to Lilly. They were sitting close to each other, and he was too intent upon her answer to hear the door open behind him. When she raised her eyes to his he put his arm about her shoulders. A noise made him swing round. He was face to face with Mrs. Levinson, Dr. Dane and his assistant.

"At last," said his wife calmly, "I've caught you, and I have witnesses. Here you are in this girl's room—and with your arms about her."

"Well, what do you intend to do?" Levinson tried to speak in a matter-of-fact tone.

"I'm going to divorce you," his wife answered. "I had you put here to force you to terms, but now force is not necessary. I have the evidence I have always wanted.

"Who is this—this woman?" She looked at Lilly contemptuously.

Levinson was angry. "Try to divorce me and I'll have you arrested for abduction."

"Very well," Mrs. Levinson returned wearily. "My life is ruined anyway. There's no happiness left for me. I'll see that you and this woman are kept prisoners here. You'll suffer as you made me suffer once."

She started to walk away resolutely.

"Think of me!" It was Lilly's voice; and her hands were on Levinson's shoulders. "For my sake—our sake! Oh, do something—" and she began to weep hysterically.

Levinson's fighting instinct was subdued. He did not care for his wife, and he did care for Lilly. And she had as much as promised to marry him.

"Stop!" he commanded. "You may have your divorce. You have gotten the best of me. I know when I'm beaten." He did not feel beaten, however, for would he, too, not benefit by a divorce?

"Then," said Mrs. Levinson, "write a letter to your lawyers, saying the suit will be undefended. You are not to give your address, and you are to remain here until the matter is settled." She turned to Dane. "Doctor, I will expect you to watch him until I let you know."

"I don't like the matter," the doctor replied. "When he gets out he'll make trouble. And don't you know he could have the decree annulled by proving force?"

Lilly turned to Dane. "Don't worry," she put in. "Mr. Levinson and I are to be married. We shall be only too glad to forget."

"Of course," replied Levinson.

"And you can give me a check for my dowry," added his wife, "now." The check was gladly given. Once he was out and married to Lilly, he would threaten his wife with arrest and he would make it hot for Dr. Dane also. He had no fear of losing the money.

ONE week later the doctor came to him and told him he was free to go. Miss Franklin also was being released. Lilly said she must go home at once, but would come to him to the hotel the next day.

Levinson hurried back to the beach.

Here he read that his wife had obtained a divorce on the grounds of desertion. He was satisfied and waited eagerly for the return of Lilly. —But when at nightfall she had not put in an appearance, he drove to the address she had given him. To his horror he found it to be a vacant lot. He telegraphed to his bank and found that his check had been cashed six days before. He hurried to the police, and they went at once to Dr. Dane's Private Sanatorium, only to find, when they burst open the door, that the house was empty. The real-estate agent informed them that he had rented the house to a Mr. Harry Franklin for a month.

There his knowledge ended.

What Levinson never found out was that Mrs. Levinson six months later became Mrs. Red Bernheim, thereby unconsciously aiding the police to do away forever with one of America's most shrewd and successful crooks. And it would have done Levinson no good had he found out. For there was no evidence on which he could proceed. Since then Harry has taken his own name (which, of course, the author would not under any circumstances divulge), and is living a quiet and happy life near Red and his wife—a life such as pleases the woman's heart of Lilly.

# ANNEX A:

# The Crime of Constance Kent: A Challenging Mystery

In the entire history of criminology, there are few cases as fascinating as the Constance Kent murder. The crime itself was amazing. The technique was even more amazing. And the psychological elements involved were nothing short of staggering. The various ramifications, and the  sequences of events which followed the discovery of little Francis Kent's decapitated body, have kept criminologists busy for decades and filled innumerable volumes.

The crime took place in Wiltshire, England, in 1860; but despite the confession and conviction of the murderer, the details of this bloody affair have never been completely cleared up. Indeed, it runs a curious parallel to the famous Lizzie Borden murder in Fall River, Massachusetts, in 1892. It was a crime of abnormal psychology, and the truth concerning it will forever be lost in that most abysmal of shadowlands—the tortured human mind.

A girl of sixteen—a strange, inhibited, determined creature—murdered her little brother of four by practically severing his head from his body, in circumstances so ghastly and unusual, and with a coolness and premeditation so astounding, that the story reads more like a distorted and maniacal dream than a transcript of actuality. And yet the record is undeniable; and the confession of Constance, five years later, is undoubtedly authentic, despite its inconsistencies.

One person at least knew the truth at the time of the murder—Inspector Whicher of Scotland Yard. But so fantastic was the truth, and so incredible were the circumstances, no one would believe him; and he was practically forced to resign from the Yard for his foul suspicions. In those days, little was known of the sexual abnormalities of puberty. *Frühlings Erwachen* had not been written and Freud and Stekel were unknown. Inspector Whicher was a martyr to the psychological ignorance of his time.

Nor did the charming and demure Miss Kent herself aid in the advance of the science of psychology when she confessed. She admitted the crime, but her account of the modus operandi, as well as the reasons she gave for murdering her brother, will scarcely hold water. She was apparently as ignorant of her actual mental state as the jury which originally acquitted her. Or else she deliberately concocted a grim romance.

Because of these astonishing factors, because of the sinister aspect of the case and its terrible and mysterious unresolved equations, because of the extraordinary and haunting moments during the process of the murder, the crime of Constance Kent will always remain a fascinating horror story of unbelievable ghastliness for the layman and a continual challenge to the criminologists.

# ANNEX B:
# The Gordon Murder Case

The final case to be investigated by S. S. Van Dine was the murder of Vivian Gordon. She had been born, Benita Franklin, in 1891 and forty years later her body was found in New York's Van Cortlandt Park early one morning in February 1931. She had been strangled with a clothesline. This was twenty-four hours before she was due to appear as a witness in a judicial inquiry where she was expected to testify against certain police officers accused of corruption. The case was never solved and, as well as Gordon, it cost the life of her daughter, Benita Bischoff, who —apparently —committed suicide less than a week after her mother's murder.

There were clues —many, many clues —and the press were quick to make this the focus of the ultimately (and unsurprisingly) unsuccessful investigation. Her estranged husband John E C Bischoff was suspected, as was Joseph A Radeloff, a leading attorney who had had a relationship with the murdered woman. Neither man was ever charged. Finally, a taxi driver identified two gangsters, Harry Stein and Samuel Greenberg who he claimed had murdered the woman in the back of his cab. The men were arrested but at their trial the witness proved unreliable and both men were acquitted.

Wright wrote:
"However, when she offered to expose the police, he had a handmade alibi, so to apeak, and took immediate advantage of his opportunity; for lie knew that the first reaction of the public would be to blame the police, who might fear her exposure, Such cases of crimes, deferred until an opportune moment, arrives are common in the history of criminology.

### Psychological Clues.

"The psychological clues pointing to this theory cannot be wholly ignored. Vivian Gordon's body was placed in a spot where almost immediate discovery was inevitable, whereas a murderer who did not want the body found could have made a much better job of hiding it.

"It appears almost as if the murderer wanted the body to be found. He pointed up tn his alibi too neatly and too obviously—he was a trifle too eager to cast suspicion elsewhere.

"The crime, therefore, instead of being a logical result of an obvious cause, shows the illogical elements of a mind attempting to build a false relationship between cause and effect.

"In the mystery screen story, "The Blue Moon Murder," which I have just written, I used a similar murder, treated from the reverse angle, in which the detective unearths the true culprit by the very fact that suspicion pointed too directly toward the person whom the murderer had sought to involve.

"There are two other points which might be considered in formulating a theory of Vivian Gordon's death.

"First: Strangling, or garrotting, is not, and never has been a popular Anglo-Saxon method of murder,

"Secondly;—Strangling is rarely if ever a method of purely Impersonal or expedient murder—that is, murder without personal wrath or passion. And if the killer of Vivian Gordon did seek to throw suspicions on the police, he used a psychologically wrong method of murder, in addition to emphasizing his alibi to a point where it tends to defeat his purpose."

The case remains unsolved.

THE ALMOST PERFECT CRIME

*The Almost Perfect Crime* is printed on 60-pound paper and is designed by Jeffrey Marks. The type is Bembo, a type stemming from a Renaissance era font. The cover is by Gail Cross. The first edition was published in two forms: trade softcover, perfect bound; and one hundred copies sewn in cloth. *The Almost Perfect Crime* was printed and bound by Imprint Press. The book was published in May 2025 by Crippen & Landru Publishers, Inc., Cincinnati, OH.

**Crippen & Landru, Publishers**
P. O. Box 532057
Cincinnati, OH 45253
Web: www.Crippenlandru.Com
E-mail: info@crippenlandru.Com

Since 1994, Crippen & Landru has published more than 100 first editions of short-story collections by important detective and mystery writers.

*This is the best edited, most attractively packaged line of mystery books introduced in this decade. The books are equally valuable to collectors and readers.* [Mystery Scene Magazine]

*The specialty publisher with the most star-studded list is Crippen & Landru, which has produced short story collections by some of the biggest names in contemporary crime fiction.* [Ellery Queen's Mystery Magazine]

*God bless Crippen & Landru.* [The Strand Magazine]

*A monument in the making is appearing year by year from Crippen & Landru, a small press devoted exclusively to publishing the criminous short story.* [Alfred Hitchcock's Mystery Magazine]

# Crippen & Landru Lost Classics

Peter Godfrey. *The Newtonian Egg*. 2002.

Craig Rice. *Murder, Mystery, and Malone*. 2002 eBook, $8.99

Charles B. Child. *The Sleuth of Baghdad*. 2002.

Stuart Palmer. *Hildegarde Withers, Uncollected Riddles*. 2002 eBook $8.99

Christianna Brand. *The Spotted Cat*. 2002

Raoul Whitfield. *Jo Gar's Casebook*. 2002.

William Campbell Gault. *Marksman*. 2003.

Gerald Kersh. *Karmesin*. 2003   eBook, $8.99

C. Daly King. *The Complete Curious Mr. Tarrant*. 2003 eBook $8.99

Helen McCloy. *The Pleasant Assassin*. 2003

William DeAndrea. *Murder – All Kinds*. 2003

Anthony Berkeley. *The Avenging Chance*. 2004

Joseph Commings. *Banner Deadlines*. 2004 eBook $8.99

Erle Stanley Gardner. *The Danger Zone*. 2004 eBook $8.99

T. S. Stribling. *Dr. Poggioli: Criminologist*. 2004 eBook $8.99

Margaret Millar. *The Couple Next Door*. 2004

Gladys Mitchell. *Sleuth's Alchemy*. 2005

Philip Warne/Howard Macy. *Who Was Guilty?* 2005 eBook $8.99

Dennis Lynds writing as Michael Collins. *Slot-Machine Kelly*. 2005

Julian Symons. *The Detections of Francis Quarles*. 2006

Rafael Sabatini. *The Evidence of the Sword*. 2006 eBook, $8.99

Erle Stanley Gardner. *The Casebook of Sidney Zoom*. 2006, eBook $8.99

Ellis Peters. *The Trinity Cat*. 2006

Lloyd Biggle. *The Grandfather Rastin Mysteries*. 2007

Max Brand. *Masquerade*. 2007

Mignon Eberhart. *Dead Yesterday*. 2007

Hugh Pentecost. *The Battles of Jericho*. 2008

Victor Canning. *The Minerva Club*. 2009

Anthony Boucher and Denis Green. *The Casebook of Gregory Hood*. 2009

Vera Caspary. *The Murder in the Stork Club.* 2009

Michael Innes. *Appleby Talks About Crime.* 2010

Phillip Wylie. *Ten Thousand Blunt Instruments.* 2010

Erle Stanley Gardner. *The Exploits of the Patent Leather Kid.* 2010, eBook, $8.99

Vincent Cornier. *The Duel of Shadows.* 2011, eBook, $8.99

E. X. Ferrars. *The Casebook of Jonas P. Jonas.* 2012

Charlotte Armstrong. *Night Call.* 2014, eBook, $8.99

Phyllis Bentley. *Chain of Witnesses.* 2014

Patrick Quentin. *The Puzzles of Peter Duluth.* 2016, Clothbound $29, eBook $8.99

Frederick Irving Anderson . *The Purple Flame.* 2016, Clothbound $29, Trade Paperback $19

Anthony Gilbert. *Sequel to Murder.* 2017, Clothbound $29

James Holding. *The Zanzibar Shirt Mystery.* 2018, Clothbound $29

William Brittain. *The Man Who Read Mysteries.* 2018, Clothbound $32, Trade Paperback $1922 eBook $8.99

Q. Patrick. *The Cases of Lieutenant Trant.* 2019

Erle Stanley Gardner. *Hot Cash, Cold Clews.* 2020, Clothbound $32, Trade Paperback $22, eBook $8.99

Freeman Wills Crofts, *The 9.50 Up Express.* 2021, Clothbound $32, Trade Paperback $22, eBook $8.99

Stuart Palmer. *Hildegarde Withers, Final Riddles?* 2021, Clothbound $32, Trade Paperback $22, eBook $8.99

Patrick Quentin. *Hunt in the Dark.* 2021

William Brittain. *The Man Who Solved Mysteries.* 2022, Clothbound $32, Trade Paperback $1922 eBook $8.99

John Creasey. *Gideon and the Young Toughs.* 2022, Clothbound $35, Trade Paperback $20, eBook $8.99

Pierre Very. *The Secret of the Pointed Tower.* 2023, Clothbound $32, Trade Paperback $20

Anthony Berkeley. *The Avenging Chance and Even More Stories (Enlarged with Two Stories).* 2023, Trade Paperback $19, eBook

Richard and Francis Lockridge. *Flair for Murder.* 2024, Clothbound $32, Trade Paperback $22

White, Ethel Lina. *Blackout and Other Stories of Suspense.* 2025, Clothbound $35, Trade Paperback $22

# Subscriptions

Subscribers agree to purchase each forthcoming publication, either the Regular Series or the Lost Classics or (preferably) both. Collectors can thereby guarantee receiving limited editions, and readers won't miss any favorite stories.

Subscribers receive a discount of 20% off the list price (and the same discount on our backlist) and a specially commissioned short story by a major writer in a deluxe edition as a gift at the end of the year.

The point for us is that, since customers don't pick and choose which books they want, we have a guaranteed sale even before the book is published, and that allows us to be more imaginative in choosing short story collections to issue.

That's worth the 20% discount for us. Sign up now and start saving. Email us at orders@crippenlandru.com or visit our website at www.crippenlandru.com on our subscription page.

www.ingramcontent.com/pod-product-compliance
Lightning Source LLC
Chambersburg PA
CBHW030019200726
48283CB00012B/693